THE
DEMON
REDCOAT

TRAITOR TO THE CROWN

THE
DEMON
REDCOAT

TRAITOR TO THE CROWN

C. C. FINLAY

BALLANTINE BOOKS • NEW YORK

The Demon Redcoat is a work of fiction. Names, characters, places, and incidents are the products of the author's imagination or are used fictitiously. Any resemblance to actual events, locales, or persons, living or dead, is entirely coincidental.

A Del Rey Mass Market Original

Copyright © 2009 by Charles Coleman Finlay

All rights reserved.

Published in the United States by Del Rey, an imprint of The Random House Publishing Group, a division of Random House, Inc., New York.

DEL REY is a registered trademark and the Del Rey colophon is a trademark of Random House, Inc.

ISBN 978-0-345-50392-3

Cover design by Jae Song. Inset illustration by Craig Howell.

Printed in the United States of America

www.delreybooks.com

9 8 7 6 5 4 3 2 1

for Kathy and Carl
because love should conquer all

Chapter 1

New York State,
near the Connecticut border
1779

Fourteen hundred hooves pounded the dark, muddy road, mingling with the noise of the raindrops that slapped the sodden trees and the ordinary jangle of soldiers' gear. The dark green coats of the British Legion riders blended into the backdrop of the night and pouring rain. The cavalry raid was Banastre Tarleton's first independent command, and he led from the front. Not, as he heard some whisper, because it kept the mud from being kicked up in his face, but because this was where the action was likely to be.

"They'll learn," Tarleton murmured to himself. "War requires men to act like beasts. The sooner we unsheathe our claws, the quicker this rebellion will end."

He had his own questions about the soldiers he led. The three hundred and fifty men with Tarleton were Loyalists, believers in king and Crown, but they were still Americans. Tarleton would see what they were made of when they fought their own neighbors and countrymen.

He glanced over his shoulder to take his measure of them and one caught his eye, a mere boy without even a cap to cover his draggled blond hair. He rode near enough to Tarleton to be his shadow. His anomalous red coat, like the one worn by British regulars, stood out among the green jackets. His mount was anxious, frequently tossing its head and nipping at invisible antagonists. The other horses jostled to keep their distance.

Tarleton opened his mouth to ask the boy who he was—

A chill shot through him. He spun around and peered into the dark, looking for his advance scout. It must be near dawn, and they must be close to the rebels' camp at Pound Ridge. He estimated that they'd ridden almost seventy miles from Long Island since yesterday morning. They'd come thirty miles in less than ten hours overnight, all of it through the constant downpour. Even without mud splattered on him, Tarleton was soaked through to the bone, just like his men, but he had chosen the weather to cover their attack and he was glad it held.

A dark shape filled the road in front of them, and Tarleton reared his horse back, shifting to keep his balance as it slipped in the mud. The rest of the legion thundered to a stop behind him.

His scout.

"It's no good, sir," the scout said, mopping water from his scruffy, unshaven face. "One of them must've seen me. I practically stumbled into their camp before I saw it. They've formed up a line on the road ahead, maybe a hundred men."

Damn the luck. They would be facing the Second Continental Light Dragoons, Sheldon's horse—as if rebels deserved either flag or name. A smaller force than his, but big enough to cause him trouble.

"What of their weapons?" Tarleton demanded.

"Muskets," said the scout.

"No, I mean do they have bayonets?"

"Not as I saw. You know the rebels' guns aren't fit for 'em, most cases."

Tarleton laughed aloud. "It's too wet to fire," he said. The other advantage of an attack in the rain, if the commander was bold enough. He drew his saber and waved it over his head. "Let's show them what cavalry does."

Steel whispered from three hundred and fifty sheaths. Cold metal flashed like the first hints of sunrise.

Tarleton whirled his horse and put spurs to it. The

beast jumped foward, kicking up clods of mud. The rest of the legion galloped to catch up.

They hammered down the country road, trees whipping past, sloping downward until a clearing opened ahead. A mass of men blockaded their way. Tarleton raised his saber and leaned forward in his saddle to strike. The rest of the legion surged around him, like breakers in a wave.

The men blocking the road shouted threats and raised their useless weapons.

The legion responded, their voices roaring violence.

Just before the horses smashed into them, the rebels broke, throwing down their guns as they ran.

Tarleton galloped through the empty spot where they had been and reined in his horse. He called to his men, "See, that's how it's done! Always go straight at them and you'll never lose."

The men laughed. Victory without battle was even sweeter when you could find it.

The rebel camp was little more than a motley collection of sagging tents erected at the edge of a small town. Tarleton sent a detachment off to pursue the rebels and prevent them from regrouping. He sent another group to find the rebel Major Ebenezer Lockwood's house and detain him. Meanwhile, he took possession of the camp. Some of the men were already searching the abandoned tents.

Shots sounded as the pursuit entered the town. Tarleton peered through the rain at the small cluster of houses.

"Shall we form an offensive?" asked one of his captains, a man considerably older than Tarleton. But he was only twenty-four, and many of the men were older. He had to prove himself in battle to them, and show them that he knew how to lead.

"Pursue where they show themselves, but not too far," Tarleton said. "Don't lose sight of what we came for."

"Here's Tallmadge's tent," one of the men called out. Major Benjamin Tallmadge. George Washington's spymaster. The man whose spies had been causing all sorts of trouble for the British in occupied New York.

Tarleton dismounted and handed the reins to the first person to hold out his hand. He flung open the flap and entered the tent. The rain beat like a drum corps on the taut canvas. A lantern stood on a small table beside the small writing desk. The light twitched as the flap opened again behind Tarleton. He looked up and saw a strange boy in a red coat enter and stare at him.

He opened his mouth to demand the boy's expulsion—

"Give me that bag," Tarleton snapped as he turned to the soldier.

The soldier tossed a saddlebag to him. Tarleton flipped it open and began looking through the letters inside. Many were in code, but some weren't. There was Washington's own handwriting in notes to Tallmadge. Here was a mention of a Highday—he must be one of the Americans' new spies, should be easy to find. He saw a reference to *C—r*, the spy in Seatucket, on Long Island, who was making secret movement by the British army in New York so difficult. He flipped through the sheets and saw one more.

> *Persuade Brown to return.*
> *Need his special talents.*
>   G Washington

Brown was a common enough name, Tarleton thought. It would be hard to find him. But more importantly, what were his special talents? He tucked the letters back into the bag and closed it before his wet hands smeared the ink. These would be valuable to his commanders. "Bring this," he said, tossing the bag to one of his aides.

The first soldier was still tearing through Tallmadge's

belongings. "Look here," he said. His eyes gleamed, and his smile spread from ear to ear. He held open a purse full of money.

Tarleton snatched it away. A handful of guineas, and near as many shillings, plus a variety of other coin. He wrapped the purse shut and shoved it in his belt. They had almost everything they came for.

"Where's Lockwood's house?" he asked.

Major Ebenezer Lockwood, a rebel who served in New York's provincial congress as well as the army, had a bounty on his head. Forty guineas to the man who captured him. Tarleton could make his name *and* start on his fortune. He could pay off his gambling debts and stop begging his mother to send him new shirts.

"The house is over here," said the scout, who had just returned to the tent entrance. Like most of the men here, he was from New York, the one colony where men had sense enough of their duty to stay loyal. "But Lockwood's already gone."

"Gone, you say?" Tarleton snarled as he burst out of the tent. The rain slapped him like a wet rag.

"He left his wife behind," the scout said, pointing the way to an undistinguished wooden house. Lockwood was an important man in the colonies, and he lived in this? Anger boiled up inside Tarleton. How could any of these men think they deserved to rule themselves in place of the king?

The front door had been kicked in and hung aslant on a broken hinge. Guards stood just inside the door, out of the rain. Lockwood's frightened wife shivered in the front room, a plain creature heavy from bearing children, wearing only her nightdress.

"Where is that damned rebel?" Tarleton demanded.

Lockwood's wife stared down at him. Tarleton was not a tall man—one reason he preferred horseback, where he was the equal of any. "You are the rebel," she sneered.

"You rebel against the will of God when you make men slaves to a tyrant."

One of his officers—Tarleton was going to have to learn their names—slashed at the woman with his saber. She screamed and ducked, but the heavy hilt cracked her forehead, splitting the skin. She collapsed to the floor, blood gushing from the wound and mixing with the muddy water from their boots.

The officer raised his arm to strike again, but Tarleton caught his hand in the air. "She's a woman," he said, but the words sounded far away. A part of him wanted to strike her as well. They were all exhausted from the long ride, beat down by the constant batter of the rain, on edge from the charge and the snipers' shots.

"Burn it," whispered a voice.

Tarleton turned and noticed a boy in a red coat. He had a cherubic face, even with his hair plastered to his skin by the rain. His eyes were alight and his lips pursed.

"Who are you—?"

A sob from the woman caught Tarleton's attention.

He cast the officer's arm aside, then bent down and grabbed the bleeding woman by the collar of her dress. He dragged her toward the door and flung her out into the mud. Then he turned back to his men.

"Burn it," he commanded.

"Sir?" the officer asked. He'd been willing to strike a woman for disobedience to her king, but he hesitated at burning houses.

Tarleton couldn't let them doubt his orders ever, not if he meant to lead them. "I said, burn it. What's difficult to understand?"

On their own, the other soldiers quickly loaded their arms with silver, clothes, books—any valuables they could snatch up. Many of them had lost property to the rebels, and now they wanted some of it back.

Tarleton looked the other way. He knocked over an oil

lantern and watched the greasy fluid pour over the edge of the table and run across the uneven floor to the rag rug, which soaked it up. He felt strangely excited, even though he didn't care for fire except in a practical way. Was it command? Did command always have this effect on men?

The scout picked up a burning candle and looked to Tarleton for confirmation.

He hesitated.

"Burn it" came a boyish whisper.

Certainty surged through him, and he nodded.

The scout dropped the candle into the oil and the sudden flame cut a scar across the floor. The rug caught fire in an instant, and the fire leapt from the rug to the long curtains that covered the windows.

Tarleton went outside and watched the flames jump through the windows and sizzle against the rain. Soon black smoke poured out from under the eaves.

It wasn't enough.

"Take whatever you want," he yelled to the men gathered around him. Plunder was a part of war. It always had been. Let them reclaim what they had lost to the rebels. He walked through the street as his men ransacked the houses.

His eyes fell on the church.

And suddenly plunder didn't matter to him. One of his men rode by with a torch, sputtering in the rain. Tarleton whistled, drawing his attention. The man turned back, and Tarleton took the torch from him. He kicked the door of the church, smashing his heel against it three times before it swung open. Then he walked down the center aisle, holding the torch aloft while it grew in strength.

"Burn it," whispered a voice.

Tarleton tossed the torch into the pulpit. The dry wood sizzled and cracked until it caught fire. Tarleton stood there, transfixed, while the flames jumped up to the rafters and ran like mice to every corner of the roof.

"Sir." The scout's voice, coming from the doorway, broke Tarleton from his reverie.

"What is it?" he snapped, turning and marching smartly out of the burning building. A crowd of his men had been watching from the door.

"Their colors," the scout said. He held up the regimental flag of the rebels who'd been stationed here. "We found them in an officer's bag, in one of the houses."

"I'll take that," Tarleton said. The fire in the church burned vigorously, flames licking from the windows like tongues from the mouth of a demon. Tarleton held up the captured flag to the light for a better look. Thirteen red and white stripes on a field with a painted thundercloud. The thundercloud seemed very appropriate.

Someone had eased in close, looking over Tarleton's shoulder.

A red coat. Tarleton reached out and grabbed an arm.

He was startled to find that he had a mere boy in his hand, with an angel's face and no cap on his head. The coat he wore was a threadbare soldier's jacket, something from the regulars, but cut for a drummer boy or fifer. It had holes shot through it and dark stains around the holes. The fire lit up the boy's face, transforming it into something red and eerie.

He tilted his head to Tarleton. "Persuade Brown," he whispered. "We can use his special talents."

"Who are you?" Tarleton demanded.

"William Reed. I was assigned to your command."

Tarleton didn't remember that. He was certain he had no drummer boy on the rolls. Drummer boys were for infantry, not cavalry. "Somehow I doubt that very much."

"Don't worry, I won't get in the way," the boy said innocently. "You won't notice me at all."

"The hell I won't," Tarleton said. He had the niggling

sensation that the boy had been at the edge of his perception for the past day, like a shadow rising on the horizon.

Gunshots fired from the dark around them.

"Sir, the rebels are back," the scout said.

Tarleton spun to answer the scout, then paused. He'd just been talking to someone, but who? He folded the flag and tucked it under his arm. He wanted to burn the whole town—for a brief second he had an urge to burn the whole country—but he shook off the feeling.

"We don't want another Lexington on our hands," Tarleton said, referring to the disastrous battle that had started the war. A night attack, an overextended line, and a slow retreat resulted in a British slaughter. "We have what we came for—it's time to withdraw. Where's my horse?"

"What about Lockwood?" the scout asked.

"We have their spymaster's letters. Perhaps we'll roll up another prize or two with those."

Perhaps this fellow, Brown.

More gunshots cracked nearby. Wood splintered in the side of a house behind Tarleton. His aide handed him the lead to his horse, and he sprang into the saddle. Calling his men to follow, he led them away from the rebels' camp.

As the road started to rise, Tarleton paused and looked back, letting the other men pass him so that he might admire his handiwork. The town filled a small bowl in the trees, which glowed red in the gray and soggy dawn.

No, not a bowl, Tarleton thought. A crucible. By this alchemy would the war be transformed.

He shook off the thought, wondering where it had come from. This wasn't like him. He didn't have orders to burn anything. What had possessed him to do it?

Laughter sounded nearby.

Tarleton turned to find it and glimpsed a drummer boy in a tattered red coat riding away with the last of his men. The poor boy didn't even have a cap . . .

He spurred his horse past the other riders to take the lead.

Chapter 2

Proctor Brown stood over the washstand and stared into the basin of pristine water. There had been a time when he would have used this bowl for scrying, to pull back the veil of days and peer into the shadows of the future. But he felt like every time he'd done that, it had led him astray. It was too easy to see what he wanted to see and to miss what he needed.

"What are you thinking about, darling?"

He lifted his head at Deborah's voice. Deborah, his wife, the love of his life. The New England chill had arrived with the autumn, so she rested on a chair by the fire, with a blanket pulled up to her chin and her bare feet propped up on a stool. Her belly was as round as the pumpkins out in the field, and her feet and ankles were swollen like squash. Their first baby was due to be born any day.

"I was thinking it's a shame to dirty this clean water," he said lightly, holding up his large hands, dirty from cleaning up the stalls. "I'll probably be the one who has to go out in the middle of the night to get more."

"You aren't coming near me with dirty hands," Deborah threatened.

"Ah, well, then," he said with a smile and plunged his hands into the cold water. He felt a sharp pain in his right hand, shooting through the scar of his missing pinkie finger. The finger had been cut off three years ago by a German necromancer who had hoped to enslave Proctor's soul. The prince-bishop—the only name they had for the necromancer—had escaped with both Proctor's finger and a young witch, William Reed, whom Proctor had promised to rescue. The missing digit still ached. The memory of his failure to save the boy ached too.

Proctor shoved that memory aside while he scrubbed. He reminded himself that he was glad to be back on the farm. Before the war, all he wanted was his own home and family. He had done his duty and more, serving the young United States with his special talents in whatever capacity General Washington asked of him. But now, with a baby coming, he was ready to go back to his old life.

"Someday I'm going to add a room big enough for a whole tub of water," he said, shaking his hands dry. "So we can bathe inside whenever we want."

"Putting on airs, are we?" Deborah asked. Her tone was amused. "Whatever happened to the simple farm boy I fell in love with?"

"I'm still that same fellow," Proctor said, though he knew it was but a partial truth. He grabbed a towel and wiped his hands dry, feeling the still-strange scrape of the homespun fabric over the scarred nub of his missing finger. "Only now I'd like a tub indoors."

"There's no room for it," Deborah said.

"Maybe." Proctor smiled. He and Deborah lived in the old part of the house. Deborah loved the old house because it reminded her of her mother and father. It had one big space, which served as kitchen and common room with a hearth at one end. There were three doors: the front door, which opened onto the porch; the back door, which connected to the new addition; and the bedroom door near the hearth. The bedroom—or sleeping parlor, as they were called in old houses—was a room barely big enough for a bed.

He glanced at the hearth near the bedroom. It had

been used as a black altar by one of their enemies, which made Proctor uneasy, but if living in the old house near that tainted hearth made Deborah happy, then Proctor would do it. Someday, when she changed her mind, he would put a tub in the sleeping parlor. It would be a short journey to carry hot water from the hearth to the tub. Maybe enough water would clean away the bad memories from that attack.

"You're trying to change the subject," Deborah said. "But I can tell when you're lost in your thoughts, and you are more lost than a baby crawling through the forest. *What* are you thinking about?"

He tossed the towel aside and kissed her on the forehead. "I was thinking about you." He rested his right hand on her belly. "And our baby. But no forests."

She tilted her head up at him and smiled. "Are your hands clean now?"

"Yes."

"Are you sure?"

"*Yes.*"

"Can you please rub my feet?"

"But my hands are clean now," he protested. As she gave him a mock scowl, he pulled up a chair and pressed his thumbs into her sole. Deborah leaned back and sighed. She was past nine months pregnant, due any day, and it had finally caught up with her. Today must have been an especially bad day, because she'd quit working shortly after lunch. She winced unexpectedly, and he let go of her feet.

"No, please, keep rubbing," she said.

"But—" he protested.

"Keep rubbing," she insisted, so he cupped her foot in his hand and continued, but with a lighter touch than before. After a moment she shifted position, sighed, and relaxed again. "What's making you pensive?" she asked.

Her powers had grown during her pregnancy. She

seemed to see farther and clearer than ever before. Although it didn't take talent to see through him now. "I don't know what you mean," he said.

"Is it Washington's letter?"

General Washington's letter asking Proctor to serve again—and to go overseas to do it—could not have come at a worse time. Or rather, letters. There was one from Washington, another from Tallmadge, his spymaster, plus letters of introduction for Proctor to use in the mission. It was as though they took his service for granted.

Proctor stared out the window. In the four years since he'd moved to The Farm—he heard the capital letters in his head whenever he thought the phrase—Proctor had rebuilt a run-down spread into something special. With Ezra's help, they'd built a new addition that was bigger than the original house, repaired and repainted the barn, built a new chicken coop, and dug new privies. There were new rows of trees in the orchard on the hills in back, larger gardens stretching down the hill in front, cornstalks in the field that he had converted from fallow land, and new fences ringing the pastures. And he had done all of that in bits and pieces, in between the months that he spent serving the patriot cause.

"I belong here with you," Proctor said. "I'm not going across the ocean, not for Washington or anybody. Not with you expecting. I served in the militia, I did my time as a minuteman—"

"Any man can serve in the militia, Proctor. You do things that no one else can do."

"I know, but—" Deborah winced again, and he realized the tension was making his grip on her feet too strong. "I'm sorry. Maybe I should stop."

"No, it's all right," Deborah said when she caught her breath. "This is helping me greatly."

"It's just that there's almost peace already," Proctor

argued, lightening his touch again. "There hasn't been a major battle since Monmouth, and that was almost a year and a half ago. The war's over, all but the skirmishing."

"And what about the raids in New York? The town that was burned?"

The burning had shocked them all. "That was an aberration, a onetime thing."

She sighed and shifted again. "Maybe. But what about the Covenant?"

They had seen very little sign of the Covenant since the battle at Trenton. At first, Proctor just assumed they had retired to regroup. But now it had been more than two years. "They've given up."

Deborah caught her breath and frowned, a sure sign she was about to disagree. After a moment's pause, she said, "The Covenant has been around for hundreds of years, thousands if we believe what the widow Nance told us. When you spend that much time pursuing a goal, a year or two is nothing. Sometimes it takes a year or two of study to prepare a major spell. Besides, practicing witches, especially powerful witches, are good at hiding their activities. They have to be, just to survive. I know because I grew up around practicing witches."

Proctor always felt a little envious of Deborah's upbringing when he thought about his own mother and the way she'd made him ashamed of being a witch, frightened of everything bad that could happen to them. He didn't hold it against Deborah; he wanted to bring up their child in a household like Deborah's. But his own background had taught him a thing or two as well.

"Maybe I didn't grow up around practicing witches, but I've spent some time around the army," he said. "The British army is spread too thin. They'll never be able to push inland from the coast and beat the Continental army. The Covenant can't win the war that way.

We're too far away from Europe, for the British or the Covenant. Whatever the Covenant's grand plan is, they've decided to find a different way to pursue it. They don't care what happens here."

"That sounds like wishful thinking."

"No, it's just a cold assessment of the facts." He reached over and squeezed her hand. "I'm saving all my wishes for our baby."

"Are you worried?" she asked.

He couldn't bring himself to lie and say no or to admit the truth. She'd miscarried twice already, once when she was six months pregnant, producing a stillborn boy, small as a kitten. Luckily, they'd had Magdalena to help Deborah back to health. The old Dutch woman had a gift for helping pregnancies and for birthing. He sat there, quietly rubbing his wife's ankles.

"Coward," she said. "I'm worried. There, I said it."

"Shhh," he hushed her. "Don't make bad things true by wishing them so."

"You could do a scrying," she said. "That is your talent, above all others."

Scrying. Years ago, Proctor's witchcraft had manifested itself unbidden as scrying. It came naturally to him and was the only thing he'd known how to do until he met other witches. With Deborah's help, he had learned other, more powerful types of spells—how to set protective shields, how to create illusion or alter memory, how to move and transform objects. Simple, direct, unambiguous magic. When he thought about it, he was amazed at how far he'd come. The more he learned, the less he used his scrying.

"If the news that scrying would give me is good, then there's no need to see it," he said. "If the news is bad, then there's nothing I can do to change it and I would rather not know."

"Are you sure about that?" she asked.

"We'll answer the door when the future knocks and not before."

She lowered her feet slowly to the floor, spread them apart, and grunted uncomfortably. She made noise whenever the baby grew active. It was very active tonight.

The back door opened, and Magdalena entered from the new addition where she lived with the other student witches. The last four years had been hard on the old Dutch woman from Pennsylvania. Already stooped with age, she had never fully recovered from the Covenant's attack on The Farm years ago. She used a cane to steady herself. The basket she carried had only a few small apples in it, and yet she struggled with the weight. She set the basket down on the table and hobbled over to the hearth, where she pulled up a stool and held out her hands to the coals to warm them. Proctor rose and added wood to the fire, stirring the coals until the wood crackled in the flames.

"If I wanted that, I would have done it myself," Magdalena complained. She spoke in a thick Pennsylvania Dutch accent, her W's sounding more like V's, the D's and T's similarly swapped, and all the syllables of her words sharp and clipped.

"I wanted it," Proctor answered, knowing the old woman never asked for anything.

Magdalena glared at him, but she rubbed her liver-spotted hands together and held them up to the flame until she sighed pleasantly. She shifted on her stool and looked around at Deborah.

"You are doing how?" she asked.

"My water has broken," she said.

Proctor tensed. "What? Why didn't you say anything?"

"It just happened," Deborah said. A puddle spread on the floor between her feet.

Magdalena rose and hobbled over to her side. "Good, this is very good, you are past the best time," Magdalena said. She poked her fingers against the tight end of her fist as a demonstration. "If this baby grows much larger, it won't fit."

The sound of that worried Proctor. The contractions during Deborah's last miscarriage had been horrible, racking her body. It had been a childbirth for her in everything but outcome. "What should I do?" he asked.

"Go away," Magdalena said. "This is women's business."

Deborah held out her hand. "Don't go yet," she said. "The contractions started just after lunch. It may be hours."

So that was why she'd stopped early for the day. And of course, she hadn't said anything.

"Leave," Magdalena repeated, scowling at him.

"I'll get Abigail and Lydia," Proctor said, figuring out a compromise. They were women, and if this was women's work, Magdalena couldn't object. Then he could come back with them, which would make Deborah happy.

He stepped out the front door. A steady wind was blowing from the east. Abigail and Lydia sat in chairs on the porch watching the sunset color the sky red and orange to match autumn leaves. The two women were different from each other in almost every way, but somehow found enough in common that they had become close friends. Abigail, a big-boned girl, had her shirtsleeves rolled up and dirt on her hands. A basket overstuffed with fall turnips from the garden sat beside her where she'd dropped it. When she came to The Farm, they had called her Abby, but she had grown up in the past couple of years. Though she didn't show it at the moment, rocking back and forth, grinning happily, her mouth still open in mid-sentence.

Lydia was as parsimonious with her opinions as Abigail was free with hers, though she had reasons to watch what she said. She was a black woman probably about forty, a former slave who sometimes looked even older because her life had been hard. Her face was lean, with sharp cheekbones, and her limbs knotted with muscle. She had a shawl wrapped around her shoulders to keep her warm as she worked on knitting another blanket for the baby.

"Hey, Proctor," Abigail said. "I was just saying to Lydia—doesn't it seem odd to you?"

"Doesn't what seem odd?" he asked.

"That we worked so hard to build up this place, adding extra rooms and gardens, and even a second outhouse—" She turned aside to Lydia and said, "There were more than a dozen of us living in the house I grew up in and we never had more than one outhouse"—then turned back to Proctor to finish her thought—"and now the whole place feels almost empty."

It was true. Deborah had turned The Farm into a school for witches for several years, but now most of their students were gone. Ezra and Zoe had gone back to sea. Ezra had never forgiven Proctor for allowing the Covenant to kidnap Zoe, and Zoe had never forgiven Proctor for letting the Covenant escape with the orphan boy William. The cousins—stork-like Sukey and butterball Esther—had returned home to heal men wounded in the war. Alexandra Walker had rejected magic and disguised herself as a young man to fight the British with her brothers in the army. Other witches had shorter stays: Jane Irwin had studied for a few months and didn't say five words unprompted the whole time, Edwina Chase had displayed an amazing talent with animals but left because the people made her anxious, and a Mrs. Richardson had arrived from South Carolina and departed the same day when she discovered Deborah's mother was dead. Only the five of them were left.

Soon to be six.

"They're going to fill up this place with children, I expect," Lydia said as she knitted.

"I hope so," Abigail said enthusiastically. "I love children."

"That's my hope too," Proctor said. He knew that witches often had trouble bearing children. He and Deborah were both only children, even though all their neighbors had ten, fifteen, even twenty offspring. "We could be starting on that real soon. Deborah's water broke."

"Why didn't you say so?" Abigail snapped. She jumped up and punched him in the shoulder before she ran inside. Her family was the exception rather than the rule. Abigail's mother had given birth to nine, though the talent for witchcraft ran weak in them, even Abigail, if it showed up at all.

"Aren't you going to go inside to help with the childbirth?" Proctor asked. He couldn't return to Deborah's side until Lydia came in too, but he didn't know how to tell her that.

Lydia rocked back and forth in place for a moment. "I'm not that interested in helping with childbirth, to be honest," Lydia said. "It's an awful lot of noise and mess that I don't know nothing about."

"I just assumed—" he started, and then cut himself off.

"You just assumed that because I'm a woman, I know that sort of thing," Lydia said. "Well, I don't. I served Miss Cecily from the time I was a child and she had no interest in making babies. The only other babies I had the chance to see born were slaves, and it was hard for me to do anything that'd bring more souls into slavery. Miss Cecily couldn't stand the thought of letting anyone else have control of me, so I was never forced to the spot where I had to bear children of my own. And I'm glad. I don't know if I could have brought them up without freedom."

"I had no idea," Proctor said, letting everything he'd heard sink in.

"I shouldn't have said anything," she said, keeping her eyes down. "Forget I said anything."

"No, it's fine, it's better than fine," he said. "How can I know things if you don't tell me . . . Hey, hold on a minute. How could you be with Cecily since you were a child? You're about ten years older than she is, aren't you?"

"No, I am not. She's been that same age as long as I knowed her, never a day older or younger, and not just 'cause she was vain about her appearance. It wasn't natural. Her name's not Sumpter or Pinckney either."

"I remember you telling us that, but I assumed it was because she married."

Lydia sighed. "No, she went by Cecily Aikens when I was a child, and there was a Master Aikens too, though I don't recall as he was a relation. Then we moved and she changed her name to Hayne. She didn't become a Sumpter and a Pinckney until we moved north."

"When was that?"

"When we came to The Farm with orders to spy on Deborah's mother." She folded up her blanket and tucked the needles into it.

"How old is she really?" Proctor asked.

"She's older than I care to think about," Lydia said, squinting off at the horizon. "When she spoke to old folks, great-grandmothers and the like, she traded stories with them as if she'd been there. I remember one . . ." She trailed off. The wind rustled through the orchard, sending a cascade of leaves fluttering to the ground.

"What story?" Proctor asked.

"Oh, there was a rebellion of slaves on the Stono River, back forty years ago, and she talked about the slave Cato, he's the one who led it, like she know every line on his face. I listened close to the stories about slave uprisings when I had the chance."

"Did you have many chances?"

"No, not really. Just whispers, here and there. Everybody afraid to talk openly about it, 'cause it might mean people could die."

"Sounds much like our talent, in that respect."

"Yes it does," she said. Crinkles formed at the corners of her eyes, and she smiled at Proctor. He thought it might be the first time he had ever seen her genuinely smile at him that way. "It was a lot like our talent."

From inside the house came the sounds of furniture scraped across the floor—probably Abigail rearranging things just to have work to do. The sun had settled in the sky, taking most of the color with it. Only red remained, streaked across the horizon like blood smeared across pale white flesh.

Now, that was a morbid thought. He tried to shake it off. "I've never heard you talk about those times quite so much before."

"You never seen me trying to put off helping with a childbirth," Lydia said. She pushed her chair back and stood up.

"If you go inside though, I can follow you in and see Deborah," he admitted.

"Why do you want to go and do that? Just so she can chase you out again?"

"Sure. It'll give her something to do, between contractions."

Lydia tucked the baby blanket under her arm and picked up Abigail's basket of turnips. "We better go in and see how we can help."

"Don't even think about helping," Proctor said. "If there's some way to help, that means there's something going wrong. And nothing's going to go wrong, so nobody will need any help."

"Uh-huh," she murmured.

The wind gusted, cracking a branch heavy with fruit

from one of the trees at the edge of the orchard. It fell with a thump on a patch of dead ground, soil that had been barren ever since Cecily's necromancy raised a corpse that had been buried there. Unripened apples tumbled into the dry grass as dark clouds gathered overhead.

It was not a bad omen. Proctor was in no mood to admit bad omens. "Looks like we've got extra fodder for the pigs," he said, pulling open the door.

Lydia tugged her shawl tighter against her throat. "If you say so."

Chapter 3

All the furniture had been pushed to the edges of the room and neatly stacked out of the way. Deborah walked—no, waddled—around the open space, with Abigail supporting her on one side and Magdalena on the other. Magdalena, small and frail, supported herself with her cane, and looked as if she might topple under the weight. Proctor went to take her place, but Lydia put down the blanket and basket and got there first.

"Oh, you don't need to do that—" Deborah protested, but the last word was interrupted by a wince as she felt another contraction.

"Just keep breathing through it," Abigail said.

Deborah nodded and continued her small circuit of the room. Magdalena shuffled over to a chair and collapsed into it.

"What can I do to help?" Proctor asked.

All four women looked at him as if he had just asked them how to fly. "Maybe you could go check outside," Magdalena said.

"Check for what?" he asked. "We've set spells protecting our borders against any physical intruders, man or animal, living or dead, accidental or intentional." They'd learned their lesson after Bootzamon's probing of their hideaway some years before. "It's been over a year since we heard or saw any indication of the Covenant."

Magdalena raised the knob end of her cane at him.

He threw up his hands in surrender. "I'll go check the borders," he said.

"Thank you," Deborah said. She paused and smiled at him, but the effect was weakened by the sweat beading on her forehead.

Proctor grabbed a bucket and climbed the hill to the orchard to gather the fallen apples. Clouds rolled in, deepening the gloom before he'd gathered them all, and the wind whipped through the branches, threatening to break more limbs. He plucked a ripe apple and tucked it in his pocket for Singer, their mare, then took the rest and dumped them into the pig trough with their other kitchen scraps. Inside the barn, he rubbed Singer's nose while she ate out of his hand and then checked the cows in their stalls. When he was done, he took a lantern from the wall and went outside.

He meant to light it with magic. He had almost mastered the talent, but he wasn't going to make the attempt in the barn with all the straw around. Shielding the lantern with his body, he tried the spell that Deborah had taught him.

A prickling unease shivered through his skin the moment he spoke.

Before he could stop the spell, flame exploded from his hand, a ball of fire that hung suspended in the air. Wind swirled, drawing straw and grass up in a spiral to feed the flame. The new-fed fire, leashed to the ground, wavered toward the barn, then veered abruptly at the house.

Coming to his senses, Proctor kicked and stamped, scattering the dried grasses. Deprived of fuel, the flames quickly sputtered and died.

Hair prickled on the back of his neck, but he told himself he was imagining things. Worries about Deborah had him on edge. Still, he decided that he knew the land well enough to walk it in the dark. He put the lantern down and set out to check the fences.

The Farm was hidden by an illusion that blurred its presence to passing eyes. To anyone on the other side of the fence, Proctor would seem no more than a stray shadow or a bobbing will-o'-the-wisp. There were physical barriers, thorny hedges just beyond the fence. Spells had also been set to discourage visitors from going any farther. If someone did press through the thorns and spells, their presence would set off warning bells. A variety of other protections would delay or trap them while the witches in the house responded to the warning.

In short, no man or creature not explicitly blessed or accepted by Deborah could approach them unawares. No wonder the Covenant had given up.

He finished his inspection at the gate, the weakest spot in their defenses, but he saw and sensed nothing unusual there, either. Satisfied, he passed through the gardens and returned to the house in the dark. The wind was as fitful as his mood, gusting and twisting along the ground in his wake.

Proctor entered the new wing so he wouldn't disturb the women. He couldn't wait until Deborah made up her mind to move into this part of the house. The main room was dominated by a huge fireplace built out of fieldstone and protected by an ancient spell that he and Deborah had performed on the day of their wedding.

He put logs on the grate and started a fire—using flint and steel this time. Wind whistled across the chimney top, but the shaft did not seem to be drawing smoke very well. He let the sparks burn down instead of feeding them.

He went through the back door into the old house. He saw Deborah in the bedroom, or at least he saw her knees poking up in the air. Abigail sat on the bed beside her, holding her hand.

Magdalena stepped in front of him to block the view. "Done already?"

"I checked all our boundaries. We're shut up tight for the night."

"Then go make sure we have fresh water and kindling for the fire."

"But—" He looked at the pitchers of water already full and ready, and the stack of firewood by the hearth, and then he realized it was just more make-work to keep him out of their way. He decided not to be irritated by it. "How's Deborah?"

"She's fine," Magdalena said. "Why do you think she's not fine?"

"I didn't think she wasn't fine."

Deborah's voice came from the other room, high-pitched, breathless, and short. "I'm fine."

"Is she supposed to sound like that?" he asked Magdalena.

"Sound like what?" the old Dutch woman snapped angrily.

"I'll go get water and firewood," Proctor said.

"That would help a great deal, yes."

The pitchers were all full, so he carried the kettle outside and filled that at the well. Then, since there was plenty of firewood inside already, he started moving one of the piles over to the porch where they could get at it easier.

He'd seen plenty of births—his mother had a sure hand with the lambs and calves, especially during difficult deliveries. But as an only child, he had never attended a baby's birth before. Deborah's pregnancy had been hard enough, but this—the hours of pain, sweat, and blood, the uncertain outcome . . .

Actually, it reminded him a lot of being in battle.

Best not to mention that.

He tossed the split logs onto the new pile and went

back for two more. All that mattered was keeping Deborah safe, keeping their baby safe. He wondered if they were going to have a boy or a girl. If it was a boy, he wanted to name him after his father, Lemuel. Now, that was a good strong name. Lemuel Brown.

Lydia stepped outside. "She's asking for you."

He dropped the wood. It clattered on the ground, banging off his shins, but he hardly noticed because his heart was pounding so hard. "Is everything—"

"Everything's fine," she said.

Proctor ran inside and stopped at the door to Deborah's bedroom. Magdalena sat between Deborah's feet, and Abigail frowned at him, rising immediately to block his view. "Deborah?" he said.

"Proctor, is that you?" she answered, panting between words.

"Yes, Lydia said you wanted me."

"Yes, I did," she said, gritting her teeth through a painful contraction. "Now go away."

Abigail reached out and squeezed his arm, not as a gesture of reassurance, but as a means of turning him around and pushing him out the doorway and across the room. "She just wanted to know where you were. Now she knows. Don't you have water to fetch or wood to split?"

The hearth had burned down to coals. "I could tend the fire," he suggested. It would keep him near Deborah, and no one could argue that he wasn't doing something.

"Good," Abigail said, and she shoved him out of the way.

He moved a chair over in front of the hearth and added a log from the basket. He prodded it into flame, then added more logs on top. This chimney was drawing just fine.

Lydia pulled up another chair beside him and took out her knitting. "It's not that cold outside," she said.

"It felt chilly enough when I tried to see how my wife was doing," he muttered.

The wind rattled the shutters, which banged against the house like someone knocking to come in. The wood in the fire crackled and spit, shooting sparks out into the room. The draft from the chimney drew the flames into wild and unusual shapes. Proctor stared at them, the way he might stare into someone's face, while Deborah shouted and panted her way through ever more frequent contractions.

Abigail popped her head out of the bedroom door. "I think it's time," she said eagerly.

Proctor jumped out of his seat.

"Not you," she said. "Lydia—she'll want to see the baby being born."

Lydia sighed, then put her work aside and joined the women. With all of them crowded into the tiny room, they couldn't close the door.

Deborah cried out.

Proctor plopped down in his chair and stabbed the iron into the fire. He flipped over a log, sending up a spray of sparks.

"This time, you push," Magdalena said. "Just like you're doing your business."

Deborah cried out again.

Proctor stirred the coals. Sparks shot up again, but this time a ball of fire rose with the sparks. It was just like the strange flame that had formed when he tried to light the lantern. In a split second air spiraled around it, drawing fire from the logs, making the flame larger and stronger.

And more man-like.

The flame had limbs and a head. Proctor watched, frozen, as fiery fingers formed at the ends of its arms. Eyes as black as charcoal popped open in its head. The arms and legs, rooted in the burning logs, stretched and pulled like a creature escaping a trap.

It reminded him of the imp Dickon that had kept the evil Bootzamon's pipe lit.

Only it was the size of a man, and it was crawling out of a hearth that had once been used as a black altar.

Proctor's tongue came unfrozen. "Demon!"

Deborah cried out in reply from the other room.

He tipped over the kettle on the fire. Steam rolled out of the hearth, but the demon twisted and dodged, avoiding most of the water. It was a creature of spirit—it needed the flames to manifest. If Proctor drowned the fire, he could kill it.

Proctor grabbed the nearest pitcher and doused the flames again. The creature roared and spit, but it yanked one leg free of the burning logs. If it escaped and became a free creature of fire—

"Demon—we're under attack from a demon," Proctor yelled.

He looked for more water, wishing that he'd brought in more water—why hadn't he brought in more water? He ran for the washbowl, but it was empty. He grabbed the half-empty pitcher from the stand and turned back to the fire. The demon was almost free.

"There, you're almost there, one more push," Magdalena said.

Proctor flung the pitcher. The ceramic shattered into a thousand shards, and the water washed over the rest of the logs.

Which set free the demon's other leg.

Deborah cried out, louder than before.

The demon floated above the hearth, staring at Proctor eye-to-eye. Horns rose from its head and its mouth gaped in a snarl of white flame and orange tongue. Red fire rippled from its shoulder to its waist like a coat, and it moved on legs of smoke. It glanced away from Proctor, at the bedroom, and licked its lips.

Proctor drew all the power into himself that he could

summon. Sweat poured from his body. He would smother the demon with every stone in the house. He would call rain out of the sky. The demon took a step toward the bedroom and Proctor blocked its way.

"No. You will not have my wife or my child."

The demon hesitated and fell back.

Abigail's voice sound behind him. "Proctor, it's wonderful, come see your baby—"

Her sentence ended with a scream.

The baby—his baby—cried out in the other room, its first sound, so small and vulnerable. Proctor's heart jumped, and he turned his head. Magdalena had emerged from the room, smiling, oblivious. She held a knife out handle-first for Proctor, inviting him to cut the baby's cord.

The demon lunged past him.

Proctor clutched for it, his right hand sliding down the flames until they closed on the creature's ankle. Heat knifed up his arm, and the scar of his missing finger felt like a hot coal had been hammered into it. The demon twisted and lashed at him like a frightened snake. Proctor tried to drag it toward the front door, but the pain was blinding. His knees buckled beneath him and his vision blackened like the night. Everything in the room went dark except for the flames.

Abigail screamed and screamed. Deborah shouted his name. His baby cried out, tiny and helpless.

The demon's ankle slipped through Proctor's hand. He was holding on to no more than a heel. He tried to grab at it with his other hand, but he needed it to hold on to the floor lest he spin away into the dark and the shadow. The demon twisted around and slashed at his face with red talons. Proctor rolled away from the blow, but he couldn't hold on much longer.

A cool white light, smooth and round as a pearl, emerged from the darkness.

The light came from the knob of Magdalena's cane. She blocked the way to the child. She spoke out in German, words Proctor couldn't understand, though the tone was clear enough: *Clear out.*

The demon shrank back and roared, a sound like the wind building up to a tempest. The demon pulled free of Proctor's hand, and Proctor collapsed to the ground.

Magdalena threatened the creature with her cane. The light brightened, a full moon, filling the room. The demon bounced from corner to corner, like an anxious cat, desperate to escape and equally ready to strike.

"Grab it," Magdalena shouted, and Proctor realized she was shouting at him. "I told you to grab it und hold it!"

He lunged for it, and the demon dodged away. The baby hiccuped in the other room, and the demon seemed to cry in anguish, a whistling sound like the wind scraped over a roof's edge. Proctor grabbed at it again with his left hand but it was hot to the touch and he flinched. It slipped through his fingers.

The demon, swollen with flame, charged at Magdalena. Proctor yelled out "No!"

"You will not have this child!" she cried.

The demon tried to bull past her, but she stepped into its way and slammed the knob end of her cane into its face. The white light hit the shadowy fire of the creature like water hitting hot oil. The sizzling crackle was followed by a burst of power that knocked everyone to the floor.

When Proctor pushed himself upright again, the baby was wailing, the demon was gone . . . and Magdalena lay broken at odd angles on the floor, surrounded by the shattered pieces of her cane. Lydia knelt over her a moment, then shook her head.

Magdalena was dead.

"God, dear God in heaven, what was that?" whispered Abigail. She sat in the corner, knees pulled up to her chin.

The baby squalled.

Deborah! Proctor lurched up and lunged to the doorway. He flung it open. Deborah sat there in a pile of wet and blood-tinged sheets, holding the baby to her breast with the uncut cord snaked across the bed. Tears wet her cheeks.

"I wanted this to be a happy day," she said. "I wanted this to be our happiest day."

Her voice wasn't sad or scared. It was angry.

Chapter 4

The unblinking sun peeked through the windows as Proctor scraped the mortar off the face of the stone. He chose another one from the pile at his feet and fitted it into the gap.

"Do you really have to block up the hearth?" Abigail asked.

"I'm not going to risk another attack," Proctor said as he troweled mortar onto the stone. "I think the demon tried the other hearth first but couldn't come down it because of the protective spell."

"Why can't you put a protective spell on this one?" she said, wrapping her arms around her chest.

Because it had only been two days since the attack and none of them had gotten much sleep. Because Deborah was trying to learn how to nurse a newborn and didn't have time to prepare the spell. Because he had spent yesterday digging yet another grave at the orchard's edge, this one for Magdalena—their enemies were necromancers, and he wasn't about to leave a dead body around to tempt them.

"Because," he said, using the butt-end of the trowel to tap the stone a little tighter into place. One more and he'd be done. "Because I don't trust this hearth. Because I will never trust this hearth. Because I want us to be safe."

He met her eye as he chose another stone, challenging her to deny him.

"You doing all this work to make us safe doesn't make

me feel very safe," Abigail said. "I can bury a body or brick up a fireplace as well as anyone, but I can't do the kind of magic that you and Deborah do. I can't stop a demon. So if you want me to finish up this chore while you prepare a spell, I'd feel a lot more safe."

He chipped a corner off the stone and forced it into the last hole. That was the problem. He didn't know what kind of spell would keep them safe. Deborah and Magdalena had already placed spells on the hearth once before, after it was tainted, and those spells didn't hold.

Abigail turned and stomped away.

He tossed the trowel into the mortar bucket and stared out the window at the orchard. The graves were all unmarked, Quaker fashion, because that's what Deborah and her parents believed. But Proctor knew where they were, every one of them. Every one of the graves represented a failure. He had failed to protect Deborah's father from the assassins. He had failed to include the house in the protective spell that saved his life from the reanimated corpses, and it had cost Deborah's mother her life. He had failed to stop the demon and it had killed Magdalena.

But not Deborah. Not their daughter.

He had done that much. This time.

He went outside and scraped his bucket and tools clean, then washed his hands and found his hammer. He meant to nail the old house shut. He didn't trust the hearth, and he didn't trust the old house, and they weren't going to use any part of it. When he had time, he would tear it down to the ground, no matter what Deborah thought.

The wood was old and hard, and he bent half a dozen nails boarding the front door shut, but soon he was done. The new addition had a kitchen door. He tucked another board under his arm and went in there.

The diapers drying on the rack by the fire left a faint

scent of soap in the air, and made him think of his daughter all over again.

He went to the back door that connected to the old house and slapped the board across it. He fished a nail out of his pocket and was tapping it into place when a voice spoke behind him.

"Proctor?" Deborah said softly.

He jumped. He'd been so focused on his work, he hadn't noticed her sitting in the bent hickory rocker across the room. She held their sleeping daughter to her chest. *Their daughter.* So tiny in her mother's arms, a face in swaddling, topped by a tousle of black hair. Dear God, he wanted to build a wall around her and never let anything hurtful come near her again.

"I'm sorry," he said, setting the board down and slipping the nail back into his pocket. "I didn't mean to hammer so loud. It's just . . . the noise comes with the hammer."

"No, that's fine," she said. "I've been thinking about her name."

Elizabeth Prudence, after their two mothers. Or was she going to be Prudence Elizabeth? Both names sounded good on his tongue. He liked their diminutives too. Betty. Prue. "Either one is fine with me," he said.

"Maggie," Deborah said.

"Who?"

"Maggie," Deborah repeated, staring down at the little girl while she rocked. "Her name is going to be Maggie."

After Magdalena. Proctor set the hammer down and walked over to kiss Deborah on her forehead. She leaned into his lips. He liked the smell of her.

"Maggie, huh?" he said as he straightened. "I like that."

"Maggie Elizabeth," Deborah mumbled.

Proctor frowned. "You never were one much for Prudence, were you?"

"If I was going to name a daughter for a trait, I think it would be Courage. Or Independence."

Proctor started to laugh and then the laugh died on his lips. It was too soon after Magdalena's death to welcome that sound. "Courage and independence will serve us—and our daughter—well. But it would still be prudent to look to our defenses. Abigail was talking to me—"

He paused. A doorway opened onto the kitchen. Abigail and Lydia stood framed by the jambs, listening to Proctor's and Deborah's conversation. Lydia wiped her hands on a towel.

Abigail's face, normally full and square with rosy cheeks, looked drawn and wan. "I told him the same thing I told you, that only witchcraft can protect us from other witches."

Deborah rocked in her chair, staring down at Maggie. "I've been thinking about what you said. Demons are spirits without flesh—that's one reason why they're so eager to possess men. It gives them power in this world. Babies are most vulnerable at birth, when the soul enters with the first breath. The demon doesn't have to be invited to possess, doesn't have to fight to enter the body, because the newborn child is already open to spirits."

"How do you know that?" Proctor asked.

Deborah sighed. "My mother treated a woodcutter possessed by a demon once, and we discussed everything she knew. Every word for 'soul' means 'breath' in its original language. That's why babies always cry when they take their first breath—because it hurts to have a soul."

"So the demon was sent specifically to possess your baby?" Lydia asked.

A lump formed in Proctor's throat at the thought, but it was the only explanation that made sense. "Maybe it's the only thing they could get past our defenses. They've tried just about everything else in the past."

"No, the Covenant wants their demon to possess a witch," Deborah said. "Whatever their plan is, it requires great power."

Proctor's right hand was a fist. The thought of anyone trying to hurt his child or possess it for evil . . . "Demons are creatures of fire, soot, and ash," he said. "That's how they use chimneys to enter homes. But this hearth is protected. It tried to enter here and couldn't. I witnessed the attempt, but I didn't understand it at the time. Nothing can come through the other chimney now, not even a bird. No fire, no soot, no ash. No demon."

"I'm sorry, but that makes no sense," Abigail said.

Proctor started to protest that no, he was sure the hearth was blocked, but Abigail continued.

"Why possess the baby? We don't even know if she has any talent, and we won't know until she starts to become a woman. The Covenant's plan was to possess the baby right in front of us and then wait twelve years to do anything with her? What did they expect us to do the whole time? Twiddle our thumbs and wait for them to show up?"

"Maybe they could use the baby to kill us," Proctor said, his voice lowered as if to say it might make it true. He watched Maggie and Deborah with a sharp edge of worry.

"The demon was already powerful enough to kill us if it wanted," Abigail said. "Or didn't you notice that it killed Magdalena?"

They weren't sure how the demon had killed Magdalena. When they examined her, her face had been . . . almost peaceful. It was the first time Proctor could remember seeing her without the tightness of pain marking the corners of her mouth and eyes.

"I'll tell you what they wanted," Abigail said, coming out of the doorway into the room. "They wanted Deborah. The mother is also at her most vulnerable when she's giving birth. The demon could have possessed her right at that moment without her being able to stop it. Then it would have a witch who could do its bidding."

Proctor's gut knotted. *That* was a horrible thought.

Deborah reached out and took hold of Proctor's hand. He started to squeeze back to reassure her, but she held it up in the air to study his missing finger.

"They wanted something else to hold over us," she said in the tone of voice she used for teaching when she didn't want to be questioned. "They wanted a way to make us do their bidding."

"Now, that makes sense to me too," Abigail said. Her shoulders slouched, deflated. Proctor could tell she had really wanted her explanation to be right. "You would do anything for Maggie. We all would. They have to know that."

Deborah dropped Proctor's hand. She stopped rocking and leaned forward on the edge of her chair. "But what do they want us to do? Why do they need our power?"

They all looked at Lydia. She had spent her life as a slave of Cecily, who was a member of the Covenant. She folded the towel and tossed it onto a bench. She turned her body away as if she meant to leave, but then she crossed her arms over her chest, with her hands on her shoulders so they formed a scissors at her throat.

"When we were with the prince-bishop, he talked about the circle of misery," Lydia said. She shivered. "He used to chuckle when he said it. It's power that depends on forcing someone unwilling into the circle. Cecily drawing on the power of a slave gave her greater power to control others. When the prince-bishop drew on the power of that orphan boy, who was an innocent, it gave him greater power to corrupt others."

"That's black magic," Abigail murmured. Lydia shifted uncomfortably at the phrase.

"Maybe there's a better term for it," Proctor said.

"How about *evil*?" Deborah asked.

"If they're doing the same thing here," Lydia said, "then I expect that by destroying your belief in the cause of liberty, they could tap into your power to destroy the cause. Whatever circle they're trying to form requires patriots to complete it."

"It's not enough just to protect ourselves," Deborah said. "I have to believe that ultimately we can turn their hearts . . ."

Proctor had his doubts about that, but he withheld them.

". . . but in the meantime, we must take additional steps to protect ourselves," she finished.

"That's what I've been trying to tell you," Abigail said. The baby startled in Deborah's arms, and Abigail lowered her voice. "I'm sorry."

"Mama Chamba," Lydia said.

Proctor didn't understand what she had said. "Mumbo jumbo?"

"Mama Chamba," Lydia repeated. "She was an old slave woman on the Aikens plantation where I lived with Miss Cecily for a time. Came straight from Africa and still spoke the old tongue from there. She was a healer, like Deborah's mother. She'd use the afterbirth of a baby to help protect it."

Deborah leaned forward in interest. Maggie stirred in her arms. One tiny hand had wormed loose from her blankets and groped blindly in the air. "I know of the afterbirth from one child being used in a spell to ease the birth of the midwife's next patient," Deborah said.

"That's not what my mother does," Abigail said, eager to contribute. "She wraps it up in a clean white cloth and buries it. If the baby's a girl and she wants her to grow up to be a good seamstress, she might run a needle through the cord first. Or if it's a boy, and his parents want him to be a good carpenter, she might use an iron nail or a wooden peg. But that was only rarely. Mostly she said we should be careful never to put the afterbirth in fire or water, lest the child end up burning to death or drowning . . ." She noticed she was rambling. "Maybe that could help us too."

Proctor watched his daughter stir between wakefulness and sleep. "So what do we do to protect Maggie?"

"I can only tell you what Mama Chamba did," Lydia said. "She would take the afterbirth to a tree on the plantation, a hidden tree used only by the slaves and not the master. It was usually a fruit tree, sometimes a nut tree. She would bury the afterbirth among the roots. Then only those who had sworn to protect the child were allowed to eat from the tree."

"Did it work?" he asked.

Lydia dropped her arms to her sides. "Mama Chamba planted a tree for me when I was born. I'm still trying to decide whether my life has been protected or not."

That seemed like a fair thing to wonder, Proctor thought.

"It's a powerful focus," Deborah said. She was rocking again, and Maggie had settled back down to sleep. "It's connected directly with life, with the protection of a mother for her child, with the entrance of a new soul into the world."

"I saved the afterbirth," Abigail said. "Wrapped in waxed cloth, in a box of cedar chips."

"Is that why you wanted those cedar chips?" Proctor asked.

"No," Abigail said. "I wanted them because there were moth holes in my sweater. But then I thought about what my mother did with the afterbirth, and I wrapped it up so I could ask Deborah what we should do later."

"Thank you," Deborah said. "I didn't even think about it."

"You had other things to worry about," Abigail said,

stifling a yawn. Within a moment he and Deborah were both fighting their own yawns. Deborah's stretched on until she squeezed her eyes shut.

"We're all exhausted," Proctor said. "And not as sharp as we need to be. Let's sleep on this tonight and prepare a spell tomorrow."

Now that they had some kind of plan, maybe they could actually get some rest.

The new addition had two stories. The kitchen and the parlor were downstairs, with a pair of good-sized bedrooms up. Abigail and Lydia shared one, and Proctor and Deborah took the other.

Proctor wanted to talk to Deborah privately about the Covenant's possible plans, but by the time he finished checking all the doors and windows and climbed the stairs to join her, she was already curled up in bed asleep. Maggie nestled in her arms, eyes closed, mouth puckered as if she was ready to be fed. Or soothed.

He reached over and stroked her soft, perfect cheek with his thumb. "If you ever have a brother, he's going to be named Lemuel," he whispered.

Nothing could soothe Proctor. He kept thinking about the Covenant's last plan to destroy Washington's army. They had put a curse on the soldiers, binding their souls to the ghosts of the dead. Proctor and Deborah had been able to defeat them after months of trial and error, and only because they had the help of their whole circle. Magdalena, Ezra, Sukey, Esther—they had all played a part, and they were all gone. Magdalena was dead and Ezra had gone back to the south China seas, both of them out of reach. Even Alexandra had played a role, and she was off in the army now.

If the Covenant summoned demons and possessed the army the same way . . . He had to stop dwelling on it. They had tried. They had failed. That was it.

Except he knew now for certain that the Covenant would try again. Not only would they try to destroy the army, and the cause that he believed in, they would try to use his family—*his* family, *his* wife and daughter—to do it.

They had stopped the Covenant's ghosts. They had stopped this demon. Knowing the Covenant, they already had another plan prepared. He had been simple to think they were through. It had been wishful thinking, just like Deborah said.

He watched Maggie in the dark, so tiny and trusting, unconscious of any danger.

She looked like her mother. The same eyes, the same firm little chin. He never expected that he could feel so protective of someone. In some ways, the feelings were even stronger than his feelings for Deborah, magnified both by the love he had for Deborah and by Maggie's own helplessness. He was afraid that something would hurt her. He was even afraid that he might roll over on her in the middle of the night.

But he had to sleep.

He patted his pillow down in the space between the two of them, nested his head in the crook of his arm, and settled down as close to the edge of the mattress as he could get. The mattress was old and flattened at the sides, so he felt like he was constantly on the verge of rolling off the bed. He braced one arm against the bed frame and forced himself to stillness.

Sleep continued to evade him like a beam of light cast by a mirror, dancing out of the grasp of a kitten. His thoughts tossed and turned until finally, in the darkest part of the night, he rose again.

The bedroom door opened onto a hallway much longer than he remembered, and the steps downstairs seemed to stretch and curve in front of him, leading into the old house. When he stepped off the bottom stair, he passed through a doorway and landed in the parlor at the exact spot where Magdalena had died.

Magdalena stood there, her back to him. Her plain black dress and dark gray bonnet had been replaced with a silver robe and a gleaming white cap. She leaned on her cane, which was whole and unbroken. She faced the bricked-up hearth.

Behind the stones and mortar, something tapped at the barrier.

"Don't worry," she said. "I won't let it in."

"Magdalena," Proctor said. He fought back the tears he hadn't let himself shed before now, but they seemed to flow down his throat, swelling until they threatened to choke him. "I'm sorry."

"Don't be," she said. "What happened was meant to be. I believe this to be true, now more than before. Listen to me closely, Proctor."

He tried to take a step toward her, but his limbs were heavy and sluggish.

"Look at your hand," she said.

She didn't say which one, but he knew what she meant. He raised his arm slowly from his waist, fighting the weight of it, and turned the palm over. His hand was whole again, the finger there as it had been before.

"Why do they want Deborah and the rest of us dead?" he said, his words as thick as water.

Magdalena turned around. Her face was young again, her skin as smooth as a baby's and her features free of any pain. Proctor would not have recognized her had he not already known her voice, her clothes, her stance. She held up her cane, bouncing it lightly in her hand.

"Not they, but he," she said. "He wants you dead because you have the power to stop him. He has stretched his life for centuries, building toward the fulfillment of his plan. He must bring it to fruition soon or he will wither like a tree that failed to bear harvest in its appointed time.

He will do anything he must to bring his plan to fruit. He will use you against your loved ones, use your loved ones against you."

"Who? The necromancer—the prince-bishop?"

"Beware this one," Magdalena said. She took her cane and scratched a figure in the floor.

D

"Who is 'D'?" Proctor asked. Did she mean Deborah? "Who's 'D'?"

Magdalena had her back to him again. He tried to call out to her, but the pressure of the air weighed on him. The words rose into his mouth, but went no farther.

Behind him, he heard Deborah calling him. He turned to answer her and tripped. He fell, unable to raise his arms to catch himself. He closed his eyes and flinched, but when he hit the floor, it was soft, and yielded under him like a pile of wet straw. A black pit opened beside him. His arm and leg dangled in the air over a hole that dropped all the way to hell.

Chapter 5

"Proctor?" Deborah whispered again.

He opened his eyes. He was in bed at the edge of the mattress, with an arm and leg dangling over the side. His chin was slick with drool. "Whuh?"

"You're mumbling in your sleep and thrashing about. Are you all right?"

He wiped the drool off his chin and the sleep from his eyes. He rolled over and saw Maggie suckling at Deborah's breast. She looked so small. The idea of anything happening to her—especially because of him—was too much to bear.

"I was dreaming," he said.

Her posture tightened, rigid enough to interrupt Maggie for a second while she suckled. "What were you dreaming about?"

He hesitated before answering. He wasn't sure he wanted to share all his fears with her. She had enough to take care of already. But he was terrible at hiding things from her when she stared at him that way. "I dreamed about Magdalena."

"What did she look like?" Deborah asked.

"She looked young again. She was wearing a silver dress and a white cap, and she could stand without leaning on her cane." He sat up and nodded at their daughter. "Maybe it was because I was thinking about Maggie."

Deborah lifted Maggie away from her breast. The

baby's mouth puckered on open air, and her tiny hands waved frantically while Deborah shifted her to the other side and helped her latch on.

"Maybe it wasn't a dream," Deborah said.

"What do you mean?" he asked.

"I also dreamed of Magdalena."

Her nightcap had fallen off, and her hair was loose, spilling down over her cheeks and covering her face enough that he couldn't see her expression. But he could tell that something was wrong, that she was worried or upset. He reached out and touched her arm. "Deborah?"

She brushed the hair out of her eyes and tucked it behind her ear. "I didn't think I'd ever fall in love," she said out of nowhere. "I knew for certain that I was going to end my days an old maid."

"You mean you weren't one already when I met you?" he said, meaning to tease her. The tone was wrong, but she understood what he was trying to do. She reached over and pinched the back of his hand, and he jerked it away. "Ow."

"Let me have my say," she said.

"All right. You were going to end your days an old maid."

"Yes," she said, stroking Maggie's hair. "And then my parents would die and I wouldn't have any family or relatives. I would hide in their old house while it slowly fell down around me, invisible to the world. The years would pass, and I would turn into the very caricature of a witch, an old hag, begging from house to house in Salem village, bitter and angry, muttering petty curses under my breath at the townspeople who kicked me off their doorstep or sent their dogs to growl at me."

"You didn't dwell on it much, did you?" he said, sitting up beside her.

"A passing thought, once or twice," Deborah said.

Maggie tugged her little head off Deborah's breast and emitted a tiny, wet burp. Deborah held the baby to her shoulder and patted her back.

Proctor leaned forward and pressed his lips against the back of Maggie's delicate head. She smelled sweet, like milk. She sighed and fell instantly asleep against her mother's shoulder. "This is a fair approximation of what I always wanted out of life," he said.

Deborah looked at him, surprised. "Is it?"

"I wanted to serve my country, and I've done that, more than I ever expected. I wanted a build a prosperous farm, and we're on the way to that. I wanted to build a new house, and even though Ezra did most of the work, we've got a pretty good start on that." He met her eyes, which were the brightest thing in the room, as if they were only a shade covering the light inside her. "I wanted a beautiful wife and a family."

Deborah smiled. "And now you've got that too."

"No, I'm still hoping that will come around some-day—" Her hand jumped up to pinch him again and he flinched, grinning. "Yes, yes, now I've got that too." He leaned over to kiss her. She turned her head to the side, and he kissed her cheek. "That's been the best part," he said.

"You better say that's the best part," she said.

"That's the best part."

She leaned over and kissed him on the mouth. They leaned together carefully, protecting Maggie between them. Deborah reached up and held her hand against his cheek. Finally, she sighed and pulled away.

"That wasn't a dream," she said finally.

He closed his eyes and leaned his head back against the wall, trying to brace himself as the world rushed away from him. "No, it wasn't. Her spirit came to visit us."

"To warn us."

"I know."

"The demon they sent, that's unlike any magic, good or evil, that I've ever witnessed or heard account of," Deborah said. "And I barely glimpsed it. We'll have to be more careful than ever. Set up stronger protections, take fewer risks beyond the bounds of The Farm."

"That won't be enough." He swung his legs off the bed and rested his bare feet on the wide planks of the floor. He leaned, elbows on his knees, and rubbed his face. "It's no good waiting for them to come find us. I've got to go find them."

"And kill them?" Deborah asked.

"If I need to," Proctor answered.

"You can't solve all our problems by killing people."

"Maybe—but sometimes it's a good start."

He tried to respect Deborah's Quaker background and her rejection of violence, so he regretted the words as soon as he said them. He stood and walked over to the closed door. He braced his hands on the jambs and pressed his head against the rough wood.

"I don't like what it does to you," she said. "Every time you hurt someone it takes a little part of you away."

"Like a finger?"

"That's not what I meant."

He spun around. "But it's the truth. I'm a danger to you and to Maggie. That necromancer can use it to turn me against you. As long as he has my finger, he has a trigger on a gun that's aimed at both of you. We have no idea when it will fire."

"It doesn't have to fire," Deborah said. "Just because a man owns a gun doesn't mean he has to use it."

"But that decision isn't up to us," he said. "And if we sit here and wait and do nothing—"

"Who said anything about nothing?" Deborah said. "We'll strengthen our defenses. We'll find a way to be prepared."

"We can't solve everything with magic, not if all we do

is react to them. They create protective charms, so we break the charms. They curse the army, so we break the curse. They send demons for us, so we find a way to defeat the demon. They *attacked us in our home,* despite all our protections." He felt like his heart would dam his throat and block his words, so he talked faster, pouring the words out. "Sooner or later, they'll try some magic that gets past us. If we stay here, while they're out there making their plans, we're just like fish in a barrel. We're trapped here on The Farm, and that's precisely where they want us. It leaves them free to pursue whatever they want while we don't do anything."

"We don't have to leave The Farm to learn things," she said. "I . . . I can learn to spirit-walk. I'll find a way to reach Magdalena again. I'll ask her to explain her warnings to us."

She could learn to spirit-walk, but what did that leave him to do to protect his family? Wait until they were in danger again and react? "What exactly was Magdalena's warning to you?"

Deborah dropped her eyes and sighed. She pulled the blankets up around her and caressed Maggie's head. "I didn't mean to argue with you."

"I tell you what her warning was—she told you we were a danger to each other. She told you that our enemy would use you against your loved ones, use your loved ones against you."

He saw the tears rolling down her cheeks and the shudder in her shoulders and hated himself for saying anything. But it was the truth, and they had to face the truth if they were going to survive. He squeezed his eyes shut. Dear God, they had been attacked inside their own home. And the fire that the demon used to attack them had been stoked with his own hands.

"Love is never a danger in itself," Deborah choked

out. "It is the fear of losing love that drives us to do evil. The only solution is for us not to be afraid."

He went to the bed and sat beside her, wrapping an arm around her and pulling her close. She pressed her wet cheek against his shoulder. "I'm not afraid of love," he whispered. "I'm afraid of seeing the people I love get hurt. I'm afraid of doing nothing while evil men seek ways to hurt us. I want to find a way to stop them. I have to stop them or we'll never be safe again."

"I understand that," she said, wrapping her arm around him and squeezing. "I understand that you must follow your own light and do what you are led to believe is right. Just give me a moment to grow accustomed to it."

She shifted Maggie so that she rested half across her lap and half across Proctor's. They sat there quietly, and Proctor listened to the quiet sounds of their breathing. He wondered how the world could feel so perfectly right and so terribly wrong at the exact same time.

If he was going to take the fight to the Covenant, he would have to follow them to Europe—to Hesse or England or wherever they might be. It would take him away from his family, but it would also take them out of danger. He couldn't be used to hurt them.

A soft tap sounded at the door.

Deborah scrubbed her cheeks dry with a sleeve and gathered up Maggie. "What is it?" she asked.

"Proctor? Deborah?" Abigail's voice. She sounded frightened.

"Coming," Proctor said. He jumped to the door and pulled it open.

Abigail stood in the hall in her nightdress. Her hands were shaking. Lydia stood behind her.

"It's Magdalena," Abigail said. "She came to visit me." She indicated Lydia. "Came to visit us."

"I told her it could wait until morning," Lydia said.

"Can it wait until morning?" Proctor asked. He didn't know how many nights he had left to spend with Deborah and Maggie, and, with the prospect of leaving looming over him, he suddenly found that every moment with them was precious to him.

But Deborah appeared at his shoulder, her cap firming on her head, a sweater over her nightgown, and the baby in her arms. "Let's talk now," she said. "We're all awake, it'll be dawn in just a few hours, and Maggie needs a diaper change."

She pushed past them and headed downstairs to the kitchen. She must have left all the diapers drying on the rack beside the hearth. Abigail followed her instantly. Lydia shrugged and went after them both.

Proctor sighed. Once Deborah made up her mind to do something, she set about doing it. It was one of her better traits, when it didn't drive him mad.

He dressed and followed them all downstairs.

They were gathered around the table. A lively fire snapped in the hearth, throwing a confusion of light and shadow around the room. One of the clean diapers was missing from its spot, and a dirty one sat in a pail by the back door. He wondered if he would have time to get used to the smell.

"I was scared," Abigail was telling Deborah. "But only when I woke up."

"Were you frightened?" Deborah asked Lydia. Maggie was fussing, her eyes open, trying to focus on the things around her.

"No, I was happy," Lydia said. She stared at her hands, resting on the table. "I was sitting on the porch, a night just like the other night, perfect as could be, thinking how happy I was. All the work done for the day, a nice bed to sleep in, and no one to answer to but my own self. Magdalena came and sat beside me. We didn't say anything for a while, but then we saw a shooting star burn across the sky. And Magdalena said that she was sorry, that I would pass through blood and fire. I asked her what she meant, if I would come through it. But then I looked and she was gone."

"That was all?"

"Ain't that enough?"

Who wanted to hear that they were going to pass through blood and fire? Still, Proctor would have taken that as a comfort compared with hearing that he was a danger to his wife and daughter. Deborah rubbed her nose against Maggie, playing with her while she thought. It made Proctor happy to see them together, acting normal even when things were anything but.

"I was walking through the orchard," Abigail said, and then she hesitated.

"Go on," Deborah told her.

"There were strangers, men—well, young men, boys really—walking through the rows on either side of me. I kept trying to spy them through the trees, but I couldn't see their faces. I starting calling out their names, and I remember I was laughing, like we were playing a game." She grinned, remembering the dream, then noticed everyone else looking at her and her expression grew serious again. "I chased one of the boys. I couldn't see him clearly, just glimpses of him as he rounded the trees, always ahead of me. I was holding up my skirts in my hands, and they were feeling very heavy, and I ran around one of the apple trees, and suddenly it was night. Magdalena was standing there, only she was dressed in white and silver. She looked young and she was laughing with me."

"I don't know that I ever saw Magdalena laugh much," Proctor said.

"She suffered constant pain from her injuries after the Covenant's first attack on The Farm," Deborah said. "She and my mother laughed together often, but that was years ago. I was a little girl."

Abigail leaned forward earnestly. "It seemed perfectly normal in the dream."

"Did she say anything to you?" Deborah asked.

"I think she was going to, but I was so excited to see her that I turned around to call you. That's when I woke up. And that's when I became scared. Realizing that it was a dream, but not a dream. Well, that and Lydia, sitting awake, staring out the window as if she'd seen a ghost."

"And didn't I?" Lydia asked.

"What did you dream, Deborah?" Proctor asked.

Deborah stared at Maggie and started to rock back and forth. "Magdalena was at the foot of the bed, and I was still in labor with Maggie. I pushed and pushed." She kissed Maggie's forehead and the baby grabbed at her face. "But Maggie refused to be born. Magdalena looked over my swollen belly and said, 'You and the boy will be a grave danger to each other.' "

"Boy?" asked Abigail. "Like the one I saw in the orchard?"

Lydia snorted. "I think any man too young to have gray hair was a boy to that old woman. I heard her call Ezra *young man* once when she was mad at him."

But Proctor's heart had already sunk in his chest. "She meant me," he answered. He held up his scarred hand, turning it from side to side to show the missing finger. "The necromancer still has a part of me. As long as he does, I'm a danger to Deborah and Maggie, I'm a danger to all of you. That's what Magdalena's spirit told me."

No one said anything for a moment. No one looked at one another. The only sounds in the room was the crack of a log in the fire followed by Maggie's coo.

"What are you going to do?" Abigail asked. Her hands had bunched into fists, as if she was ready to protect herself and Deborah that very instant if needed.

Proctor had no doubts about her fierceness. Just as he had no doubts about his own. "I'm going to go after the Covenant," he said. "I'm going to find the man who maimed me—the prince-bishop, this German necromancer who serves the Covenant. I'm going to find him, I'm going to destroy his gruesome little collection and him, and I'm going to claim what's mine so that nobody can ever use me or my spirit to harm those I love."

"But didn't he sail for England?"

Proctor went over to their writing desk and opened the lid. He hooked the chain to hold it up, then sorted through the small stack of letters. He found the one he wanted and held it out to the group.

"General Washington asked me to follow—here, let me read it." The paper crackled as he unfolded the letter. General Washington's precise but hurried script, telling him that his special services were needed yet again. With it was another page in Tallmadge's handwriting, laying out the details. Tallmadge had an agent who left the letters in a hollow tree outside the gate where Proctor could retrieve them later. "They want me to accompany John Adams on a diplomatic mission to France and the Netherlands. Adams has been given authority to negotiate with England directly, so they hope he may even be welcomed onto their shores. Washington's worried about a secret effort to wreck Adams's diplomacy. They are certain there is a spy following Adams and they hope my talents can uncover him." He looked at the date of Adams's approximate departure and his heart fell. There was a small bundle of letters with the original, introductions he could use if he chose to go.

"It's even possible that the spy is a member of the Covenant," Lydia said. "Looking for one may lead you to the other."

"That sounds like a good plan," Abigail said, her fists still at the ready.

"Yes, it's possible that the Covenant will be behind the effort to wreck Adams's diplomacy. Yes, accompanying

Adams is a good plan." It was their only plan. He folded the letter and slapped it on the table. "You'll all be safer when I'm gone."

Deborah had noticed his gesture with the letter. "How soon must you go?" she asked. Her voice was flat, deliberately emotionless.

"Today," he said. "Maybe tomorrow. They're expected to sail by week's end."

Another uncomfortable silence with averted eyes followed this announcement. It was one thing to know a departure was imminent, and another to find out that it had to be immediate.

"But you don't even know what you'll do when you get there," Deborah said. "You have no idea how you'll find the Covenant."

"I'll think of something. I always do. I just . . . I have to start someplace." He rubbed his face and tried to think. "Most of the harvest is in already. It's more than enough to carry you through the winter. Abigail and Lydia can help out with anything else that needs to be done. I don't expect you'll run low on firewood, but if you do there's plenty of deadfall in the trees behind the field corn."

"I'm going with you," Lydia announced.

Abigail grabbed the other woman's arm. "No, I don't want you to go."

"If I have to pass through blood and fire, then I best make sure that blood and fire is as far away from you as possible. And think about it—I spent my whole life serving a witch who served the Covenant. I can recognize them, and I know how they do some of the things they do. It only makes sense that I go along."

As soon as she said it, it seemed obvious to Proctor, so much so that he wondered why he hadn't considered it himself. Still, he had reservations. He didn't know what he was going to face and didn't want to put anyone else in danger. "You don't have to do that," he said. "I don't know how we'd explain the two of us traveling together."

Lydia rolled her eyes. "Believe me, you don't need to be a witch to be invisible. I'll go—" She hesitated, as if the word was hard to spit out. "I'll go as a slave. If people think I'm your slave, I'll be as good as invisible to them."

Deborah shook her head firmly. "I don't care for even the appearance of slavery. It does irreparable harm to both the master as well as the slave."

Proctor agreed. "Now that you have your freedom, I could never ask you to act the slave again. I won't do it."

"It is a false pride not to do what must be done," Lydia said. "All those years I traveled with Miss Cecily as her slave, I pretended to myself that I was free. Now that I'm free, I can travel one more time, pretending to the world I'm a slave. Especially if it will defeat men who would make slaves of us all."

Deborah would not let go. "For all we know, there may be blood and fire here as well," she said. "You don't need to go looking for it on our account."

"That may be true," Lydia said. "But you've been good to me, better than I have had any reason to expect, after what Miss Cecily did here. If I go away, and blood and fire shows up here as well, at least I'll know it's not because of me."

Proctor would not argue that point with her. It was too similar to his own motivations for going.

Deborah turned to him, her chin set firm, her voice trembling and bitter. "I thought you were done doing work for Washington, done with making sacrifices for your country."

"I'm still a patriot. I still want to see our country free, and I'll do my part to make that happen. But let's be clear about one thing." He looked Deborah in the eye and fought to control the emotion in his voice. "I'm not doing this just for Washington or my country. I'm doing it for you and for our daughter, and God help any man on any side of this war who gets in my way."

His traveling bag hung on a peg by the door. He rose and put the letter, with its accompanying papers of introduction, into the bag. A gesture to make his decision final.

The fire had burned down and now cast the room in a dull, even glow. Outside the window, the sky quickened toward dawn. Maggie squirmed in Deborah's arms. Deborah's face, for once, looked bleak and defeated.

"It's as good a time as any for us to do the spell," she said at last. She turned to Abigail. "Will you go fetch the box with Maggie's cord and all the rest of it?"

Chapter 6

Dawn rose on a tiny crib set in the shelter of a tree.

They gathered at the edge of the orchard. Deborah had positioned them at the four points of the compass, around the dead patch of ground where Cecily's black magic had once raised corpses.

"Are you certain this is the right place to do this?" Proctor asked. He could see the same question on Abigail's face, though Lydia's expression was hard to read. At one time, Deborah would have worked to bring everyone to a consensus, but for this spell she simply told them where it was going to happen.

"Absolutely," she answered. "We will confront evil directly wherever it attacks us. On this farm, we will always answer fear with love and the blunt force of violence with the irresistible persistence of peace. When they leave a mark of destruction, we will turn it into a garden of hope."

It was a message for him. It would be more convincing if she didn't sound angry when she said it. She wasn't going to change his mind. He didn't think the Covenant was going to be stopped by love or peace or hope. It wasn't that kind of world.

Maggie made noises for attention, but they sounded more curious than distressed.

"Proctor?" Deborah said.

He stepped forward with the spade. Suppressing a spasm of revulsion at the memory of the vile thing he'd fought here years ago, he jammed the spade into the ground and dug the hole. The soil was dead and full of gravel. A barrow full of garden compost, black with leaf mold and alive with worms, sat off to one side. Proctor scooped several spadefuls into the hole.

"Abigail," Deborah said.

Abigail held a small box wrapped in cloth. Maggie's afterbirth and cord. She knelt by the hole and gently lowered it to the bottom. When she stepped out of the way, Proctor dumped another spade of compost in the hole. Clumps of dirt pattered over the box.

"Lydia," Deborah prompted.

Lydia had a small apple tree at her feet, a large root-ball with three and a half feet of slender trunk. It had been her memory that led to this spell, so Deborah had asked her to choose the tree. She knew exactly the one she had wanted, and Proctor had dug it up in the dark.

She bent over, grabbing the trunk by the base near the roots. She swung the tree back and forth for momentum, shedding dirt each time it brushed against her leg. She let go when it was out over the hole and it dropped solidly into place. The top of the root-ball mounded just over the lip of the hole. Proctor made a circle of compost around the tree, moving clockwise and filling in the edges. After he patted the dirt down, continuing his clockwise motion, he placed the spade outside the circle and then returned to his position.

Deborah held a pitcher of water. She circled the tree in the same direction as Proctor, pouring until the pitcher was empty. Then she set it aside with the spade and returned to her position. She stood at the north point of the compass, Proctor at the east, Lydia at the south, and Abigail at the west.

Maggie's cries had grown a little more insistent. Proctor looked over to make sure she was fine, but Deborah said, "Everyone stay with me for a moment longer."

She held out her hands. Proctor closed his hand around hers and felt Lydia grab his other. The power started with Deborah and flowed through them, like water moving a mill wheel, but returning with more strength every time it passed through. He counted four slow pulses of energy, marked by the tingling of his skin and the hair rising on his neck. As the fourth pulse completed the circle, Deborah spoke.

"Deliver us from our enemies, O our God," she said, and they all repeated the phrase after her. "Defend us from those who rise against us. Deliver us from the workers of iniquity and save us from bloody men. For lo, they lie in wait for our soul."

When he chorused the last phrase with the others, he felt a sting in the severed joint where his finger had been, and he realized that she intended the spell to protect him as much as she meant it to protect The Farm. Maybe she wasn't even protecting The Farm at all.

"Fight against those that fight against us," she said, quoting the Psalm, and they repeated the phrase. "Take hold of Your shield and buckler, and stand up for our help. Let them be confounded and put to shame that seek after our souls."

The final chorus ended and the flow of power subsided. Deborah let go, and they all dropped their hands. The ghost-sting in Proctor's finger faded. Maybe he had just imagined it. Knowing Deborah, she had worked the spell in her head to encompass him, Maggie, and The Farm. But dividing the focus that much might weaken the spell. It might leave her unprotected.

"Let this tree be dedicated to Magdalena Elizabeth Brown," Deborah said. "Let no one eat of it who is not willing to shelter her when she needs shelter, feed her when she needs food, comfort her when she needs comfort, and protect her when she needs protection."

She would never ask anyone to take a vow or swear an

oath, so *willing* was as strong as she would make her statement.

"I am willing," Proctor said with the other two.

"Let this tree grow as Magdalena grows, let it be a shelter when she needs shelter, a source of fruit when she needs something to eat, a comfort and a protection to her all her life."

The tree itself seemed to respond to Deborah's words. The branches twisted upward, turning their leaves, already gold with the season, toward the morning sun.

Magdalena's fussing had finally turned into a persistent cry. Deborah said, "That's all, we're done," and turned to go get their daughter, but Proctor reached her first. "It may be my last chance to hold her for a while," he said as he picked her up. She continued to fuss.

"Hold her closer to your body," Deborah said, pushing his arms up against his chest. "You won't break her." She stroked the baby's head. "You come back soon, and you come back whole. It's four to six weeks' sailing either way. I want you back here by spring, in time for planting."

"I'll take care of things as swiftly as the circumstances allow," Proctor said. "And I'll write to you if I can. You can send letters to me also, care of the American legate in Paris."

Deborah hated letters. Her mother had taught her that witches should never put anything down in writing, lest it be used against them. "She's hungry," Deborah said, taking Maggie from his arms. "I should feed her."

"I should go pack," Proctor said, though he lingered by Deborah's side as he said it.

She reached out and grasped his hand. "I want you to know that you're ready to face the Covenant. You've grown in power, and I trust you to use that power wisely. They don't know what they're in for."

"Brave words." He hoped they were true. He didn't

have as much power as Deborah, but he hadn't had a lifetime of learning to use his talent either.

She let go and pushed him away. "Go already. You can't harvest the field before you plow it. The sooner you leave, the sooner you'll return."

He wanted more time, but he was afraid that if he took it, he would lose his resolve to go and instead try to find some way to protect his family here. That way was a trap. He looked up and saw the other two witches standing nearby. "Lydia?" he said.

"I'm ready," she said.

He took one last look at Maggie suckling. "Then let's grab our bags and go."

The road to Boston was barren and unpromising. The sky was an expansive gray slab, spackled along the horizon with brown leaves, among which were scattered a few sere reds and yellows. The ground had not yet frozen, but it was stiff and unyielding. Every clod of mud was hard enough to turn an ankle.

"It's going to be a harder winter than I thought," Proctor said.

Lydia was wrapped in a heavy cloak that she held tight around her thin frame. "What you call summer here feels like a hard winter to me."

"It might be even colder where we're going," Proctor said. "I'm sure it won't be any warmer."

"Were I looking for someplace to spend the rest of my life, I might take that into consideration," Lydia said. "But I'm going because there's a job to do."

"Just confirming," he said, but he watched her closely.

Lydia wore her forty years more heavily than she used to, while her clothes hung a little looser. The lines on her face had been etched more by pain than laughter, and the last two years on The Farm could not erase that. When she reached up to pull the hood down around her

face, her sleeves fell to her elbows, revealing arms that
looked like corded rope. Nor was she afraid of hard
work.

He was glad that she had decided to come.

It was a long walk to Boston in one day, so they spent
the night with Quaker friends near Malden and continued on their way the next morning. When they came to
Boston, they found more life. Proctor had been to the
city before the war started, and it was both the same
and completely transformed. They crossed over on the
Charlestown ferry, and he led the way through twisting
streets, dense with buildings, noting the differences. The
main ways were as crowded as ever before, and the mixture of familiar voices and foreign accents the same, but
the British Redcoats were absent, replaced by Continental soldiers in blue and buff. Ships still crowded the harbor, their masts and rigging a forest that surrounded the
city, but the Union Jack no longer snapped in the wind
and the flag of France, a white cross on a blue field, was
as common as the banners of the states. Closer to the
docks, where the air smelled of fish and garbage and the
seagull cries filled the air, merchants sold items imported
from halfway around the world—coffee beans, cane
sugar, and pimientos—but what they had for sale de-
pended on which British trade ships the American privateers had recently captured. He couldn't help thinking
about the way he had also been transformed by the Revolution. He was both the same as he had always been
and yet completely different.

"Proctor?"

He felt Lydia's hand on his forearm and jerked to a
stop as a carter with a wagonload of firewood clattered
past.

"Are you all right?" she asked.

"Just thinking about where we need to go." He pointed
to the long wharf extending out into the harbor and the

dozens of masts and hulls that lined it. "It should be one of the ships out there."

Their destination, the French frigate *La Sensible*, was all the way out at the end. It was more than a hundred feet in length, as long as the British ships of the line that Proctor had seen sailing around Manhattan, but sleeker, with only two decks instead of three. It was painted black, with a yellow band around the gun deck and ports for sixteen cannons.

"This is promising," Proctor told Lydia. "This could outrun any ship big enough to beat it, and beat any ship fast enough to catch it. Must be why they named it *Sensible*."

"You think the Covenant will attack it during the crossing?" Lydia asked.

"The British will, if they get a chance," Proctor said. "But yes, if the Covenant is committed to stopping the Revolution, they're likely to do something to stop Adams, who is authorized to negotiate that peace."

"I hadn't thought about that," Lydia said. "We might be attacked even before we land in France."

"It's not too late to change your mind," he said. "You can go back to Deborah. She'd welcome you."

"I'm not afraid," Lydia said. "I'm just wondering what else I hadn't thought of yet."

"You and me, both of us," Proctor said.

They walked down to the gangplank and looked up at a deck crowded with several hundred people. Casks of fresh water dangled overhead as sailors lifted them by ropes from the dock to the hold. Other sailors climbed in the rigging and among the furled sails. A group of passengers stood at the railing arguing with the ship's captain. One of the passengers was a man of average height and stout girth, with a balding head shaped like a cannonball onto which human features had been impressed. He kept slipping into halting French while the French officer answered in fractured English. Neither tactic seemed to make either speaker better understood.

Proctor stepped aside to let Lydia lead the way up the gangplank.

"Don't be stupid," she snapped under her breath. She yanked his bag out of his hand and carried it as well as her own. "If I'm going to be your slave, you will ignore me except to tell me what to do. You will never step out of the way to let me go first."

That was something he hadn't thought of right there. He was taken aback by her vehemence, and it was hard to fight his own nature, but he could see what she meant. "I'll remember that."

"See that you do," she said quietly but fiercely. "And don't look at me that way."

He waited while a mob of laughing dockmen, loads on their shoulders, surged around them and stomped up the sagging gangplank to the deck. "What way?"

"As if I'm an equal, as if I'm someone you've offended." She kept her voice low and her eyes averted. "I'm not a person to you and you can't treat me like one or you'll put us in danger."

"I've seen men treat their slaves like people. Washington has a servant, William Lee—"

"You're not Washington," Lydia interrupted. "And you don't know near as much as you think. A ship is a small town, where every word that is spoken is heard and every action observed. If anyone suspects I'm not your slave, they may—" She hesitated, and Proctor could see that she did not wish to put into words something bad that had happened to her before. "They may kidnap me as an escapee when we get ashore and then resell me," she said finally. "And I will not be put on the block. So I must have no more feelings in your mind than your cattle."

He started to protest, then turned away without uttering the apology already formed on his lips.

"Good," she whispered tensely.

He felt foolish, but also properly chastened. They were heading into an unknown and dangerous situation. It would be foolish to add another danger to the stew. He walked up the plank without looking back, though it galled him to do so. He could tell from the slight sway of the plank that Lydia followed him.

The captain was a dignified man who gave the impression of a beaked nose framed by a powdered wig, with rows of white curls that hung over his ears like furled sails. He wore the smart red uniform and dark blue jacket of the French navy. Proctor expected to wait until he was finished talking with the other passengers, but the captain excused himself and turned to speak to the newcomers.

"Captain Chavagne, commanding *La Sensible*, what may I help you?"

The loud, round gentleman with the cannonball head blustered impatiently, but the captain ignored him. Proctor presented his letters of introduction. He would have to use his and Deborah's savings to pay for their passage, but the letters would bring him money in Paris, and Tallmadge would see that he was reimbursed when he returned.

The captain stared at the letter, concentration written in the crease of his brow, then folded the papers and snapped them back to Proctor's open hand. "The ship is too full already. Are not you certainment—another ship?"

"I must be aboard this ship to France," Proctor said.

"The young gentleman does not want to come," the captain asserted, looking over Proctor's shoulder at Lydia. "By His Majesty's decree, no slave may enter France. To do so may mean the slave will be taken away."

Lydia tensed noticeably at this last sentence. Proctor had never heard of the decree, and wasn't sure how they could enforce it. He knew that other Americans had taken their slaves with them to Paris. "We do not plan to stay in the country. We will enter and leave. I'm sure it will be fine."

The captain sighed. "I would like to help you," he said. "But I cannot offer you the berth I possesses not. There is no place for you to sleep."

"There is no problem," Proctor said. He jingled a purse full of coin. "I'll sleep anywhere there's a spot for me, on the deck if I must."

The captain raised a dark eyebrow that stood out in sharp contrast with his powdered hair. He took the purse from Proctor's hand, peered inside, and pocketed it. "Very well."

Proctor realized he had made another error, revealing himself to be neither a gentleman nor a man used to owning slaves. Men of that class demanded a certain level of luxury just as a factor of their status. Proctor had reacted out of reflex—after all the hardship he'd seen soldiers endure during the war, it seemed selfish and indulgent to insist on luxuries. He tried to cover up his error by changing the subject. "If that's settled, you could help me by directing me to Mister John Adams."

"I'm John Adams," the round gentleman said. Proctor realized that the group of passengers were the men attached to his mission and other hangers-on. "I hope you'll oblige by introducing yourself—hold on there."

"Yes, monsieur?" Captain Chavagne replied, caught in the act of trying to slip away.

"We are not resolved on this question. Tomorrow is the Sabbath, and thus not a fit day for travel. Can we not delay our departure one more day and set sail on Monday?"

The captain shrugged. "If God does not wish us to sail on the Sabbath, then He should suspend the tides."

Adams sighed in defeat as the Frenchman walked away, then turned back to Proctor. Proctor offered him the letter of introduction prepared by Tallmadge. Adams unfolded it and began to read. "You know the Chevalier de la Luzerne?" he asked incredulously as he scanned the page.

"I met him but once, while I was in service to General Washington."

Adams folded the letter and returned it to Proctor. "And what employment do you expect to find in Paris?"

"I was a secretary in General Washington's headquarters during the campaign of 'seventy-six," Proctor said. "Do you have need of one?"

A plain man with a pinched face and a shabby suit pushed forward. "His Excellency already employs a capable and experienced secretary, and one with a whole hand I might add."

Adams motioned the other man to silence. "You seem like a good Massachusetts man," he said to Proctor.

"Born outside Concord, late of Salem, lived my whole life here," Proctor answered.

"Excellent," Adams said. "You must admit that men of our state have taken the lead in the fight for freedom, from the battle at Lexington right down to today."

"That's true . . ." Proctor wasn't sure what Adams was getting at, but he felt confident he wouldn't like it.

"Perhaps you can explain this to me," Adams said. "It does not seem to me that the passion for freedom can burn as strongly in the breasts of men who deprive their fellow men of freedom." He held an open palm in the direction of Lydia, inviting an explanation. "What has been your experience?"

The worst part was that Proctor shared Adams's feelings

on slavery but dared not let on. This was the crux of his problem, ever since he had been drawn into the society of witches some four years before: he was always pretending to be someone he was not.

But he remembered Lydia's warning and knew that now was not the time to change that.

"I don't know if I care for your implication," he said, trying to sound like an affronted young man of class. "It has been my experience that the men from our southern states are every bit as ardent in their love of freedom as are we men from Massachusetts, and are as equally willing to sacrifice their all to achieve it. Or are you trying to imply otherwise? Your own words would cast doubt on men like Washington, Jefferson, and even Franklin."

Adams frowned. "Of course I mean to imply no such thing. We all share an ardor for our native land and its freedom. But I hope you will take no offense when I tell you that I see no position for you in this mission. Mister Dana, my secretary"—he indicated the man with the pinched face and worn suit—"is satisfactory in every regard. I have a servant I know and trust well, as does Mister Dana, and I have already engaged a tutor, Mister Thaxter, for my two sons." He seemed to realize that he was starting to run on but proved incapable of stopping. "While it is possible to be frugal to a fault, in this instance taking on any additional expense would represent a mismanagement of the fiduciary trust placed in me by the Congress in pursuit of the goals that they've assigned me." He cleared his throat uncomfortably. "I'm sorry."

That wasn't the ideal situation. It would make things much harder. Proctor reached into his pocket and clutched his focus—a lock of Deborah's hair tied in a gray ribbon made from the same fabric as her favorite dress.

"Don't worry," he said. "You won't even know we're here."

It was a simple spell of redirected attention. He could stay close to Adams, but Adams wouldn't notice him. Adams looked at Proctor as he mouthed the words of the spell, and then through him.

"Where did the captain escape to?" Adams asked. "We never resolved the issue of the Sabbath, and I hate to travel on the Sabbath unless I absolutely must." He started for the quarterdeck and bumped into Proctor with his first step, startling in surprise that someone stood there. He excused himself and hurried away, followed by his mob.

"Where did you learn that particular prayer, Master Brown?" Lydia asked in a subservient tone of voice that gave Proctor an unexpected chill. By *prayer* she meant "spell."

"Deborah taught it to me," he said, not looking directly at her. "It was one of the first things she taught me."

"I would not be so quick to use it," she said. "Miss Deborah learned it from my former mistress, and I do not think she was of good faith."

The spell was dangerous just because Cecily had used it? "Surely the intentions matter," Proctor said.

"I'm certain you know best," Lydia said, her eyes downcast. "But I never knew my former mistress to have a good intention." She set Proctor's bag down at his feet. "I best go find a spot for myself in steerage."

"Steerage?" Proctor asked.

"The lowest deck, with such other servants as may be on board." She looked around at the crowded ship, which probably contained between three and four hundred sailors and passengers. "Good berths will be hard to come by. I will come up again in a little while to see if you need anything."

"The Covenant may try to get at Adams while he's on board the ship," Proctor said. "Keep an eye and an ear open down there for anything unusual."

"I can do that," she said

She stopped at a gangway and asked a negro sailor for directions. He called down the open hatch to someone below. Lydia descended below the deck.

A voice at Proctor's side startled him. "How much for the darky?"

"What?" he said, turning to answer the man. A huge sailor stood behind Proctor. He had shoulders as broad as a yoke and whiskers black as coal. His sunburned skin was etched with a variety of scars, everything from the jagged cuts of splinters to the clean lines of a blade.

"I said how much for the woman?" the man repeated.

"She's not for sale," Proctor said.

"G'wan," the man said angrily. "I'm not trying to buy her. More in the line of I'd be interested in renting her a time or two during the voyage."

"She's not for rent, either," Proctor said.

"You can't expect me to believe that you'd keep that all to yourself," the man said. "Not really your quality. I never knew a man like you who didn't bring dark meat to the table if he wasn't planning to eat. But you look like you're on hard times and could use a bit o' coin. So I'm going to ask you one more time, how much for the woman?"

Proctor closed the space with the man, intending to force him to back down, but the sailor just stood there until Proctor was close enough to smell the beer and onions on his breath. Proctor realized he should have tried a different tack, using words or appeals to the captain instead, but it was too late to change his decision now. "I think you should just walk away."

The sailor glared down at Proctor as if he could smash him at will. He was clearly not intimidated in the least by anyone he considered a gentleman. "My coin, your loss," the sailor said. He cleared his throat and spit a big wad of phlegm at Proctor's feet, then turned and walked away.

Proctor grabbed one of the barefoot ship's boys as he ran past. He pointed to the big sailor. "Who is that?"

The boy's eyes went wide with fright. "His name is Jacques," the boy said in a thick French accent. "Jacques Tar."

Proctor let him go and he scampered off. So the sailor's name was Jack Tar. Very funny. British sailors were called jack tars. It seemed too obvious for him to be an agent of either the British or the Covenant with a name like that. More probably, like many sailors, he was hiding his true identity because he had committed some crime on shore.

Proctor had undertaken this journey to find his enemy. It seemed he had already made a new one.

They departed with the tide on Sunday, despite Adams's reservations. By Monday morning they had sailed well north. The sails were only partially unfurled, but they were filled with the crisp wind, and the great mainmast, taller than the ship was long, strained like a horse in harness, pulling the ship forward through the waves like a plow breaking the soil.

Proctor stood at the rail, with the wind biting his ears and the salt air already drying his skin. He watched the rocky outline of Cape Ann diminish in the distance. The port of Gloucester was situated on Cape Ann, and from Gloucester it was but a morning's walk to Salem town. Deborah and Maggie were at home just outside Salem.

He went to find Lydia. He needed to share that last sight of home with someone.

As he climbed down to the lowest deck, the smell of human bodies grew more oppressive. The ceilings were much lower too, and Proctor had to duck his head not to bump it. As he reached the bottom level, the smell of seawater grew stronger, overpowering the other scents. The sound of voices echoed from another part of the hold. His eyes strained to pierce the murky darkness, but it was difficult coming straight down from the sun-glittering waves.

"Lydia," he called.

"Coming, sir," she said.

He climbed down into a narrow passage between the barrels of biscuit, meat, and water. His feet hit water and he was soaked to his ankles. He saw Lydia coming toward him with her shoes in her hands and her dress held up to her knees. The captain and several officers sloshed along behind her, through water as deep as their shins. The captain recognized Proctor and frowned.

"I thought the water was supposed to be on the outside of the ship," Proctor said.

"There is always leaking a little," the captain said. "No thing to worry about."

He smiled, but his narrow face looked pained to wear the expression. He squeezed past them and climbed out of the hold, shouting orders as he went.

"For men with nothing to worry about, they all looked a little worried," Proctor said. "If it's bad, they'd turn back to shore, wouldn't they?"

"I'm certain they would," she said, eyes lowered.

The tone of her voice said she was certain of no such thing. But he had to reconcile himself to the fact that she wasn't going to speak freely to him as long as they were aboard the ship. "Come up to the deck, I want to show you something," Proctor said.

On their climb up, they passed the ship's pumps. Two large elm handles, curved like the haft of an ax, were connected to pipes that pierced the deck on either side of the mast and reached down deep into the hold. Jack Tar and several other sailors worked the pumps, spraying water from the hold across the deck. Other sailors scrubbed the already pristine planks and mopped the water over the sides. Jack stared at Proctor coming up from belowdeck, and his frown said he blamed Proctor for the leak.

"What did you want to show me?" Lydia asked.

To the west, Cape Ann had sunk below the horizon. Protected or unprotected, his home had passed beyond his sight and his power. They were at sea. "Nothing," he said. "I guess it was nothing."

Chapter 7

The creak and slosh of the pumps sounded as regular as the ship's bell as they sailed for several days under clear skies. Proctor asked the crewmen about it one morning. "Is it usual for a ship to be running the pumps this frequently?"

The crewmen looked to one another to see if they should answer that kind of question from a passenger. The English-speaking crew members explained the question to those who only spoke French.

An older crewman, a fellow with long brown streaks of tobacco juice striping his gray beard, said, "It's not usual, but in our case it's only sensible."

The crewman's expression was dead serious and Proctor was willing to take the answer at face value. His past experience with ships had kept him close to shore, seldom out of sight of land, and he didn't want to presume what was ordinary or not.

But the ship's boy swabbing the deck with the pumped water started to snicker, and Proctor finally got the pun. Only *Sensible*. He chuckled, and the crew nearby burst out laughing.

The chuckle died on his lips as he realized the old sailor was implying that *Sensible* was a leaky ship. The crew, apparently seeing Proctor's discomfort, laughed harder. After that, whenever Proctor paced that part of the deck, one of the crew members would repeat the phrase *only sensible* and they would all laugh again.

They had the chance to do so fairly often. Proctor needed some kind of work to do. He didn't expect to find trouble or the Covenant until they reached Paris, but he was not going to miss anything on the way. So he prowled the deck, hoping to feel that familiar tingle that told him someone nearby was performing magic. The Covenant wanted a British victory as part of their plan to build an empire that circled the globe. If they had sent an agent to wreck Adams's mission, Proctor would find him and stop him before the ship reached French shores.

From the first day, he began to narrow the possible choices. The ship's officers had all been assigned to the vessel before Adams began his voyage, but the sailors were a different story. They were a mixed crew of Frenchmen and newly recruited Americans, a wicked-looking lot on the whole, scarred by sun and steel. All day long, dozens of sailors sat along the yards in the masts, their feet dangling as they rolled back and forth with the waves, an audience in the balcony to the play on the deck below. He saw their eyes follow him as he paced, and he was keenly aware that they were just as well placed to watch Adams.

He had been observing them for a week, his eyes turned to the mast, when a voice startled him.

"I see you spying on us," Jack said. He was looking the other direction, as if he were talking to someone else. "Better keep your eyes in front of you, or you might fall overboard. And who'll own your property then?"

"Toi, là-bas, remets-toi à travailler," the bosun yelled at Jack.

"Oui, mon major," Jack said as he knuckled his forehead and moved off.

Proctor thought that would be the end of it, but the bosun eyed him suspiciously as he continued his circuit of the deck. When Proctor glanced back over his shoulder, he saw the bosun talking to the lieutenant, and both of them staring at him.

The problem was that Proctor did not act like the other passengers, though he placed himself in their company as much as possible. They gathered on deck daily, a loud mob of worry merchants trading old news and rumors as if both were coin of the same weight. The war would be over before they could turn a profit. The war would drag on forever, killing trade. They all had some intention of making money off either war or peace, and this entitled them to judge how others were fighting it.

It was the worst-kept secret on board that Adams had been named minister plenipotentiary, which gave him the full authority of the United States to negotiate with foreign countries. Opinion was divided between those who thought Adams intended further agreements with France and those who thought he meant to negotiate peace with Britain.

Proctor thought either case unlikely. It was clear from Adams's brusque treatment of the officers that he neither trusted nor liked the opulent French, while the British had no reason to negotiate. Henry Laurens, the former president of the Continental Congress and the American diplomat sent overseas, had been captured by the British and was currently imprisoned in London. The same fate might easily await Adams.

And then there was the Covenant. They would go to any length to assure a British victory.

Proctor remembered the demon attack and shuddered. He worried about Deborah and Maggie, and wondered if they were still safe. If he allowed himself to think about them too much, he grew panicky. If trouble did come for them, there was nothing he could do to help. So he told himself to stay focused: find an agent of the Covenant, follow him back to his leaders, destroy them, and return home.

Day after day, into the second week, the ship made its

way east, accompanied by the periodic creak and slosh, creak and slosh of the pumps. Proctor turned his attention to those closest to Adams.

The diplomat was a crowd unto himself. With his secretary, both their servants, his two boys, their tutor, and several others claiming some connection to the American mission, Adams was always at the center of a dozen or more people, usually gathered at one railing or the other.

Proctor lingered at the edge of this group looking for their enemy. They stood at the port bow, watching a group of distant fishing boats gathered in a spot where the ocean's green-tinged waves collided with a blue current. Silver churned the surface of the water. A secondary cloud of diving gulls hung over the boats to snap up scraps of bait and other cast-offs.

"But I thought we saw the Grand Banks yesterday," said the smaller of Adams's two sons, an anxious boy of about ten named Charles.

"That's why they're called Grand—it means very large," the older son replied.

"An excellent observation, John Quincy," Adams said. One hand rested affectionately on the shoulder of each boy. The ship plunged through the fitful waves, as one slapped the side of the ship and sent spray over the railing. Everyone jumped back—the water was bitter cold.

Charles's eyes brimmed with tears as his face turned a shade of green. Proctor felt sorry for him—homesick and seasick was an awful combination. "Are the waves grand, too?" he asked. "Can we leave the Grand Banks now, Father?"

Adams stared at the sky and the wind-driven clouds coming in from the northwest. "There might be a storm, but it's nothing to worry about," he said reassuringly. The chickens did not share his opinion: they squawked and pecked anxiously at the latches on their coop.

Proctor spotted Lydia on deck and went to see her. "Have you felt any prayer?" he asked.

"Not one amen," she answered. Another cross-wave rocked the ship, and she grabbed hold of Proctor. As soon as he steadied her on her feet, she pulled away and, with eyes downcast, said, "I'm sorry about that, Master Brown, sir. Do you think—the weather?"

The shock of her formal address unnerved him so much it took a moment for the question to register. He looked at the storm clouds gathered overhead. He'd seen witch-craft move weather half a dozen times before, but this felt natural. "There's no one aboard the ship who's pow-erful enough," he said. He included himself in that esti-mate.

He had the same thought when the gale smashed into them that night. He knew he could do nothing to avert it.

The ship climbed and crashed the swells like a great, uncomfortable horse. The planks groaned all around them, as if the sides of the ship were gasping for breath. The crew moved walls and stores around on the gun deck. Proctor was herded into a forward cabin, where he sat on the floor pressed arm-to-arm with the other American passengers, including Adams and his party. A single lantern dangled from a hook, swinging as the ship tilted. Light and shadow lurched from one side of the cabin to the other and back again. A storm, but an ordi-nary storm, the kind he'd weathered before on land.

A normal storm was no comfort to Adams's younger boy, Charles, who was racked by the dry heaves. The lingering odor of vomit indicated that it probably had not started out dry. John Quincy had an arm around his shoulders and tried to comfort him, though he appeared just as miserable. Their father was nervous, and, as some men did, Proctor noticed he talked continuously to cover up his nerves.

"A ship is like a nation, and wars are a storm to be

weathered," he told his sons. "Just as America has weathered the storm of revolution, the *Sensible* will weather this storm as well. Thucydides was the first to make that comparison, though I find it very apt to our situation. I highly recommend Thucydides as a good foundation for young men. If your Greek continues to improve, John, I will purchase for you your very own copy in the original language."

"Thank you, Father," John Quincy said heavily.

"Can't you make the captain stop the ship?" Charles moaned.

"There, there," Adams said. "Just as we trust war to our generals, and diplomacy to wise men, so, too, must we trust the ship to the captain. He knows what is best—"

The cabin door slammed open. John Adams's servant braced himself in the doorway. The storm howled louder through an open hatch, seeming to come at them from all sides.

"Joseph," Adams cried. "What's happened?"

Joseph was soaked to his knees. "The hold is filling up with water. The carpenter told us not to worry, it was normal to take on some water in a storm like this. But he had us all come up to the higher deck. May we come in?"

"Of course," Adams said, shooing other passengers aside to make room for his men.

Outside the door, men clambered up and down the open hatch, shouting frantically. The pump gears echoed through the ship, steady as a metronome during the repeated crescendos of the storm. Lydia was the last one to enter. Proctor made room so she could squeeze in beside him. Her dress was wet to her waist, smelling of salt water and bilge.

"What happened?" he whispered, leaning his head close to hers.

"I overheard the carpenter say that the caulking in the hold was bad, and it can't be fixed except in port," she whispered back. "At least that's what I think he said. Le calfatage a été mal fait. Je ne peux pas le réparer avant qu'on arrive au port."

"How do you know French?"

"Miss Cecily wanted to learn it at one time."

"Is it prayer work?" Proctor asked, meaning the damage to the caulking. The merchant on the opposite side of him shifted and jabbed Proctor with an elbow.

"I don't know."

The light swayed dizzily overhead, flickering as if it might go out.

Proctor realized how foolish he had been.

The Covenant did not need to use magic to achieve their goals. Hadn't they sent ordinary assassins to kill them once on The Farm? This was no different. It would have been easy to hire someone in Boston to come on board under some pretense and then sabotage the ship. The problem would not show until they were in heavy seas, and no one would know for a long time that the ship had sunk. It might be weeks or even months before Adams was missed, and longer yet before another man could be charged with negotiating peace.

"We have to do something," Proctor whispered.

"We should pray," Lydia said.

He had the same thought. But what kind of spell would strengthen the ship and ease their passage? He couldn't change the weather and didn't know how to stop the leaking, but he had to do something. "What can we use as a focus?" he asked.

"No, I meant we should *pray*," she said. Her voice was shaking as she folded her hands together and bowed her head.

The ship crashed down a swell, bouncing them both off the cabin wall. Outside, the wind renewed its fury, sending wave after wave against the hull. The lantern, spinning around, sputtered and went out. The dark lasted through the night and the next day while the storm raged outside.

When the last winds finally ran away and the sky cleared, the air was much colder. The damp had settled into everything, soaking every corner of the ship, so that Proctor felt chilled even after the cookpots were fired up and the passengers served their first hot meal in two days.

They were out of the storm but hardly out of danger. On deck, the two pumps on either side of the mast operated constantly. The crewmen worked in shifts, day and night, swinging the great elm handles up and down, spraying water over the sides of the ship. Proctor peered over the side for signs of damage. The ship rode noticeably lower in the water and seemed likely to sink at a moment's notice if he looked away.

"This is no good," Adams said nearby. He was talking to himself, which he often did. "If an English ship comes along, we'll be unable to outrun it. They'll snatch us up in a heartbeat."

He ran off to complain to Captain Chavagne, who was standing by the pumps. Proctor followed him.

Chavagne, his eyes bloodshot and his cheeks ashen, had lost his wig and hat somewhere during the storm. He had close-cropped black hair and a receding hairline. Though clearly doing his best to keep up with Adams's rapid flow of words, the expression on his face revealed how much he was also missing.

Proctor interrupted. "What can we do to help?"

Adams looked at him, startled, as if he had appeared, a stranger, out of nowhere.

"There is nothing but the pumps," the captain said. "The pumps and repairs."

"I can pump," Proctor said. "It'll free up someone to work on the ship."

Chavagne looked at Proctor and pasted a false, tight-lipped smile on his face. "No, monsieur, I can't allow—"

"I'm no gentleman," Proctor said. He had failed to think like the Covenant, failed to foresee or prevent their methods. He had to do something. "Let me take a turn at the pump."

Chavagne shrugged indifferently and gestured him toward the pump.

Jack stood at the near handle. He was shirtless, despite the bitter cold, and sweat poured down the corded muscles of his back. His hair was plastered to his face, and the ship's boy stood there with a ladle to pour water into his mouth whenever he asked for it. He looked like he'd been pumping for a very long time.

"If you think you can do it," he told Proctor. "I could use a break for a minute or two." To the other crew, he said, "Faites place. Ce monsieur veut faire notre travail— laissez-le essayer. On the count of three now, ready? Un, deux, trois."

On three, he pushed the lever down and stepped out of the way. Proctor caught it on the upswing, turning the motion into the next downward pump. His arms, soft from two weeks of not working, strained with the first stroke. Jack laughed at him.

But Proctor got into a rhythm, like splitting wood or cutting wheat, and he blocked out everything else—his mistake in underestimating the Covenant, his memory of the demon, his fears for Deborah and Maggie—and he pumped over and over again, sending water sluicing across the deck and back out into the ocean.

He wasn't sure how long he'd been at it, but his shirt was stuck to his back, and his breath was shallow and ragged. A voice at his side said, "All right, that's good enough, more than your turn. I'll take it now. On the count of three."

The count slid past and he staggered out of the way. Jack was watching him, and he frowned, the way a man does when a dearly held belief is shattered. He turned and walked away.

Lydia was waiting for him with a blanket. "You'll catch your death of cold," she said.

Water ran across the deck and past their feet. "Better than catching my death of wet," he said. "I'll take my chances."

Other passengers volunteered, but within a day the voluntary work became mandatory, a matter of life and death. With both pumps running constantly, the water in the hold stayed level. The minute the pumps stopped, it began to rise. Nothing could be done to plug the hold because the whole ship was leaking. It would have to be repaired in port, assuming they made it to port.

Adams took his turns at the pump, and even John Quincy lent a hand. He tried to talk to his father about public service, and everyone contributing, but he soon ran out of breath.

Assuming they avoided British ships, assuming there wasn't another storm, assuming they could find a port, their chances looked good, Proctor thought.

Until the first pump plugged. The crew had to disassemble it, clearing out all the bilge and muck that fouled the pipe. Proctor watched them work, fearful of the rising water in the hold. As they were putting it back together, he overheard two of the American crewmen.

"That'll do, at least until the box fouls," one said.

"Pray that doesn't happen soon," said another. Both had their eyes east, looking for a shore.

The pump, Proctor discovered, had a filter box at the bottom in the hold. When it plugged up, the best they could do was take the rest apart, bang a pole around the box from topside, and hope it dislodged whatever was blocking the filter.

Not the most reassuring method Proctor could imagine.

It was the middle of the night two days later when the box plugged.

Proctor lay awake belowdeck when he overheard the crewmen talking to each other. "There's nothing coming through," the first one said.

"Pump harder," the second one replied.

"It's plugged," the first one snapped back. Proctor recognized Jack's voice. He took more than his share at the pumps because of his size and strength. "We cleaned the pipes a few bells back, but we'll have to do it again."

"The water gained six inches on us the last time we stopped the pump, and we haven't made up the difference yet."

Proctor rose and climbed up through the hatch. "I'm fresh," he said. "Let me take a hand at the pump. Maybe it will jar something loose."

The pump handle stood dead. "If you can loosen it up, I'll eat whatever comes out of this end," Jack said.

"You're just trying to sweeten the deal, aren't you?" Proctor said.

He bent his back into the pump and could feel the plug at once. The handles moved, the gears ground, but only a trickle of water came through. There was no suction. He took a deep breath and drew on his talent. It was one thing to move rocks that he could see, but another entirely to shift shapeless muck hidden way below him. He used the rhythm of the pump for a focus, closed his eyes, and sent his will down the pipe.

"The gentleman should leave off now, sir," a crewman said. "We've got to take it apart, as quick as we can."

Proctor kept pumping. He tried to draw the muck through the screen and couldn't, and it affected him in turn—he tried to draw a breath and felt as if his lungs were blocked. The flow of water decreased from a trickle to almost nothing. Without the sound of water, the noise of the metal pump gear grinding grew even louder.

"It's no use," Jack said. "Now stand aside."

He felt the muck break apart through the screen. He almost had it. It was like pulling on a thousand tiny rocks all at once. He was thinking: from a little fountain was made a great flood, from a little fountain was made a great flood.

A heavy hand fell on his shoulder, breaking his focus.

What came out of his mouth was a scream of raw frustration, and what surged through his hands was a burst of power.

Water hiccuped out of the pump. Wet sludge flopped onto the deck, followed by a gush of slimy water. Proctor didn't break his rhythm. He closed his eyes and fell into the work, bringing muck up through the pipe until the water flowed smooth and fast.

He meant to pump a long time, the way he always did, but the spell had weakened him and he staggered back, falling onto his rump.

A big hand reached out to pull him up. Proctor took it and came face-to-face with Jack. He glared at Proctor angrily, like a man shamed by being wrong or bested in strength by another. But he put a cup of undiluted grog in Proctor's hand and jabbed a thumb toward the captain, standing watch on the quarterdeck. The officer favored Proctor with a reluctant nod of approval.

"You still need to eat that sludge," Proctor told Jack.

"What do you think I put in your grog?" he grumbled, then walked away.

Proctor smiled and sat on the chicken coop. The hen ruffled her feathers, squawking at him. The chill air settled around him as he savored the grog. No taste of sludge.

For the next two weeks, the ship limped slowly eastward. Proctor took regular shifts on both pumps, keeping the water flowing smoothly before the box could be blocked. There were cheers when land was sighted, but not from Adams. Proctor thought he had the most to cheer about, with his children aboard. He followed Adams when he went to complain to the captain. Lydia followed him.

"—is it true that we're going to put into a Spanish port?" Adams asked. "That's a disaster."

"A disaster is what happens if we don't put in at the nearest port," the captain said.

But for once Proctor found himself agreeing with Adams. He had no money left. He had expected to borrow in Paris with Tallmadge's letters to Franklin. Those wouldn't help them in Spain at all. Adams faced a very similar problem.

"I don't know how we'll get to France," Proctor told Lydia. "If we wait for them to fix the ship, I don't know how we'll eat."

"We can walk or beg if we must," she said.

"It might come to that."

Still, when the ship raised land and came into the ship-builders' wharves at Ferrol on Spain's northern coast, Proctor's relief was genuine and unblemished. The crew stopped pumping as soon as they tied up, and the ship responded by starting to sink. Proctor was standing on deck with the other passengers, who momentarily ceased sorting out their travel options to watch the ship's steady descent in place and decide whether they should make a desperate leap to the docks. While they argued, a crewman popped his head out of the hatch and called to the officers.

"Il y a plus de deux mètres d'eau dans la cale!" Crewmen ran to the hold while others went to man the pumps.

"What did he say?" Proctor asked.

"I think he said there's almost seven feet of water in the hold," Adams answered. He stared at Proctor for a moment, as if wondering who he was, but then, as if struck by the enormity of the news, he continued. "And that's in less than an hour. We barely escaped with our lives. If even a mild storm had followed the first, it would have carried us to a grave beneath the waves."

Exactly what the Covenant had hoped for or even intended. "Thank God they didn't think you worth a little more effort," Proctor murmured.

Adams's brow furrowed as he overheard Proctor's comment. Without another word, he turned away to gather his sons and servants.

But Proctor was too lost in thought to give it more than passing notice. The essential thing was this: the Covenant had failed, and though Adams was a thousand miles from Paris, he was not yet dead.

"What's troubling you, Master Brown?" Lydia asked.

"We're a thousand miles from Paris, with no idea how to find the Covenant from here." It was early December, and his plan to find and finish the Covenant quickly so he could return home to Deborah and Maggie had already gone astray.

"I wouldn't trouble about that too much," Lydia said. "If it's anything like home, I expect they'll find us."

Chapter 8

At first, Proctor and Lydia stayed aboard the frigate while the crew and shipbuilders undertook repairs to fix the leak. He offered the excuse that they intended to continue to France when the ship resumed sail, the same excuse that Adams offered as he stayed aboard the vessel, and it allowed Proctor to stay close to him. But as soon as the crew stopped pumping, the ship took on water. *La Sensible* would not continue on to any other port soon.

Adams and his entourage disembarked and took lodgings in town. Proctor and Lydia could not afford to follow him, and as word came back after a week that Adams had hired a train of mules to begin the overland route to France, Proctor grew desperate.

"Just go and ask him for help," Lydia said.

"I can't do that," Proctor replied.

"Certain men have a need to appear great by helping out others, and by doing favors that leave men in their debt," Lydia said. "I saw it when I was in the Carolinas. Adams wants other men to see him as a great man."

"All that may be true," Proctor said. "But the attitudes of Massachusetts are very different from those of the Carolinas. New Englanders put a value on independence and self-reliance."

The words felt bitter on his tongue as soon as he spoke them. Proctor put a value on independence and self-reliance. He had begged Emily Rucke, his former fiancée, for help in New York City after the fire, and he wasn't sure he could bring himself to beg anyone for help again. He felt worse for taking charity than he did for going without.

"When you come up with a different plan, you let me know," Lydia said and stomped away. It was the least servile she'd pretended to be since they left Boston. Proctor didn't realize how much he'd missed the old Lydia until that moment.

Of course, she was right. He had to swallow his pride and go beg Adams for the favor of accompanying him to Paris.

The diplomat had been meeting with the dignitaries of the city, making his name and status known to anyone who might help him, and taking tours of such sights as the city offered. Proctor and Lydia went ashore and began inquiring after Adams. The answers led them toward the church of San Julian and its twin bell towers rising over the surrounding rooftops. The modest church, like many of the houses around it, seemed relatively new, and leaned toward a simple and functional design of stone and plaster. The two towers framed an entrance of three plain arches. The windows on either side of the arches and above them were squares of plain glass instead of the gaudy colored illustrations he had heard so often described. In all, the exterior could have been a meeting-house in Boston.

"It's not what I was expecting," Proctor told Lydia as they leaned against the cool stone wall opposite the entrance to the church. "I thought there would be more popery."

"Popery?" she asked.

"Gilded idols and graven images, that sort of thing, I suppose," he said. "I expected big statues of Our Lord, and carvings of Mary, draped in gold and jewels, with people kissing their marble feet."

"You sound disappointed," she observed.

He considered his reaction. "You realize that you are in a foreign country when the things you are sure of turn out to be untrue."

"Then we are, all of us, always in a foreign country."

"Perhaps," he admitted, though the thought unsettled him.

Even though it was December, the leaves had not yet been visited by frost. Men, women, and children alike wandered the rocky, muddy streets barefoot and in short leggings. The people were dark-haired and dark-skinned, not as much as Lydia, but enough to look different to Proctor. Men and women alike wore their dark hair in plaits down their backs, reaching the waists of some men and the knees of some of the women. Proctor stood out as a foreigner, just like the men in Adams's party or the French officers. Despite the differences, when Proctor saw a young couple strolling past the church, with the wife carrying an infant no older than Maggie, he felt a kinship to them and a sharp desire to be home.

The young man stepped away from his wife to say something in Spanish to a hunchbacked old woman lingering on the doorsteps of the church. She was wearing a ratty black robe, little better than rags, even by the poor standards of the country. Lank strands of loose white hair spilled out of her hood. She answered him angrily in a different language, flicking her hands at him and turning her back. He shoved her away from the church doors, shouting at her as he drove her down the street.

Proctor stepped away from the wall, intending to intervene, but Lydia put a hand on his arm and he stopped. "What?"

"You can't solve every problem," she said.

"But what he did, that wasn't right," he said.

"It's what happens to old women," she said, a little bitterly. "I've seen old slave women given their 'freedom' when they're too old to work, turned away from the plantations they served their whole lives. They have to live in the woods and the swamps, taking such charity as the other slaves can spare. If they show up in public, they're driven away. They call them witches and conjure-women, whether they are or not. It's the way of the world."

His jaw tightened. "Is that what you expected to happen to you?"

She glanced down and turned away.

"You can't think we'd do that to you, turn you off The Farm?"

"It is harder than I expected, pretending to be a slave again," she said, still not meeting his eyes. "I thought that bending my neck was my first nature, but when I put it on again it fits me like a pair of outgrown shoes, all pinched and hurting."

"So you understand why I don't think that man should be allowed to beat that old woman?"

"I understand that if you don't catch Mr. Adams and convince him to take us to France, we'll never do what we need to do to protect your wife and child, we won't be able to save the Revolution, and we'll never get home again. Look, there he is, and you would have missed him."

The door to the church was pushed open, and Adams emerged with his two sons. He was followed by an entourage that included a priest, several local officials, and some French naval officers. Proctor hopped across the street, slowing down to appear casual. "Mr. Adams, what a coincidence. It's good to see you again."

Adams's round face turned to Proctor in surprise, a mixture of recognition and confusion written on his features. "And you are?"

"Proctor Brown, sir. Your fellow passenger from the *Sensible*."

"You remember him, Father," John Quincy said. "He worked more shifts at the pumps than any of us."

"Ah, well, yes, thank you for that," Adams said. "How may I help you?"

Proctor stood up straight and clasped his hands behind his back. "As you may know, it will be some months before the *Sensible* resumes her journey to France. I hear that you are traveling over the mountains in order to get there sooner. I was hoping that I might be able to join you."

"It is reported to be a difficult journey. The governor of Galicia himself warned me not to take my children along because of the danger . . ."

While he was speaking, a cat appeared out of an alley, a thin black thing with white whiskers and a streak of white fur along its head. It ran straight for the children. Charles and John Quincy bent to pet it, and it purred enthusiastically as it swirled around their ankles. The elder Adams trailed off, annoyed, and a tingle of anxiety shot through Proctor.

"I think I would be a great addition to your journey, surely in no more danger than anyone else, and quite able to help if the need arose."

"What?" Adams said. "Oh, yes, of course you could. No doubt. How is your Spanish and your French?"

"I have neither," Proctor admitted. "It is one reason why I'm eager to join the company of someone like yourself, more capable of communication with the local peoples."

Adams's face grew less enthusiastic. "If you know Latin, then Sobrino's Spanish dictionary should provide you with an able vocabulary with only a few weeks' application."

"Father," John Quincy interrupted. "May we bring the cat along with us? Look how thin she is—we could feed her scraps from our own meals."

"In a moment," Adams said, still watching his son.

"I'm afraid I don't know Latin either," Proctor said. "But I have letters permitting me to draw on funds once I reach Paris, and will gladly repay you the cost of mules and board for the journey—"

Adams started at Proctor's voice. "I'm sorry, but did you say that you were expecting me to pay for your transportation?"

"I would repay you in full. I can show you my letters." He could show Adams his letters again, as he had already presented them once on the ship. He had his hand in his pocket for the letters, and his fingers fell around the lock of Deborah's hair. The spell that he had used to make Adams forget him had worked too well. Maybe a different setting would erase the effect.

Adams held out his hand to forestall the letters. "Forgive me for being blunt, but I don't know you. It would be a dereliction of my responsibility to the government I represent to use its hard-raised funds to support a private citizen on the promise of repayment. If you can acquire funds and join us on your own account, that would be one thing, but under the circumstances—"

The cat was vigorously rubbing against the ankles of Charles and John Quincy, and nipping at their fingertips. "Father—"

"I'm sorry, but we can take on no strays!"

The boys' faces fell, and Adams winced at seeing their expression. But Proctor understood that the words were intended for him. "Please, sir, I beg you—"

"It doesn't become a healthy young man to beg," Adams said. "Nor does it reflect well on our young nation, which must learn to stand on its own two feet and contribute to the well-being of the community of nations of which we hope and expect to be a part. Please leave the cat behind, boys."

Adams turned and led his children away. Lydia came

up and stood behind Proctor as the rest of the group followed Adams in a slow trickle down the street. "You did the right thing," she said.

"I did not do it successfully," he said. His heart fell as he thought about Deborah and Maggie. He was a thousand miles away from taking his next step to finding the Covenant and defeating their plans. "How do you feel about walking to Paris?"

"It's better than swimming," she mumbled. "Which is what I thought we might be faced with, when the ship was sinking."

"Monsieur Brown?"

They turned at the voice. Proctor did not recognize the gentleman at first, until he imagined a uniform filling out the man's spare form, and a cockade and wig framing the beaked nose. "Captain Chavagne," he said, bowing his head.

"I could not help but overhear the difficulty of your situation," the captain said. "Since we did not deliver you as agreed, I am afraid that we cannot keep any payment." He reached out for Proctor's hand, and Proctor felt the hard coin-filled knot of his purse pressed into his palm.

"I don't know what to say," Proctor stumbled. "Merci?"

"Oui, c'est ça, 'Merci.' Très bien. De rien." The captain nodded respectfully. "I have never seen elm pumps work so long without plugging. I believe that you earned your passage to Ferrol. Good day and good wishes, monsieur."

Chavagne walked away, taking long steps that carried him back to the other group as it disappeared down the street.

Proctor held up the purse. "It looks like we can pay our own way. Adams cannot refuse us now."

Lydia sighed with relief. "God is looking out for us. Did you drop something?"

Proctor had been spinning around, searching. "I was

looking for the cat. I thought I ought to buy something else for another stray, just as an offering of thanks, but it's gone."

Despite Adams's protests that he did not like to travel on Sunday, they began the journey to France on a Sunday afternoon, the day after Christmas. The skies were gray and foreboding, and the air was cold enough to leave one feeling miserable all the time.

It had been six weeks since Proctor left Deborah and Maggie, and the thought of them enjoying Christmas dinner in front of a warm fire, with snow on the ground outside and without him, made him feel lonely and sorry for himself. He would have been willing to start for France on Christmas Day if it meant that he'd return home sooner.

Adams came out to begin the journey. Proctor tipped his hat, only to have Adams ignore him. The diplomat had been put out to discover that Proctor had found means of paying his own way, and though he would not go back on his word to allow Proctor and Lydia to accompany them, he remained frostier than the air.

Adams had hired three calashes, but they were older than any Proctor had ever seen in Boston, and in worse repair. The leather, whether in seats or harness, had never known the touch of oil, and was sunbaked and cracked. The tack was falling apart and knotted together with twine. The calashes were a perfect match for the mules, the only animals that could be bought or hired in the area. The mules were lean and shorn from ear to tail of almost all their hair to prevent the infestation of parasites. Adams and his sons took one calash, Adams's secretary and the boys' tutor took another, and two other Americans who had attached themselves to Adams took the third. The servants rode mules, as did Proctor and Lydia. Mr. Lagoanere, the American agent in northern

Spain, accompanied them on the first part of the journey. Lagoanere was the sort of man who weighed a little
too much for his frame, paid a little too much for his
clothes, and drank a little too much at meals: in short,
the sort of congenial companion who made almost anyone feel superior in his presence.

Though it was described as the easiest part of their
passage, Proctor found the roads in such poor repair
that he thought the country abandoned. It was different
from going across the remote parts of America—those
had a feeling that they were waiting to fill up. The Spanish countryside gave an impression of long occupation
and ultimate surrender. Men had tried to live well here
and, after many generations, had failed. Now the only
people who remained were those too stubborn to try
somewhere else.

The steep ascent was mountainous and rocky, and
they finished it near dark. The calashes groaned and complained as they bounced over the deep ruts and fallen
rocks, until Proctor thought something would crack. The
mules proved sure-footed in the harsh terrain, but the
ride was jarring.

When they arrived in Betanzos, an ancient city set on
steep slopes, Proctor turned to Lydia. "I think that's
about twelve miles done. Only nine hundred and eighty-
eight more to go."

"If they're all as rough as these, can I go back and wait
for the ship to be repaired? I promise to meet you in
France."

Mr. Lagoanere helped them find rooms for the night.
"The very best that are available," Lagoanere told all the
Americans. Proctor didn't understand the apologetic tone
in the agent's voice until he saw the rooms. The floors
were bare ground, carpeted with straw, while the walls
and ceiling were covered with soot from the open-floor
ovens. Everything smelled like smoke. The mattresses

were dirty cloth stuffed with smashed straw and crawling with fleas. Proctor would have complained, but the family who owned it ended up sleeping on the floor in another room.

Lydia did a very discreet spell that caused the fleas to leave the mattresses. "Just like Moses, chasing off the plague of flies," she said. It was the least they could do for the family they displaced. "But if every night is like this, I am definitely going back to the ship."

The Adamses were in a different house, since John Adams was unwilling to share quarters with someone who wasn't part of the official American party. That was fine with Proctor. He stood in the doorway to see how Adams and the others were doing. Charles and John Quincy sat in the doorway of their house, silhouettes playing with a thin black cat. "Isn't that the same cat we saw in front of the church?"

Lydia came and stood at his side. "How can you tell in the dark? There are black cats anywhere you go."

Lydia was right. It was just a passing fancy. He turned back into their own room. "It will have to be better tomorrow."

The roads the next day were steeper and rockier. It was still early in the cloudy morning, and they were twisting around a narrow road with a steep drop on one side when a loud crack sounded. The black cat leapt from the calash carrying Adams and his sons. At the same instant, it pitched abruptly to one side with a snapped axle.

The mules knew their business, however, pulling instead of panicking, and they dragged the carriage to a safe spot before the momentum carried it over the cliff.

Proctor looked for the cat, but it had disappeared. "It had a white streak across the head, just like the one outside the church," Proctor said, stretching in his saddle.

"I thought you were imagining it," Lydia said. "But now I'm not so sure."

Something large and wet hit Proctor's face, and he looked up to see if a bird was flying overhead. Another drop hit him and another. Just what they needed—rain.

By the time they fixed the axle and continued on their way, the rain was steady and dismally cold. They traveled no more in the whole day than they had in half a day before. The town they arrived in that night was smaller, the houses were cruder, and the mud-floored rooms were shared by people and their animals. The ventilation was so poor the rooms filled with smoke, and the room that served as the bedchamber was also the kitchen and storeroom. Baskets of rapeseed, oats, and Indian corn lined the walls.

"I overheard Mr. Adams talking with his secretary," Lydia said as they looked at their beds.

Proctor was trying the spell to chase the fleas away. He remembered reading how Aaron had caused a plague of lice on the pharaoh, and he thought again how much miracles were magic by another name. Lydia had been the first one to tell him that. He bent to peer at the mattress to see if anything was crawling on it. "What did the secretary say?"

"He said we were lucky the broken axle and the rain happened today, as this is still the easy part of our journey."

Proctor snapped up a speck with his fingernails, but it was only dirt and not a flea or bedbug. "I know this may sound like simple raving—" he started, then stopped.

"But you want to keep an eye on that cat," Lydia finished for him.

Their eyes met. She had been thinking the same thing, and he did not feel so mad after all. "Familiars sometimes take on the appearance of their masters. We should look for someone like the cat."

"How?" Lydia asked. "Everyone in this country wears

black wool and little else, and white hair is as common as old people."

She had a point. "We'll just keep an eye out for the cat then," he said.

But the cat did not appear the next day nor in the days after that. Proctor thought they had left it behind as they traveled from village to village. The new year came and they stayed up late with their hosts for that night, eating grapes at midnight around a bonfire. But the next morning they resumed their journey just like any other day. As the week passed, Adams had a stubborn determination to reach Paris as soon as possible. The roads grew even worse as they wound through mountains that had been cleared of trees. The farms were small and scattered, the people were poor and dirty, and the cities marked by a lack of industry and commerce. The only signs of wealth were the old churches and monasteries, vast in size, rich in decoration, and containing the only fat men to be found anywhere in the country.

"That is the popery I was warned about as a child," Proctor said, rocking in the saddle of his mule as they passed the long stone walls of a monastery.

"You sound disappointed," Lydia said.

"Sometimes you realize you're in a foreign country when everything you heard to be true proves to be the case," he said. He kicked his mule, which made its way slowly ahead to Adams, who was riding with his secretary and the tutor. They had traded transportation with their servants, finding the mules more comfortable than the carriages. The face of Mr. Dana, the secretary, was more pinched than before, as if he needed to squeeze everything in his body together just to stay seated on the mule. Mr. Thaxter, the tutor, owned one item of note, an extravagant velvet hat so black it was nearly blue, accented by a silk headband of matching hue. He rode with one hand on the reins and the other firmly holding the hat to his head to prevent its blowing away.

"How did Spain become this reduced?" Proctor asked as he joined the three men.

"What do you mean?" Adams replied curtly in the manner he used whenever Proctor joined his party.

"Was not Spain the richest country in the world as recently as two centuries ago?" Proctor asked. "We see the signs of its wealth all around us, in the churches and buildings. But its present poverty is overwhelming. America is a young nation, never wealthy, and yet our meanest towns and poorest houses are not this squalid. How does a country go from being the richest country in the world to one of the poorest?"

"It is the inevitable fate of any nation that attempts to become an empire," Adams answered, warming up to the question. "Look at the present case of England. Money spent abroad on the military and on mercenaries is money lost. Spain became poor the same way it became rich: it built an empire overseas, plundering the labor of the people that it conquered. In turn, the empire squandered the wealth, wasting it on armies and bureaucrats. I daresay we see England reaping the same fruits from its colonies in America. Empire bankrupts a nation. In a democracy, we will never have that problem because the people will keep the government honest."

"So the governments of Spain and England are not honest?"

"Sometimes they are and sometimes they are not," Adams said. He glanced at Mr. Dana and Mr. Thaxter as if expecting the confirmation of his opinion. "There are no checks on the power of royalty. America will never oppress other nations because the people provide a natural check on the ambitions of our leaders. Can you imagine our militias being called up to fight overseas?"

"No, I can't," Proctor said.

"That is why America will never become an empire nor bring ruin to itself. We merely wish to be left alone to pursue our own interests in agriculture and commerce."

Mr. Dana began to expound on the superiority of the militia to a standing army, which, if it existed, must have wars to justify its existence, while Mr. Thaxter offered observations on the armies of the Romans. They came to a narrow place in the road; Proctor let Adams go ahead. The other two men squeezed in front to cut him off, leaving Proctor with his thoughts. He had never served in anything else but the militia, and here he was, pursuing an enemy overseas. He stared across the largely barren plain in front of them, the herds of sheep crowded behind mud walls, and wondered what Deborah was doing, whether Maggie was starting to crawl. He hoped he had made the right decision in leaving them to pursue the Covenant.

When they arrived in San Juan Segun that evening, Proctor was so sore that he almost welcomed the squalor. The tavern keeper was eager to rush them indoors, repeating a warning to them several times.

"What is he saying?" Proctor asked.

"It is just superstition," Adams replied. Though hardly shaped for hard travel, he bore it as well as any of them, stretching his arms and legs at the end of the day as if he had been only a short while in the saddle. "He is telling us that we must be careful, for it is a Friday night and the sorginak are about."

Proctor had an uneasy feeling. "The sorginak?"

"Witches, men and women who fly off to their black Sabbath every Friday night. He is not a local, but comes originally from Biscay, where I am told they have their own peculiar beliefs. As I told you, it is mere superstition."

Superstition or a hint of truth? "Why are the sorginak to be feared? Does he say?"

"I suppose they are to be feared because they do what all witches do everywhere—they worship Satan and fight the will of God."

Proctor opened his mouth to argue and then snapped it shut. He thanked Adams for his information and then joined Lydia to make arrangements for their own rooms for the night.

"What was he saying?" she asked.

"There are witches among us," Proctor said.

She shouldered her own pack and lifted Proctor's. "What are the chances?"

"Flying witches," he said.

"If that were possible, we'd be in Paris already."

"I hope he's right," Proctor said. "Because if there are witches about—other witches—maybe it's the connection we need to find the Covenant."

Chapter 9

The next morning when Proctor went out to mount their mules and carriages, Adams and the other travelers stood in the cold light, scratching their newest flea and bedbug bites. They had purchased their own mattresses, pillows, and sheets, lugging them from one town to the next, but it only reduced the problem rather than eliminating it. As soon as Proctor had the chance, he meant to rid their bedding of vermin.

He looked west, in the direction of home, but a cold fog obscured even a glimpse of the mountains or any perception of distance. Perhaps weeks in this harsh landscape had hardened him. In truth, he felt only a regret that Adams's sons suffered with him.

"Father!" John Quincy said. "Look, it's Priscilla."

The boy was bending to pet a thin black cat that rubbed up against his leg. Proctor tensed. Certainly he was imagining things. It couldn't be . . .

Adams turned away from supervising the servants' loading of their baggage. "Priscilla?"

"I called her that because she seems so ancient," John Quincy said. He lifted the animal and held it up for his father's inspection. It was unmistakably the same cat as before, with white whiskers and a white streak across its head. "Look, it's her."

"Don't be an enthusiast, John," Adams chided affectionately. "There are so many cats in Spain that they aren't worth remarking. It just happens to resemble every other old black cat."

John Quincy started to protest, pointing out the mark on its head, but Proctor had walked over for a closer look. As soon as he came near, the cat hissed and squirmed out of the boy's hands. He and his brother Charles began chasing it around the wheels of the calash.

Proctor felt a familiar tingle run across his skin. The cat must be a familiar, like Bootzamon's Dickon. Proctor scanned the narrow street and stone houses, the laborers in black wool shifts going about their work, the curious faces under broad-brimmed hats. There was a witch somewhere nearby.

He walked back to Lydia, who stood with their mules. Proctor's mount nipped at him as he came close, and Proctor missed Singer. He had ridden a thousand miles from Boston to Virginia in a fortnight on that horse. They had been on the road more than a fortnight already and were barely halfway to the French border.

"Looks like the sorginak may be around after all," Proctor told Lydia under his breath. "I think the cat's a familiar. Will you keep an eye on it?"

She nodded. "Looks like someone wants to make it easier for me, too."

The cat had crawled into the calash, where the boys were persuading their father to take it along while the servants braved its claws in an unsuccessful attempt to dislodge it.

"Oh, very well, you may bring it along," the elder Adams said. "But you must promise not to be upset if it leaps out the first time you rattle over a rock or rut."

"We won't," Charles promised earnestly.

Adams's servant had just snatched the creature up and it dangled by its scruff, twisting and hissing. Perhaps the cat had just reacted to Proctor the way it would to anyone that might approach it. "Let it down, Joseph," Adams said.

Proctor still hoped that the cat would run away. No doubt Adams did as well, but when Joseph dropped it to the ground, it immediately ran back to the boys' calash and jumped in among their bags. Proctor scanned the street for anyone who might be the creature's master, but saw no one.

Adams sighed heavily. "I forbid you to think too much about the creature, or become too attached, do you understand me? You must treat her well and see that she is comfortable. But she's liable to run off again at any time, and you must accept that we will not expend one moment looking for her."

"Thank you, Father," John Quincy said. He guided his brother into the carriage and quickly followed him before his father could change his mind. Proctor felt sorry for the boys. They were as bored and exhausted by the journey as anyone. He promised himself to spell the fleas off their sheets and mattresses.

Except that a spell might alert the cat's master to their presence, if he or she did not already know that Proctor and Lydia were witches.

Adams mounted his mule and encouraged everyone to get moving. The carriages creaked into motion, followed by the gentlemen riders, followed by Proctor and Lydia on their own mules. Soon they were outside the town and into a thicker fog. The damp air settled on Proctor's skin, raising more ordinary goose bumps.

The air stayed chilled and damp all that day. When they arrived at a town for the night, both the boys had developed colds and could not stop coughing. Proctor and Lydia watched for the cat to slip away, or the master to come find it, but it stayed curled up in the laps of the children. There was a cat on the farm that did the same thing with Deborah whenever she was the least bit unwell.

Adams would not let Proctor or anyone else come near his sons, but it did no good. By the time they reached the town of Sellada el Camino, which was little more than a roadblock meant to slow down travelers, everyone in Adams's party had developed a cold.

Another night in a mud-floored house with only coals for warmth and no chimney to let out the smoke could not be good for the boys. Proctor went to the house that lodged Adams and his children, and begged an audience, doing his best to explain to the uncomprehending expression of the Spanish host that he wished to help. The sounds of persistent racking coughs came from within. Finally, the host drew Adams to the door. He had a blanket wrapped around his shoulders and clutched his ribs as if they ached. "What is it?" Adams gasped out during a lull in his own coughing.

Proctor couldn't answer him immediately. The faint image of a skull had formed behind Adams's face. It shimmered and faded, but before it was gone it reminded Proctor sharply of the widow Nance's spell during the siege of Boston that had brought sickness on the militiamen surrounding the city.

"Perhaps Lydia can help you," Proctor said when he found his tongue again. "She's nursed many people back to health before. I'm sure she can ease your discomfort."

He was careful not to refer to her as a slave, but Adams could not let it pass. "I will not benefit from slave labor," he said. "It offends the principles of freedom on which our nation is founded. I'm sure we'll improve when we reach better dwellings in the city of Burgos tomorrow. Good night, Mister—"

Another burst of coughing interrupted him before he could finish, but he covered his mouth and closed the door on Proctor anyway.

"It's not a natural sickness," Proctor told Lydia when he rejoined her. He described what he had seen and how it resembled the widow's spell at the beginning of the war. "I think I've learned enough from Deborah to undo the spell, especially before it's had too many days to do its work," he said. "But you're a better healer than I am."

"I'll need to get close to the children and the others to do it."

"And we need to catch that cat," Proctor said. "Perhaps we can learn something from it, whether its master appears or not."

The next day did not give them any opportunity to approach Adams. He climbed into the calash that morning with his boys, pulled the canopy shut, and forbade anyone's approach. Proctor's last glimpse of them was the cat curled in a blanket on John Quincy's lap, smiling as if it had just eaten a juicy mouse.

Proctor and Lydia were forced to ride in the bitter weather. A constantly changing mix of rain and snow soaked through their clothes, which then stiffened with the cold. The other members of Adams's party, especially the servants relegated to riding mules after days in the calashes, were sullen and ignored any attempts at conversation.

Proctor shared their mood. It improved slightly when Burgos appeared on the road ahead of them. The river that split the city was crossed by several impressive bridges. Even from a distance, Proctor saw the ruins of a castle, the spires of numerous iglesias, and the compounds of several large monasteries, all within the small compass of the city.

When they arrived at their destination, which was, supposedly, the best tavern to be had, his hopes fell again. There was again no chimney, which left the rooms smoky despite the petty heat offered by a brass pan of coals. The sound of the children, coughing until they were near to vomiting, echoed through the building. Proctor found Adams at a table, making notes in his diary to calculate the remainder of their journey. He wadded a handkerchief in his free hand and covered his mouth with it as he wrote. The image of bones showed through the backs of his hands.

"Mister Adams," Proctor said. "Whether you approve or not, Lydia is a skilled healer. For your children's sake, please let her see if she can ease their coughing."

Adams looked up from writing, his eyes red-rimmed and watery. He was coughing too hard to answer, so he waved Proctor on, giving him permission to try.

Lydia went to the boys' room, which had a stone floor for the mattress they shared. Mr. Thaxter and Joseph were there. Proctor talked with them about the city and its churches, distracting them while Lydia watered down a cup of wine and heated it over the coals. She offered each boy a sip, touching his hand and saying a healing spell as she helped him hold the cup. When she was done, she heated undiluted wine for the men, making excuses to touch their hands and say a similar spell.

Proctor turned to the boys. Charles had fallen asleep as soon as his coughing stopped. It seemed almost too easy.

"Where has your cat got to?" Proctor asked. "Priscilla, right?"

John Quincy wrapped the blanket up to his chin. "Father said we must leave her outside. She is a hunter, or she would never have grown so old, and she can fend for herself."

"He's very wise, your father," Proctor said.

"She tries to sneak in the kitchen door, Joseph told me," John Quincy said. "If you see her, will you make sure she has a warm place to sleep tonight?"

"I will," Proctor said.

When he and Lydia stopped in the hall, she shook her

head. "It was a poor prayer," she said, referring to the spell she had broken. "Like the imitation of a better prayer, heard once, a long time ago. I had no trouble with it."

"It seemed that way to me too, with even the little I know about healing," he said. It nagged at him. If these were the same people who had sent a demon after his wife and child, why were they making such a poor effort here? "Let's see if we can find Priscilla."

They stopped to leave a cup of warmed spiced wine for Adams, telling him it would ease his coughing. Lydia laid a sympathetic hand on his wrist and said she was praying for him. He was so absorbed in his notes that he returned a perfunctory "thank you" and went back to work. Proctor led her through the kitchen.

"The boy says the cat's been trying to sneak in this door," Proctor said. "Do you think you can catch it?"

"Easier than you could catch a cold," she said.

He frowned at her, but waited until she was in position by the door, then reached out with his long arm and pushed it open. The black cat darted through the gap before he was ready for it.

Lydia's hand snapped out lightning-fast and caught the cat by its neck.

The creature howled in fury, twisting and slashing with front claws and back. But Lydia held it at arm's length while Proctor pinned its back legs in one hand and its front legs in another. Its howl changed to a cry that was almost human in its misery and pitifulness. It was a skinny thing, its legs barely more than bone, and its bones barely more than sticks. Proctor doubted it weighed much more than a kitten.

"Now what do we do?" Lydia asked.

"We can take it to our room and—"

He stopped in mid-sentence because the cat suddenly grew ten times heavier. He and Lydia were pulled toward each other as the cat's sudden weight dragged it to the ground, but neither one of them let go. Not even when it started to grow and transform in their hands. As they held tight, the squirming, struggling creature turned into an old woman in a raggedy black dress. Strands of lank white hair escaped from her hood. She writhed and slapped at them, speaking in a strange language neither of them understood.

Proctor had a firm grip on her shoulder and arm, which felt as fragile and brittle as the cat. Lydia let go and glanced around, expecting someone to answer the old woman's cries for aid.

"What do we do?" she asked.

Proctor clamped a hand over the old woman's mouth, wincing as she bit him. "There was an empty stall in the stables—"

"Let's go," Lydia said, banging the door open.

The old woman kicked and scratched as Proctor dragged her out the door and through the alley, but she was thin and weak, frail to the point that Proctor feared she might break in half if they shoved her too hard. The mules flicked their ears as Proctor and the old woman passed them. Lydia followed behind, scattering the straw over the marks created by the old woman's dragging heels.

The new location had the smell of manure and the buzz of flies, guaranteeing, he hoped, some greater measure of privacy. "We have to question her," Proctor said. "But I have no idea what she's saying."

Lydia stood by the stall door, biting her lip. "I know a prayer . . ."

The old woman bit Proctor's hand again, the soft spot between his thumb and forefinger. If she'd had a few more teeth, it might have hurt enough to let go. "I'm listening."

"I learned it from observing Miss Cecily," Lydia said.

That explained her hesitation. "Your intention is not to do harm, it is to stop harm."

The old woman struggled harder, thrashing her legs and scratching at Proctor's hand, trying desperately to pull it away from her mouth. The mules shifted uncomfortably at the struggle.

Lydia covered her ears with her hands. Proctor thought it was to shut out what he was saying, but then he could feel her working a spell. The old woman stopped her struggles and watched Lydia with wide eyes. When Lydia reached out and touched the old woman's ears, she began to tremble in Proctor's grip. Then Lydia touched Proctor's ears and he felt a piercing sting.

Maybe there was something to the idea that some magic was by its very nature evil, regardless of intention.

Lydia bowed her head and folded her hands together. "Dear Father, let us by the manifestation of the Spirit be given to us to profit withal, to the understanding of tongues, that we may know what this woman says, and that she may understand us, that we may ease her fright and discover her purpose."

The old woman's body began to shake with sobs. Proctor let go of her mouth, though he was ready to cover it again the instant she started to scream or cry for help.

"Please don't hurt me," the woman said, her voice little more than a whisper. It was odd: her words still sounded strange and foreign, but Proctor found he understood them. "Don't hurt me."

"Who are you?" he asked.

"Emazteona, but I am called Urraca. How—?" She tried looking over her shoulder at Proctor, but she was afraid to take her eyes from Lydia. Her question trailed off in a mixture of uncertainty and tears.

"Don't be frightened, Urraca," Lydia said. "Why did you make the Americans sick?"

"A great sorcerer came to me in a vision of fire while I was in my town of Etxebarri. He hates the American rebels, wants to see all the American rebels destroyed. He promised . . . things . . . to anyone who would help him. I went to the coast, to the sea, because I thought, if Americans come here, that is where they will land."

"How were you to get in touch with him?"

"He promised he would find me, flying like a spirit in the dark."

Proctor tensed. Could it be the prince-bishop? The man who stole his finger and held a leash on his soul. "What did he look like, this man?"

"Very old," Urraca said. "But not old. He was thin, and wore long robes, and had a beard . . ." She dissolved into tears again, the way she did every time Proctor spoke to her.

Proctor looked up at Lydia. "That doesn't sound like the German."

"An associate of his, perhaps?"

"Yes, one of the twelve," Urraca said, licking her lips nervously. "He said there were twelve spots at his side, twelve places for the immortals. I am old, and have no one, but if I helped this sorcerer, then I might be young again, I might be rich." She looked at her bare feet, covered with sores and calluses. Her toes ended in cracked and yellowed nails. "I could buy a pair of shoes. And a mule to carry me so I never have to walk again."

She sighed and collapsed pathetically. Her body sagged against Proctor, weighing no more than a bag full of rags and sticks, just like Bootzamon.

"What is the sorcerer's name?" Proctor demanded.

She glanced from Lydia's feet to Proctor's to her own. Proctor's shoes were scuffed and scraped by the hard mountain roads, but he suddenly felt very wealthy to have them. Urraca sobbed into her fists, unable to answer.

"I want to feel harshly toward her," Proctor said to

Lydia. "She meant to sicken Adams and his sons until they were dead, but she seems so small and hopeless and afraid."

The old woman clawed ineffectually at Proctor's hand, which still gripped her. She muttered "I hate you, I hate you, I hate you" as if it were a rosary.

"I think that this is what our enemy does," Lydia said. "He plays on people's fears to make them use their talents for him."

Proctor could see what she meant at once. "He doesn't need one big plan or one agent—he prepares thousands of them. Everyone with a talent who hides it out of fear, every old woman who possesses one or two spells and nothing else, anyone with a grievance who is willing to use a charm or focus prepared by someone else. One man sabotages a ship in Boston, an old woman makes someone sick in Spain, a third person waits already at the next spot on the road."

"He can have an army at his command," Lydia said.

But Proctor had spent time in the army and around it. "It's not the same. He doesn't organize everyone to work together toward a goal. He winds them up and sends them out on their own, to accomplish it however they see fit. An army can be defeated by another army. But how do you stop a thousand different agents?"

Lydia shrugged.

"You have to defeat the leader," Proctor said, answering his own question. "So we have to find out who he is. You spent your whole life with Cecily—do you have any idea?"

She shook her head. "Cecily was rising through their ranks. She was an apprentice to the widow Nance until you and Deborah killed her. Then the prince-bishop found her and she became his protégée. Unless he's the leader, the man we're searching for—"

"I don't think he is," Proctor said. "But he's near the

top, of that I am certain." The old woman was still weeping, weak and limp in his grip. "Can you put a binding spell on her, something to keep her from harming anyone? Or hold her, and I'll do it."

"No, I can do it," Lydia said. She pulled a thread from her hem, then tore one from Proctor's coat, and took a third from the old woman's dress, braiding the threads together. "She has only a small talent and shouldn't be that dangerous. What if she goes to the sorcerer she described and brings him to us?"

"Then we've found the man we were searching for," Proctor said.

Lydia tied the braided thread around the old woman's wrist, and put a binding on her to do no harm to anyone. The old woman tried to untie it and pulled her hand back as if stung. Proctor released her and she sprawled into the straw, crawling out of the stall on her hands and knees like an animal. It was one of the saddest things he had ever seen.

"It seems wrong somehow," he said, thinking about his mother, and her fears of being discovered for a witch. Of Deborah, and her fears of being an old woman, kicked from door to door, muttering petty curses out of spite. "That we faced a demon in our own home and have come this far in search of its master only to face a woman as sad as this, one we would try to help in any other circumstance. I wish—"

"What do you wish?"

Lydia stared at him, expecting him to continue, but he could scarcely see her. The manure and flies had already faded from sense, and the walls of the stable were flimsy gauze, and Lydia was little more than a ghost. Dizzy, he groped for something to hold on to, trying simply to stay upright. Then he felt himself falling.

It was as though a hand reached inside him and grabbed him by the breastbone. He felt himself skimming over mountains in a blur of light and snow, then out over an ocean as smooth as glass over sunken stars. A second later, he was falling through clouds like a wounded bird. The clouds parted and the land opened up below him. He was dropping toward The Farm.

He saw Deborah through the walls of the house. She was lying on her bed, eyes closed, arms folded on her chest. Abigail stood over her, holding Maggie in her arms. Maggie had grown so big. She was holding her head up, leaning toward her mother. Abigail had to pull her away. What was happening—was Deborah dead? Proctor plunged from the sky and reached through the wall to touch his daughter.

And then he sensed it. A presence waited for him, a spirit lurking at the edge of his mind, ready to break in. Behind the vision of Deborah, something else waited for him. It lunged at him like a serpent, and he could feel the poisonous fire of its fangs scrape against him.

Back in the stall, so far away it was like it was happening to a different person, he felt Lydia take hold of his hand.

As the presence lunged at him, he pulled away and snapped back to his body like a bowstring released by an archer. His spirit flew like an arrow, back to his body, but when it pierced his chest and he landed there, he couldn't move his limbs. His stomach churned nauseously and his head pounded as the light faded to black. The last thing he felt was Lydia's hands wrapped around his, but it was as though they were both wearing heavy mittens. The last thing he heard was her voice, muffled and far away, as if calling from another room.

"Proctor—what just happened? Proctor!"

Chapter 10

Six hundred hooves pounded the dusty Carolina road, a steady drumbeat to the melody of the songbirds in the trees and underbrush. The dark green jackets of the British Legion blended in with the foliage, and the hard black caps on their heads gleamed like the carapaces of predatory insects.

Only they were no longer called the British Legion. They were now just as often referred to as Tarleton's Raiders. Banastre Tarleton, the brash young commander of this group of American Loyalists, took pride in the appellation. They had been forged into a single unit during that first raid together on Pound Ridge, New York, the year before. The new year meant a new campaign in the South as British forces finally made progress against the rebel armies. Tarleton had already made his name. The right victory would cement his reputation and might even make his fortune.

A voice chuckled behind him.

Tarleton turned and noticed a hatless boy with an unruly tousle of blond hair. He wore a red coat, like the British regulars, which was as out of place among the light dragoons as his age. The boy's eyes were unsettling. When Tarleton met those eyes, he felt as though someone—or something—else were looking at him from behind them. A shiver ran through his spine.

His horse nickered and tossed its head. Tarleton turned to it and looked at the road ahead. He had the

sense that he'd just a moment ago been thinking about
something or someone . . .

He spurred the horse ahead of his men. He had a reputation for leading from the front to uphold. The men
looked to him as their model. The rebel forces were
nearby, and Tarleton meant to catch them.

The scouts reported that the rebels' Colonel Buford
had come with three hundred and fifty or four hundred
Continental soldiers, the entire Third Virginia detachment, to reinforce the Americans at Charleston. They
hadn't known that Charleston had already surrendered—
the greatest British victory of the war since Brooklyn. A
whole army lost to the rebels, thousands of men. When
Buford's men had found out that Charleston was lost,
they'd turned tail and headed back for Virginia as fast as
their horses would carry them.

But not, hopefully, as fast as Tarleton's Raiders could
catch them.

It would be worthwhile just to spank them for the
spoiled colonial brats they were. But John Rutledge, the
pretender to South Carolina's governorship, was with
them. Catching Rutledge would take all the wind out
of the rebels' sails. Following the loss of their army at
Charleston, it might break the colonies' back. String up
a few of the leaders, and the followers would fold. The
bloodshed would be over. America and Great Britain
could return to the natural state that history and logic
preferred for them.

As he hopefully considered that prospect, Tarleton
looked back at his own men. They were called the British
Legion, but every man of them was born in the colonies
and came from America. The difference between his
men and the rebels was that his men knew where their
true allegiance and interest lay.

Well, that, and they could fight. He'd take one of his
men to lick two or three of the rebels any day.

At the edge of his vision, he glimpsed a boy in a red coat, out of place among all the green jackets of his men. Tarleton had no idea who the boy was or where he came from, but he meant to find out . . .

Hoofbeats galloped on the road ahead, and he turned to see who was coming. The newcomers were hidden by the hills and the dense trees.

A figure rounded a bend in the road. Matthews, his shaggy-haired, perpetually unshaven scout. The man's beard grew in so fast, the shadow returned to one side of his face while he was shaving the other. Tarleton held up his hand, bringing the men to a stop. Matthews reined in his horse at Tarleton's side.

"Report," Tarleton said.

"They're just short of the crossroads a couple of miles ahead," Matthews said. "Closer to four hundred than three."

Tarleton looked back at the hundred and fifty men riding with him, and could feel that they were on edge. Almost four hundred rebels. How much did he believe his own braggadocio? Was every one of his raiders really as good as two rebels?

"Go kill them," whispered a boy's voice, almost in his ear. "Go kill them all."

Tarleton shook off the shiver that ran through his skin. He had a second group of men coming four or five miles behind. He nodded to Matthews. "Go back and tell the reserves to get their asses up here. If they can't run, they damned well better sprout wings and fly. I want them here *now*."

The scout snapped a crisp salute. "Yes, sir."

Tarleton returned the salute, and the scout peeled away, wheeling his horse around the other men in the narrow, tree-lined road. Matthews had been fortunate enough to find a good horse, one bred for racing, after all their animals had died during the gruesome ship's voyage from

New York. He could not forget the backbreaking work of shoving all the dead horses overboard, nor the feeling that it had been unnecessary, that they were plagued by something that delighted in death.

Now they took whatever poor screw they could find, the men rode the horses to death, and no one knew how his mount would act in battle. No wonder the men were on edge.

"Captain Kinlock!" Tarleton shouted.

David Kinlock had been with the legion since '78. His curly red hair originally led Tarleton to expect a man with either a temper or a sense of humor, or both. Kinlock had neither. He was a good soldier, and played poker with one of the straightest faces Tarleton had ever seen. In typical fashion, he waited a moment, then walked his horse slowly out of line up to Tarleton's side.

"Sir," Kinlock said.

"These colonials were too cowardly to join real fighting men like those in the legion," Tarleton said, raising his voice enough to carry all the way back the line. The comment brought a few grins. "Therefore I want you to take a flag of truce and see if they're willing to surrender. It'd be a shame for us to have to hurt them."

That won a few snickers, but the men still sounded nervous.

"And Kinlock," Tarleton said.

"Sir," Kinlock said, not having moved or reacted since Tarleton's original statement.

"Why don't you make the decision easy by telling them we've got seven hundred troops here? We outnumber them two to one. They'll see the wisdom of surrender then." He watched the men nod to one another and sit back in their saddles. In the short run, this group always appreciated craftiness over praise. "Tell Buford that, resistance being vain, to prevent the effusion of human blood I make offers that shall never be repeated. He has but one chance." Tarleton surveyed his men and saw their approval. Turning back to Kinlock, he said, "What're you waiting for, Captain?"

"You, to make sure you're done talking," Kinlock answered laconically.

That sort of cheek would be insubordination in the regular army, but among colonials it was a sign of affection. Tarleton waved Kinlock off unceremoniously, and the captain unfolded a white handkerchief and tied it to his gun barrel as he trotted away.

Tarleton sent out flankers through the trees to keep rebel scouts or their local allies from discovering his true numbers. Then he formed up the men he had and pushed ahead, hoping Matthews would bring up his reserves before Buford crossed the border into rebel-held territory. With luck, he could bluff Buford and the colonials into surrender.

"There will be bloodshed," whispered a voice beside him.

Tarleton was startled to see a strange boy in a red coat riding beside him. He went without a cap, and unruly blond hair covered his head. "Who are you? What did you say?"

The boy licked his lips, like a cat at a cream saucer, and smiled.

On sudden impulse, Tarleton trotted ahead of his men. What had he just been thinking? Oh, yes. Likely enough he could bluff Buford and the rebels into surrendering. But if he couldn't he knew the legion could fight.

Before long Kinlock came galloping back along the trail. Tarleton called the men to a halt.

"What did Buford say?" he asked.

Kinlock sat up straight in his saddle and, in a fair imitation of Buford's voice, said, "Sir, I reject your proposals. I shall defend myself to the last extremity."

Tarleton considered this for a moment. "He said *defend myself*?"

Kinlock pushed his tongue in his cheek, thought about it to be sure, then nodded.

So Buford was thinking more about himself than his men. Their will was split. Best to find out their battle plans, see if there was a weak spot. "What did they do after you rode away?"

"I don't know about after," Kinlock said. "But before I left, they were already marching north again."

"Marching?" Tarleton couldn't believe his ears. What kind of fool would turn his back on an enemy and march when he was about to be attacked?

"Marching," Kinlock said. "Hightailin' it for the border. But they'll have to hoof it pretty quick to reach Virginia before we catch 'em."

"If they're retreating, then they aren't prepared to fight," Tarleton said aloud. He wanted the men to hear his thoughts, although his mind was already decided. "All right, attend me closely."

The men pressed forward on their horses until they were all in earshot.

"If we wait for the reserves to come up, these Virginians will still outnumber us. And they may have settled down a bit, and not be quite as scared. It sounds to me like they're frightened, and it sounds to me like they're running. So I say we do what the hounds do whenever the fox is running scared, and we run them down."

All the humor had gone out of the men, and most of the nervousness. Tarleton saw resolve in their eyes, and in that moment he thought, by God, he loved this bloody fighting legion. They were good men.

"We're going to run them down from behind," Tarleton repeated. "We're going to break their line and capture Colonel Buford and Governor Rutledge. If you capture Rutledge, withdraw with him at once so he doesn't get hurt. But that'll take the fight out of them. If they don't have sense enough to surrender after that, we'll withdraw and wait for the reserves to join us."

The men took a moment to check their weapons. Tarleton heard clapping, and he turned and saw a boy in a red coat with a gleeful expression on his face.

"This is going to be so good," the boy said, grinning.

Tarleton was about to demand to know who the bloody hell he was when Kinlock spoke.

"Food, sir?"

"What?" Tarleton asked. "Oh, yes, of course, give the men permission for a bite to eat if they wish." He had grown weary of corn pone and hominy, which was what the corn pone was before they baked it. The two formed nearly their entire diet. But he carried several small loaves of pone in his pack, and he broke one in pieces and ate it.

They had the advantage of horses and of Buford's lack of resolve, and that should make this quick and easy even though they were outnumbered. If it wasn't quick and easy, they could always pull back.

He signaled his troops into the formation that he wanted and had them move forward at a trot. As they came through the hills, and past the crossroads, he saw faces in the windows of the farms, latching the shutters and hiding from view. The fear was strong. Fear was his ally.

They heard the echo of a drum through the trees, and soon afterward raised sight of Buford's troops half a mile or so ahead of them. He waited until the rear guard spotted them and all the marching heads were looking back over their shoulders. When the audience was large enough, Tarleton put out false signals to both his flanks as if he were communicating with a much larger force.

Then he sent a single rider in clear view over one of the hilltops to give orders to their imaginary reserves.

Buford's men took the bait. The cadence of the drum doubled, and the men moved at a quick march instead of turning to fight.

Tarleton pulled out his saber and waved it over his head. "We've got them on the bloody run, boys. Ride them down and bring me Rutledge."

The horses cantered forward as a mass, picking up speed as they went. The road widened out into fields on either side, and the horses spread out around Tarleton in a thundering, ironshod wedge.

As soon as the charge began, Buford called a halt and his men spread a hasty line across the road and into the fields. They had only minutes to react. Tarleton did not slow, but he knew that a couple of rounds into the cavalry at this distance could break the charge. With only a hundred and fifty men instead of seven hundred, that loss of momentum could be fatal.

But Buford didn't fire. In what was perhaps some mistaken memory of the tactics at Bunker Hill, his voice rose above the field yelling, "Hold, hold!"

At a hundred yards away, Tartleton bent down over the neck of his horse and spurred it to a full gallop. In the last seconds before they crashed into the thin American line, he scanned the ranks for some sign of South Carolina's rebel governor.

Finally, Buford's voice cried out, "Fire! God damn you, fire!"

The muskets erupted when Tarleton's men were ten yards away. Tarleton felt one ball whiz by him, heard others zip over his head. Most men were tossing their weapons aside even as they pulled the triggers, and the volley was wasted.

And then Tarleton smashed through the line, his men

on either side of him. They discharged their pistols at point-blank range and slashed with their sabers. The rebels went down, some under the hooves of the horses and some beneath the sudden impact of lead or steel. But most, thinking they were outnumbered, fell from fear.

Tarleton felt the fear now too. A dread, like the dread they felt on the storm-rattled ships when all the horses were dying. Overpowering dread, a flood that washed away all reason.

The rebels had thrown down their weapons and were surrendering everywhere that Tarleton looked. But still he felt the urge to shoot one, any one of them, just to kill someone, to see the blood flow, to watch it stain the ground and soak in like water for an evil garden.

Buford himself stepped forward, waving a white cloth in his hand. One of his aides held out his musket in surrender. Tarleton sheathed his saber. It was over. The British Legion, outnumbered more than two to one, had defeated the rebels.

Tarleton raised his unfired pistol.

A voice in his head whispered to him to shoot.

Only the voice wasn't in his head.

It was an angelic-faced boy in a red coat. His eyes were wide, his lips parted hungrily. "Shoot," he demanded. "Kill."

Tarleton would not obey that voice, but he could not refuse it either. He lowered the pistol against the back of his own mount's head and fired.

At the crack of the weapon, the horse reared and then collapsed. Tarleton was thrown to the ground.

"They shot the colonel!" someone yelled.

And someone else, "They murdered Ban!"

By the time Tarleton had staggered to his feet, a slaughter had commenced. His men, full of fear, driven by the same demonic voice, emptied their weapons into the prisoners and then began hacking at them with their sabers. They chased from horseback and dismounted to attack. Dozens of rebels were already dead, more wounded. Tarleton saw men cut down from behind as they tried to flee.

The little boy stood with his arms at his sides, the cuffs of his red coat hanging down over his hands. His head was tilted back at the sky, his expression as sated and vacant as a drunkard's.

Tarleton grabbed him by the lapels and shook him. "What have you done? Make it stop!"

The boy's eyes had rolled back in his head so that only the whites showed. A red light shimmered in the sheen of his whites, like a fire that danced in the caverns of his skull.

Tarleton flung him aside and ran among the men, grabbing their weapon hands to stay them. But the men tore free of his grip, using his name as their battle cry.

"I'm alive, I'm alive," Tarleton screamed, running from man to man.

The men, as if jerked suddenly to their senses, staggered to a stop. But it was too late. More than a hundred rebels already lay dead. Another hundred or more crawled wounded among the corpses, crying out for aid. One man rolled over at Tarleton's feet, with a dozen bloody slashes to his face and arms, begging for mercy as blood gushed from a wound that lay open the bare bone of his jaw.

"Brownfield!" Tarleton bellowed. The surgeon was with the reserves, so Brownfield would have to do. "Where's the surgeon's mate? Brownfield!"

The British-born Brownfield answered Tarleton's call. He was pale as a flag of surrender as he dismounted his horse. He glanced around him, helplessly, and his voice wavered when he spoke. "The carnage . . ."

"Pull yourself together," Tarleton snapped angrily. "Save as many as you can. Treat all the wounded alike, ours and theirs."

They were hollow words. He didn't see any of his men among the wounded, though he supposed there must be a few. The surgeon nodded uncertainly and knelt by the wounded man at Tarleton's feet. At the sight of the wounds, his eyes lifted toward the commander in horror.

"Do what you can," Tarleton said. He walked away to escape the accusation in Brownfield's gaze. "Kinlock!"

The laconic captain, never excitable, answered Tarleton's call. His arms were splattered with blood to his elbows, his boots were bloody to his knees, and his saber's point had snapped off. He seemed as surprised by his appearance as Tarleton was. "Sir? We're so glad you're—"

"Where's Rutledge?" Tarleton demanded. God forbid they killed a governor, even a rebel governor, in this mindless slaughter. He would never be able to justify that to Cornwallis.

"He escaped, sir," Kinlock said. "The rebels say he went his separate way hours ago."

Tarleton turned away to hide his fury. All this blood and for nothing! He looked for that smirking boy, that strange boy in the red coat. Tarleton remembered him now. He had been hanging around ever since they burned that town in New York.

The boy saw him coming. He knelt over a dead American, rent by horrible wounds. When he lifted his head, a crimson smear was slashed across his angelic mouth. He sighed like a dog after eating its fill.

"Balfri is coming," he said. "And I am his herald. This is the blood of his new covenant, which is shed for many."

Tarleton recoiled. "Oh my God—"

The boy laughed. "If you want to remember me, you can." He offered a scarlet hand to Tarleton. "Take, drink this blood, in remembrance of me. Take and eat of this body, in remembrance of me."

"You blasphemous monster!" Rage whirlwinded

through Tarleton. He drew his saber, intending to smash the unholy creature trapped in this boy's body, and—

"Colonel Tarleton!"

He spun around to answer the voice.

Brownfield was wandering among the wounded with a train of volunteers, treating and aiding any man still alive. When he spied Tarleton, revulsion washed over his face. "Even savages do not commit these kinds of atrocities."

Tarleton noticed the bloody saber in his hand—he must have slashed someone when they broke the line—and wondered why he had drawn it. He slammed it into its scabbard. There was an explanation for all of this, he was certain.

As if hearing someone else's voice come out of his mouth, Tarleton said, "My men saw my horse fall, shot out from under me after the rebels had already surrendered." Yes, that was it. That explained all their actions. "They reacted accordingly. Who could have restrained them?"

Brownfield bent to help another victim.

Somewhere behind Tarleton, a boy was laughing. Tarleton spun around, trying to find him, but no one was there.

Chapter 11

The post chaise rattled over French roads in the cold, dismal morning. Proctor shifted in his seat and looked out the window of the enclosed carriage. Another charming village and yet more vineyards. He had never seen so many vineyards as he had in France.

He leaned his head out the window and called up to the coachman, "Are we near Paris yet?"

The coachman pulled down the scarf that protected his face from the cold. "Nous sommes à une heure de moins que la dernière fois que vous m'avez posé cette question, il y a une heure de cela. Vous devez être gentilhomme puisque vous avez les moyens de vous payer une esclave et un carrosse, mais vous avez la patience d'un ivrogne qui attend sa bouteille. Si vous avez plus de questions, peut-être pourriez-vous les poser à mon cul, parce que mes oreilles sont gelées."

"I beg your pardon," Proctor said. "En anglais, s'il vous plaît."

The coachman looked at him and offered a small smile. "I said, 'We are very near to Paris.'"

"Ah, good," Proctor said. He pulled his head back through the window and shifted to the other side of the seat.

"That's not what he said," murmured Lydia. She sat in the seat opposite him, so still and silent at times it was almost possible to forget she was there.

"Do I want to know what he said?"

She thought about it for a moment. "No, not really."

"What did he say?"

Lydia shook her head. "No, you don't want to know."

She was dragging it out, trying to distract him, but he was in no mood to play along, so he fell back into silence. He shifted in his seat again. No matter how many times he changed position, he could not stretch out his legs comfortably or ease the aches that resulted from the constant jarring of the carriage. The squeak of the wheels was like an itch in his ears that he could not scratch.

"You've done everything you can do," Lydia said.

"If by *everything* you mean fall down sick, let Adams get away from us while I recover, and then spend a month crossing France in a post carriage that is supposed to be the quickest transportation available, then yes, I've done everything I can. Forgive me if it doesn't feel like enough."

Lydia was too schooled in hiding her feelings to register any reaction, but Proctor knew as soon as the words were out of his mouth that he'd spoken too harshly.

"I'm sorry," he said.

She shook her head. "There's no reason to go sorrying me. You see your wife and child in danger, someone or something attacks you and you barely escape, and the man you're trying to protect goes off without you because he doesn't even know you've been protecting him."

"We," Proctor said. "We were protecting him."

Lydia shifted uncomfortably, perhaps because she had never been permitted to take credit for her work, especially her witchcraft. Or perhaps because the seats were hard, the roads were bumpy, and she was as tired of being confined inside a carriage as Proctor was. "It's a full plate of unhappiness, sitting on the table in front of you. That's all I'm saying."

"I've got no appetite," Proctor said.

Lydia stared out the window. "I know you're worried about Deborah."

"When I saw her, at first I thought she was dead," Proctor said. They had talked about it before, but hour after hour, day after day of riding left him with nothing else to do but play the whole scene in his head over and over again. It had left him as weak as a newborn, and he didn't know whether that was a reaction to the magic or to the thought of Deborah dead. He still had not fully recovered his strength.

"You know it's not real," Lydia said.

"Do I? It felt real, it looked real. Who am I to say what is and isn't possible?"

"The Covenant plays upon our fears. You saw it with that old woman, you know it's true. There's nothing you fear more than something happening to your wife and child, and that's a natural way for a man to feel. But don't let our enemies go using it against you."

"Adams was supposed to lead me to them," Proctor said. "What if something's happened since he left us?" At least Adams had been easy to follow. Once they reached Bilbao and the bigger cities, there were stories about him in every newspaper. *El Caballero Juan Adams miembro del Congreso Americano y Su Ministro Plenipotenciario la Corte de Paris.* The echoes of the thirteen-gun salutes still sounded in the trail of gossip that he left behind.

Lydia shrugged. "Then we'll find them another way. Don't your letters introduce us to someone in Paris—"

"Benjamin Franklin?"

"Yes, Doctor Franklin. He'll find some way to help you."

He hoped Lydia was right. He'd find some way to pick up where they left off. Part of the problem was that he had been so weakened by the attack. The constant riding, the lack of exercise and work, left him little means of recovery. He felt like he was growing weaker instead of stronger.

"It's already been more than three months. I promised Deborah I'd try to be home in three months."

"Oh, don't worry about that," Lydia said. "She said it, 'cause that's what's in her heart. But she knows that what you're planning to do might take a might bit longer."

"Maybe," Proctor said, propping his elbow on the arm rest and leaning on his hand. "But *I* wanted to be home that soon. That's why I promised it."

Although the coachman had given the same answer— "Yes, we are very near to Paris"—many times over the past few days, this time his answer proved correct. After a short stop for lunch, they arrived in the village of Passy. Amid the quaint cottages and smaller houses rose a building as large as any of the great churches they had visited in Spain or many of the castles and châteaux they had glimpsed from a distance on their journey across France. As they came closer, Proctor saw that smaller pavilions surrounded the main building, which had wings that framed a beautiful courtyard. It was an edifice of gray stone, elegantly proportioned and delicately cut, with windows larger than any he had ever seen. The whole building was encompassed by a terrace and formal gardens with hedges cut in geometric forms surrounding fountains and beds for flowers.

Lydia pressed against him with excitement. "Look," she said.

Beyond the building they could see all the way to the river, with the magnificent spires of Paris spearing the cold, crisp sky. "I think I recognize this place from the descriptions I've heard," Proctor said. "But I asked him to take us to the dwelling of Franklin."

"Perhaps this is on the way," Lydia said.

Proctor could not argue with her. His knowledge of

French geography was limited to its general location—across the ocean—and the parts of it he had seen from their carriage.

The coachman pulled the post up to the terrace where several gentlemen dressed in velvet and lace descended the steps to inquire about the new arrival. Proctor assumed they were diplomats, perhaps members of the nobility like the Marquis de Lafayette, whom he had seen with Washington once. When the coachman came down from the boot and opened the door for them, Proctor gratefully stretched his legs and stepped out.

"I'm sorry," he said. "Je suis désolé. But I wished to be delivered to the house, la maison, of Benjamin Franklin."

"And this is the house of Doctor Franklin," the coachman said.

With a sweep of his hand, Proctor indicated the palace, the gardens, the sweeping vista. "It isn't Versailles?"

The residence of the king. He believed that he had been taken, for some reason, to the king's palace.

The coachman gave a knowing look to the well-dressed gentlemen, a look of shared suffering. And Proctor realized at once that the men he thought gentlemen were merely servants. He looked at the residence a second time and saw a lightning rod projecting from the roof. One of Franklin's lightning rods.

This was not the king's palace. *What did the king's palace look like?*

"Doctor Franklin welcomes his American guest," the head servant said, bowing. He lifted his eyes and caught sight of Lydia in her plain, travel-stained dress. If he had any contempt or disregard for her, he did not let it show. "If you wish, I may show your servant to the rooms in which you're welcome to stay. Monsieur Franklin regrets that you are too late to join him for dinner today, but he will welcome a visit from you later this evening."

When Proctor felt a little less embarrassment he said, "Is the post office nearby? I wish to see if I have any letters."

The servants spoke to the coachman in French, too fast for Proctor to make out any individual words, and then the coachman said, "I will take you there and return with you."

"It's all right," Lydia said. She picked up their small packs in either hand. "I'll go prepare our quarters."

"Thank you," Proctor said, and then wondered if he'd made a mistake to thank his slave. He had no idea what the social rules were in France.

He had asked Deborah to write him care of the American legate in Paris, but he understood that he would have to go claim the letters for himself. The coachman took him on a quick ride through the village to an official-looking building that might have served in America for courts or even the legislature. When he went inside, he was relieved to find someone at the desk whose English was as good as his own. He reached into his pocket and turned his focus—the lock of Deborah's hair—over and over in his fingers.

"You look familiar," a voice said behind him.

Proctor turned and saw the round features of John Adams, displaying considerably less strain than they had during the voyage or the trip across Spain. He had been so eager to hear from Deborah that he had forgotten Adams for a moment, and he found himself relieved and happy to see him standing there.

"Proctor Brown," he said. "We were shipmates on the *Sensible* and traveled part of the way across Spain together."

"Ah, yes," Adams said, though Proctor wasn't sure how much he remembered. It could be dangerous to do forgetting spells on those you might need to know in the future. Adams waved over one of the clerks. "John Adams, minister for the United States."

"How are your sons doing?" Proctor asked. "The last I saw of them, they were ill with colds."

"Yes, the same thing that delayed your journey, if I recall correctly," Adams said. He looked at Proctor more closely, as if some of the memories were pushing through. "Both Charles and John recovered very well, and they're now enrolled in Monsieur Le Couer's boarding school here in town with Mister Franklin's grandson. Splendid instruction in Latin and French, although they are also attempting to introduce the boys to fencing and dancing." He shook his head. "Who are you expecting to hear from?"

"My wife, Deborah," Proctor said.

"My Abigail writes me frequently. Her thoughts and conversation, no matter the distance, make my heart throb like a cannonade." Adams seemed lost in reverie for a moment, but then he looked up at Proctor earnestly. "You must be very careful what you write your Deborah in reply."

Proctor was taken aback. "Why?"

"The French read and copy all the mail that is sent through the post, everything that might be of use to them against the English, or in their negotiations with us. Above all, be not too intimate in your expressions." Proctor's face must have registered the puzzlement he felt, so Adams continued. "You'll understand once you have been in the country awhile. The French are a very immodest people. A tender word in a letter is no different from a public display of affection, and who would have prying eyes spying on his most personal moments?"

"Here you are, Monsieur Adams," said the clerk.

He handed a bundle of letters, neatly tied with a red, white, and blue ribbon, into Adams's hand. Adams undid the ribbon with a single tug and flipped through the letters. "Ah," he said, clearly disappointed.

"Nothing from Mrs. Adams?"

"No, mostly newspaper clippings from my agent in

London. I should go and peruse them carefully. Good day to you, Mister Brown."

"Good day, Mister Adams," Proctor said, considering whether he ought to follow Adams.

"Here you are, sir," his clerk said. "We were able to find but this one letter."

All thoughts of Adams fled from Proctor's head. A letter from Deborah! He stepped outside in the cold sun and tore it open at once. The script was large and more confident than precise, looking as if it had been completed in a hurry, with lines marked out and written over. In short, it was very like Deborah, and he felt as though he were holding her in his hands. It was dated the first day of December, just weeks after he left.

> My dearest Proctor,
>   I am writing you because I promised to do so, but it goes against everything in my nature to commit words to paper.

That was true. It had been Deborah's habit, and her mother's and grandmother's before her, to commit nothing to paper, so that nothing could be a record against them if the witchcraft trials ever resumed. Deborah's notes were usually brief and direct.

The letter continued,

> If you see Mr. Adams, I hope you will express my very great disappointment that he has stolen my right to vote. When I inherited my parents' property, I became eligible to vote under the law of Massachusetts, at least until you and I were married. But my point is that the new constitution, written by Mr. Adams before his departure, has stripped women of that right, which we so justly deserve if we meet the same qualifications as the men. Only

now it appears that being a man is the necessary qualification.

The writing in this part of the letter was sharp and angry, the letters slashed across the page.

As I know that women have given as much to the cause of liberty, and have suffered as much if not more than the men, I am greatly upset by this news.

Proctor glanced in the direction that Adams had gone. Perhaps Proctor would keep that complaint to himself.

Do you remember the last visit from our dear friend Magdalena, the day after little Maggie was born? I have been thinking about how the distance between us is unbearable. I would like to be able to visit you the same way, just to see how you are doing. Do not be surprised if I appear unexpectedly.

The section was much crossed out and written over, but the meaning was clear. He flashed back to the stable in Spain, when he had been carried away. What if he hadn't been attacked at all? What if that had been Deborah, trying to reach him by means of spirit travel? And he had fought her. He had pushed her away.

Maggie is doing very well, although her appetite is insatiable. I am dependent on Abigail for everything. She sends you her best wishes. I already regret writing this letter, but since it is written, I will send it. But I beg you to burn it when you are done. I may not write again unless I hear from you. It is too much, this feeling that I am casting words to the wind like autumn leaves and hoping they are carried to you. But I shall watch the road for you every day until you return.

She had signed it simply with her name.

He had to rush back to Lydia to ask her opinion. It was possible he had frightened Deborah by pushing her away. Maybe he had even hurt her. He had to find a way to make things right again.

The coachman was patiently standing at the edge of the road with the carriage door held open.

"Back to—" Proctor started to say Versailles and then corrected himself.

"L'hôtel de Valentinois," offered the coachman. "Doctor Franklin's residence."

"Oui," Proctor said.

He read and reread Deborah's letter on the ride back. He settled his account with the coachman, thanking him for his service, and then one of the well-dressed servants escorted him to a furnished room in which the bed alone, a large elaborately carved frame with columns supporting a heavy canopy, was likely worth more than all the furniture he had ever owned.

Lydia stood at the ready in an open door. Proctor saw that it was a pair of furnished rooms—Lydia's chamber, smaller and plainer and without the great windows, adjoined his.

"This is the sort of existence Miss Cecily always wanted," Lydia said.

"With an empty purse, an uncertain friend, and an enemy wanting her dead?" Proctor asked.

"No," Lydia said, frowning at him. She made a circuit of the room, running her hand over the carved chair, the finely painted porcelain, the heavy plaster picture frames around singular works of art. "She could have had it too, if she had been willing to marry the right man. Or become the right man's mistress. But she had to go about it her own way. I'm still afraid of her."

Proctor saw how quickly Lydia had performed that binding spell on the old woman in Spain, and he knew that she had been practicing in case they met Cecily again. "I fear her too."

There was a knock at the door. Lydia opened the door before Proctor could reach it. The servant outside proved to be an American as soon as he opened his mouth.

"Doctor Franklin wishes to discover if Mister Brown is available to call upon his parlor," the servant said, looking firmly into the air past Lydia.

"Mister Brown?" asked Lydia, turning to Proctor. She stared meaningfully at his shirt, which had not been changed nor washed in several days.

"I can go right now," Proctor said. After weeks in a carriage, he was eager to move, to feel like he was doing something, even if it meant meeting Franklin in a dirty shirt.

The servant ushered them into Franklin's rooms. They were larger than Proctor's but appeared smaller because they were crowded with furniture. Tables were lined with cut glass, tools for measurement, small models in wood and metal, and what Proctor could only assume were other scientific apparatuses. Shelves were filled with books and other books stacked sideways in front of those books, old tomes with cracked leather bindings and new volumes that had yet to have their pages cut. A writing desk was placed near windows offering good light and a spectacular view of the gardens. It had numerous drawers, slots, and compartments, and was stacked with papers, some in neat piles and others in various stages of being sorted.

Franklin was seated at this desk. He rose when the servant announced Proctor and Lydia. He did not have the appearance of a man in his eighth decade. On the contrary, his cheeks had good color, he looked fit, and his hands were steady, even as he tilted his head to peer over the tops of his spectacles.

"Welcome to Paris," he said. "You'll not find a more

amiable city anywhere. I am to understand that you have letters?"

"Thank you, I'm pleased to meet you, and yes, I do, here they are." Proctor hoped that he had responded to everything.

Franklin smiled, accepted the letters, and then pushed the spectacles back on his nose as he started to read them carefully.

Proctor formed a quick impression of Franklin while he was reading. On the surface, he was dressed much like Proctor—a chestnut coat, a simple linen shirt, his natural hair. But on closer examination, he resembled the Frenchmen just as nearly. Although his jacket was of American fabric and cut, the craftsmanship was of a different quality: every seam was flawlessly sewn, it hung on Franklin's frame without a bunch or wrinkle, and neither cuff nor collar showed a sign of shine or fray. The shirt was of linen like Proctor's, but fashioned as carefully as the jacket from the highest-quality fabric Proctor had ever seen, unmarred by a single slub or knot. It was ironed smooth and still crisp, even this late in the day, and held an odor of soap and spices. And though Franklin wore his hair unpowdered, the long tresses were neatly and precisely combed, arranged down his back. Proctor ran his fingers through his hair, tucked in the threads at his cuffs, and smoothed the wrinkles in his shirt.

"You may leave us," Franklin told his servant. He moved a stack of papers off the extra chair and indicated to Proctor that he should sit. Handing the letters back to Proctor, he said, "I deduce, from everything these don't say, that you are one of Tallmadge's boys."

In other words, a spy. "I'm not here on orders from Colonel Tallmadge."

Franklin looked over the tops of his glasses and tapped the side of his nose. "And yet you know which

Tallmadge I mean and his rank in the army, and you speak of orders even though you are clearly, according to these letters, a private citizen." Proctor winced and opened his mouth to explain, but Franklin silenced him with a shake of his head. "May I offer you some advice?"

"I would be most grateful," Proctor said.

"You will do best outside the safe bounds of our own nation, and better within, if you assume that everything you do is spied upon." Franklin leaned back in his chair and rested one arm casually on his desk. "For example, I assume that the French allow me to stay here because it's easier to observe me. I assume that some of my friends are spies for the English and that someone on my own staff copies every word I write and sends it to our enemies."

"I don't understand," Proctor said.

"If I assume that everything I do will be scrutinized, then I don't have to attempt to conceal anything. Take, for example, the matter of visiting Americans. I invite every one of my countrymen in France, friend and stranger, well-born and apprentice alike, to come visit me here and bring me news of home. Because all of them come, and I give all of them an audience, there is nothing remarkable to report. It is impossible for either our allies or our enemies to keep track of all of you. A visitor from Colonel Tallmadge might thus be hidden in plain sight by not being hidden at all."

Proctor saw the sense of it at once. It was like Deborah's insistence on using Bible verses for spells and calling them prayers. That way they could be hidden right out in the open, like everyone else's prayers, and it became impossible to make accusations of witchcraft.

Franklin, perhaps seeing comprehension dawn in Proctor's face, leaned forward, warming up to his topic. "Similarly, I dine out with friends six nights a week and invite as many friends as I am able to dine with me on the seventh, and these friends come from all walks and classes of life. As a result, any guest whom I share a meal with becomes unremarkable, part of the ordinary routine, and it is impossible to distinguish any degree of importance between one guest and another. Do you begin to see?"

"With surprising clarity," Proctor replied.

"If you will allow me to make a suggestion then, it will behoove your labors here to develop habits that will dull the scrutiny of those who observe you. A young man such as yourself, without a fortune to spare, might choose to avail himself of the delightful public gardens that abound throughout this part of France. If you walk in them daily, no matter what the weather, and make a point of conversing with strangers whenever your paths cross, then those types of conversation become unremarkable."

"Does the Covenant mean anything to you?"

Franklin reacted as though he'd been asked for a scientific treatise. "A covenant is a contract or agreement. It can be constituted among a group of men, it can be reached by agreement between two men, or it can be used to describe the sacred relationship that exists between man and his Creator. But you're a bright young man, and from Massachusetts—surely you're familiar with the word in all these contexts, so . . ."

"I am," Proctor said, not sure how much more to add.

Franklin pushed his glasses back up and reached for Proctor's letters again. "I'm going to wear the skin off my nose if I continue this habit. I've asked Mister Sykes to cut another set of doubles lenses for me, so that I can make do with a single set of spectacles. But until they arrive . . ." He reread Proctor's letters, but what he was looking for, he did not say. He handed them back to Proctor again when he was done. "Are you a member of any lodge?"

The Masons. Somehow, Proctor was never surprised when it came back to the Masons. "I was introduced at St. Andrew's Lodge in Boston by Mister Paul Revere."

"Paul?"

"Yes."

"Ah," Franklin said, clapping his hands on his knees, as if this explained much to him. "But you were not initiated?"

"No," Proctor said. "It wasn't clear that I could travel regularly to the meetings, nor that I could afford the dues. I didn't want to start something that I couldn't finish." And then there was the fact that he carried a secret. It was a bad idea for a man with so many secrets to join a brotherhood that was supposed to be without.

"It would make things easier here. I belong to the Nine Sisters Lodge here in Paris and have a position such that you might be initiated again if you wish to pick up where you left off."

Proctor wasn't sure that would be the best use of his time. He had no desire to settle in for a long stay in Paris. He wanted a quick solution, and a ship home. "Your invitation is very gracious. May I reflect on it before I answer?"

"Indeed, I hope you will. Clearly you have reason to be circumspect. But we must consider ways to introduce you to the groups where you're most likely to meet those you are seeking." He tapped the desk thoughtfully and looked at Proctor from the corner of his eye. "It might be better to introduce you to the Egyptian Rites Lodge and the followers of Count Cagliostro. But in that case, it would be best if you were already at least a magus."

Franklin watched him closely, but Proctor didn't twitch. He knew already that *magus* was the word for one of the intermediate levels of Mason. When Proctor sat there perfectly still, offering no reaction at all, Franklin responded with a very small smile. "May I offer one additional piece of advice?"

"I am eager to hear whatever you have to say," Proctor replied.

"Be forthright and direct in any letters you may write," Franklin said.

That surprised Proctor. "But Mister Adams just advised me to say nothing. He said that any letters I write will be read and copied before they're sent on through the post."

"I suggest that you consider his reasons rather than his reasoning," Franklin said. "He is quite correct about one thing, and that is you must assume that anything and everything you write and send through the mail will be copied and read."

Proctor was confused for a moment, and then he thought about the idea of hiding something in plain sight. "So if I'm known to be looking for someone, that someone may come looking for me."

"If I were you, I would express a serious interest in the Egyptian Rites, as practiced by the Order of the Strict Observance," Franklin said. He stood and offered Proctor his hand. "It was a pleasure to meet you, Mister Brown. I will consider what else we may do to help you."

His grip was confident and strong, despite his age. Proctor held his hand for an extra second, probing to see if Franklin had any spark. He didn't feel one and finally released his hand. "You've already done more than I expected."

Chapter 12

Days later, Proctor sat at the desk in his room and sharpened the end of his quill. One shredded feather already lay in a pile by the inkwell. Every day the post came in, he went to check for another letter from Deborah. So far, she had kept to her promise not to write again until she heard from him.

He held the sharpened quill above the inkwell. He had put off writing the letter to Deborah for as long as he could.

First, he had dithered over the problem of delivery. He dared not send it by way of Tallmadge or any of his agents connected with the army, for fear of drawing attention to either the spies or Deborah. Best keep those two apart. He also did not feel he could send it care of Paul Revere, who actively served in the war. Ultimately he decided to send it by way of a friend on the Quaker Highway, the secret route that had moved accused witches from Massachusetts to places like The Farm where they could be trained to safely use and hide their talents.

He dipped the quill in the ink and tapped his thumb on the rim of the bottle. The extra ink coalesced in a drop and fell back inside.

Intending to write still did not give him something to write. Neither Adams's advice to reveal nothing nor Franklin's advice to be direct seemed helpful. Every day he left behind wads of crumpled paper from his failed attempts. He pressed the tip to the paper and began with the easiest part.

> My dear Deborah,
>   We had a difficult voyage and a long journey through Spain, but have been in Paris now for some time, where we are guests of Dr. Franklin at the Hotel Valentinois. I hope to finish the business I came for and return to you soon.

A drop of sweat beaded on his forehead and fell, smearing the ink in *finish* where it splashed. Why did this have to be so hard? He wiped his forehead on his sleeve and continued with the part he knew he had to write.

> I remember Magdalena's last visit very well, and while I would welcome the opportunity to see you sooner than expected, I would never wish to put you through the hardship she experienced. Please think twice before setting out. I feel confident that I will be home by the start of summer.

If Deborah was as drained by the visit as he had been, still assuming that it had been her attempting to draw him back, then she would just be recovering her full strength. If—no, *when*—the Covenant attacked again, they would both need their full strength. As much as he wanted to see her, he did not want to put either of them in any danger. Any additional danger.

> I miss you. I fear that Maggie will not know my voice when I return home.

This is where he usually broke down and wadded up the paper. He picked up his knife, intending to resharpen the point of his quill yet again. The knife slipped and he cut the quill in half. He pushed it over to the pile with the other and picked up a third.

> *Lydia has been strong and dependable as always. She sends her regards to you and Abigail, and wants me to remind Abigail to clean under her nails.*

Lydia was always teasing Abigail about forgetting to wash her hands, and even as he wrote it he could imagine Abigail just in from getting the eggs, with a straw in her hair and dirt on her fingers.

> *Please remember me to her as well.*
> *I have met a great many people here. A Scotsman named William Alexander visits Dr. Franklin every day. He is an outspoken supporter of our patriotic cause. Dr. Bancroft, who is Dr. Franklin's assistant, and from Connecticut and before that Westfield in Mass., took an interest in my business here but has not been able to help me. Dr. Franklin has offered to introduce me to the Masons' lodge in Paris, which he thinks will help make suitable connections, but they only meet once per month. He has also mentioned an Egyptian RitesLodge, founded by an Italian count and countess named Cagliostro, which admits both men and women. The lodge was founded in London, but Count Cagliostro recently returned to the Continent again.*

Everything about Count Cagliostro pointed to the Covenant. Alexander and Bancroft, among others, had filled in details for Proctor. The Egyptian Rites Lodge openly embraced magic symbols. Its goal was immortality for its members. Cagliostro himself claimed to see spirits and speak to the dead. The count and countess had moved to London just a few years before—when the Covenant was increasing its activity—to start the lodge. But Cagliostro and his wife had recently fled England and had been traveling around the Continent, speaking to royalty's dead. Rumor had it that they were on their way back to France, or headed for the tsar's palace in Russia.

Proctor stopped when he considered that. In America, people like him and Deborah still lived in the shadow of the Salem witch trials. Anything tainted by a hint of witchcraft was considered evil. But in Europe, it appeared there were different rules. Or maybe there were different rules for the nobility. Proctor wondered if ordinary men were tolerated as much as counts like Cagliostro.

If the letter was read, Proctor hoped it would help scare up Cagliostro in France. He wanted to go home again.

> I will write you when I make progress, which should be any day now.

And that was it. If he tried to write any more, he'd get overwhelmed.

He signed it carefully and deliberately, imagining the way that Deborah might run her fingertips over the signature just to feel connected to him. He had nearly rubbed her name off her letter, the one that he had not burned despite her request.

Even though he had scarcely said anything personal at all, even though he wanted the letter read, so that someone would spread the word to Cagliostro, he resented the thought of someone besides Deborah opening his letter. So when he sealed it, he placed a splinter in the wax with a pinch of gunpowder. It was a trick his mother had done, to keep him out of her medicines when he was small. Deborah would notice the spell at once and render it harmless. But if anyone besides her opened it, they would get a little surprise.

Lydia waited for him in the hall outside his door. She was wearing a much finer dress—still plain, in what Proctor was beginning to think of as "the American style," but of excellent fabric and elegantly cut and sewn. It was a gift for her arranged by a friend of Franklin.

She greeted him by staring at his jacket. "When are you going to let me take that and have it cleaned and repaired?"

"Soon," he said. "I keep thinking that we may have to leave at a moment's notice."

"And go where?"

"Wherever we will find the Covenant." He would climb Franklin's lightning rod and shout the word from the rooftop if it would help them move forward.

She glanced at the walls. "Perhaps we should continue this during your walk."

"I was planning to go into town to the post," he said. He held up his letter. It felt very thin in his hand, and he almost wadded it up, convinced that he should have written more. Or else nothing at all. But he resisted the urge.

It was a short walk into town and Proctor felt silly for having taken the carriage that first day. The clerk at the post office accepted his letter and informed him, after checking, that no other mail had arrived for him.

Lydia was holding the door for Proctor—he was still having a hard time forcing himself to allow that—when a bang sounded from the back room. Lydia jumped, and all the clerks from the counter ran to the back. They were jammed in the door and then shoved out of the way by a jowled man with thick glasses. He was sucking angrily on his thumb. The faint, sharp smell of gunpowder followed him.

Proctor waved to the clerks. "Merci!"

"What was that?" Lydia asked under her breath as they walked out to the street.

"I'm not sure what you mean," Proctor said. "But I imagine that the gunpowder was just for effect, to frighten whoever opened the letter. The splinter works as a sting regardless of the noise."

Even as he said it, he imagined a variation on the same spell, in which the splinter was coated with a poison. The wrongful letter opener would be—

"It reminds me of Miss Cecily's work," Lydia said. "It smacks of delight in the hurt of another."

Proctor stopped and turned on her. "They're reading my letter to Deborah."

"Which you knew they were going to do, and which you wanted them to do, if you included that part about the count and countess—"

"I did," he said. "That was the whole point, right?"

"That poor scrivener, the one who got hurt by your prank, he doesn't have anything against you or Deborah or maybe even America. It's just his job, working for the court. What's going to happen if they blame him for damaging your letter? He'll lose his job, his family won't be able to eat, and they'll just find somebody else to do it for them."

"All right, all right." He surrendered. "I shouldn't have done it."

"We are not judged on the basis of what we should have done, but on what we actually do," Lydia said.

"I admitted my mistake," he snapped.

He was used to talking to everyone on The Farm as equals, but it was another thing to do it out in public, in a foreign country, where his every move was watched. Lydia's questioning of him and his motives made him angry. But everything about this place and his situation was making him angry. He spun away from her and looked at the waters of the Seine, muddy and opaque. A pair of swans sat on an island in the middle. One raised its wings and flapped them menacingly as a boat passed on the river.

"Do you feel up for a longer walk today?" Lydia asked.

"Yes, I'm fine, I've fully recovered," he said. Every day, he had been taking longer and longer walks in the garden and then the neighborhoods of Passy to regain his strength. They had been short walks, limited in part by frequent rains. The weather today was chilly but dry, and the skies were clear. "Shall we go see the gardens at the Palace of Tuileries that everyone keeps telling us about?"

"If you wish," Lydia said, bowing her head.

He almost snapped at her for it, but then he saw that she was looking sideways out of her eyes at a small group that was watching them. They walked silently along the tree-lined bank. The branches were covered with a frill of green, emerging leaves.

"What I did with the letter may have been wrong," Proctor whispered after a long while. "But I'm not evil. I'm not trying to kill people." Even as he said it, he started to think about the men he had killed, from the assassins on The Farm to the battles at Concord and Bunker Hill. Not to mention souls he may have condemned, like Rotenhahn when he was freed from Bootzamon's shell. But all of those had been necessary. He didn't do harm unless he had to. Did he? "I want to hear the truth from you," he said. "Always."

"It is our first nature to give back what we are used to receiving," Lydia said. "After a lifetime of constant correction . . ." She let her sentence trail off unfinished. "I'm sorry. I'm afraid to end up in a situation again like I was with Miss Cecily. Have you made any progress?"

"None since last night. Franklin wants us to stay in Paris a little while longer."

"Why?"

"I don't know, but he asked me to stay when he found

out I hadn't written any letters home yet. I begged him to help us find a way into England. And you, any progress?"

She shook her head. "Even the servants have their pecking orders here, and I'm not fine enough to pass among them. To be honest, I'd be happy to go someplace where I belong."

"I know what you mean about not belonging here. I just want to find the Covenant, crush them, and go home again."

They stepped aside at the last minute to let pass a group of young French gentlemen in animated conversation. Carriages rattled by them on the street, and a man in servant's livery cantered by on a horse. When they had gone, Lydia led Proctor across the road, following a stream of other people.

"Have you any better idea how you'll stop them?" Lydia asked.

He kept hoping it would be obvious to him when the time came. "First I have to find them, don't I? If Franklin doesn't help me soon, I'll go to Alexander or Bancroft and ask them to introduce me to someone who can help us reach England."

"How soon?"

"It depends on how long it takes to see if my letter had any effect," he said. The prospect of more weeks of waiting daunted him. The weeks in Paris so far had done nothing—"What's that?"

"The entrance to the gardens," Lydia said.

Two huge statues of white marble stood on either side of the street, riders on horseback, with the horses reared above shields and weapons and symbols of war. The horses had wings, so realistically and convincingly carved, from the flare of the nostrils to the tense muscles to the hair of the pinfeathers, that Proctor was convinced at once that the creatures had existed, had been captured in life and turned into stone. One of the riders was a naked boy, holding a trumpet with a stem so long and delicate it looked like a wind might snap it. The light seemed to be absorbed by the stone, which radiated it back with a cool warmth that made it seem like living skin. Proctor had seen small busts of stone and images carved of wood, but he had never seen anything like these, not even on the churches in Spain. Nothing, not the clothes or language or food, had made him feel more like he was in a foreign country.

"Those wings—who would think to put wings on a horse?" he asked.

"There are more statues," Lydia said, pointing toward the garden. "It's what it's famous for."

Pools of water formed an axis from the horses to a distant palace, which was wider than any building Proctor had ever seen. It formed a wall at the far end of the gardens, with a domed block directly opposite the entrance. The wings on either side of the entrance rose like the wings on the horses. Between the horses and the palace, on either side of the pools, there were sixty or seventy acres of trees and flower beds, all formally arranged amid carefully designed paths.

"And all this is for the public?" Proctor asked. It was a reflection on the greatness of a nation, if true.

"From what the other servants tell me, it was built for one queen," she said.

"But I thought the king and queen lived at Versailles," Proctor said.

"Oh, they don't live here anymore, although guests might stay here. That's why it's open to the public now."

They walked into the garden, stopping at another group of statues around a pool. One was a giant man, reclining while a dozen tiny children crawled over his figure like a group of men climbing a hill. As they walked from statue to statue, Proctor felt increasing awe and greater disorientation. He did not recognize any of the images from the Bible stories he knew, and he couldn't imagine who or what had put these ideas into the heads of the artists. He abhorred the expense of wealth, the indulgence of the nobility in building this garden, and at the same time he was delighted by it, by the order, the vividness, the focus.

A place like this could be a powerful focus for channeling the untapped magic of a city and a nation's people.

He felt a prickle on the back of his neck at the thought. He turned to say something to Lydia and saw her standing, still as a statue. He touched her arm and she didn't move. Her eyes stared straight ahead, blind to him. He spun around. All throughout the garden, people had stopped mid-movement. Even the birds had fallen silent. There was only the trickle of water.

Blue, as pale as ice in the moonlight, flashed between the trees.

Proctor ran toward it. His skin was electrified, covered with goose bumps. He rounded a corner and stopped.

There, in the middle of the path, was the most striking woman he had ever seen. Her face was a symmetry of full lips, delicate nose, and large eyes, with skin as pale and perfect as marble, with her lips painted red, her cheeks rose, and one black dot below the corner of her left eye. Her hair was piled atop her head in the French manner, her dress was cut shockingly low, and the fabric was trimmed with lace that sparkled with tiny jewels. Her neck, fingers, wrists, and ears were adorned with jewelry, and every piece carried a charm or spell. He could feel the power of it.

"Bonjour, Monsieur Brown," she said. "I understand that you have been looking for me."

"And you are?"

"The Countess Cagliostro," she said. She glided over

to him, hooking her hand familiarly around his arm. "But you may call me Seraphina. Let us walk and enjoy the garden while we talk."

"Where is the count?" Proctor said, looking over his shoulder as they strolled past a row of motionless visitors. Even the air was still, as if they had somehow stepped momentarily out of time.

"At the palace in St. Petersburg by now, I hope," she said. "Although he can be easily distracted and is loath to bypass a single opportunity, so he may have stopped anywhere between here and there. But I thought you were seeking members of the Covenant?"

He tried to pull his arm away, but it felt pinned to her hand. She wasn't strong enough to hold him. He suspected one of the charms in her bracelet.

She smiled without showing any teeth and tapped him on the wrist. "You wanted to find me, and you have found me. Do not run away or you will not find me again."

"But I thought—"

"Have you ever seen a charlatan perform, one of those who call themselves magicians?"

He didn't answer. He felt out of his depth, and out of control, and he was more than a little frightened. He didn't even know if Lydia was all right.

"Stage conjurors use misdirection to fool their audiences," the countess continued after his uncomfortable silence. "They perform one action over here with their hands"—she flourished her free hand in the air, and he immediately looked at it—"while they perform the trick with their other hand over here."

In the hand looped around his arm she held Deborah's lock of hair, taken from his pocket. In place of the plain gray ribbon that had tied it before, there was now a ribbon of black silk, embroidered with a vine that snaked around its edge. It curved in shapes that seemed to form letters, though Proctor did not recognize the words.

"Interesting," she said. "If you pull it out by the roots, it will have much more power as a focus. But this woman has talents . . ."

He snatched it back from her. It was still Deborah's hair, but it felt tainted to him now, as if there were a layer of oil on the lock. He slipped it into the opposite pocket.

"But my point is that those of us with talent are in constant danger," she said. "People fear us because they are jealous of our power and unable to oppose our will. That is why it can also be useful for those of us with a true talent to practice misdirection. While everyone watches my dear husband the count and follows his every action, I am free to pursue my own purpose."

"And those are the purposes of the Covenant? You are the leader?" If she was the leader, the one who had orchestrated all the evil they'd done so far, could he do what was necessary? Would he kill her?

"Oh, heavens, no. Though I was one of the twelve and came to London at his call in 'seventy-six to add my power to his. But I think that he's gone mad with his focus on your pitiful country." She indicated the gardens and the palace with a sweep of her arm. "There is no culture there, no power there. Why build a single empire around the world in that direction, when, if he but turns east instead, a civilized land lies before him? I have severed my ties with the Covenant."

She spoke confidently, but Proctor detected a slight tremble of fear in her voice. If she had cut her ties with the Covenant, then she was looking for new allies.

An old man in a dusty wig sat on the edge of a fountain, his outstretched hand offering bread crumbs to pigeons that were frozen in their eagerness to reach the meal. The countess gestured with her hand. The pigeons scattered, squawking, the noise harsh in the unnatural silence. The old man looked up startled, as if woken from a dream, and, after one glance at the countess, averted his eyes and hurried away through the other people still frozen like statues. The countess spread out her dress and took a seat.

"If nothing else, it takes magic to remain comfortable in these dresses," she said. "Please, sit."

"I think I'll stand," he said, rubbing the cold spot on his forearm where she had been touching him. "If you are no longer loyal to the Covenant, then you can tell me who they are."

"I'm not going to give you names," she said. "If you can't discover them on your own, you're not worthy of the task."

"What will you tell me?"

She considered the question for a moment. "The Covenant was a pact formed over two hundred years ago by a group of necromancers who wanted to achieve immortality in this world. They believed we are the children of the Nephilim, the offspring of men and angels, and so they sought ways to speak to the angels to learn their secrets. There was one leader and twelve disciples, and each disciple was to recruit another twelve disciples, and so on, all of them channeling their power to the leader."

"I don't understand the connections to the Masons."

"We don't have enough power. We can extend life, but not cheat it entirely. We need more. The symbols of kings and nations are one way to focus the untapped magic of the people," she said. "Religion is another, which is why the church has expended so much energy pursuing and defeating those who practice outside the bounds of its guiding hand. Both try to extend their reach around the world, do they not? And both come up against other armies and other priests. But free associations, like the order of the Masons, are a new route to power, one that has no natural opposition, and can pass the borders of any nation and welcome those of any religion."

"For men eager to cheat death, they have been profligate in dealing it out."

"Don't pretend to be better," she said. "Your hands have also laved in blood, that of men and women both. We are the scions of angels, the divine children of a higher plane, set here among the mortals. What are their lives to such as us?"

The barb about the blood on his hands hit home. Was he already becoming more like the witches of the Covenant? Was Deborah? He resisted that thought. "We are all children of one God, divine in our reflection of His divinity."

"Not all children are created equal," she answered, as if this were self-evident. "Only one child may inherit the title and the estates. Why should those of us with gifts not be the proper inheritors of the earth?"

"And so the Covenant proposes to bring the earth under its empire," he said. "But I thought you had gone your separate way?"

"I do not wish to consort with demons to gain power," she answered with a forced smile. "Again, I think you've seen them. I think you know the danger they present. You've spent some time around witches, I know. Tell me, have you known more women or men?"

On The Farm, the numbers had never even been close. "Women."

"And who have the most powerful of those witches been?"

He hesitated, remembering the menace he felt when the prince-bishop stood over him sawing off his finger. "Women."

"The women are often stronger than the men, and yet the men lead. How curious." She closed her eyes and inhaled deeply. "But I sense that you are thinking of one woman in particular. Her name begins with a D . . . Deborah?"

Proctor took a step back, tensed, ready to strike.

The countess laughed at his reaction. "You mention her name in your letter."

"How have you seen that already?"

She waved his question aside and rose, smoothing her dress. "Come, I have one more thing to show you."

He did not follow. "If you are no longer with the Covenant, will you tell me how to find them, so I can stop them?"

"Come with me, and I'll tell you anything you wish to know."

They walked through the garden, where living statues mingled with the stone. They sidestepped a nurse holding two small children by the hands, bypassed a group of Englishmen made conspicuous by their non-Parisian clothes, and circled a noblewoman chasing after a very small dog, all of them frozen. The countess spoke continuously.

"The Egyptians were great worshippers of the dead, and their rites are a powerful focus for immortality. Have you ever considered a trip to Egypt? The pyramids are the greatest buildings ever made by man." She nodded toward the façade of the Tuileries in the distance, looking unreal against the backdrop of the clear and frozen sky. "They dwarf these palaces in conception and execution, rising above the landscape, providing the same inevitable gaze upward from every direction."

"How does this help me defeat the Covenant?"

She stopped at the foot of a statue. "You can't defeat the Covenant. You don't have the power, the experience, or the numbers. That is the point I wish to make. But if you are willing to join with me, you might survive. I am drawing together a new power through the lodges, one where men and women will both contribute. You may invite some of your friends if you will join me."

"No—"

"Do you recognize this statue?"

He looked up at a beautiful young woman with a quiver on her back. She held a small stag by the horns and was reaching for an arrow. "I don't."

"Her name begins with a D, just like your Deborah. She stayed away from men her whole life, and then one fell in love with her."

"What happened?" He had a feeling he wasn't going to like the answer.

"She hunted him down and killed him. Women can be so cruel, can't they?"

Thunder rocked the clear sky, startling them both. It sounded again, and this time lightning stitched a seam from the ground to the heavens. The countess spun around. A figure in a fine chestnut coat was walking toward them through the frozen people. He came closer, and Proctor recognized the long gray hair and spectacles.

"Doctor Franklin," the countess said.

"How gratifying to see you again, Seraphina," he said. They kissed each other and embraced. Franklin's hand lingered on the curves of her body. When they pulled apart, Franklin sighed happily. "You are as lovely as ever."

Despite his casual tone, the countess was as tense as a cat. "Why are you here?"

"Although news chases your husband the count like a pack of wolves, I had heard a rumor that you were here in Paris. I need to know what you are up to, and whether you are working for America or against us."

"I am pursuing my own interests," she said.

He nodded judiciously and gave some thought to what she said. "Those interests do not include this boy."

"I will be going east to join the count very soon," she said. "I do not want to be here when the blood starts."

"If you would help us, perhaps it need not flow."

"It will flow. Mark my words, these gardens will drown in it." She turned to Proctor and leaned forward for a kiss, but he ignored her. She pulled back with an expression of mock woundedness. "Poor Monsieur Brown. You will regret that you did not take this opportunity."

"You'll regret not helping me when you had the chance," he said. "It's not too late to change your mind. She should change her mind, shouldn't she, Doctor Franklin?"

He looked over his shoulder for confirmation, but Franklin was gone. He spun back to the countess but she had disappeared also.

And then, in a blink, he was right back where he'd started, standing next to Lydia. He was dizzy and staggered off-balance, almost falling to his knees. The smell of the mulch, the chatter of the birds, the spray of water in the air falling chill across his face, all rushed back on him at once. He heard children talking in French, Englishmen arguing, and a small dog barking.

"Proctor, are you all right?" Lydia said.

"I think so," he answered, even though his legs were weak, his heart pounded, and his breath came short. He thrust his hand into the pocket where he normally carried Deborah's lock of hair, but it was missing. He reached into the other pocket and found it. He rubbed his thumb across it and felt the black silk ribbon, embroidered with words shaped like vines.

"Ah, Mister Brown," said a new but familiar voice.

Proctor looked up. There, through the gardens, came Benjamin Franklin again. The chestnut-brown coat, long gray hair, and spectacles stood out among the crowd. He leaned on a cane as he walked.

"Doctor Franklin," Proctor said. "I was hoping we could *count* on one new ally today. What do you think our chances are?"

"Anything could happen," Franklin said. "How could I have ever predicted you showing up so usefully on my doorstep?" A pair of well-dressed ladies walked by, followed by servants. They looked over their shoulders at Franklin as they passed. "The gardens are wonderful. A young man should enjoy the beautiful women of Paris. Do you know how to kiss them?"

"I'm sorry?" Proctor said, confused.

"It is not the mode in Paris to kiss either the lips or cheeks, for the first is considered rude and the second may ruin the art with which the ladies adorn their faces. So you must kiss them on the neck, and this provides the opportunity to embrace them, which, I have discovered, they heartily embrace in turn." He sighed contentedly, just as he had after embracing the countess. "It is like being a man who loves mutton and finding oneself in a land of sheep. Perhaps it would be best to help you to my chaise? It is waiting for me near those marvelous statues of Pegasus."

Proctor was relieved that a ride was available. "Yes, that would be good," he said. "I hope that you are able to help us with our goal."

Franklin smiled. "There are some men come over from England, one in particular, to whom I wish to introduce you. If you wish to go to England, he is the man."

"And if we seek a Covenant?" Proctor asked.

"Oh, he is most definitely the man for that as well."

Chapter 13

During the short ride back to the hotel, while Franklin chatted amiably about this and that aspect of Parisian life, Proctor sat silently and tried to decide what had happened. Had the countess visited him, or had he just imagined it? Did Franklin really arrive and confront her, or was that just another part of his dream? Franklin's comment about kissing could have been innocent—or not-so-innocent—advice. Or it could have been a winking acknowledgment that he was there with Proctor when the countess offered him the chance to kiss her.

He slid his hand into his pocket and touched the lock of Deborah's hair. The ribbon was different. That much was real. She seemed so far away. It was not just the ocean that separated them.

When the carriage arrived in Passy, Franklin invited them up to his room. Proctor looked at the walls again, this time noticing how many of the symbols and items had magical significance. A square and compass hung on the wall, and though they were the tools of a builder, they were also the marks of the Mason, and a focus for their power. There was a sketch of an eye tacked to a corner where it looked over the entire room. A sun, whose rays formed a hexagram, was suspended over the door.

Proctor looked at Franklin again, but he gave off no spark or sense of talent. If it was there, it was perfectly concealed.

Franklin sent his servants out for additional chairs,

then turned immediately back to Proctor. "I'm not sure where the other gentlemen are," Franklin said. "Perhaps they took a walk down to the gardens. I hope they are not taken by the same spell as you."

Proctor twitched. "Spell?"

"The dizzy spell, the one that left you feeling weak," Franklin answered, looking at Proctor over the tops of his glasses. "I've neglected your comfort. Do you require refreshment?"

"I could use something to drink," Proctor answered.

Franklin popped his head out the door and called to one of the servants in French. Returning to the room, he smiled at Proctor and Lydia. "It's not the day for ices, but they make marvelous lemon ices in the kitchen here, and I asked them to bring some of those for us as well."

"What do you know about magic, Doctor Franklin?"

There. He asked it directly. If he was going to make a good decision about where to go next, he needed to know exactly where he stood.

"Magic is the subversion of natural laws by a power higher than nature," Franklin said. "That makes it coterminous with the scope of religion."

Proctor glanced at Lydia. She had said something very similar to him once, when he first went to The Farm. "So *magic* is just another word for 'miracle,'" he said.

"That's a perceptive way to put it," Franklin said. He sat down, indicating to them that they should sit on the chairs available. "The longer I live, the more proof I see that God governs the affairs of men. If a sparrow cannot fall without His notice, can an empire rise without His aid? I think not. We are assured in sacred writings that unless the Lord builds the house, they labor in vain that build it. I think all those who work without His concurring aid have no better chance to succeed than those who built the tower of Babel."

Was he referring to the political house of America? Or

to the plans of the Covenant? His meaning could apply to either. "So you do believe that magic is possible?"

Franklin smiled. "It is like a bicameral legislature, is it not?"

Proctor shook his head, not understanding. In Massachusetts, he was more familiar with the town meeting.

"A bicameral legislature provides for checks and balances, the voice of the people, looking to immediate needs and problems, and the voice of experience, taking a longer view and holding to a course with higher aspirations. The natural and the spiritual work in the same way." Franklin, perhaps sensing that Proctor didn't follow, leaned back in his chair and lost some of his tone of eagerness. "I have dedicated my own life to understanding the laws of nature. The supernatural is, in its own way, lawless. Its rules are mutable and subject to change. But the natural world admits no such caprice. It is a better discipline to follow, and will keep a man lawful. Scripture assures me that on the last day, we shall not be judged for what we thought or believed, but for our deeds. If I prevent fires or build a better stove, if I provide for better education or just government, that helps all men, and I expect to be judged accordingly. I trust in the higher power to take the longer view and hold me to that course with higher aspirations."

Proctor realized that Franklin could be extraordinarily slippery. Unlike Adams, who flew at you like a cannonball and attempted to batter down your resistance. "I think I understand now," Proctor said.

"Do you play chess, Mister Brown?"

"The game? I have never had much time for idle amusements."

"Chess is more than an idle amusement. Several very valuable qualities of mind may be acquired and improved by their application to the game, and subsequently become habits that prove useful in all aspects of life."

Lydia fidgeted uncomfortably, scuffing her feet on the floor. She looked to the door, but neither the servants nor the other guests had appeared.

"What kind of qualities?" Proctor asked.

"Foresight," Franklin said, holding out one finger. "Chess teaches us to look ahead and anticipate all possible decisions of one's opponent." He unfolded a second finger. "Circumspection. Chess prepares us to consider all the possible consequences of our own decisions." He unfolded a third finger. "Caution. Chess develops the habit of proceeding carefully until we are certain of the outcome."

Proctor shrugged indifferently. "I think I've learned the same things from farming. Although my opponents were weather, sickness, and bad luck."

Franklin shook with laughter. "I would contend that the farmer must proceed without certainty of outcome, but point well taken," he said when the laughter subsided. "But consider this. We also learn from chess not to despair in the present state of our bad circumstances, but to keep our eyes open for the favorable chance and to persevere in the secrets of our resources."

Proctor wasn't sure what the last phrase meant—*the secrets of our resources*—but before he could ask there was a tap at the door. Franklin rose at once and went to answer it. Proctor noticed that he limped, favoring one leg over the other. He had not limped in the park at Tuileries when he first appeared and interrupted the countess.

Franklin opened the door. Servants entered with two more chairs, a tray of refreshments, and a pair of guests. The chairs were arranged and cups of shaved ice were passed around with spoons. Proctor slipped a bite into his mouth and was startled by the sharp lemon flavor. He was caught with his mouth full as Franklin presented introductions.

"Israel Potter, Thomas Digges, this is Proctor Brown," Franklin said. The servants left and Franklin bolted the door shut behind them.

The man introduced as Potter seemed a bit simple. He had a blunt, honest face, bespeaking goodwill and bad luck. So it seemed out of place that he wore boots with considerable heels, on which he carried himself awkwardly, like a man on a ladder unused to heights. As he stepped across the polished inlaid floor to shake Proctor's hand, he slipped. His companion's quick hands caught him and held him upright. Potter smiled and said, "Pleased to meet you, Mister Brown."

"And you," Proctor replied. The second man had a long face with a high forehead framed by long wavy hair, and, Proctor noticed, eyes like a doe's. Even the small beard he wore failed to soften the overall feminine features of his face. The talent was not strong in him, but he had it and was aware of it. He let the spark fill him the way a small candle in a bottle could scatter light throughout a room. Proctor held out his hands. "Mister Digges."

"It's best if I'm called Church, W. S. Church," Digges said peevishly. He looked to Franklin as he explained. "It's not just that I must hide what I do from the British, who, if they catch me, would send me to the hangman in a moment. It's that my name could draw unfortunate attention from other quarters as well."

"Of course," Franklin said. "I always recognize your handwriting in an instant, but I never bother to look at the signature anymore because the name changes so often. Mister Brown, allow me to introduce Mister Church."

Because Proctor did not believe that Franklin made casual errors, not after his speech on chess, he was sure that Franklin wanted him to know Digges's true name, and also that he was hiding something.

This time, Digges acknowledged Franklin and Proctor,

but did not accept Proctor's proffered hand. Instead, he took his glass of shaved ice and went to sit in the chair farthest from the others. He arrogantly stretched out his thin legs.

"I thought we agreed to send away the servants," he said, nodding at Lydia. He swirled his spoon around the edge of glass and brought a large scoop of ice to his mouth.

Lydia stood back in the shadows, motionless, her hands folded at her waist. Her face remained a blank slate, expressionless.

"She's not his servant," Franklin said. "Though she poses as one. *Companion* is also the wrong word, or creates the wrong impression. In any case, gentlemen, I give you Lydia Freeman. She and Mister Brown are, as we all are, working for the cause of freedom."

Proctor tensed. He had never said anything to Franklin; nor, judging from Lydia's slight widening of the eyes, had she.

But neither of their guests seemed to notice the reaction.

"Nice to meet you, ma'am," Potter said. He had plopped down in the chair closest to hand without any ice at all and pulled off a boot. It dangled awkwardly from his hand as he looked up, uncertain whether he should jump up to complete the introduction.

Digges—or Church, as he preferred—crossed his legs at the ankles, but made no other change to his posture or expression. "I see," he said.

Franklin motioned Proctor and Lydia to take their seats, which they did. "Mister Church is originally of Maryland," Franklin said.

Digges snapped upright. "And late of London, and in between, of all the world between. Must we go into my personal history?"

Franklin leaned forward in his chair and clapped his

hands on his knees, a gesture Proctor had seen him use several times when he wished to bring men to agreement. "Those whose lives depend on one another's trust have cause to know the foundation on which that trust is laid."

Digges set down down his empty glass—he was not one to take his time with things or go at them halfheartedly. He looked at Proctor and Lydia from the corner of his eyes.

He knew. He could sense the talent in them as surely as Proctor sensed the talent in him, and it made him anxious.

And Franklin knew.

Proctor had no time to consider the implications as Franklin then launched into further introductions. He explained how Proctor was from Massachusetts and had served with the army from Lexington to Trenton, and how he had served at length with Washington, who trusted him completely.

At Washington's name, Digges relaxed. "We grew up across the Potomac from each other," he said.

"Was you at Bunker Hill?" Israel Potter asked. He sat with the boot on his lap, one foot on the floor elevated by a heel and the other sliding back and forth in a worn stocking.

"I was," Proctor answered.

"I knew it!" Israel said, slapping his thigh. "I was there too. You stayed to the end, right by Doctor Warren, while the Redcoats came over the wall. We was out past the hay bales, with the shot flying thick around us, and saw you come running away. You and that black fellow."

"Peter Salem," Proctor said.

"I don't know his name, but that was something, I can tell you," Israel said.

"Fine, we know each other now," Digges said. "Shall we get down to business?"

Israel held up his boot, grunting as he twisted open the heel to reveal a hidden compartment. He offered the boot to Franklin. "I figured it was time for me to go back to my friends in England," he said.

"Indeed it is," Franklin replied. He dabbed the corner of his mouth and set down his empty glass. While Franklin rose and went to his desk, Proctor looked at his own glass. The ice had melted to water. He lifted it to his mouth for a sip but the taste proved too bitter and he set it down unfinished. He glanced over at Lydia. Her hands were empty. No one had thought to serve her.

Drawers scraped open and shut as Franklin searched through several compartments for the item he wanted. Israel noticed his own glass of ice and slurped it down, smacking his lips. Eventually Franklin found what he was looking for, a packet of paper folded very tight. He wedged the packet in the heel and sealed it shut again. When he was done, he handed the boot back to Israel and took his seat.

Digges held out his empty hand. "I would not have been able to help Mister Potter, nor any of a hundred other American sailors, slip through the bars of prison without the liberal application of grease in the form of . . . cold, hard currency."

He stumbled over the end of his sentence as the figure of speech that he had so carefully constructed unraveled like a poorly knit sweater.

"Of course," Franklin said, rising more slowly on this occasion. Once again, he poked through the many drawers and compartments of his elaborate desk, moving aside papers, bottles, and pieces of scientific equipment until he found a small purse. He opened it, counted carefully, and then removed a few coin, which he tossed into a randomly opened drawer. "This should be sufficient for your purposes."

"Not if I am to be a nursemaid to all three," Digges

said, with a contemptuous nod at the other people in the room. He watched them sideways to see what kind of response he received. Proctor disliked the man.

"It is sufficient," Franklin said.

Digges frowned, counted the coin, and settled back in his chair. "It's not as if we can hire the Dover packet to deliver us across the channel."

"No, but the money you've expended in helping so many men escape from Forton Prison ought to serve as a down payment on their favors in return."

"Perhaps," Digges allowed.

"I will thank you to convey Israel to London as you did before," Franklin said. "These two are pursuing a different goal, but may be dropped off there as well. You should use everything you have remaining to aid more American sailors. Any other munitions or technology you can steal will also be welcome."

"There is no way I can come away with a loom," Digges said.

"If you can't steal the loom, then steal the weavers. We need the English textile technology even more than we need the weapons." He tapped the side of his head. "Remember, all true wealth is carried in the purse that rests between our ears."

"I do not know if I can persuade the Dutch to carry it for us again."

"I have utmost confidence in your powers of persuasion," Franklin replied impatiently. He rose. "Now, if you will all excuse me, it is nearly time for dinner, and I am never late for a meal."

Potter rose and shook his hand eagerly, thanking him profusely.

Franklin interrupted him. "Gratitude may never be too profuse when offered to God, but to man it should be limited."

Digges remained cold and distant, exchanging no words

of parting. He and Franklin shared a working agreement, but there was no love between them. Or perhaps no trust. He was clearly uncomfortable conducting his business in front of so many witnesses. Just as clearly, Franklin wanted Proctor to witness, if only to force him to form his own impression of Digges.

Franklin put his hand on Proctor's shoulder as he escorted him to the door. "Do not go looking for trouble, but beware when it comes looking for you."

"Foresight, circumspection, and caution," Proctor replied.

Franklin smiled. He embraced Lydia, kissing her neck in the manner of the French. She went rigid in reply and did not return the gesture, but Franklin merely stepped away and sighed. "Madame, I know that the French servants have been threatening you, telling you that the king will confiscate you as an illegal slave. You will be out of the country before that happens, but still it will be best if you do not return, and so I do not think that we shall meet again. Therefore I wish you safe travels and the blessing of your name."

A whole range of emotions had flashed across her face while Franklin spoke, but she only responded to the last thing he said. "My name?"

"Freeman," he replied with a smile. "That is your name, is it not?"

She held her mouth firmly shut. Proctor tried to meet her eye, to ask her why she had not said anything about the threats made by the French servants, but she would not look at him.

They stepped outside into the hall with Potter and Digges. The door snapped closed behind them. Digges spun on them. He held his talent at the ready, like a match suspended over a fuse.

"How soon can you be ready to depart?" he asked.

Proctor still felt wobbly from the encounter in the

garden. Though it had only been that morning, a few scant hours before, it seemed almost a lifetime ago. He thought about Franklin's description of chess, and he wondered whether Franklin was teaching him how to play the game or subtly informing him that he was just another pawn on a very large board.

He looked Digges in the eye. "How soon can you be ready to escort us, Mister Church?"

They departed from a small dock outside Calais, in a small boat, on a dark night. The crew was British, though Israel Potter recognized one as an American, a fellow sailor who had been captured, like him, by the British when their ship sailed out of Boston.

"William," he exclaimed innocently. "How come you to be here?"

The other sailors, whom Proctor took for smugglers, scowled. William glanced at Digges, who refused to recognize him. "I escaped the hulk at Spithead, same as you," he said.

"I presumed that much," Potter replied. "No, I mean here on this boat now."

William jerked a thumb at the other smugglers. "My mother's brother's sons."

One of the men cuffed him, and he turned back to his work. Proctor considered how many families were divided by the war. English and American, they were still one people in many ways, united by a common past and present relatives despite the war and wide ocean.

The small crew worked quietly and efficiently, scarcely whispering to one another as they raised a dark sail and slipped out of the small cove. Lanterns hung from patrolling warships bobbed in the distant night, but the ship moved quickly over the waves, and even those signs of civilized life soon faded away. The dark surrounded them, the moonless and star-spangled sky above, and the black water with its light-tipped waves below.

Digges stared at the sky. "Tell me who you are and what you mean to do, or I'll tip you both overboard and let you swim to shore."

Proctor started at the open threat. When he looked over and saw the crewmen's heads sunk to their chests in apparent sleep—Potter was sleeping too—he tensed. The waves lapped the sides of the boat in an irregular rhythm.

Digges rose and moved over to the rudder, taking it in hand. "They'll be fine that way for a while," he went on. "My talents are small compared with some I've seen. Compared with the two of you, I suspect. I can persuade people, but only to do things they might already have done; I can lull men to sleep, but only if they're already tired. What can the two of you do?"

Lydia held out her hand and closed her fist. A wind rushed at them, snapping the sail taut and tipping the boat to one side. She did not like to be threatened.

"This and that," Proctor said. "A small talent must lead to a large fear, because the danger is the same if we are discovered, no matter our talent."

"You have no idea what I'm afraid of," Digges sneered.

Proctor regretted his remark, and decided it would be best to be honest and direct. "We are seeking a group called the Covenant."

"To join them?" Digges asked tersely.

"To destroy them, if we can. They mean an end to American freedom, and they have killed our friends and our families in pursuit of their goal." He looked down at his own scarred right hand. He left off, *They have tried to possess us with demons and have my own soul on a leash.*

After a moment's pause, Digges said, "They're English?"

"We don't know that they're English," Proctor answered, still distracted. "In fact, the members we've encountered have been English, American, German, and Italian. We're told that there are thirteen, although maybe there are now only twelve. Although each member of the twelve supposedly recruits twelve more, all of them channeling their power toward a single sorcerer in an attempt to achieve immortality."

"It wasn't a question. I'm telling you, they're English." Digges stared off into the dark, drawing his fingers across the point of his beard. "The name has changed, but they are the modern version of the *pactum in saecula saeculorum.*"

"The what?"

"*Pactum in saecula saeculorum,*" Digges said. "The Pact, Forever and Ever. It was mentioned in the papers of my great-great-great-great-grandfather and namesake, who was an astronomer and mathematician. And more. Two hundred years ago, he was invited to join."

"And did he?"

"He did not. What profits it a man to gain the world and lose his soul?" By the catch in his throat, the phrase clearly had a personal meaning for him too. He pointed at the stars. "He was the best student of the best astronomer in Queen Elizabeth's England, but he was an even greater mathematician. He proved, mathematically, that the stars lie beyond the orbit of the moon. Far beyond the orbit of the moon. He proved that the stars themselves are suns, and that there are an infinite number of them."

Lydia sat shoulder-to-shoulder with Proctor in the small boat. She pulled a blanket around her against the cold. Proctor felt a chill go through him that no blanket would fight off.

Digges noticed their reaction. "That's not all. He contended that all those infinite suns have worlds whirling about them much like our own. It sounds mad, doesn't it?"

"If I believed that, it would make me feel very small and insignificant," Proctor said.

"Ha," Digges laughed. "If you want to feel small and insignificant, you should have such a man in your family tree, along with poets and professors, astronomers and royal governors." He leaned back and looked at the stars again. "Actually, I take great comfort in that thought. I fear great and powerful men much less when I think that, compared with the infinity of space, we are all small and insignificant."

Lydia shook her head sharply in disagreement. "The human spirit is no small thing," she said. "Every spirit burns as bright as one of them stars."

"Can you believe that there are an infinite number of them?" Digges asked.

"God is infinite and eternal. If He created the stars, He could make an infinite number of them," she replied. "In God all things are possible."

"Yes," Digges answered. "That is what I tell myself when I am confronted by people with our talent. This too comes from God, even among those who use it for evil."

"So far our efforts to find the Covenant have been like searching for a needle in the hay field," Proctor said.

"Then perhaps you need a larger magnet."

The sail had slackened, and the boat drifted. It hit a larger wave side-on and bucked like a wagon jumping a rut. Cold spray came over the side, hitting their skin like ice. The three of them grabbed the sides of the craft to hold on, and the crew, along with Potter, jerked awake. The oldest smuggler cuffed the other men and cursed them for napping. He looked at the rudder in Digges's hands and snatched it away. Within moments the ship had been righted, the sail filled, and they were zipping toward England once again.

Digges crowded into a spot next to Proctor and Lydia. He leaned back and stared at the stars. "I do know someone who fights the same fight as you, who may be able to help you find that needle."

"Is he in London?"

"He has been traveling across the country working to this end. But I know a place we can stay just outside London, where we will pass unnoticed until he returns."

"I would rather be in London, if that's where we'll find . . ." He glanced at the crew. "The other men we're looking for."

"It will be safer for you outside the city," Digges said. *You*, not *us*.

Israel Potter grinned at them from his place near the bow. His high-heeled boots looked out of place among the other simple shoes in the wet bottom of the boat. Proctor did not think him simple, but he was clearly everyone's earnest pawn. Digges smiled back at Potter, then pulled his hat down over his face and leaned back as if to sleep.

Proctor met Lydia's eyes and saw reflected in them the same doubts that he felt. He gave a slight jut of his head toward Digges and quirked an eyebrow. Lydia answered with a simple shrug, as if to say, *What else can we do?*

What else could they do?

Digges was hiding something from them, but he struck Proctor as a man who, despite his youth, had been hiding so many things for so long that it was second nature to him. He couldn't help but compare him with the earnest but inept spy they'd met in New York, that poor blond boy who regretted that he but had one life to give for his country just before they hanged him. Digges was determined to hold on to his life and do something with it.

His story about the stars was fantastic and unreal, but Proctor looked up at the moonless, cloudless sky and found that he believed it. And he found that he believed the rest of it too. Digges did oppose the Covenant, and he would introduce them to someone with the same purpose.

Despite that belief, Proctor sat there awake until the dark shape of England rose in the west. The crash of breakers pounding on the shores matched the pounding in his head. He had been trying not to think about Deborah, but the ocean of his pulse slowly wore away the wet sand of his resistance until she stood out stark and vivid in his thoughts like bright white cliffs.

The sun rose suddenly, as it did over the ocean, on a sea full of ships, hundreds of them, large and small, more than Proctor had seen off the shores of New York when the British landed thirty thousand troops on Long Island. British warships towered over them as they joined the fishing boats sliding in toward shore.

Chapter 14

Proctor was walking through the farmhouse looking for Deborah and Maggie. From room to room to room he went, every room empty but for ruins. The furniture was broken, the dishes were shattered, sheets and clothing torn to shreds and scattered. The new wing opened into the upstairs opened into the barn opened into the kitchen, every room the same. He screamed their names—*Deborah, Maggie, Deborah*—until the door he had nailed shut burst open and he entered the old wing of the house.

He walked without moving his feet, gliding over the floor like a child sliding on the ice, until he stood in front of the old hearth. The one that Cecily had used for her black altar, the one the demon had come through seeking his child, the one he had bricked in. The place where he had last seen Magdalena standing guard.

Magdalena had vanished. The splinters of her cane lay scattered on the floor.

And in the hearth, the bricks were broken. The hearth stood open like a sooty mouth ringed with black and rotting teeth. The stench of smoke was everywhere, choking Proctor's breath, and ash fell out of the air like filthy snow. Heat pressed in at him from all sides, as if he were surrounded by fire.

His head pounded, like it had been pounding for days. It pounded like the drums of approaching legions. He had to find Deborah and Maggie and escape.

Deborah?

Why did his voice sound so far away? Where was she? Why didn't she answer him?

Deborah!

"I'm here," replied her voice, quiet and present, with a hint of laughter, directly behind him. He spun around, filled with relief and joy, ready to embrace her and carry her away.

A demon stood there in her place, with heavy horns above its thick brow and a bloody smear across its scissored smile. A red coat draped over its broad shoulders, with a sword tucked in its waistband and a pistol in its taloned hand.

"Balfri is here," the demon mocked in Deborah's voice. "Send forth the herald and summon the footman to do my will."

It opened its sooty-toothed mouth and laughed.

Proctor jerked awake.

Beware of D.

D, for Deborah. D, for demon. D, for despair. Which was it?

His head pounded, just as it had been pounding for days, only it had grown worse. To the throbbing pain had been added a sharp one, as if someone held a nail against his temple and was tapping it into place before driving it home.

Tap-tap-tap.

The sound was so real and present, it startled him a second time, and his heart, already racing from the nightmare, thumped faster. He looked over and saw an ash-black raven on the windowsill, tapping at the glass. He sat up on the edge of the bed.

The raven cocked its head to one side knowingly and stared at Proctor with an eye that glittered like a poisoned gem. It leaned over and tapped at the pane again harder, *tap-tap-tap,* and the window nudged open. In triumph, the raven perched on its toes and bobbed along the ledge.

"Hallo, Hallo, Hallo," the raven said, in its mockery of a human voice. "You're a devil, You're a saucy devil—what's the matter here?—You're a devil."

"Grip, be a good boy, Grip," called a voice from outside.

The raven beat its wings against its sides, and then against the window. It hopped off the window ledge, but not before uttering a final, "You're a devil!"

Proctor staggered to the window and leaned on the frame. In the road outside the inn stood a balding simpleton. He laughed and clapped his hands like a delighted child, and the raven flapped its wings, hopping along the ground and then up into the air to alight on his shoulder. The raven croaked, and the simpleton nodded his head vigorously as if he understood.

"Good morning, Barnaby," Proctor called.

"Good evening, Mister Brown," the simpleton replied. "I do hope Grip didn't disturb you."

"Not at all," Proctor said, and he squinted at the sky. It was late afternoon. He thought about Deborah, and he wondered what time it was in Salem and what she was doing. "Take care."

Barnaby waved, and then strolled down the road, talking to the next person he saw. The eerie screech of the raven echoed down the street.

"I thought I heard your voice," Lydia said.

Proctor turned, startled again, and saw her standing in the doorway. He sagged into a seat by the window.

"Still not feeling well?" she asked.

"My head won't stop throbbing," he said. Nothing had happened since they'd arrived in England except his headaches. "I finally fell asleep, but either dreams or Barnaby's raven woke me. Have we heard any word from Digges? I mean, Church."

"The owner of the inn thinks his name is Warburton," she answered. She folded her arms across her chest and looked out the window. "But no, nothing. He said that he was going to find Gordon, the man he was telling us about, but I don't think he had any idea where Gordon might be."

Proctor had the same impression. "I think that our friend, Mister Digges Church Warburton, is a man with his fingers in an awful lot of pies. He could get distracted, and we might not see him again for weeks. London is only a dozen miles away. We can walk there and see what we can find on our own."

He looked out the window at the village. It stood on the edge of Epping Forest, and in many ways it reminded him of the small villages he knew in Massachusetts. There was an inn, a small plain church, a smithy, and a handful of houses. But in other ways, it wasn't like home at all. It felt ancient, older than the oldest man he had ever known, and infirm with its age. The inn had almost as many gables as windows, all slapped on haphazardly, as if the building had grown from a shed over the centuries by slowly accreting rooms. Chimneys zigzagged from the rooftops as randomly as the additions. Outside, a thirty-foot maypole of slender ash rose higher than the rooftop, its simplicity a stark contrast with the building itself. The rest of the village matched the inn in character and style. There wasn't a straight line anywhere: every door was lopsided, every wall leaned, every rooftop needed repair. The people of the village were bent odd by their own weight, an accumulation of misery, of death, loss, and betrayal. Digges told them that Proctor and Lydia had come from the Bahamas, and were looking for a quiet place to recover from some unspoken tragedy, and the people accepted it without question.

He squeezed his head to stop the pounding. Darkness

swam before his eyes, and his stomach rolled over and over, even though it was empty.

"You won't be able to walk anywhere until you get well," Lydia said.

"I'm not sick," Proctor replied. "I'm just—"

He fell forward off the chair onto his hands and knees.

"Proctor!"

"Stay back," he said, panting for air. "I can stand up—"

He fell over on his side and his temple slammed into the floor. The world around him went dark except for a single line of light, lashed at him like a whip from a distance beyond reckoning.

He rolled over, trying to dodge the whip. But the cord slashed into him, bright and painful, winding around his soul like a windlass reeling in an anchor.

He blindly grabbed at the floor, but though his nails scraped the joins, the smooth wood offered no serious purchase for his fingers. He could feel himself being pulled away, out of the inn and out over the green hills of England, just as he had been before, the time in Spain when Deborah tried to reach him. She hadn't received his letter. Or she had, and she was calling for him anyway. There was a rush and desperation to this call. Despite his resistance, he flew across the ocean in a blink. Though he was only a spirit, he felt the wind and the power of the lash that reeled him in. He wrapped his hands around the cord of light, to keep it from slicing him in half, and clenched his jaw to keep from screaming in pain.

His eyes popped open, and he was standing in the farmhouse. This was not the dream, this was not anything like the dream. A bad floorboard sagged beneath his feet, he smelled the bucket full of diapers by the door, and Maggie squirmed in his arms, slapping her tiny palm against the window.

He wanted to look at her, wanted to see his daughter,

but he could scarcely see a thing. It was as black as a bad night, heavy with storms. The throbbing pain in his head was gone but it had been replaced by a thick and ominous sense of fear.

He stared out the window. He knew it was daytime, so he expected daylight, but everything was dark. Not dark like an eclipse, but dark like the sun blotted out forever. The smell of smoke was everywhere.

That much was like his dream. He tensed, expecting the heat of invisible fires to press in on him at any second.

A voice, muddled by distance and panic, sounded behind him and he turned. Abigail held two candles. She offered one to him.

The candles barely lit the room. He could see the noon meal sitting uneaten on the table, a rack of diapers hung to dry beside the fire. He turned back to the window and the darkness. It made no sense. He could not even guess what was happening. It was as if the day had arrived without a sun. It felt like the end of the world was happening.

But that wasn't possible. The world wasn't ending in England—it had been an ordinary spring day there.

It wasn't possible for the world to be ending, but it was fact.

As he moved across the room, from window to window, from the outer door to the boarded-up door to the old house, he realized that he was with Deborah. That she had called to him and brought him to her.

The darkness alone did not explain the level of panic he felt coursing through her blood. He wanted to reassure her. She wasn't reaching out to him for reassurance, though. She needed help. She needed power.

But why? He felt stretched too thin to understand, like yarn wrapped around the spindle of her spirit, pulled off a wheel the size of the world. The colors were drained from everything, and the world revealed itself in shades of charcoal, bone, and ash.

He—she—handed Maggie to Abigail, whose face was marked by the mixture of determination and fright that seemed so characteristic of her. Then he—she—ran to the door that he had nailed shut. He saw Deborah's small hands in front of him grab hold of the board, but he felt his strength flow through her arms as she gritted her teeth and yanked. The nails screeched as they came out of the wood, and she cast the board aside. She ran into the old part of the house and stood in front of the old hearth.

Blood flowed through the mortar, just like the blood splattered there by Cecily when she made a black altar of it. Drums thundered from far away, echoed by the tramp of countless boots, as if legions were marching on The Farm. With each beat of the drums, the stones that blocked the fireplace shook as if they were hit by a hammer. Little pieces of mortar dust fell to the floor, leaving a thin coat of dust across the drops of blood.

Deborah!

He called to her, wanted to warn her, wanted to tell her to run, to flee.

But she couldn't—or wouldn't—hear him. Instead, he could feel her drawing on him, trying to reel him in. He felt a tingling, a tickle, running over an invisible skin stretched across the sky.

He could see the lines of power forming as she performed her spell. They lit up the gray world like lightning illuminating the night. She drew power from the protective spell the two of them had laid together on the new hearth, flowing it through the beams and the joints of the house, running it over the paths worn by their feet in the floor. She drew on all that power and patched it over the old hearth like a poultice over an open wound.

The analogy was apt—the bleeding stopped. The stones

pulsed but his masonry held. The drums continued but the tramp of marching footsteps halted.

He—Deborah—ran back through the door, closing it behind her and barring it. When had she put a bar on it? She did another quick spell to seal it as well. She was working too fast—he was spread too thin—for him to follow her work.

She ran back to the window.

Outside, the dark sky churned like soup brought to boil. The sky was black with clouds, but they were no ordinary clouds—it was like smoke from a fire so vast and so distant that it rose up and blotted out the sun. He reached through the window and tried to brush the smoke away. If he could wave his arms, he could clear it away. Instead he felt it flow around him, sticking to him like a film on the back of his neck.

Not the smoke. He didn't feel the smoke. He felt a presence in the smoke.

Suddenly he was back in the house again, behind Deborah's eyes, desperately trying to reach her, to help her understand. She had to seal off the house, from the smoke and the thing hiding in it.

Tiny flakes of ash fell from the sky like filthy snow.

The window frames rattled, not from any wind, but from the punch of an invisible fist just like the blows that crashed the hearth. The drums intensified. The legions resumed their march.

Abigail rocked Maggie in her arms. Oh, God, Maggie was so much bigger than he remembered. She had become this little person, and she desperately wanted her mother. She was flinging herself out of Abigail's arms, straining to reach Deborah. Abigail clutched her tighter, her mouth set grimly as tears streamed from her eyes.

And he was there.

He—Deborah—shouted at Abigail for salt but Abigail

stared at the window and didn't respond. He—Deborah—
ran to the cupboard. He took the bag from the shelf
and felt the rough grains trickle through his fist like sand
through an hourglass onto the windowsill. They stuck to
the sweat on his palm but he didn't pause to brush them
off. He ran to the next window and poured salt along
that sill too. He felt the words shape his mouth, almost
understood what he was saying, but something distracted
him, a tickle at the back of his neck.

Somewhere, far away, he could feel the flames feeding
these clouds of smoke, and those flames had the form of
a demon wrapped in a red coat of fire. Its heavy brow was
topped with horns, and it wore a mocking grin across the
bloody smear of its mouth. The clouds of smoke spread
over the landscape like a vast, scaly arm. At the end of the
arm was a taloned hand, and the hand was stroking the
back of his—Deborah's—neck. The fingers were sliding
around his—Deborah's—throat.

Choking off the words of his protective spell.

Stealing his breath.

No.

Choking off *Deborah's* words, stealing *Deborah's*
breath.

Proctor shook off the paralysis of fear. The demon
wasn't a creature of flesh, but a creature of spirit. Deborah could never seal the farmhouse as long as she was
tethered to Proctor's spirit and his spirit was tethered to
his body across the ocean. Like lightning running down
a kite string to a key. It was her connection to him that
made her vulnerable.

He could feel the demon crawling, all calluses and
nails, down his back to get into the house. The stump of
his missing finger burned as badly as if it had just been
cut off all over again.

Proctor immediately tried pulling away from Deborah, but it was like trying to crawl out of his own skin.

In the weird split perception that he had, he felt Deborah's emotions alongside his own. She sensed him trying to pull away, and she held on to him more tightly, angry that he was abandoning her, tying his spirit to hers with knots.

The tie would prove to be a noose for them both if he couldn't make her understand, if he couldn't pull away.

His spirit thrashed, like a fish on a hook hoping to snap the fisherman's line.

The demon laughed—a sound that pierced the white-water noise clogging Proctor's ears—and clawed its way hand over hand, moving inexorably toward Deborah and the house. Something in Proctor's fear and panic reached Deborah, and her own fear accelerated. She looked toward Maggie, wailing in Abigail's arms.

Proctor had a glimpse of the demon's bloody intent: use Proctor to reach Deborah, possess Deborah and use her to sacrifice their innocent child, then draw on the power of the child to summon its loyal host, the legions of demons that would emerge from a hellgate in Salem to march across America.

Everything the demon needed was present: a link to the spirit world, a powerful witch for its host, the blood of an innocent to feed its evil power.

Let . . . me . . . go . . .

Proctor tried to force the words out of Deborah's mouth. She doubled over, coughing as if there were something in her throat.

Abigail came over and knelt beside her, trying to help her. Maggie's tiny hands reached out from Abigail's arms and grabbed fistfuls of her mother's dress.

The demon came closer. The flames on the candle flashed brighter as it approached.

Proctor forced his—her—head up.

"Let . . . me . . . go . . ."

The words came out like a croak, but they broke

through the noise of the rapids in his ears. Abigail stared at him—at Deborah—with wide eyes and asked what he—she—meant.

Maggie dragged herself out of Abigail's grip, spilling onto the floor.

Deborah could not pick up her daughter. Her fingers tore at her throat, trying to breathe.

The candles on the table and the mantel flared, shining as bright as torches, melting all the wax into puddles in seconds. The room plunged into darkness.

Proctor—Deborah—crawled on her hands and knees across the floor. Proctor tried to pull away, tried to climb out of Deborah's skin, but she wouldn't let him go. The more he struggled to escape, the tighter she held on.

Maggie's wail pierced the pitch black. Abigail called out Deborah's name over and over.

The walls of the house shook as though a great wind would smash them to matchsticks at any moment. Outside, the outhouse exploded in a shower of splinters. The barn rattled, near collapse.

And Proctor realized that his spirit was tied at two ends, one in England and another here at home at noon on the darkest day he'd ever known. If he couldn't break the bond on this end in time, cutting off the demon's path past Deborah's wards, he could unravel the knot at the other end and board himself inside the house with her.

It might mean the end of him. It might leave his body a dead shell. But it was worth it to protect his wife and daughter. If this was how D was a danger to him, so be it—he'd always been willing to lay his life down for her.

He sent his mind back through his spirit. Past the wall of the house, between the darkened earth and the polluted sky. When he reached the vast cloud of smoke, he found the gloating visage of the demon in the red coat. Proctor darted one way, feinted the other, then shot past it like a wild creature escaping from some corner trap.

For a few seconds his world was a blur of sky and ocean, green hills and pale stars.

The demon let him go. Proctor was still tethered to Deborah, and the demon climbed down the other end of that rope.

Then he was back in his own body. It felt as strange and foreign to him as occupying Deborah's body did. Immediately he tried to pull free his soul.

Behind him, he felt Deborah trying to reel him back, trying to draw on his power.

She could have it, have it all, as soon he undid the last thread that connected him to his mortal body. His flesh felt reluctant to give up his ghost, so he tore at it, fighting against himself in a suicide's attempt to save Deborah.

No!

It was her voice in his head, less in words than in presence, imploring him to stop, demanding that he quit.

I have to, he answered. It was all the explanation he could manage.

He found the frayed end of his soul, wrapped around his heart like a ragged rope. He took hold of it with his right hand, and the hand was complete and whole again. He braced himself to pull free. When he joined Deborah inside the house, he would lend her his power, and they would fight off the demon's attempt to enter—

Oh.

Deborah understood. She understood the demon's plan, or her own danger, or Proctor's intention, or something. But whatever she understood, she flung him loose, like a child letting go of a kite in a strong wind. He had already pulled free the rope end of his soul, and so he sailed away across the sky, buffeted this way and that, helpless to return to his body or to go join Deborah.

The demon roared in frustration and aimed a wild slap of raw power at Proctor, then made a furious lunge for Deborah and The Farm. Proctor clutched at the hem of its coat, just to slow it down, but the demon's blow had sent him spinning wildly into a darkness no sight could pierce, cut off from Deborah and lost to his own self.

If this was it, if he wandered lost forever, it was worth it to save Deborah.

If he had saved her.

I love you, he said, less in words than with the last essence of his spirit, even though there was no way for her to hear.

And then he felt Lydia reach out and pluck him from the void, a hand catching a string in the wind. She wound in the string, hand over hand, cutting her flesh to pull him back.

When she tucked him into the heart of his own flesh, he opened his eyes and saw her frightened face, lit by candles. Hours had passed. She leaned forward over him.

"Is she safe?" he whispered, his voice weak.

Lydia shook her head. "I don't know. I don't know what just happened."

He was too exhausted, too weary, to explain. So he didn't try. He fell again, like a man stepping off a scaffold into a different darkness, black like the soil, heavy as a mound of earth.

Chapter 15

Proctor slowly crawled his way back into the world, but when he reached it his first sensation was falling, like a man in a dream with no ground to catch him. From time to time, he heard Lydia's voice, felt her hands roll him over and change his bedding, hold warm broth to his lips.

He could feel his spirit growing stronger at the same time his body wasted away, and he wondered if they would cross paths, like two strangers headed opposite directions, or if they would stop just short of meeting each other.

From time to time, he fell again through darkness, and a time came when he fell again but the ground rushed toward him. He closed his eyes and braced for the impact, but he landed as delicately as the falling snow. He woke in a bed with a mattress so soft it felt like a trap.

But he was awake. He turned his head to the side and saw large windows thrown open to an overcast sky. The unfamiliar trees outside had filled out with leaf. He felt thirsty and sore, but he was alive. He had survived. Lydia had saved him.

Had he saved Deborah?

An ash-black shape flapped out of the air and landed on the sill. Proctor's heart pounded, but the appearance of the bird fixed his location. He was still at the inn on the edge of Epping Forest, and the bird was only the simpleton's pet raven. It cocked its head at him sideways and tapped the sill.

"Hallo, you're a devil," it squawked. "You're a saucy devil."

Proctor pushed back the covers and slowly sat up on the edge of the bed. "Shoo," he told the bird. "Go on, shoo."

"Shoo yourself, shoo your god-damned self!" the bird replied, beating its wings.

Suddenly it flapped away as quickly as it had come.

The door cracked open quietly behind Proctor, as if someone wanted to sneak up on him. He knew he was too weak to defend himself, so he drew on his power. There was no time for a protective spell, but he might be able to fling objects at an attacker, and stop them with a lucky blow. A ceramic pitcher sat on the wash table. It rose in the air and flew over to the door, hovering where he could drop it on someone's head.

The door creaked wide.

Lydia stood there. "Thank God you're finally up."

Proctor breathed a sigh of relief. The pitcher dropped suddenly, grazing Lydia as it fell. It shattered on the floor in a burst of water and ceramics.

He held out his hands. "I'm sorry, I didn't know it was you—"

"Are you—?" she asked.

"I'm sorry."

"Are you yourself? Are you—?"

"I'm myself," he said. "Is Deborah safe? Do we know what happened to her?"

She stepped over the pieces of the broken pitcher, latching the door behind her. Then she crossed to the window and shut it as well. "I don't know what happened to Deborah," she said, turning back to him. "I thought she was trying to spirit-talk to you again."

"She was. But she was doing it because she wanted—needed—help. The Covenant summoned a demon." *Bal-*

fri. He didn't want to say the name, in case invoking the creature called it to oneself.

Lydia was skilled at turning her face into a blank wall that hid her feelings, but this time Proctor could see her wondering if he had been hurt or if maybe he was touched in the head. She crossed her arm over her chest and covered her mouth with her hand.

"I don't know if I can explain what happened," Proctor said. "When I arrived at The Farm, and saw it through her eyes, the whole world was wrong. It was noon, but the sky was so dark you could only see inside the house with candles."

"Like an eclipse?" Lydia asked.

Proctor tried to remember what he'd seen and felt while he was there. "It felt like there was a great fire, as if all the forests in Canada were burning, but it was a fire set to summon the demon. A black cloud blotted out the sun. The air was so thick with smoke you couldn't breathe. Ash fell out of the sky like dust. Do you remember the demon in the fireplace?"

Lydia glanced toward the hearth in their room and nodded once.

"Imagine that but on a larger scale—a rowboat compared with a warship, a spitball straw compared to a cannonade." He shook his head. "No, even that doesn't do it justice. It filled the sky."

"But why?" Lydia asked.

Proctor pushed himself to his feet. His legs were wobbly, but he could stand. He was wearing only a nightshirt, and his bare legs looked thin. His skin was a sickly yellow. He touched his head. His hair was long and greasy. "How long have I been unconscious?"

"Weeks," she said.

"Weeks?"

"I told the innkeeper you were suffering a relapse of malaria," she said. "You've had a fever. His wife sent up broth for you at every meal, and his son came up every day and we helped you walk around the room to keep up your strength. How much do you remember?"

"I remember falling," he said. Maybe the sensation of falling had been the daily walks around the room. "That's all I remember is the falling. What about Digges?"

She shook her head. "I haven't seen a hair or heard a rumor of him. But the innkeeper says that he disappears for weeks or months at a time and then shows up with one guest or another, much like he did with us."

"The Covenant is desperate to finish the war," Proctor said. "They want to crush the spirit of freedom, to force everyone to declare allegiance to a single sovereign. It's a focus to bring all the power they can draw together."

"But . . . demons?"

He paced the small room, walking from the window around the bed and back again. "Maybe it's a scorched-earth policy, a true scorched earth." He thought about the way the countess had described America. "Our continent is not a real place to them, not part of civilization. They don't care what happens to it."

She picked up a towel draped over the edge of the bed and used it to wipe up the water and collect the shattered pitcher into a single pile. The pieces clicked and screeched as they tumbled together. He stared out the window while she worked, trying to sort out the explanation.

"So you think that King George is behind the plan?" Lydia asked.

"I don't know," Proctor said. "I don't think so. The prince-bishop, Countess Cagliostro, they're not even English."

"They're royalty."

"But the widow Nance wasn't and neither is Cecily," Proctor said. "Besides, if what the widow said was true, if Rotenhahn told the truth about his age and the prince-bishop's, if Digges is right about his ancestor, then this has been building for centuries, long before King George was born."

"That's a heavy load of truth to accept from a group of known liars." She bundled the pieces of the pitcher together and set them on the washstand.

"It is," he admitted. "King George may only be a convenient tool for the Covenant's purpose. Think about it. Of all the Covenant's agents we've fought, only one, Major Pitcairn, had a direct connection to the Crown. And his magic was only a minor protective charm." Funny to think it minor now—when Proctor first encountered Pitcairn and his protective charm, it had seemed the height of sorcery. "But the people behind the Covenant may very well be advisers to the king, or connected to the Crown in some other way. We just don't know."

Their voices, which had begun as whispers, had risen to normal pitch, carried along by the energy of their discussion. The sound of feet shuffling in the hall outside the door brought their conversation to a sudden halt.

Proctor's hand jumped up from his side and he looked for something to fling now that the pitcher was broken.

Lydia covered her hand with his and pushed it down.

"It's an inn," she said. "People walk in the halls."

His nostrils flared and he tried to settle his breath. "Maybe we should take a walk outside. Is there someplace . . ."

"The forest beyond the village is usually empty. I take walks there almost every day."

"That's what we'll do," he said.

He sipped a cup of broth and ate some cold lamb stew while he dressed himself in the same clothes that he had been wearing for months. Lydia had washed and patched them, but there was no hiding the worn fabric or the frayed hems.

"Are you sure you're well enough to do this?" she asked.

He wiped his mouth. "Yes," he said. "I must regain my strength. If Digges doesn't return, we should go to London to look for the Covenant." He looked out the window at the trees. Winter had passed by swiftly, and spring was already on the verge of summer. He had no idea if Deborah was safe or not. "I thought we would sail over here and find the Covenant as easy as finding a street in Philadelphia or a farm in Virginia. I expected to be home by now."

Lydia stood with her arms crossed and stared out the window also. "This hasn't been what I expected either."

There was a meaning in her words that Proctor knew he missed, but he decided it would be better to pursue it again when they were outside and away from casual listeners. "Shall we go?"

"The sooner the better," she said. Then she snapped to her senses. "Oh, you mean to take our walk. Yes, of course."

On their way through the common room, an old man in an apron stopped wiping the tables and waved to them. "It's good to see you up and about again, Mister Brown," he said. "That malaria, it's something awful. The missus, she says she'd like to go to the Bahamas and try our hand at an inn there, but I say no thank you. Give me a healthy climate and something I know. I trust my Joe has given you good service."

"He has, excellent service," Proctor assured him. "The best thing for me now is fresh air and exercise."

"Oh, we have plenty of both here, never you mind," the innkeeper said. He walked around the tables to continue the conversation, but Proctor smiled and banged through the door out into the street.

The village was much as he remembered it, a small cluster of buildings dominated by the inn. Down the wagon-rutted road, the simpleton—Barnaby, that was his name—leaned in a window to talk to someone. The raven bobbed on his shoulder, cocking its head at Proctor. He recalled a manor house nearby as well, but it wasn't visible because the forest surrounded everything. The air held the crisp, fresh smell of greenery and dew.

"Which way?" Proctor asked.

"This way," Lydia said, leading him off the road.

The woods were unlike those Proctor knew in America. There was no underbrush filling the forest floor, no thickets of wild berries or brush piles covered with vines. Instead, the ancient trees rose high above, providing a roof so thick that only a slight carpet of grasses grew beneath. The trees were not quite laid out in rows, but they were regularly spaced, as if they had been carefully selected over time while their brothers and sisters were cleared away. Even the roots had room to stretch out, half exposed, along the surface. Proctor saw piles of deer scat here and there, but the profusion of wild animals of all sizes that he'd expected when he entered the woods was nowhere to be seen. It was like thinking he was going into a crowded tavern and instead finding himself in an empty church. But there was something peaceful and restorative about it at the same time. Although they had chosen the forest as a place to talk, instead they found themselves walking for a long time in silence.

"I belong nowhere," Lydia said.

"What?" Proctor asked, shaken from his own worries for Deborah and Maggie.

"Except maybe Deborah's farm," she said. "I felt at home there, like I belonged in my own right, equal to everyone else."

"We all belonged there," Proctor said. Dogs barked in the far distance. The direction was indiscernible because of the way sound was amplified and distorted by the open space beneath the trees. "I feel better now that I'm out in the fresh air," Proctor said. "Maybe another day or two of rest, and then we'll leave for London to search for the Covenant."

"Of course," Lydia said. "We'll do whatever you want."

"What exactly is that supposed to mean? Isn't that our plan?"

Before she could answer, the dogs barked again much closer. They stopped and searched the trees, but couldn't see them. "What do you think that is?" she asked.

"Some hunters," Proctor offered, not really thinking about the question.

"I don't think Englishmen are allowed to hunt in their forests," she said. "The deer belong to the king. I saw some men out here yesterday."

"Let's head back to the inn," Proctor said, looking around.

"I think that's a wise idea."

They turned and started walking back the way they'd come. Proctor thought they were headed in the right direction, but it was difficult to tell because of the uniformity of the trees and the landscape. The dogs barked more furiously, and without saying anything to each other Proctor and Lydia started walking faster.

"Where's the road?" he asked.

"Just a little farther that way," she said.

He shook his head in understanding. He had overestimated the fullness of his recovery. His stamina was pressed by the exertion, and he had no breath left for talking.

"There she is," yelled a man behind them.

Proctor glanced over his shoulder to see a group of men with a pack of leashed hounds. The dogs erupted in a frenzy of barking, and the men gave pursuit.

"Run," Proctor gasped.

Lydia pulled up her skirts and started to run and he stumbled after her as fast as he could go, though he didn't know why the men were chasing them. He was dizzy and couldn't concentrate. He reached in his pocket for Deborah's lock of hair, but it felt slippery and tainted in his fingers. He thought he saw the road up ahead and, through the trees, the rambling rooftop of the inn.

Over his shoulder, he saw the hunters unleashing the hounds.

He tripped over a root and went sprawling on the ground. Lydia turned back at the sound, then looked up and saw the dogs. There was a wild fear in her eyes like he had never seen, and then she left him and ran. He had risen to his hands and knees when the dogs reached him, nipping and barking, and he cowered, covering his head.

Not twenty yards away, they cornered Lydia as well.

There were four men, one with a shotgun tucked under his arm and the others carrying pistols. They were not ragged or desperate enough to be outlaws, though they were clearly men who lived on the rough side of order. A fifth man accompanied them for the dogs. He gathered them up and returned them to their leashes while the other four guarded Proctor and Lydia.

"See, I told you I saw her out here," one of the men said smugly.

"I think there's a mistake," Proctor said.

"Oh, there is, and you made it," the man said, jabbing the barrel of the shotgun at him.

"My name is Proctor Brown. I'm from the Bahamas and this"—he hesitated before he said the next words—"is my slave, Lydia."

All five of the men laughed. They had heard his hesitation and it confirmed something they suspected. "If she's your slave, then show us your papers," the smug one said.

"What?"

"Show us your papers of ownership," the smug one said. "We checked into you. We know you're staying at the Maypole Inn. We'll follow you back there while you get the papers."

"I've . . . I've been ill," Proctor said. "We didn't expect to be here so long. I don't have the papers with me."

"Oh, that's all right," the smug man answered with a jerk of his thumb at Lydia. "This here's valuable property. If you're a gentleman, you won't mind producing a surety for her until her papers can be produced."

Proctor could not tell if the man was serious or bluffing. He didn't know the laws in England. He looked at Lydia to see if they had any money left, but he already knew the answer before he glimpsed the frightened zeros in her eyes. If they had been at the inn for weeks without word from Digges, they were broke and running up a tab.

The smug one saw the exchange and recognized it for what it was. He laughed again; they all laughed. "Let me tell you a story," he said. "What I think happened. You can tell by her nice dress that she was a house slave. That's good fabric. Nobody dresses their slaves like that unless they value them. Now look at you, on the other hand. Your clothes are plain and threadbare and twenty years out of fashion. You aren't a gentleman, and I'd be surprised if you ever owned anything more than what you're carrying on your back right now."

"That's not how it is," Proctor said.

The man thumped Proctor's chest with the barrel of the shotgun. All the amusement was gone from his face, replaced by greed and anger. "I'm telling the story, so you're going to shut up and listen. I figure she was somebody's house slave somewhere, and maybe you worked in the stables, mucking out the stalls. You decided to run away together."

The dogs grew restless, yipping and tugging at their leashes.

The leader looked at Proctor and Lydia as if sizing up their differences in age and station. "I guess there's no accounting for affection. So you show up here with some wild story about the Bahamas, and that would have been just fine if you were passing through on your way to someplace else, but then you fell sick, and she can't produce any papers or letters for you, and nobody knows anything about you."

He expected some kind of confirmation from Proctor, but Proctor was busy calculating their chances of escape. He and Lydia needed not only to throw off these men, but also to make sure they didn't follow or spread an alarm. And then the two of them would need some kind of coin when they continued on their way. The only solution he could come up with involved leaving all five men dead in the woods, rifling their pockets, and hoping for the best. He thought he could lift and aim the guns, then pull the triggers, but the noise would draw everyone from the village.

When Proctor didn't respond, the smug one continued. "So this is how it's going to be. If you tell us who she belonged to, we'll find them and return her for the reward, and we won't say anything about you. You can go free on your way. If you don't say anything, then we have to go to the trouble of finding papers for her so we can sell her. And that's more work for us, so after we do it, we turn you in for a thief." He looked at Proctor's hand, with its neatly missing finger. "Which maybe you already are, and in that case you're just as likely to go to the hangman as to jail."

Proctor looked at Lydia and saw that she held her power at the ready. He drew on his own. The dogs barked and struggled to get free, and he wondered if they could sense it. He would have to try to use the guns as bludgeons. His plan was to strike down the leader first, and then the other men with guns, leaving the houndsman for last.

"Are you going to say anything?" the leader asked. Proctor wanted him to step forward and thump him in the chest with the gun one more time. It would be easier to redirect if it was already in motion, and the man would be less prepared to stop it.

Proctor spit at his feet. That finally did it—

"Oh, hey, hello!" called a voice from off through the trees. "Look, I think they're over here."

A small group of men came strolling through the woods. Proctor recognized the shorter one in front as Digges. The second man was tall, Proctor's height at least, but thin and sallow. His hair was long, lank, and red. He was obviously a gentleman of some sort, because only a gentleman would dare dress so peculiarly, matching red plaid trousers with a black velvet coat. He was flanked by a pair of servants.

The four men holding Proctor and Lydia prisoner quickly hid their guns beneath their coats. "Lord Gordon," the leader said. The others ducked their heads and echoed, "Lord Gordon, sir—Good to see you—Hello, sir."

"Good day," Gordon said. "It's good to see you too. I recognize some of your faces from the last meeting of the Protestant Association. Will you all put blue cockades in your caps and join me in the march on Parliament?"

"Planning to do that, sir."

"Absolutely."

"You can count on us."

"Excellent," Gordon said. "I am on my way to London now, in fact." He sized up Proctor as he spoke, staring absently for a second at Proctor's pocket, then glanced from Digges to Proctor to the group of ruffians. "So what exactly do we have here?"

"We caught this runaway slave and this thief," the leader said, jerking a thumb at Proctor and Lydia.

"Oh, he's not a thief," Digges said.

"He's not a thief," Gordon said. "He's . . ."

"He's Mister Brown from the Bahamas," Digges said. "And this is his slave, Lydia."

"But you all know as well as I that slavery is illegal in England," Gordon said, his face registering concern and surprise. "The court case of James Somersett settled—"

"We know no such thing, and never heard of no Somersett," the leader of the ruffians said. His coat slipped open and his gun showed.

Gordon's man stepped in front of him. His face showed no sign of concern or worry, but made it clear to the ruffians that they could not, and would not, threaten his master. Proctor glanced at the ruffians to see if they would back down.

The leader, at least, refused to be cowed. "There'd be no abolitionists if there was no slavery, now would there?" he said. "What do Sharp and Wilberforce go on about freeing the slaves for, if there's no slavery?"

"Sometimes men exaggerate a situation to make a point," Gordon said.

"So His Lordship is suggesting that the Catholic threat has been exaggerated—"

"No, I'm suggesting no such thing, of course not—popery is a danger to every free man in England," Gordon said at once, smiling. When he smiled, Proctor felt like a lamp had been lit just for him. Though Gordon spoke in a low voice, Proctor could hear every word as though it were whispered for him alone. "Would you be satisfied if the gentleman provided a surety for his conduct and that of his companion?"

"Well, that's the problem in a nutshell, isn't it?" the leader said. "They're running up a bill at the Maypole with no apparent means of paying it. So you look at them, and she's dressed well enough, but his clothes are worn to rags. We've searched their room, and there's not a shilling in any crack in the floor. We've emptied their pockets too, and unless money's made of lint, they don't have any."

Proctor squeezed the lock of Deborah's hair in his fist. There might still be a fight.

"We'll settle his account and pay the surety for him," Digges whispered to Gordon.

"Oh, absolutely, we'll provide the surety for him," Gordon insisted. He glanced again at Proctor's pocket. "After all, they're all coming to London with us for the march on Parliament." He patted his own pockets, then glanced at his two servants, who made no response. To Digges, he said, "Thomas, I'm terribly sorry, do you mind?"

"Of course not," Digges replied. He opened up the purse that Franklin had given him, now visibly lighter, and counted out enough coin to buy the silence of five men.

Once all assurances were made, and the men departed, Gordon turned to Proctor.

"We're going to London with you?" Proctor asked. He had still not relaxed.

Gordon clapped a hand on his shoulder. "Thomas tells me that we share a common enemy. I am on my way to London to see if I can wreck their plans."

for a palace of the king. Indeed, if King George was afraid of attack, it would make sense to stay in a defensible spot like this. In one of the gardens, he glimpsed strange animals—a horse with black and white stripes; a cat like a panther but twice as large with a great ruff around its neck. Suddenly he realized where they were, recognizing it from descriptions he had read.

"When you said *the tower,* you meant 'the Tower of London,'" Proctor said to Gordon.

"Of course," Gordon said. "But we're in London, so the phrase *of London* is rather superfluous, is it not?" He tugged at his collar and nervously loosened a gold chain around his throat. "I have to speak to the king's warden. Will you help Grueby carry this bag up to the room there, the one overlooking the garden?"

The request made Proctor suspicious. He looked at his clothes, but then he saw Gordon's brother outside, and Grueby, and all sorts of men who knew them both. What had Lydia said? No one who knew them both would ever mistake them for each other. "I'll carry this up to the room, but that's all I'm doing until you make me part of your plans," Proctor said.

"I'll ask no more of you," Gordon promised. "You've already done more than I could have ever expected, and I am deeply indebted."

Proctor climbed out of the carriage with Gordon's bag. Guards stared through him as if he weren't there. Gordon's family averted their eyes or peered into the carriage where Gordon still sat.

Grueby held the large chair. "The rest of the furniture will be sent along shortly, I am told. Come on, let's get this done with."

He sounded uncharacteristically gruff, even a little unhappy.

"What's going on with Gordon?" Proctor asked. "He's acting very strangely."

"Hrmph" was all that Grueby would say.

Proctor was very uneasy now. As soon as they dropped off the items, he planned to confront Gordon and force an answer from him. If Gordon didn't have a plan that was more specific than "Look after the king," then Proctor would formulate his own. Guards led them into a small tower above an archway leading to the river. They climbed up two flights of steps to a large but empty room.

"We'll take it from here," Grueby said.

After a moment the guards withdrew to the bottom of the steps. Proctor sensed something very wrong now, so he hesitated at the door. Grueby entered the room and dumped the chair over by the window.

"There's Gordon, speaking with the warden now," he said.

Proctor crossed the threshold to look through the window, and instantly felt dizzy. The room seemed to whirl around him. He dropped the bag as Deborah's lock of hair twisted and jumped in his pocket. He reached for it, but it crawled out of its own accord and dropped to the center of the room like a living thing. The black ribbon—the one that the Countess Cagliostro had given him, the one he was always forgetting to exchange—untied itself and scattered the hair in a circle at Proctor's feet. It slithered like a flat snake toward the window, where it shivered and withdrew. It did the same thing at the door. It ran to the corners and turned back each time, before rushing to the center of the room, where it whirled in a circle at Proctor's feet, caught fire, and burned. All of Deborah's scattered hairs caught fire, twisting and burning like a hundred tiny snakes.

It was over in a moment. All that remained of his focus was a swirl of ash marks in the floor.

"Well, that's interesting," Grueby said.

"I can't touch it," Proctor said.

"Not with it all burned up like that."

"No, I can't touch my talent—it's as if there's nothing there." It wasn't like when another drew on his talent and he felt it flow away from him. He reached for it and nothing was there. Like a dry well. He turned and ran for the door, but Grueby reached it first and stopped him.

"Before you leave, I'm supposed to tell you about this room," he said.

"What about it?" demanded Proctor. His pulse raced and he felt sweat beading on his brow.

"This is called the Bloody Tower. Not because of all the blood shed here, though that's what everybody thinks. It's called the Bloody Tower because the mortar was mixed with blood, and all the stones are inscribed on the inside with marks that shield against the use of witchcraft."

"What?"

"This tower was built during the reign of King Henry the Third. The first witchcraft trials in England occurred during the reign of his father, King John, but it grew worse in Henry's day. There was a pirate, Eustace the monk, who ruled the channel, first serving England, then France, wherever profit or whim suited him. Do you want to hear this?"

"Do I have a choice?" Proctor said, but he knew there was a lesson here about witchcraft and kings. A room where no magic could be performed might be useful in stopping the Covenant, though he wished Gordon had just spoken to him directly.

"Eustace was a necromancer. He used blood magic to make his ship invisible. At this same time, there was a witch who served in the English fleet, a man by the name of Stephen Crabbe. When English ships challenged the French, they could gain no advantage. Their arrows would rain down on the open boats, killing the

Frenchmen, but then before the victory, the English ships would have their hulls shattered, turn by turn, and sink."

"Eustace and his invisible ship," Proctor said.

"Exactly," Grueby answered. "Crabbe, though, he had the vision, just as you and my lord do. Let those who have eyes see, right? He jumped out of his own ship. It looked to the Englishmen around him as if he were walking on water. As he danced over the waves, he swung his ax about him, like a woodcutter in the forest. Men thought him mad."

"But he wasn't."

"No, he walked across Eustace's deck and killed men right and left, until the spell was broken. Eustace's last act, before he was beheaded, was to summon demons. The demons came and tore Crabbe to pieces where he stood. But he was a hero. He saved England from a terrible magic."

"And then King Henry built this tower to protect his throne against similar magic."

"Right again," Grueby said, tapping Proctor on the chest. "And now we face a similar situation. An enemy using witchcraft and demons, and Britain's very survival threatened by our foe across the ocean."

"A Catholic foe, and the friend of America," Proctor said.

"There is that," Grueby answered. "But Gordon feels outnumbered by the Covenant. So he thought that he might use the Tower to help even the odds."

"What was that ribbon?" Proctor asked.

"It was a token. The embroidery was written in Enochian, the language of angels that Dee and his followers have learned to speak. Members of the Covenant use those tokens to recognize one another."

"And Gordon has taken me for a member of the

Covenant," Proctor said. He slapped his forehead and felt the ache slam all the way through his hand. "How stupid am I, really? Be honest."

"Not so stupid as all that," Grueby said indifferently. "After what you saw last night, most men wouldn't be able to think straight. You were sick, and then you didn't eat right or rest for days. I've been exhausted just trying to keep up with you."

"What's this then?" Proctor said, taking the pendant in his fist.

"I wouldn't try to take that off if I were you," Grueby said.

The warning came too late. Proctor tried to snap the chain, and it wrapped around his throat like one of those snakes that suffocate their prey. Black spots were swimming before his eyes and he was falling toward the floor before he could let go. Grueby caught him and helped him back to his feet.

"I figured you for the type that would have to learn for yourself," Grueby said.

"Why does it work when other magic doesn't?" Proctor gasped, his hand at his throat.

"Because there's almost no magic in the necklace itself, as I understand it," Grueby said. "Gordon has it all focused in the matching necklace that he wears. This tower aside, he was very concerned that you not notice any spell when you put it on. Try to say your name or explain who you are."

"Must I?" Proctor asked.

"I figure you will, sooner or later. But the effects are the same."

"So this makes me look like Gordon, and Gordon look like me?"

"Near enough. I should go get the rest of your possessions. You're going to be here for a long time."

"Not damned likely," Proctor said.

"That's what they all say when they enter the Bloody Tower," Grueby said. "I heard those were Sir Walter Raleigh's exact words as well. But to be blunt, this here's a prison, and you should plan on staying for a while."

He turned to go. "Wait," Proctor said.

Gordon's servant stopped.

"You saw me. I heard you tell Gordon how I attacked the Covenant. If you've been following me, you know that they're my enemy, too, and I'll do anything I can to destroy them."

"That might be."

"It is! So why would you help lock up an ally? Why would you help put away the one man you can trust to help your lord's cause?"

Grueby shrugged indifferently. "Because I was told to."

"And you always do what you're told?"

The stoic thought about it for a moment. "Depends on who does the telling. And what they tell me to do. And if I feel like doing it. But yes, almost always."

He left the cell, closing the door behind him. Proctor ran through the two rooms, looking out over the river on one side and the courtyard garden on the other. Gordon's carriage was rolling away, with Gordon still inside it.

Proctor ran to the door and found it unlocked. He opened it and ran down the steps. The guards waiting at the bottom caught him by either arm. When he tried to tell them who he really was, the necklace constricted around his throat at once.

He came to as they were laying him on the floor of his cell. He looked up to see one of them swirling a finger at the side of his head.

"His secretary warned the warden," the guard whispered. "This one's gone a little mad. He'll bear close watching."

They left the room, locking the door behind them.

Proctor went over to the window and kicked the chair. There was no way he was going to stay in prison for any length of time.

Chapter 20

One hundred hooves trotted along the road lined on either side by live oaks. The green uniforms of the British Legion had been faded by seasons of weather and wear, matching the leaves still clinging to the trees in November. The hard black caps on the heads of the men were marred by months of woods and war.

Banastre Tarleton, leading his men from the front, glimpsed a splash of red from the corner of his eye and turned in his saddle to see what it might be. But by the time he cranked his head around, the color was gone.

He heard a boy's chuckle and decided that he was imagining things. There were no boys in his cavalry, and his men had no reason to chuckle.

The battle at Waxhaws had been an overwhelming victory against a superior force, but ever since then Tarleton and his men had been hard-pressed by southern partisans, men little better than outlaws, who attacked in the twilight and faded back into the swamps. Rumors of one such force had been little more than another wild goose chase, which was no more than Tarleton expected. More than likely, the partisans had hoped to draw the legion away from the plantation they occupied. The autumn harvest was in, and soldiers on either side needed food and fodder to get through the coming winter.

The road opened out on a plantation up ahead, the place locals called Big Home. Size was the only thing that distinguished it. In every other particular, from its rough wood to its brutish proportions, it resembled the rude shacks that seemed to be dropped at random throughout this wild, unsettled, and unsettling country. Tarleton was ready to welcome anything, adapt any tactic, that would bring an end to this rebellion and allow him to return home to the civilized parlors, theaters, and clubs of London.

He felt an urge that made him want to turn away from the road and face toward London. That was strange. He'd left men here—

"Go on," whispered a voice. "Go on to the Big Home."

Tarleton noticed that the horses had all slowed to a walk. "Let's go," he said angrily, and kicked his own horse forward, expecting the others to follow him.

This plantation was protected by luck or something. Despite the ruthless foraging by armies on both sides, no one had plundered it. Even with no man at home to protect it—the owner had died recently—it had remained untouched.

Well, that wouldn't last.

The rest of the legion was spread out across the grounds of the plantation, their horses in the pasture, soldiers taking their ease on the broad porch. His men were good, loyal men, who fought hard for him. They, too, deserved peace and a chance to reclaim the homes and lives stolen from them by the rebel rabble.

A fresh grave stood in a little cemetery just outside the entrance of the plantation. The rebel general, Richard Richardson. He'd had the cowardice to die of natural causes a month ago, before Tarleton could hunt him down and kill him. It seemed too convenient to be true, but when the legion had alighted unannounced on Richardson's home, his wife was in her widow's dress and his children, especially his ten-year-old son, seemed genuinely grieved. More so than Tarleton had been at the age of nineteen when his own father died.

"Captain Kinlock," Tarleton said as he dismounted by the house. "Did any rebels appear while we were gone?"

"Not one, Colonel," Kinlock said.

"We didn't see any either," Tarleton admitted, handing his horse off to one of his men. "It was a feint, meant to draw us out from the plantation. What do you think they want here?"

"Same as we do, I reckon—fresh grain, a good meal, supplies."

"Chasing a fox through the swamp is a losing venture. So maybe it's better to sit on the henhouse and wait for the fox to appear."

Kinlock grinned. "And here we sit."

Tarleton studied Richardson's grave. "This was the house of one of their most respected generals. You don't think there's anything else here?"

"Lost pride, perhaps," Kinlock said.

"Perhaps," Tarleton answered.

But as he climbed the steps of the house, he had a different thought in mind. There was something about Richardson's widow that made him uneasy. She was hiding something. It might be as simple as the family silver, but his instinct told him it was something bigger.

He kicked open the front door, making sure his boot left a big black scrape across the wood. Inside, a girl gasped in shock, only to have someone quickly shush her.

"Is my dinner ready?" he yelled. The words echoed through the big, hollow rooms.

He made his voice as imperious and grating as possible. An angry woman or furious child was likely to say things in temper that they would otherwise hold secret. Men would do the same, but there were no men on the farm. All the more reason to suspect a connection to the rebel partisans.

Richardson's widow, wearing a black dress as simple as an ordinary death, appeared in the doorway. She was preternaturally calm as always. Tarleton dearly wanted to find some way to rattle her cage and uncover her secrets.

"The gentlemen may be served in the dining room," she said.

Kinlock and Tarleton's other officers smirked at being called gentlemen. They were anything but gentlemen and they knew it. But they followed her into the dining room.

"James," Tarleton called, looking into rooms and around the corners of doors. "Where's James?"

The widow stopped and turned around. James was her ten-year-old son, the one so upset by his father's death.

"I sent him to his room. He was misbehaving."

Tarleton threw his arms open in an extravagant gesture of disbelief. "How, madame, may a boy his age misbehave? Everything they do at that age is the outgrowth of their natural curiosity and desire. I want him. Fetch him to me."

He expected her to balk, like a horse approaching a bad jump.

But, calm as ever, she ducked her head. "As you wish, sir. James, come here please."

His head appeared over the railing on the landing of the stairs. He was a handsome boy, with intelligent features set in a face framed by curly hair and a cleft chin. "Yes, Mother."

"Colonel Tarleton requests the pleasure of your company for dinner," she said.

"But I already ate my—"

His mother's stern look conveyed an unmistakable message.

"Yes, Mother, I'll be right down."

The Richardsons' dining room was a plain rectangle of whitewashed plaster of uneven application. The table filled the room so near to its edges that there was little room for servants to pass behind the officers, much less for each of them to be waited on individually. Kinlock and the others didn't expect it, so it was not a problem, but it only served to reinforce Tarleton's impression that he was in a wilderness that wore its civilization like a borrowed overcoat that might be reclaimed at any moment.

Tarleton took his place at the head of the table, while his officers took the other seats. The last chair, at the end opposite Tarleton, sat empty. For a moment, Tarleton thought he glimpsed a blond boy sitting there in a red coat. Then he looked again and the boy was gone.

James appeared in the doorway in a clean shirt and jacket. Inwardly, Tarleton approved. The boy had the makings of a gentleman at least.

"Come here and stand at my side, James," Tarleton said.

James looked at his mother.

Tarleton hammered his fist on the table, causing boy and mother to jump. "You do not look to her for permission," he yelled. "I command here. When I tell you what to do, you must learn to do it."

The boy swallowed hard but mastered his fear. "Yes, sir."

"Very well," Tarleton said, softening his voice. "Now come stand at my side. You will eat some of every dish put in front of me."

James opened his mouth to protest, then looked at Tarleton's eyes and snapped it closed.

Excellent. Tarleton would not put it past these partisan sympathizers to poison the men they served at their table. From their constant raids and ambushes, he thought them capable of anything.

But Mrs. Richardson made no unexpected change in the service of her meal. Plate after plate came out to the table. James obligingly swallowed his bites, and then she served the other men. Tarleton, who had grown weary

of corn pone and hominy, enjoyed the uncommon pleasure of a real meal. Each bottle of wine, obligingly sipped
first by James as it was uncorked, was better than vine-
gar. A bargain at the price he paid for it, which was nothing, though Tarleton would not give it much more credit
than that. In all, he was almost enjoying himself.

As he wiped his mouth with his napkin between each
course, he noticed that Mrs. Richardson watched the
empty chair at the far end of the table with the avidity of
a hawk. With each serving dish that made its way around
the table, she obediently placed a scoop on the plate.

Tarleton did not know what she was up to, and, not
knowing what she was about, he was furious. He watched
her closely, looking for a clue, but could discover none.
While the other men conversed in general terms about
the campaign and British victories, Tarleton grew ever
more sullen. He would only blink or glance away for a
second, but every time he did, she found some way to clear
the plate of the food she had just placed on it. Some way
to empty the glass of its wine.

And none of the other men seemed to notice or, if they
noticed, care.

Finally, as Mrs. Richardson stood to the side of the
empty seat, ladling a spoon full of cobbler into the bowl
there, Tarleton lost his temper.

He wadded up his napkin and flung it on the table so
hard it knocked over his wineglass, which cracked,
spreading a red stain over the linen tablecloth. He kicked
back his chair and stood up.

"Madame," he said. "If you are so eager to serve an
extra seat, let me give you someone to serve."

A boy's chuckle echoed in the room, though James's
face, green with too much food and wine, registered only
fear.

"I want no one to move or leave this table," Tarleton
snapped.

He scarcely knew his own thoughts as he stomped out the front door until his eyes lit on the grave. Then it all came together. Yes, he would rattle the widow's cage and make her sing. He scanned the faces of the legionnaires until he saw the worst men of the lot, a pair of thieves, throat cutters who delighted in hurting men when they had the chance. Every unit in every army had a man or two of their type, Tarleton told himself, and it was for jobs like this.

"Grab some shovels, boys," he said, pointing to the two men. "General Richardson will be joining us for dinner."

They appeared puzzled for a second, then one whispered to the other, and they snickered like men in on a joke. In moments, they were flinging dirt aside. When they got down to the plain pine casket, they scraped the top clean and then pried the lid off. They looked up at Tarleton, disappointed.

"The silver's not in here, sir," the first one said.

"There's nothing in here but the old man's corpse," the second one said.

"You fools," Tarleton replied. "It's the corpse I want. Bring it in and prop it up at the end of the table."

Their shocked expressions transformed in a moment to the nervous laughter of men who set cats on fire to amuse themselves. The two men shrugged, and one of them reached under the general's arms while the other wrapped up his legs. The general had been buried in his uniform, which held the pieces of him together, more or less, as they carried him up the steps and into the dining room, leaving a trail of fallen dirt and scurrying insects along the way. Kinlock and his other officers looked on in a mixture of disbelief and horror, but Tarleton heard the young boy's chuckle again and he snapped at James.

"This is no laughing matter!"

The boy, whose eyes were wide with terror, had his hand clasped over his mouth, but not to keep from laughing. Instead, he turned to the corner and vomited up his dinner, the acid stew of meat and cheap wine splashing all over the wall, from the chair rail to the floor.

"Sir?"

Tarleton spun back. His two throat cutters were having a hard time propping up the corpse. Every time they set it up in the chair, it tilted to one side, leaving them to catch it before it spilled to the floor. They held it at uneasy arm's length between them.

"God damn it," Tarleton cursed like a man possessed. "God damn every man of you, if you do not do as I command."

The corpse's arms dangled to either side. He grabbed it by the wrists and pulled it forward, elbows across the table, and pushed the chair in so that it couldn't fall over. The head leaned forward, falling on one arm, like a drunk asleep at the table. Putrid flesh fell out of an eyesocket. White maggots squirmed like tears down a desiccated cheek.

"That's all—now get out," Tarleton said. The two men fled, pausing in the doorway to look back. "I said, get out!"

They shut the door behind them.

Tarleton walked calmly back to his seat at the head of the table. He picked up his napkin and wiped the dirt from his hands. Then he pulled down the front of his coat and tugged the cuffs of his sleeves back into place. He took his seat and cleared his throat.

"James," he said.

"Yes, sir," the boy said weakly, still huddled in the corner.

"I still expect you at my side."

"Yes, sir." The boy trembled as he shuffled over to Tarleton's side, staring at a spot on the ceiling so he wouldn't have to look at the table.

Richardson's widow stood next to her husband's body,

squeezing her hands to stop them from shaking. If Tarleton had entertained a notion that it might not be the general in the grave, one glance at the corpse disabused him. Even in death, the imprint of the general's features matched his son.

"You wished to serve someone in that seat," Tarleton told the widow. "I pray you continue."

Anger flashed across her features and hardened into resolve. She picked up a serving bowl and unceremoniously dumped a large wooden spoonful of potatoes on the plate. The bowl rattled when she dropped it on the table. She stood there rigidly staring straight ahead over the top of Tarleton's head.

Yes, said a boy's voice. *Yes, that's it, push her now, push her.*

Tarleton decided to push her.

"Feed him," he said, with a wave of his hand. "Go on and give him a spoonful."

Her chin trembled and her lips narrowed, but her hand was steady as she lifted a spoonful of potatoes to the dead man's mouth. She placed the spoon to the lips, held it there a second, and then put it down again. When she was done, she resumed the same rigid stance as before.

Tarleton slammed his fist on the table and the plates jumped. Kinlock and the other officers twitched in their seats, but said nothing.

"I said, feed him. Feed him the whole thing."

Yes, said the voice. *Yes, yes.*

Dutifully, she did as she was told. She stabbed the spoon into the potatoes, scraped it off on the dead man's mouth, then did it again.

His officers began to shift in their seats and clear their throats.

Tarleton was furious. He reached for the plate of mutton and tossed it down to her end of the table, spilling half its contents. "He looks like he needs some meat on his bones. You better feed him some meat."

She set the spoon down and without a word, picked up a fork and knife. After cutting a small piece of meat, she placed it on the fork and shoved it into the dead man's mouth. The metal scraped against the teeth as she pulled it out again empty. Kinlock winced at the sound. She took up the knife and began to cut another piece.

Rage shot through Tarleton. Could nothing shake her? He kicked his chair back and stood to yell at her again when a new voice, a man's voice, spoke.

Enough.

The room was frozen. Kinlock and the other officers had their faces turned toward Tarleton, or the corpse, or their eyes averted entirely, but their eyes, whatever direction they faced, were still and unblinking. Beside him, James stood with his chin elevated, caught in mid-sob.

Richardson's widow stood at the far end of the table as still as ever, but, as Tarleton watched, she tilted her head toward her dead husband's body.

A blond boy in the regulars' red coat stood on the opposite side of the general, mirroring the position of James at Tarleton's side. He had food stains on his shirt. His hair was a wild, unruly tangle of knots. His eyes glittered with an unearthly fire.

He placed his hand on the dead man's shoulder, and the corpse moved, animated by the spirit of the general, visible behind the bone and rotting flesh. Tarleton jumped. *What was this?*

"God forgive me, all my sins," Kinlock whispered.

James screamed and turned away, hiding his face. The widow covered her mouth, choking off a sob.

Don't tell them anything, my beloved, the corpse said.

"Tell us everything," said the boy in the red coat. "We know that you know the Salem witches. We are calling all of them—calling you—to our service."

"I'll never serve you," she said.

"What's going on here?" Tarleton asked.

They ignored him. He had gone from the man orchestrating this gross charade to a mere observer, and he didn't understand how or why. He had the feeling that he recognized the boy, that the boy had been his shadow since New York. But as hard as he tried, he could not call any of those memories to mind.

"Who would have thought you would be willing to serve a corpse," said the boy. He laughed, a sound wrong in its cheerfulness. He reached out and scooped a handful of potatoes off the corpse's chin and smeared them on the woman's shoulder. "And yet, you did exactly that, didn't you?"

"Go to hell," she said.

"Why go to hell, when I can bring hell here? Consider that I can consign your husband's soul to an eternity of torment if you do not do as I ask."

I can suffer anything, the dead man said. *Do not aid this beast.*

"God alone holds power over the afterlife," she said. "He will not allow it."

Tarleton felt sick. The enormity of what he had just done caught up with him. He was a soldier, yes, and war sometimes called for brutal and extraordinary measures. But this was unnatural, this was not who he was. He had been used by a demon. The smells of the room rushed in on him—the cheap wine, the vomit, the corpse—and he felt polluted.

The boy in the red coat shrugged. "If that's what you want to believe, fine. I cannot change your mind in that." With a smile, he skipped around the table. The corpse's head swiveled in the dead socket of its neck, looking to the wife, to the son.

The boy went behind James, draped his arms over the other boy's shoulders, and grinned, cheek-to-cheek.

James shrieked again and began to tremble, unable to move.

"No," the mother said.

You wouldn't, said the spirit in the corpse.

"But I'm so lonely," said the boy in the red coat. "I could use a playmate. Someone just like me. And what does it matter what I do in this world? God holds power over the afterlife—He will not allow any harm to befall the boy's soul. Would He?"

The woman reached out her hand, and the corpse reached up and clasped it. She shook her head in mute protest.

The boy took a step back and laughed.

Tarleton swung his fist with all his strength. The back-handed blow connected knuckles to jaw and knocked the boy in the red coat against the wall. He grabbed the boy by the lapels of his jacket and shook him like a terrier with a rat.

"I want all this undone," he screamed. "I want all evidence of this wiped away, do you hear me?"

The boy wiped the back of his hand across his mouth, smearing blood from his lip to his ear. His eyes glittered like the tips of sabers.

"If you're sure that's what you want," he said.

Tarleton blinked and he found himself outside the house. Richardson's widow huddled with her children as torches were set to the farmhouse, the summer kitchen, and the outhouse. His men were driving all the farm animals into the barn—the cattle, the pigs, even the chickens and geese. When they were done, they barred the doors shut and set that on fire too.

"Sir," Kinlock asked. He had a confused expression, as if he were forgetting something. "Are you sure we're doing the right thing?"

I want all the evidence wiped away, said a boy's voice. Tarleton looked to see where it came from and saw nothing. "Yes," he said. He must never show a weakness or doubt in his decisions. "They've been giving aid to the rebels. We saw proof of that. We can leave the neighborhood now, and know they'll render no more aid when we've gone."

"Yes, sir," Kinlock said. But there was a doubt behind his words. At some level, he knew that he was not asking about the barns and the stores.

Despite the sureness in his own voice, Tarleton felt tremors of doubt shiver through him. The cattle lowed mournfully and the hogs squealed in terror as the barn burned. The corncribs and the granaries, all of it was set aflame. Great clouds of black smoke rose, stinging Tarleton's eyes and blotting out the sun. He turned away and wiped tears from the corners of his eyes.

That's when he saw a woman walking toward the house.

She came down the oak-lined road, alone, wearing no more than a plain gray dress, but glowing like a torch brighter than the burning flames beneath the clouds of smoke. She walked through the anxious horses of his men, and they shied away from her. She walked past his men, and they shielded their eyes and turned away their heads. She walked through the rain of sparks and ash until she stood in front of Tarleton.

No one walked toward him, not this way, not in this country.

"Who in the damned hell are you?" he demanded.

"My name is Deborah Brown," she said. "And I've been summoned."

Chapter 21

It was the middle of the night. Proctor still had not grown accustomed to his imprisonment, and not even the luxurious bed that Grueby had delivered for him could tempt him to sleep. So he was awake and pacing when he heard a distant door creak, followed a short time later by the soft pad of footsteps outside his door.

A key snapped into the lock, tumblers turned, and the door opened. A hooded man stood there in a heavy cloak, his features lit by the light of a candle atop a heavy candlestick.

"May I help you?" Proctor asked. Although the better question was: will you help me?

The man pulled the hood off his head. He had a round face with a somewhat dull but pugnacious appearance. His cheeks were chapped red from exposure to the wind, and Proctor imagined him as a rather single-minded gardener. He went to take a step across the threshold and stopped.

The demon sat on the man's shoulder, with one hand thrust wrist-deep into his skull. Its face was a twin to the candle's fire, the emotions jumping across it as quick as a flame. It was the demon that Dee and his followers had released during the fires of the riots. It would be invisible to anyone not practiced in the spirit world, but Proctor could see it.

He retreated to the back wall of his cell. He couldn't face the creature without his power. He would be helpless if it wanted to possess him. He looked around frantically for a weapon and saw none.

But the demon wasn't interested in entering the room. It glanced at the walls where the wards were hidden, and it hissed and bared its teeth and tried to pull its host back. The man started to sweat and his hands to shake. When he spoke, he stammered.

"L-l-leave me al-l-lone, you p-p-petty vile thing."

Despite the uncertain delivery of his words, he spoke with the confidence of a man who expected to be obeyed. The demon shrank at his command. Proctor rose from his spot against the wall and came forward. Maybe this man could help him. As he stepped forward into the light, the man startled.

"You—you're not Lord Gordon."

Proctor was almost too stunned to react. "No, I'm not! You can see that?" He held out his hands in supplication. "Please—tell someone. Help me get out of here."

"I w-w-wanted Gordon," the man said. He jerked the hood up over his head and then slammed the door shut.

Proctor threw himself against the wood as the key turned in the lock. "No, please—I can help you just as much as Gordon." He pounded on the door with his fists. "I can help you more! Come back! Don't leave me here."

He pounded and called until the guard came down the hall. "What's with all the noise in there? Other people are trying to sleep."

"Who was that? Who just came to see me?"

"There's been nobody here," he said. He voice softened now that Proctor had stopped screaming and pounding. "You were dreaming, having nightmares. It happens often to men their first weeks here. It will get better." He kicked the door. "Now go back to bed and leave the night to sleep in peace."

Proctor could not fall asleep. He was fairly certain that he had just met King George.

*   *   *

"They hanged more of the rioters," the guard said.

Proctor stared out the window at the tower walls, but said nothing. Weeks had passed and he was still in prison.

"Don't you want to know who?" the guard asked. "They're hanging because of you."

"They're hanging because of their own bad decisions." Proctor held on to the bars as if he were holding on to the truth of that statement.

"I suppose you're right," the guard said. "Today they hanged a simpleton, a fellow from some village outside the city. He was the one who carried Gordon's flag. He murdered a man in front of Parliament."

Barnaby? Proctor shook his head in denial. Barnaby was a kind soul, harmless.

"Oh, and they hanged some black men too. Or two black men and a black woman."

Proctor spun around. "Who? Who was she?"

"The woman? How should I know? She never gave her name, but there were enough witnesses who saw her during the riots to convict her. She was outside the distillery when it burned. God, that was a horror. Why does it matter to you?"

Proctor ran to the door to grab the man and shake him, but he stopped short. "What did she look like?"

The guard laughed and shut the door. "What do they all look like? She was black."

Proctor's head sunk. He had failed.

Proctor went back to the window. A group of ravens perched on the tower wall, dropping into the yard to feed. A black shape flew over the rooftops. The other birds flapped their wings and called to it, and it swooped in to join them.

"Hallo, you're a devil, you're a saucy devil. Hallo."

Barnaby's raven, with its master dead, had sought someplace else to live.

"Hallo, you're a devil."

Proctor ran to the window and screamed. "Be quiet! All of you be quiet!"

The noise disturbed the ravens, who lifted into the air, wings flapping, but then settled back down again. Barnaby's raven strutted across the yard in front of them, tilting his head at Proctor's window.

Hallo, you're a devil.

He had come to accept that this was no mistake, no nightmare. He was trapped here, by the power of the world and the power of magic both. No one would come to admit their mistake. No one would come to save him. He had to escape, not just for his own sake, but for his wife and daughter. Because there might still be a chance to help his country.

Proctor walked to the center of the room and knelt down by the floor. He could see faint marks of ash where the last of Deborah's hair had burned away when his focus was destroyed.

He tore open the scab that had formed where Dee peeled back the scar on his finger. Pain shot through his hand, but he gritted his teeth, and as the blood flowed over the raw bone of his knuckle, he smeared it along the lightest and faintest of the ash marks. With his thumb, he rubbed it into the stone, holding in his mind the image of Deborah—the sharp intelligence of her eyes, the reluctant smile on her lips, the flower that she'd tuck behind an ear and then forget.

"This is my blood," he said. "Shed for you."

The dark stain on the dark stone stared back at him like a frowning mouth, bloody and mute. He reached up and tried to remove the necklace, and immediately it choked him until he let it go again, and fell to the floor, panting for breath.

*   *   *

Day after day, Proctor stood at the barred window and studied the grounds, the austere strength of the high White Tower, the sturdy presence of the thick walls, the stagnant odor of the moat. He could hear conversations in the room below his, where the Bloody Tower's other prisoner was kept. His appetite faded and he ate only the amount necessary to keep going and gave the rest to other prisoners who couldn't afford their meals, or sent it to the poorer families who lived inside the Tower walls.

Grueby, come to check on him each day, frowned at the unfinished plates of food. "We're working to delay the trial as long as possible," he said. "To let the memory of the riots fade some in the city's memory. But that delay won't last forever. You should keep your health up."

"So I can walk to the scaffold under my own power?" Proctor asked.

"If you must face the hangman, you should face him like a gentleman," Grueby said. "But I do not expect it to come to that. The guards say that no one unexpected comes to visit you."

"Some friends of Gordon come from time to time, but if I try to tell them who I am or what has happened, they treat me like I'm raving and beat a hasty retreat," he said, remembering the number of times he had choked and collapsed. "Must be the 'fits.' "

"You have poor friends who would leave you here," Grueby answered.

"I have excellent friends," Proctor said. "But they have no idea where I am."

"I could take letters perhaps," Grueby replied.

"Give me the money and I will purchase what I need from the warden," Proctor said.

Grueby said, "I don't want to trouble you. I will buy it myself and return with it sometime. In the meantime, you should take your exercise out in the gardens."

"I have been told there's a fee for that as well," Proctor said.

"The more money they think a man has, the more they try to get out of him," Grueby answered. "I'll talk to the warden and see what can be done."

Proctor watched him as he left. He had a routine, where he stopped and checked in with the warden, the guards, the other staff. Using them to spy on Proctor, no doubt. But what was he looking for? And if Proctor gave it to him, would they let him free?

One of the servants brought word that His Lordship, George Gordon, was permitted to walk in the Tower grounds while under guard. The guards were for his own protection, as there was still much hard feeling about the riots and their aftermath.

On his first day in the gardens, the guards were talking about the news from America. Generally, the guards didn't speak to the prisoners directly, not in public. But if there was news they thought the prisoners would like to know, they would share it with one another so the prisoner could overhear.

"Cornwallis has turned up the heat in the colonies," the guard said. "Ever since they captured the American army at Charleston, it's been one victory after another. They could crush the rebellion by Christmas."

"It's not all Cornwallis," the second guard replied. "I read that most of it is Colonel Banastre Tarleton. He defeated a force twice his own size at a place called Waxhaws, and he's had victories in every other place that he's faced the enemy."

"I met him once at Oxford," the first guard said. "And I wasn't that impressed. Something must have got into him since he went to America."

"Whatever got into him knows how to fight," the second guard said. "He's got Washington's army on the run. It'll take longer than Christmas, I suspect, but it will get done—"

They spoke in more details about the war in America, and Proctor grew increasingly anxious. Had the plans of the Covenant succeeded so quickly? How had the war, a stalemate when he left, shifted so suddenly and decisively toward the English? He suspected that the answer involved black magic, and was not the doing of the English at all.

His walk brought him to the farthest part of the gardens from his room. He reached up and grabbed the necklace, expecting he could break the spell that hid his identity.

He woke up on the grass, with the guards splashing water in his face.

There had been so much blood shed within these walls that the power of the spell, centered in his room, extended as far as the grounds.

"Your strength will come back in time," they said. "Fresh air and exercise, that's all you need."

He needed more than that, but maybe it was a start.

The Tower was a city within the city, a complex of twenty towers built over centuries, surrounded by a wall and moat. To escape, he needed to get out of his room, which he had done. Then he needed to escape his own guards, which he had confidence he could do. Then he had to pass a series of gates and walls and a moat, all guarded, and where he would be refused passage at each point. Once he had escaped the walls, he would be loose in London, without resources or allies. All alone, he would have to find the Covenant and defeat their plan before returning to America to make sure that Deborah and Maggie were safe.

If he tried to think about all of it, he was overwhelmed. So he would have to take it one step at a time. He was walking in the garden one day still early in the summer, followed by a pair of fusiliers and lost in thought about how to solve this problem, when he felt something heavy bump his hand. He turned, expecting a dog, and jumped. It was a lion, with a huge mane and powerful shoulders. Proctor had never seen such a creature before, like a cat, or a panther, but as big as a black bear. He tossed his head and made a sound between a roar and a bark.

"He's just looking for something to eat," one of his guards explained.

"And if I don't have any?" Proctor said.

"He might decide you are something to eat," the guard replied.

"How much would he have to pay for me?" Proctor asked. "It might be worth the price."

He meant to ask how much he could get for just a hand or a foot when he saw a familiar face walking across the yard. Thomas Digges, wrapped in a heavy coat, glanced once at Proctor and then quickened his pace. Proctor took after him.

"Don't run away, you'll only agitate him," the guard called.

Proctor glanced back and saw the lion bounding alongside him. He stopped, startled, and the lion turned just as quick and batted at him with a front paw. The guards ran into its way, threatening it with their guns, and it backed down. Proctor thought he might use the moment as a distraction, but other guards came to separate him and the lion, and both were watched just as closely. They called for the animal keepers, who came out with some freshly butchered meat to draw the lion away.

"Can I pet him?" Proctor asked.

"Sure, go on," his guard said. "He's a good-natured cat, but it's best not to excite him. When the children come to see him, we always make sure he's well fed and sleepy first. And we have them keep their distance. He's never bitten anyone who matters."

Proctor stroked his hand deep through the lion's mane. "There was a man crossing the garden," he said. "Where was he going?"

"I don't know," said the first guard.

"He must be visiting the American," said the second.

"There's an American in the Tower?" Proctor asked, continuing to pet the lion.

"Henry Laurens," said the first guard. "Don't you read the news? He was sent as a diplomat to the Netherlands, but we caught him on the way. It's why we've gone to war with the Dutch. We're not allowed to let him speak to anyone, except those approved through diplomatic channels, but there are plenty enough of those come to visit him."

"Ah," Proctor said. "Would that he were the only American to ever grace this prison."

The guards looked puzzled, until one of them said, "Oh, because there'll be no more America?"

Before Proctor could respond, the lion suddenly turned its head and snapped at him, and the guards quickly pulled him and the lion apart.

"Maybe you shouldn't pet the lion anymore," the guard said.

"I think that's best," Proctor answered. "I'll go back to my room now."

When he was escorted back to his quarters, and the door was shut and closed, he opened his hand and looked at the lion's hair he had gathered. It was pulled out by the roots, which should give it more power as a focus. He took one of his candles and set one hair on fire, burning it in the center of the floor where Deborah's hair had burned.

Then he hesitated. Blood magic was black magic. He thought of the rioters dying in the street, in fire and blood, and the way that Dee had used it to summon a demon. By using fire and magic the same way, was Proctor pulling himself closer to their world? Was he aligning himself with their magic, their way of changing the world?

Did he care?

He was trapped by blood magic. He could see no other way out. He sorted his memory for Bible verses about lions, setting aside those that had lions laying down with lambs or comparing Satan to a lion. He scratched open the scab on his finger and smeared a stain of blood across the floor, overlaying a stain he had already made once before.

"The righteous are as bold as a lion," he said. "Let me rise up, as bold as a lion. Let me not lie down until I have taken the prey and tasted the blood of the slain."

He felt a tingle flow through him, faint as a fly's wing brushing his skin, but it made him think that he had touched the source of magic. He reached up and grabbed the necklace, hoping to remove it and break the spell.

He awoke on the floor. When he touched his neck, he could feel the deep gouges left there by the chain of the necklace.

It had been a good thought.

The days passed into weeks, and the weeks into months. The long days of summer grew ever shorter and darker. The trees gave up their fruit and the leaves turned color. Proctor walked in the garden every day to build his strength. When he was alone in his room, he lifted the heavy furniture over and over to keep strong. Every day Grueby visited Proctor, and every day they had a similar exchange.

"You promised to bring me paper and pen," Proctor said.

"I forgot," Grueby said. "But I'll make a note and remember to do it soon. In the meantime, I hope you continue your walks in the gardens."

So every day, Proctor took walks in the gardens and studied the marvelous animals in the menagerie. Quagga grazed on the grasses. They were a sort of wild horse from Africa, with black and white stripes in front and brown behind. The keepers explained that it helped them blend into the scrub where they were found. Monkeys ran among the trees, pulling hats off the visitors and flinging things at them. The ravens gathered on the wall, where the keepers clipped their wings so they couldn't fly away.

Proctor thought he saw Barnaby's raven, Grip, but though the bird marched back and forth and stared at him familiarly, it never spoke again.

A month passed before he spied Digges again. Their eyes met, and though Digges kept on walking, Proctor felt like a promise had been made between them. He lingered among the peacocks near the garden gate, boring the guards with his silence and inactivity, and waited for Digges to leave.

"You don't look well, my lord," Digges said, pausing to watch the flock of birds.

"I'm no one's lord," Proctor said, tugging at the chain around his neck. He had to be careful with what he said.

Digges did not look up. "Gordon?"

"Let those who have eyes, see. Are you Church now?"

"Warburton."

"What brings you here, Mister Warburton?"

"To check on the welfare of Mister Laurens and see if there is anything he needs." He glanced at Proctor's injured hand, but it looked complete to anyone seeing him through the illusion. "I am not amused by your prank, sir."

Proctor searched his brain for something that only he would know, that Gordon wouldn't. "Franklin doesn't like you much. Israel Potter would walk more easily in boots with lower heels."

Digges shifted uncomfortably. "Brown?"

The necklace twitched at his throat like a living thing. "I can't speak of it. Can you get me any money? I must buy everything here for my own needs, but I don't have Gordon's income at my disposal."

Digges stroked his beard to a point. "Oh, good. I thought you'd ask for something difficult, like a winged horse or an army to command."

Two of the guards had noticed Digges lingering near the man they took for Gordon and came over to investigate. "Is there something we can help you with here?"

Digges shook his head. "Be careful," he said. "You can never tell when a peacock might be a common raven in disguise."

He exited the grounds, leaving Proctor behind him without an answer or a promise.

As Proctor watched him go, he spied Gordon's man Grueby lingering among the Tower visitors. He turned away as Proctor glanced in his direction.

Weeks passed, and Digges did not return. It was a cold dismal fall. Proctor saw the American, Henry Laurens, walking in the gardens under guard. He was not supposed to speak to anyone else, but Proctor arranged to go outside, and then immediately left the path he had promised his guard he would take and approached the American as he paced.

"Excuse me, sir," he said.

Laurens, his face drawn and angry, looked up, startled. "I don't believe we've been introduced."

"George, Lord Gordon," Proctor said, thrusting out his hand in a typically American gesture. "Pleased to meet you."

Laurens looked up, startled, while his guards attempted to place themselves between the two men. "I'm sorry, sir," one said to Proctor. "But I must ask you to refrain from speaking to the prisoner."

"Surely, you can permit us a simple civil exchange," Proctor said. Gordon's guards had arrived and now placed themselves between the two men. Proctor spoke over them. "We are both prisoners, we both wish an end to the mutual hostilities of our nations, and we share a mutual friend, a Mister Warburton."

Laurens's brows drew down and his face shut off any emotion. "I don't have any idea who you mean."

The guards pushed them apart, very angry with Laurens. "My mistake," Proctor yelled, though he doubted it would do Laurens any good.

If Digges didn't come through for him, he was going to have to find some other way to get the things he needed. He looked out his window toward the Traitor's Gate and wondered if there might be some way to escape by way of the river.

Grueby did not appear one day; a different servant from the kitchens brought Proctor his plate of food. Proctor stood at his window and gestured toward the table. "Leave it there," he said.

"Yes, Your Lordship," came the reply.

Proctor spun at the voice. It was Digges, his face dirtied and his clothes matching those commonly used by the servants. A guard stood in the hall. Digges placed the serving tray on the table, blocking the guard's view with his body, and lifted the lid on the plate. A heavy purse sat there among the food.

"It's a rich meal, Your Lordship," he said. "If you eat it all, you shall gain a hundred pounds."

"I'm feeling a bit thin," Proctor said. "Thank you."

Digges ducked his head and made his way out. Proctor pocketed the purse, wondering where he should hide it and what he might want to buy.

He looked at the plaid pants he was wearing and decided the first thing he was going to buy would be clothes.

* * *

More than seven months had passed. Christmas came and went, with no news of a final victory over the Rebellion. Some guards still spoke of Tarleton's successes; others talked about his cruel excesses. The winter brought frequent visitors to Laurens as the Americans tried to negotiate his release. Proctor stood at the window, listening to the muffled sound of their conversation in the rooms below, when Grueby arrived.

Proctor did no more than glance at him until he set ink and paper down on the table.

"We can put it off no longer. Your trial is scheduled to begin in days," Grueby said. "If you wish to escape here, I suggest you write your true friends."

Proctor's heart leapt up. "Finally," he said. "The chance that I've been waiting for."

Grueby stood over him while he wrote two letters addressed to his wife and daughter. When he finished, he handed them to Grueby, who scowled, tore them up, and fed them to the fire.

"You can't write those things," he said. "No one will believe that you are not Lord Gordon. No one will believe this talk of blood and demons."

"But it's the truth," Proctor said, looking at the pages curling in the hearth. He touched the necklace. "Interesting, that I can write the truth to someone who already knows it and not fall down choking."

"Is there no one else you want to write to? No code you wish to employ?"

"None," Proctor said. "Is this what you were told to do, Mr. Grueby? Is it what you feel like doing?"

Grueby snapped up the ink and paper. He looked around for the quill but, not finding it, stormed out of the room.

Proctor rushed to the fire and pulled out the charred bits of the paper. He carried them cupped in his hands to the spot in the center of the room, already dark with ash and blood. Deborah's hair had marked a sunburst pattern in ash there. Proctor had written over every mark in his own blood, day by day across the weeks. He had slowly and meticulously repeated the marks with the lion's hair for strength, the quagga's hair for disguise, the monkey's hair for cunning, and none of it had worked.

Now he knelt down over the sun formed of ash and blood, and in a passionate rush he smeared the ash into the lines he had marked before.

"Ye shall know the truth," he said with each hurried mark of his thumb.

When he was done, he took the quill from the pocket where he had hidden it and jabbed it into the unhealed scar on his hand. Only the tools of those who had trapped him in the necklace and imprisoned him could break the spell and set him free. Drawing blood onto the end of the quill, he scooted around the floor in a circle, slashing red lines over the marks in ash.

With each slash of the pen, he said, "The truth shall set me free."

He could feel the lightning running through his whole body as he completed the circle. He cast aside the quill and stepped into the middle of the circle.

Blood magic could be defeated by blood magic. Slowly, over the months, he had shed enough to create one spot here in the middle of this room that the spell on the Tower could not touch. Or so he hoped.

He grabbed hold of the necklace and felt it sting his hand.

Bracing himself for the worst, he pulled on it and felt it tighten against his neck. He gritted his teeth and prepared to be choked unconscious.

But it was only the normal pull of metal against skin. He yanked and the chain broke. The light went out in the gem on the pendant.

He ran to the window and gasped for breath. He could hear the voices below, saying their farewells to Laurens.

Had he done it? Had he broken the spell?

He would only have one chance to find out. He had bribed one of the servants to bring him ordinary clothes, cut in the plain style of the Americans, and paid her extra to keep silent about it. He hurried and changed and then went to the door. The guards did not stand outside his room, but watched the Tower exit.

Proctor hurried down the steps and joined the group of merchants, religious men, and diplomats representing the American interests in London. They looked at him oddly but said nothing as he followed them to the exit.

The guards at the exit stared at Proctor for a moment and he thought that all was lost.

Then they turned their heads away. Clearly they didn't recognize him, and in a group with the Americans they let him pass through gates and over the moat.

He looked up at the gray sky and felt the cold drizzle of rain on his face.

He was free. If he did not feel the weight of months of preparation, the sharp pain of the scar on his hand where he'd drawn so much blood, he would have called it easy. But the hard part was only just beginning.

Where did he go next?

Grueby would know.

Chapter 22

Proctor was sure he could find his way to Gordon's house on Welbeck Street, but if everyone thought Gordon was in prison, it was doubtful he was staying there. Grueby still took his orders from Gordon, and he would run back to his master as soon as he found Proctor missing.

It was the next day before Grueby returned. Proctor watched for him from a doorway opposite the Tower entrance. It wasn't until he saw Gordon's man go strolling through the gate with his breakfast that he felt all the anger flood through him. Eight months of his life lost in prison, and who knew what had happened to Deborah or Maggie in the meantime.

He forced himself to calm down. His time in the Tower had taught him that skill. He had to decide whether he wanted vengeance on Gordon for locking him away, or vengeance on the Covenant for the success of their plans. How much of his old life could still be salvaged? And if all that remained was wreckage, did he want it?

Grueby returned through the gate very shortly with a bundle of items under his arms and made his way down to the riverbank. He tied a rock inside the bundle and hurled it out into the river. Dumping all the evidence of Proctor's escape. That was neatly done. Proctor respected Grueby as a practical man.

Grueby mounted a horse and took off through the streets. Proctor jogged after him. Little chimney sweeps, covered with sores and black dust, laughed at him as he ran. One stuck out his pole to trip Proctor, but Proctor moved his hand and knocked it out of the way. He had gone another block before he realized that he had done the spell just by thinking of it. All the months of working on the blood magic of the Tower had increased his power incredibly.

When Grueby turned his horse down Bond Street, Proctor thought he might be going to Gordon's house after all. But then he turned again, into a neighborhood of mansions that dwarfed Gordon's house in size and ornamentation the way that Gordon's house dwarfed a poor man's farmhouse. A broad park lined with trees—was it called a commons here? Proctor wondered—sat at the heart of the neighborhood. Grueby entered a large house of beautiful formal proportions at the southwest corner of the park.

"Excuse me," Proctor said to a stranger. The gentleman ignored him and walked on by. Proctor tried again, this time addressing a man in servant's clothes. "Where am I?"

"If you ask me, you're lost," the servant answered.

"I'm sorry," Proctor said. "I've just arrived in London."

"You ought to turn around and go back where you came from," the man said, walking away. "Not much has been right here since the riots."

"What's this neighborhood?" Proctor persisted, following alongside him.

"Berkeley Square. Now if that's all—"

"And that house?"

The man stopped, frustrated but plainly willing to answer one more question if it meant Proctor would stop accosting him. "That's Lansdowne, the earl of Shelburne's house," the man said. "I've worked in his gardens. Don't even think about robbing him."

"I'm not here to rob anyone," Proctor said. "I followed a man I know, someone I don't trust, and saw him enter there."

"Shelburne's a politician. They're always in deep with men who can't be trusted. And the earl, he considers himself enlightened. Keeps company with scientists and philosophers and all sorts of unsavory, untrustworthy folks." He tipped his cap to Proctor. "Now good day. And don't get caught hanging about or they'll take you before the bench."

Proctor stood in the park and watched the house while trying not to look like a thief. What were Grueby and Gordon doing here? And did Proctor have to worry about magic again?

He shook his head at that. Gordon wasn't coming near him.

The house was surrounded by trees and formal hedges. Proctor waited until a carriage had passed, then crossed the street and walked toward the front of the house. With a glance over his shoulder, he slipped into the trees and ventured a small spell to avert any watchful eyes.

Not that there were many watchful eyes. As he circled the house, it appeared to be empty. There were no servants anywhere—even the stable in back was empty except for horses and a carriage. The curtains were all drawn shut as well.

He watched the house, considering what to do next. As he watched, he saw the draperies shift. Someone inside was impatiently watching the street at the rear of the house. Proctor was willing to bet it was Gordon.

He went up to the servants' door and tried the handle. It was unlatched. He stepped inside and closed it quietly behind him. Voices came from the room where the draperies had moved. One of them was Gordon's.

Proctor calmed himself. And walked to the doorway.

Three men stood inside the room: Grueby, Gordon—still wearing plain clothes and an air of despair—and a third man dressed more like the French noblemen Proctor had seen. He assumed he was the earl of Shelburne. The walls were lined with furniture of elegant proportions, all spaced evenly and regularly.

Gordon shrank away from the sight of Proctor. "Restrain him at once," he ordered Grueby.

Proctor knotted his hands into fists.

But Grueby shook his head. "No, sir, I don't feel like it." With a look at Proctor, he said, "Thought you would get here eventually. Didn't think it would be so fast."

"Mr. Grueby was just describing your remarkable escape from the Bloody Tower to us," Shelburne said. He was a handsome man in his forties, neat and orderly, with a calm and rational tone to his voice.

"Did they tell you why I needed to escape?" Proctor said. He took a step forward. His hands were still knotted into fists.

"I'm sorry," Gordon said. "You carried a token of the Covenant. I had to be sure you were not one of their allies."

"Fighting them, trying to stop them—that wasn't enough?" Proctor asked.

"You have to understand," Gordon explained. "A witch appeared, out of America, with more knowledge and power than one would expect from such a place. There is no one there to teach you, no one but the Covenant."

"You don't know Deborah," Proctor said.

"And then you came from France, which is Britain's enemy. And you—"

Proctor held up his right fist, turned so that Gordon could see the bloody scar of his missing finger. "I've bled to stop the Covenant. Have you? Because I would be glad to help you."

Gordon fell silent. Grueby rolled his tongue through his cheek.

"You can attack us if you wish," Shelburne said calmly. "You can expend your first breath of freedom and possibly your last breath in pursuit of revenge—"

"I was thinking of it in terms of justice," Proctor said.

"Fair enough," Shelburne answered. "Or you can use your power to help us defeat the Covenant. It is why we are here today. Mister Brown—and please forgive me for forgoing the formalities of introduction—I appeal to your rational side."

Proctor slowly unballed his fists and crossed his arms over his chest. "I'm listening."

"We have come here today to save the king. Your talent and experience may be of practical assistance."

Proctor boggled. "What cause do I have to save the king?"

"The cause of freedom. You oppose the Covenant. I have spent my whole life fighting the machinations of that occult cabal, just as my father did before me. Yet they are closer now to taking their next great step to power than they ever have been before. For almost two hundred years, their goal has been to build an empire that circles the globe. If they can possess His Majesty's will, as is their intention, nothing will stand in their way."

"Nothing but the will of the American people to be free."

"You may believe that if you wish. And given the evidence of your own desire to be free, and your ability to achieve it, I would hesitate to underestimate our American cousins. But if His Majesty's will is possessed by the Covenant, you can be sure they will turn all their attention to subjugating America."

"It seems like that was exactly what was happening when His Majesty's will was his own," Proctor said.

There was a tap at the door.

"They're here," Grueby said.

Gordon looked as if he wanted to run to the doorway, but was afraid to pass Proctor. He cupped his hands to his mouth and called, "In here."

Shelburne met Proctor's eyes. "I appeal to your own self-interest. I appeal to your love of your native country. If you will not help us, do not hinder us. But the choice, of course, is yours."

"It always has been," Proctor said.

Shelburne took this rebuke with magnanimity, bowing his head slightly and opening his palm.

Two men appeared in the doorway, one of them cloaked and hooded. Proctor recognized him at once from the visit to the Tower, even before he removed the hood and revealed the leering demon squatting on his shoulder. The demon chuckled. He had one ethereal arm plunged into the back of the man's head. He was accompanied by an Anglican priest.

"Your Majesty," said the three men, all of them bowing.

"One of them is looking at me," the king whispered to the priest. "Why is he looking at me?"

"I don't know who he is, Sire," the priest said.

"He's an American, Sire," explained Shelburne.

King George pounded his fist into his palm. "Americans. Y-y-you've been a thorn in our side these past few years—"

"Sire," the priest said. He was a compact man with sun-darkened skin; despite his delicately framed spectacles and scholarly air, he appeared to be someone who spent more time out of doors than secluded in some dark chapel or musty library. He also held great power. "We are here for a reason. We don't know how long our attempt will take. Perhaps we'd best get started."

"Yes, right, of course, that's why we're here," George said. "Where are we going to do this?"

"In the dining room, Sire," Shelburne said, indicating the way with a gesture of his hand. "We have been preparing it for several months."

King George's face fell. "I thought it might be best to do it at some sacred place of great power like Stonehenge."

"Stonehenge is aligned with the stars," Shelburne admitted, "which does give it great power. But it was built thousands of years ago, and I am reliably informed by our astronomers that the stars no longer align."

"How can that be?" the king asked.

"Given a great enough span of time, everything changes."

The men spoke as they followed Shelburne through the halls. Gordon stayed close to the king and the priest. Proctor followed at the rear, behind Grueby. He felt lost, as if he had walked into the middle of not just a conversation, but one in a different language.

The king sighed. "So even the firmament is not so firm as we once believed. But isn't that where our friends have been at work on our behalf?"

"If you mean the white horse at Cherhill, Doctor Alsop has seen to its completion," the priest said.

"I'm sorry," the king said, pausing at a closed door. "We seem to have forgotten introductions. Do all of you know the special secretary to the Archbishop of Canterbury?"

"Your Reverend," Shelburne said, with a smaller bow of his head than he had offered the king.

Gordon extended his hand, but the priest did not take it. "I'm sorry, Your Reverend," Gordon said. "I didn't catch your name."

"I have no name," the priest replied. "I exist only as an office."

Gordon laughed nervously. "The office of secretary?"

"A secretary is one who keeps secrets," the priest answered. "And no secret is more important than this. Again, I suggest that perhaps we should not waste our time."

"No, of course we shouldn't," Gordon agreed. He looked to Shelburne and indicated Proctor with a nod of his head. "Should we include him in this?"

"I want to be included," Proctor said.

"Yes," said Shelburne. "If he wants to help us after the great injustice that has been done to him."

"What injustice?" the king asked.

Gordon stared at the floor. Shelburne pushed open the door to the ballroom, saying, "It is no concern of yours, Sire. It was done, it has ended, and it will be remedied."

"Any injustice that happens within the compass of my realm is my c-c-concern," the king insisted. His face had grown red, and the words came out haltingly, turning into a stammer by the end. The demon stirred on his shoulder. In the daylight, it was hard to see the creature. Proctor was not even sure that anyone else could spy it. He drew power into himself to take hold of it if he could.

"Interesting," murmured the priest with no name. He looked straight at the demon. So two of them knew what they faced. The priest held out his palm, indicating to Proctor that he should stay back. "Be calm," the priest commanded.

The king drew a breath. The demon's twitching subsided.

"How did . . . that happen?" Proctor said.

"He's looking directly at me again," the king whispered to the priest.

"He doesn't know any better," the priest said. "But you may answer him. When he saw the danger, his first instinct was to come to your aid."

"Dee, the necromancer, has been plotting this a very long time. He attempted to possess my father first, only it killed him, and I ascended to the throne in-in-instead."

Shelburne opened the door and entered the room ahead of them. It had high ceilings, with marvelous natural light. A large crystal candelabra hung from the ceiling, catching and refracting light throughout the room. The ceiling was decorated with elaborate plasterwork. The same patterns were picked up in the imprints of urns and vines spaced evenly around the walls. The walls without windows were set with nine niches. Each niche held a life-sized statue, carved in marble, as beautiful as the ones that Proctor had seen in the gardens of Paris. The neutral paints were chosen to bring out the natural color of the statues. Chairs and serving tables lined the rail along the wall.

"Yes, yes," murmured the priest in satisfaction.

As King George entered the room, his knees buckled. No one dared catch him, but he caught himself on the priest, who stood as still as a doorpost. "M-m-may we be-begin this business?"

"Are you well enough to continue, Sire?" Gordon asked.

"Yes," the king said. He mopped his forehead with a handkerchief, pasted a smile on his face, and struggled to sound normal. The demon struggled, just as it had at the doorway to Proctor's room in the Bloody Tower. "Is that Tyche?" the king asked, pointing to one of the statues.

"Yes, Sire," Shelburne replied.

"The god of luck," the king said to the priest. "Though we all know there is but one God—may He have mercy on our souls—nevertheless I think I shall prefer to be seated where I can look on Tyche and he can look on me."

"I think that's very logical," the priest said.

"This whole house is designed as a tribute to rationality and the great works of man," Shelburne said. "When we embrace the rational and scientific view of the world, we will weaken and perhaps destroy the power that Dee and others like him gain by drawing on the unwitting contributions of the ignorant and superstitious."

He grabbed one of the chairs from against the wall and swung it into position in the center of the room.

The king started to sit down, then popped up again immediately as if it were hot. "It-it-it wants me to l-l-leave—"

"Calm," the priest said, with the same motion of his hand at his waist.

The king sat, but he seemed very twitchy, as if he was fighting the urge to rise. "Is this going to hurt? I've heard that Gassner strikes his patients on the head."

Proctor wanted to ask who Gassner was, but refrained. "Maybe if we hit him hard enough, we can knock that creature loose."

"He's joking, Sire," Gordon said. "No one is going to strike you on the head."

"I will not call the German exorcist a fraud," the priest added quickly. "But I have observed him at work, and the good he does is as much by chance as it is by design. Like many men, he neither comprehends nor holds in leash his own power." He stared meaningfully at Proctor. "Sire, we need to begin by speaking with your guest."

"What good will that do?" the king asked.

"I intend to ask it to leave."

"And if it says no?" Proctor asked.

The priest leaned close to the demon, which turned and bared its teeth at him, making a sound like crackling fire. "Then I shall become persuasive," the priest said. "Will the three of you stand over there, along the fourth wall? Just as if you were three more statues. My lord, Shelburne, if you would stand in the middle. Thank you. Mister Grueby, if you will fetch my bag from the entry, please."

They took their positions while Grueby retrieved a plain canvas bag. He handed it to the priest and then took up his position again as a guard by the door. The priest removed a coil of rough hemp rope from the bag.

"I'm not going to tie you to the chair, Sire," the priest said. "These ropes will protect you from harm if your guest tries to force his will upon you."

Proctor almost laughed.

"Speak the truth to His Majesty," Shelburne said forcefully. "He is your liege and he deserves it."

The priest paused for a moment, then nodded. "These lengths of rope come from the nooses of hanged men. Or rather, hanged men and women."

"From the late riots?" asked the king.

The priest nodded.

Gordon stared at the floor again. Proctor thought of Lydia. He had avoided thinking of her for months. Whether she was alive or dead, there was nothing he could do to help her. Seeing the length of rope in the priest's hand made that feel rather selfish to him. If he had led her to death . . .

"How do they work?" the king asked.

"We hope to use them to bind your guest, but since your guest occupies a space with—"

"I g-g-get it," the king said impatiently. "I am not some coward. I am not some delicate flower that needs to be nurtured in a hothouse. Show me the enemy, put a sword in my hand, and send me to f-f-face him—"

The demon twisted its arm back and forth inside the king's skull, and the words stuttered to a halt.

"Our enemies used blood magic to set the spell, so we will use the same to break it," the priest said. "They used the blood of those shed in the riot to bring harm to you. We will use the blood of the leaders, brought to justice for their choices, to help undo the harm."

"Get on with it then," the king said.

The priest wrapped the ropes loosely around the

king's wrists and ankles. Proctor shook his head. It was only a symbolic restraint. The king and the demon represented the merging of the flesh and the spirit. It would take symbols merged with the actual to achieve a cure. It seemed so obvious.

Symbolic or not, the ropes had an effect on the demon. It twisted its arm vigorously in the king's head. His eyes rolled back in his head and he began to cough and hack as if he were choking.

The priest wore a heavy silver ring on the fourth finger of his right hand. He held it up to the demon's face. "Who is present here?"

"I count six men, six frightened men, six mortal men—"

The demon's mouth moved, but the words came out of the king's mouth, rough and gravelly.

"Who is speaking to me?" the priest demanded.

"I am." You could almost hear the mockery in the voice. If it had to answer, and answer honestly, it would also answer unhelpfully.

But the priest seemed to expect this. He was clear and patient. "Who are you?" After a long delay while the demon squirmed and grimaced, he repeated the question. "Who are you?"

Finally, the voice answered. "I am the footman."

"Whose footman?"

"I am the footman of Balfri."

"Is Balfri also known as Berith?"

"You tell me. I cannot know how others know him."

Gordon started forward, angry. "Tell him what he wishes to know."

A smile spread over the demon's face, mirrored in a smile on the king. "He wishes to know how his wife died. Whether she died thinking of him, or whether her last thoughts were of the men who held her down and—"

The priest had already jumped up and shoved wax

plugs in his ears. He ran to the other men, shoving wax in their ears as he went. The demon talked vigorously the whole time. The priest reached Grueby last; his usually stoic expression seemed shaken. Then the priest sat in front of the demon and repeated the same question over and over again until the demon answered it and fell silent.

The priest was much paler when he rose again and took the plugs from his ears. He indicated to the other men that they might do the same. Proctor was the first to have his out.

"I should have warned you," the priest said. "This demon will answer any question truthfully, but he can speak anything he pleases to a statement directed at him. If you speak statements to him, you allow him to lie, and when he lies he can be most persuasive. Although he is one demon, he commands legions of demons, all aspects of the one. I have experience with these creatures, and I beg you let me do the speaking."

"May we have chairs?" Proctor asked.

"Of course," the priest said. Proctor retrieved a chair for each of them.

"How can we help?" Gordon asked. "We want to help."

"With your permission, we may come to a point where I will draw on your power," the priest said. To Proctor, he added, "Yours, too."

"Help is where we all work together," Proctor said.

"Someone must lead," Shelburne said calmly. "The secretary has treated dozens of demonic possessions. We should let him lead."

"He can lead," Proctor said. "But this demon, or another aspect of it, tried to possess my wife and daughter. So if I can help it back to hell, I'll help. And I won't ask for permission."

"We should remove him," Gordon said, growing in courage the longer Proctor ignored him.

The priest held up his hand. "I accept that," he said. "But follow my guidance, and don't speak to the guest directly."

He settled down at the king's side again, holding up the silver ring to the demon's face. "What will make you leave?"

The king's hand flew up and slapped the priest, knocking his spectacles across the room. Grueby calmly retrieved them. The priest put them back on.

"What will make you leave?"

The king's fist moved with lightning quickness, clipping the priest on the jaw again. This time he held on to his glasses and forced the ring into the demon's face.

"What will make you leave?"

The king's hands jumped up and started to choke the priest, who hesitated to lay hands on His Majesty. Proctor had had enough. The ropes, looped loosely around the king's wrists and ankles, unraveled and reached for the arms and legs of the chair. As soon as they touched wood they wound like a windlass, drawing in the king's arms and legs and binding them tight where he sat.

The priest fell back to the floor, clutching his throat.

"Did the demon do that?" Gordon asked.

"No," the demon said. And then it roared in frustration. "The American did it—they mean to break the empire, they mean to throw down kings. Someday they mean to be greater than England. He is no friend, no friend to you."

"We must untie those bonds at once," Shelburne said as soon as he understood what had happened. He stood up from his seat.

"Oh, enough of this," Proctor said. He used his power to push Shelburne and Gordon back into their seats. He grabbed the priest by the wrist. He felt him trying to pull away, using both his physical and spiritual strength. But

Proctor was tired of letting others make the choices. He dragged the priest across the floor and jammed the silver ring against the demon's forehead. Fire shot down through his arm. "Did you try to possess my daughter?"

Words tumbled reluctantly out of the king's mouth. "Balfri wanted your child, and he sent his left hand, but he was stopped."

"Did you try to possess Deborah, my wife?"

"Balfri sent his left hand again, in power and glory, but he was stopped."

"Who or what is the left hand?"

"The footman, the herald, and the left hand—these are three aspects of Balfri. One to serve, one to announce, and one to rule."

"Does Balfri possess Deborah now?"

The demon opened its mouth and screamed at Proctor directly. It moved its hand in the king's skull, and words came out of his mouth. "She is in his presence."

It was a trick answer and Proctor would not let himself be blinded. He slammed the priest's ring into the demon's face again. "Does Balfri's left hand possess my Deborah?"

"She is with the herald."

"Is she alive?"

"Her body lives."

They were true answers, but they were not the true answers he wanted. The demon was trying to provoke him into speaking directly or lashing out. Proctor felt the rage and fear building inside him. Red swam before his eyes, and he wanted to take the priest's hand and strike the king's mouth. He wanted to beat it until it swore to leave Deborah alone.

Calm, the priest whispered. It was merely a voice in his head, not even a word on his lips.

And Proctor calmed. He realized he was squeezing the man's wrist so tight, the skin paled. He almost let go, but the priest looked at him through his spectacles. In his head, Proctor heard the thought, *Go ahead and ask your questions. Finish.*

Proctor loosened his grip on the priest's wrist but strengthened his will. "How do I get Deborah or my daughter back if you've possessed them?"

"You can't."

"How does anyone do it, how do we get you out of our bodies?"

The king's head lolled to one side. A chuckle formed in his throat then blossomed into full-throated laughter, even with his eyes rolled back. "You must kill the body to release us from the body," said the voice.

Shelburne was up in a heartbeat. "That's unacceptable."

"Surely there's some other way," Gordon said.

King and demon smiled. The demon began to describe in elaborate and gruesome detail the various ways they could kill the king. Proctor flung the priest's arm aside in disgust, and the priest rose and passed out the earplugs again.

"It's lying," Proctor said to the priest.

What do you mean? the priest mouthed. He rubbed his wrist to make the blood flow into it again.

Proctor didn't know what he meant. He looked at the king tied to the chair, the way he thrashed and pulled against his bonds, and the demon sitting on his shoulder like a coachman at the reins.

The possession wasn't complete.

If the Bloody Tower had so many protections against malevolent magic built into its walls, how many protections were built into the Crown and kingdom? Especially after a thousand years? The Covenant, for all their power, had only managed to break through part of the king's protections.

Proctor studied the demon again. When he'd seen it in

the Tower, the demon only had its hand wrist-deep in the king's skull. Now it was sunk to the elbow. Eventually, given time, it might possess the king completely. But not yet.

"Give me the ring," Proctor said.

The priest hesitated. Then he pulled it off and dropped it in Proctor's hand. It was a heavy silver ring, with the signet of the cross on it. A line from the Lord's prayer had been engraved inside the band.

DELIVER US FROM EVIL.

Proctor slipped on the ring and walked over to the demon. He calmly and deliberately rested the ring against the tip of its nose. With the ring on his own hand, the demon felt almost solid.

"What happens if we cut off your arm?"

The demon screamed at him.

"What happens if we cut off your arm?"

The king's head snapped back as if he'd been struck. His body shook and strained against the ropes, and gibberish poured out of his mouth.

"What happens if we cut off your arm?"

The king's head flew forward and he spewed vomit in Proctor's face. Proctor wiped it off with his free hand and didn't budge. When he repeated the question again, the king thrashed from side to side, spewing forth words in many different languages, some inflected, rolling like the hills, some as harsh and flat as a wasteland. The priest leaned forward, his eyes fixed on the king's lips, his own lips moving with the king's words. He seemed always on the verge of understanding. His fingers ticked upward every time he picked up a word or a phrase.

But Proctor didn't understand and had no patience to sort it out. "How do I make you explain it in English so I can understand you?"

"I'll drive him mad," screamed the demon. "I'll wring

his stomach into knots until he pisses blood. I'll steal the sense from his thoughts and the words from his lips. I'll make his life a living hell."

Proctor shoved the ring against the demon's face, bending its head backward. It twisted from side to side, trying to escape. "Will Balfri control him?"

"I will drive him mad, mad with pain, mad with desire. I will break him—"

"Will you control him?"

"NO!"

The king's head rolled forward onto his chest, and he sagged in the chair.

"How do we cut off your arm?" Proctor asked.

"Blood and silver," the demon said, its voice a wretched sob.

Proctor stepped away from the creature and noticed everyone looking at him. Gordon's eyes were wide with fear. Shelburne's face was composed and thoughtful. Grueby turned his head away quickly, staring at a blank spot on the wall.

"I need a silver knife," Proctor said.

"I have one in my bag," the priest said.

"We cannot proceed without asking His Majesty's permission," Shelburne said. "I very firmly insist. We must explain the situation to him and ask what he wishes."

Proctor nodded. If he faced forty years of pain and despair, he might choose death instead. Proctor undid an imaginary knot with his fingers, and all four ropes fell to the floor.

The priest knelt at the king's side. "Your Majesty," he said softly.

The king raised his head and sat up straight. He rubbed his wrists where they had been bound. "There is no dignity in this," he said, shaking his head. "No dignity at all. It is wrong."

"We have something we must explain to you," the priest said.

"I heard all of it," the king said. "Like an argument happening in the next room, behind only a thin wall." He looked to Shelburne. "Thank you. Your attention to propriety will not be forgotten." To Proctor, he said, "Do I understand correctly that this creature has attacked your wife and ch-children?"

"My daughter, yes," Proctor said.

The king reached out and patted him on the arm. He seemed at a loss for words, reaching up to wipe a knuckle at the corner of each eye. The demon on his shoulder had a furtive, trapped look about it now.

"I would like to be present for whatever else you do," the king said. He clapped his hands on his knees.

"Do you want to take a break—prepare for another day?" the priest asked.

"Let's be done with it," he said. To Proctor, "Can you do this?"

The demon began to thrash and struggle, trying to pull its arm free of the king's head.

"Sire," Shelburne said. "Did you clearly hear the consequences?"

Proctor guessed that the loss of reason was something Shelburne feared more than death.

"Madness and pain," the king said. "I'd rather not go into the details. But I remain my own man and England's king."

The priest handed Proctor the silver knife. He drew it across the scar on his hand. Let the wounds that the Covenant had given him be their undoing. He grabbed the demon's wrist with his ringed hand. The creature slashed and bit at him, tearing open real wounds in his flesh. The physical world and the spirit world were as one.

Proctor stabbed the bloody knife into the demon's arm where it touched the king's skull.

"Oh," said the king. "I feel that."

Proctor ignored him, sawing all the way through the arm. The demon yowled in rage. The instant Proctor severed its arm the sound vanished. The demon's arm slipped out of Proctor's grip as it floated away. A bright white light appeared in the room and the creature turned to smoke, then disappeared.

As he watched it go, Proctor wondered if he could do the same thing to Deborah and Maggie if they were only partially possessed. Could he condemn them to a life of suffering to free them from a demon?

Could he free them any other way if they were entirely possessed?

The priest stared at Proctor as if waiting to see what he would do next.

Proctor tossed him the silver knife and said, "God save the king."

Chapter 23

The priest took Proctor aside. "What you did here today was remarkable. Have you ever considered a career in the priesthood?"

Proctor was taken aback. "I have a wife and a daughter," he said.

"That is no barrier in the Church of England," the priest said.

"But I'm not English."

"Are you Christian?"

"Of course."

"That is all that matters. You must realize that your wife and daughter are in terrible danger." When Proctor tensed, the priest held up his hand. "I speak not of anything specific, nor to be cruel, but to prepare you for the unhappy fact."

Proctor did not need anyone to feed his fears for Deborah and Maggie. It was too easy to imagine Maggie as a blood sacrifice and Deborah possessed by Balfri.

"You may return home to find them not as you remember them," the priest said. "If you find them. You may not find them at all. A life of service would be a fitting tribute to their memory."

"Is that what happened to you?"

The priest blinked. Recovering, he offered Proctor a melancholy smile. "Nothing has ever happened to me," he said. "You must remember that I have no name. I am no one."

"Thank you, but all I want to do is return home."

"Please consider sending a letter to the office of special secretary at Canterbury if you ever change your mind."

"How will it reach you, if you are no one."

"Because the office is always there," the priest said. "Your letter will reach someone."

The other men had joined them. King George spoke quietly to Lord Gordon. "I w-w-will see that you have the best legal minds to advise and represent you. But you-you-you must go to the Tower and you m-m-must go to trial."

Gordon's face was grave. He glanced at the king's head where the demon had been amputated, then looked at the ground. "Yes, sir."

Shelburne stood with his hands behind his back, staring Proctor in the eye. "It is my goal to render your kind powerless. When men no longer believe in magic, sorcerers like Dee will not be able to channel the untapped talent of ordinary men to evil purposes."

"I don't believe that will ever happen," the priest said.

"W-w-we must all work to elevate reason," the king said.

Proctor watched the others seem to let that stand as the last word, but he was not content. "So how do we go after Dee now? I want to go with you."

"Dee and his followers have left the country," Shelburne said.

"It's why we finally considered it safe to bring His Majesty here," the priest said.

"Where have they gone?" Proctor asked.

King George seemed almost apologetic. "I-I-I assumed that you knew. They've gone to Am-m-merica."

Grueby brought a shay around from Shelburne's stables, and offered Proctor a hand up to the seat. "Lord

Gordon has commanded me to deliver you to the destination of your choice," he said.

"There's a farm outside Salem, in the state of Massachusetts," Proctor said.

"I believe he meant within the vicinity of London."

"I have to find a ship to America," Proctor said.

"There's a place down near the docks that I believe will suit," Grueby said. He snapped the reins, and the spritely gray mare clopped off through the streets.

Proctor was lost in thought about his next steps. It might be best to find some way back to France, maybe with some of the smugglers whom Digges knew. From France, he could surely find an American ship or at least a ship bound for America.

"If you don't mind my asking," Grueby said as they rolled through the streets. "How exactly did you turn the spell and escape from the Tower? I didn't think that was possible."

"I'd better keep that secret, in case I ever need it again."

Grueby nodded. "Gordon was convinced that you were a member of the Covenant. He thought they would come visit you in prison. I was to wait and spy on you to see if they came. The goal was to follow them back to their residence."

"And after eight months?" Proctor said.

"I don't blame you for being bitter," Grueby said, keeping his eyes on the road. "I just wanted to explain. I was coming for you today because our plans changed with Dee's departure. He just appeared in a carriage at the docks and hired a merchant ship to America for himself and several passengers."

"And you were simply going to tell the guards that I was the wrong man and they would have set me free?"

Grueby was silent as the blocks rolled past. The carriage had excellent springs. Proctor thought he had never had a smoother ride. They had passed from the London of mansions in classical styles unknown in America through streets lined with spacious homes, modest by comparison, that rivaled the best his homeland had to offer, and had come to the kind of buildings one found everywhere he'd been yet, slapped-together structures that seemed to stand up by leaning on one another like a group of drunks. They were infinite in their variety—this one had a balcony, that one had an overhanging roof, one over there had shutters on the windows—and identical in their dreariness, dilapidation, and decrepitude. The smell of water—of fish and slime and sewage—filled the air.

"I'm sure I can find a ship to America from France," Proctor said. "Are there smugglers down here who will take me there?"

"It's someone who can get you to France," Grueby said. "I'll wait while you go talk to him, if you prefer. But if this doesn't work, I'll see if we can find passage for you on one of the military ships."

"That would be less than ideal," Proctor said. "Although it would be better than prison."

"It's the door on the right," Grueby said, pointing.

Proctor climbed down from the shay and walked up to the door. Voices inside were having a hushed but heated discussion. Proctor felt like a beggar again, realizing that if he didn't have enough of Digges's money left, he'd have to ask Grueby for more. He wiped his palm on his pants and rapped on the wood, which hung so loose it rattled in the frame.

The door opened a crack. Eyes peered at him out of the dark.

"Hello," Proctor said. "I'm looking for—"

The door opened wide. Thomas Digges stood there. The sailor's jacket and breeches he wore looked as natural on him as the cook's apron he had worn when he brought Proctor food in prison. A shadow stepped out of the dark recesses of the room behind him.

Proctor threw himself through the doorway and wrapped his arms around the second person. He squeezed tight and then thrust her back at arm's length.

"Lydia! I thought you were dead. I thought I'd never see you again."

Out in the street, Grueby cracked the reins and the mare pulled the carriage away from the curb. It rolled off into the night.

Digges shut the door. "If I'm that easy to find, I'll have to change addresses again. I worried that I had been staying here too long."

"Lydia, I . . ."

"I'm glad to see you too, Mister Brown."

"Proctor. You better call me Proctor. How did you— Where did you—?"

She stepped away from him and composed herself again. "I got caught up in the riots, just as you did, I suspect."

"Were you at Newgate?"

"I was drawn there, like a bee to honey, but when they set it on fire I fled."

"I arrived as they were pulling prisoners out of the flames. And then the distillery fire—we thought we saw you there."

"I was there," she said. They all fell silent for a moment at the memory of that horrible fire, the rioters shot by the troops, the people burned alive. Finally, Lydia said, "John was one of the men they captured and hanged."

Proctor remembered the ugly craftsman with the delighted smile. "I'm sorry to hear that."

She shrugged it off. "He said he didn't mind going to his death as long as he went as a freeman. After he was killed, I begged . . ." She hesitated, and he imagined that she was leaving out the use of her talent to ease the way.

"Then I found work as a washerwoman. I'd been saving money, a penny here, a penny there, hoping to save enough to buy my way back to Massachusetts."

"But you're free here," he said.

"It's an odd sort of freedom. Most of the negroes here are runaways. They've been slaves and have escaped. The community is large enough, and the laws prohibit taking and selling them again, so most don't get caught. But it's not home. I don't really belong here."

"I found her by accident," Digges said. "She had come down to the docks—"

"To find out how much passage would cost," she said. "I couldn't get myself to Spithead, much less France or America."

"I remembered her, and approached her, and apprised her of your situation in the Tower. We'd been working on ideas to break you free—" Mentioning the Tower brought Digges to a halt. "How did you—?"

"I freed myself," Proctor said. "But now we have a bigger problem. The Covenant has sailed for America."

"Dee?" Digges asked.

"Yes, and several of his followers at the least."

"Dee's departure doesn't mean that all the Covenant has gone," Digges said. "Some of them will remain behind. They still have agents everywhere."

"If Dee has gone, then he has planned something big, some spell that requires skill and power that only he can master. That can't be good for America. I plan to follow him and stop him, whatever his plan, whatever the cost." When he mentioned cost, he wasn't thinking money, but that brought the purse to mind. He pulled it from his pocket and held it in his palm. It now bulged considerably less than it had when Digges first gave it to him. "Will that get me there?"

Digges took the purse and counted the coins. "By the

time I'm done with you, you will have cost Franklin three hundred pounds. That's a lot of American prisoners that won't be set free. That's a lot of technology that I won't be able to steal and ship in secret."

"But you've seen what Dee is doing," Proctor started to argue.

"Yes, it's worth every cent." Digges smoothed the point of his beard while he was thinking. "We'll get you there. I'm just trying to consider the best means of doing it. There's not much money left. But perhaps Lafayette has not yet sailed for America. And John Paul Jones was refitting his ships at L'Orient. I believe he plans to sail for America."

"If the best you can do is a rowboat, I'll row my way home," Proctor said.

Lydia took a step closer. "I'm coming with you. If the rowboat starts to leak, I can bail water."

"We'll do better than that," Digges promised.

Digges hired a fishing boat to carry them down the Thames, then a smuggler to ferry them across the channel on a dark night.

"I can't go with you any farther," Digges said, standing on the smuggler's strand. "But I hope to see you in Maryland someday."

"If you make it back across the ocean, I promise I'll come visit," Proctor said. Digges offered him his hand, but Proctor embraced him instead.

The smuggler deposited them in Calais, where they engaged a carriage. In less than two weeks, they had reached L'Orient, where they found the *Alliance* flying the Stars and Stripes. It was a thirty-six-gun frigate similar to *La Sensible,* but it was American.

"Who's her captain?" Proctor asked one of the dock-workers.

The man made a sour face and turned his head to spit. "Captain John Barry. And if you have to speak to him, good luck to you."

"Is that bad news?" Lydia asked.

"It could be either," Proctor answered. "Barry believes in divine providence, and does as he feels directed to do. He's obstinate and has a temper. If he makes up his mind against us, there's nothing we can do to change it."

"Is there any good news?" she asked.

"If he decides he likes us, there's nothing anyone else can do to change his mind."

Proctor had met Barry before. Back in '76, with his ship still under construction, Barry had volunteered to fight in the army. He was with the group that fought at the battle of Trenton in late December, though as an aide to General Cadwalader, which meant Proctor had not seen him there. Their paths had crossed during the battle of Princeton several days later, when Barry had led a formidable defense of the American position and was later selected by Washington to act as a courier for the wounded through British lines. Proctor remembered Barry but did not know if Barry would remember him.

The ship appeared ready to sail. The hull had been scrubbed clean of the moss and barnacles that slowed ships down; the wood gleamed through the clear glass of the water. Everything was stored on the deck, the sails were furled, and the crew, as scarred and sullen a lot as Proctor had ever seen, hung over the sides of the ship or dangled their feet from the masts.

They found the captain on the deck. Barry was a giant, standing almost a foot taller than most of the men who surrounded him. He was as broad as he was tall, with a jaw as square as his shoulders and a small mole on the bridge of his nose that made his eyebrows look perpetually folded down in anger. When he spoke, he still had the Irish accent that he carried with him from the country of his birth. He held a Bible in his hand when he thumped across the deck to speak to Proctor and Lydia.

"Proctor Brown, sir," Proctor said. "And this is Lydia Freeman. We're Americans. I served with General Washington at Trenton and at Princeton. We've been in Paris with Doctor Franklin on a mission from Major Tallmadge, but now we need passage home."

"That's a mouthful of names in one breath," Barry said. "I don't suppose you have a letter from Doctor Franklin."

"No, sir, I don't."

"I don't have room for passengers, nor can I in good conscience take them on. We may be called into battle at any time. I've had a ship battered to splinters beneath my feet and had to sink it to keep it from falling into British hands. That's one thing when we're a day off the coast of our own country, but with this ship, and this mission, it could happen in the middle of the sea, with neither shore nor rescue to be had."

"Yes, sir. We understand."

He hoped his use of *sir* reflected a military urgency to Barry. When Proctor had served with Washington, he had presented himself as a Quaker and had never used military courtesies or forms of address. But he was a different man now, in many ways.

That might have been the problem. Barry studied Proctor's face for a moment and then looked down at his right hand, where the scar was re-forming over the knuckle of his missing pinkie. If he recognized Proctor, he wasn't going to say so. Proctor opened his mouth to remind him of the courier duty with the wounded soldiers, but Barry waved the Bible in the air.

"I was just reading to the crew," he said. "It has a

salubrious effect on their disposition, and puts them in the proper frame of mind to show obedience. Do you mind if I see what the Good Book says?"

"Please," Proctor said. He sifted his brain frantically for a passage that would be a good omen, and a spell to open the page to it, but before he'd solved even the first part of the equation Barry flung open his Bible and thumped a finger down blindly on a page. When he read it, he laughed until his cheeks colored.

"Welcome aboard," Barry said, clapping Proctor on the shoulder so hard he nearly knocked him off his feet. "Welcome aboard."

"What did it say?" Proctor asked.

"John, chapter six, verse twenty-one, my friend. John six: twenty-one."

He turned away to call for one of the crewmen to find a place aboard for their passengers. Proctor whispered to Lydia, "What's John six: twenty-one say?"

She shook her head. "But maybe there is divine providence at work here. Maybe there's something back in America so bad, you're the only one who can stop it."

Proctor chewed on that thought. If he had stayed in America, then Dee wouldn't have freed the demon that attacked King George. But if Proctor had stayed in America, and Dee found some other way to release it, then Proctor would not have been there to help the king. There were too many ifs. Divine providence or demonic providence, either seemed just as likely an interpretation.

Barry came back and Proctor decided to ask him outright, as he knew the captain was not a man who changed his mind. "What is John six: twenty-one? It's the miracles on Galilee, but . . ."

Barry nodded, still grinning. "That's right. The verse says, 'Then they willingly received him into the ship and immediately the ship was at the land wither they went.' "

He pointed to a French ship at another dock. "Do you see that letter of marque?"

"Yes," Proctor said. It was an Indiaman, a large merchant ship fitted out with, it appeared, about forty guns. At least as many as the *Alliance* carried.

"That's the *Marquis de Lafayette*," Barry said. "It carries over a million livres of cargo—twenty-six eighteen-pounders, fifteen thousand gun barrels, a hundred tons of saltpeter, and uniforms for ten thousand men. That's every penny Congress has left, and it's all going to General Washington to give him a fighting chance to stop Cornwallis. So if I willingly receive you into the ship and immediately the ship is at the land we're heading for, then I say welcome aboard." He turned to his first officer, a man with a rough, functional appearance about him, much like an old doglock musket. "Mister Hacker."

"Sir?"

"Enter our passenger in the log as Mister Trent," Barry said. "He wants to serve as a volunteer in the American army. Don't mention the woman with him—I don't want to explain her—but find her a spot away from the men."

"Sir," Hacker said, and turned away.

"See, I do remember you from Trenton," Barry said. "Though you weren't regular army then, any more than I suspect you are now. Will that suit?"

"It will suit very well," Proctor said.

"I almost signed you on to the crew as a landsman," Barry said. "We've been taking every American we could find from any French ship, just to get us up to fighting strength. Which reminds me—"

Without another word of explanation or excuse, he turned to yell instructions to another one of his officers.

Lydia scuffed her feet across the deck and put her hands on her hips. "Here we are on another ship, headed right back where we came from. I lived through blood and fire. But what did we accomplish? Nothing."

"It's not nothing," Proctor said. He wasn't willing to accept that the last eighteen months had accomplished nothing. "We found out who the Covenant is. We discovered their plan." He had saved King George III—he hadn't mentioned that to Digges or Lydia. He wasn't sure he ever would. "Maybe it is divine providence at work."

"Maybe that creature possessed Deborah, and now we've got to stop her before Dee gets to her first and tells her what to do."

"Stop it," Proctor said.

Lydia took a step back and frowned at him.

"I don't believe that's true," Proctor told her.

"Don't believe it or don't want to believe it?" she said. The question hung in the air unanswered until she shook her head. "I think I'll go find Lieutenant Hacker and see where my quarters are. I'm likely to be in them for most of the voyage."

Proctor turned and grabbed hold of the rigging. The hemp rope felt as rough as a hangman's noose in his palms. Deborah possessed by the demon? He didn't believe it. But he knew that he didn't want to believe it either.

He looked for Lydia and saw a different familiar face instead: his old friend from *La Sensible,* Jack Tar. Jack glimpsed Proctor and immediately made himself busy, disappearing from view.

Barry had said that they were taking aboard Americans from French ships. But what did divine providence have in mind with this?

The winds were contrary for a week, and the French pilot refused to lead them through the narrow channel out of port. Every day, messengers came back and forth from the *Lafayette,* from Paris, from the shipyards.

Proctor felt like all of them were watching him. Finally, on March 29, under a steady breeze that smelled like bad weather, they followed the *Lafayette* to the open sea.

At dusk Proctor was standing in the bow of the ship because it made him feel that much closer to home. Now that they were under way, and home seemed like a possibility again instead of just another word, Proctor grew desperate to know what had happened to Deborah and Maggie.

There was a way he might be able to find out.

"Let a reef out of the topsails," Barry ordered from the quarterdeck in his booming voice. "Unbend the cables and set up the back stays."

The men swarmed through the rigging and across the deck to do his bidding. The ship jumped through the waves, and Proctor tasted the salt in the spray that flew over the side into his face. A sailor called out from the tops to the *Lafayette,* which sailed nearby. An answer came back over the water. Proctor couldn't understand but the man in the tops laughed. Barry ordered a light hung from the stern so that the *Lafayette* could follow them in the dark.

When the other passengers and most of the crew went belowdeck for the night, Proctor lingered above, acting as if he needed to use the head. Darkness fell suddenly and wholly at sea, and the moment it did, he made his way instead to the chicken coops. If he could get his hand on an egg, he could scrye.

He reached hopefully into the first cage, poking his hand through the straw while the hen bustled and nipped at him, but there was no egg. None in the second, either, nor the third. He checked every cage twice, but none of the chickens had laid yet.

"What's going on over here?" asked a voice, responding to the annoyed clucks of the chickens.

Proctor dived into the shadows behind the cages and said a quick spell to conceal himself. A shadow approached, paused at the cages, and then moved on.

Despite having no bowl or water or candles, Proctor felt confident he could still scrye if he had an egg for his focus: he understood now that he was sacrificing the future of the chick in that egg to see a different future. But he was willing to pay that price. If only he had an egg.

He settled down into the shadows and waited for one of the chickens to lay. As he waited, he peered through the broken clouds at the stars. If the sky was infinite in every direction, and there were more stars in the heavens than grains of sand on a beach, then could his actions make a difference? Did his efforts have any effect? Had he done the right thing by leaving Deborah to hunt the Covenant? *Were she and Maggie safe?*

The chickens began to rustle again and Proctor prepared to check the cages again, hopeful for an egg. As he rose, he saw a man clambering down the foremast while two other men approached through the dark. Proctor slipped back into the shadows.

"Patrick, is that you?" whispered the man just come out of the foretop.

"I'm going to slit your throat if you say my name again," whispered Patrick.

"I was talking to the other Patrick, Patrick Shelden."

"Shh," said a third man, Shelden. "We don't want to be heard."

"Are we ready to do it then?" Patrick asked.

"They're ready aboard the other ship," the top man said. "Their man will be waiting for our signal."

Proctor leaned toward the conversation. The other ship was waiting for what signal?

"Good," Patrick said. He turned his head and spat a fat glob of tobacco—it landed just inches from Proctor's face. "Crawford is ready, and Crooks and Mallady.

We'll kill all the officers and the passengers, everybody but Fletcher, and we'll make him navigate us to Ireland."

Mutiny? Divine providence, indeed, Proctor thought bitterly.

"Do we have to kill all of them?" Shelden asked.

"Yes, we have to kill them," Patrick sneered. "You want to wait until we come up against a British first-rate, seventy-four guns? You know what Barry does to his ships. He looks for battles, gets his ships sunk and his crews killed. Better he and a few officers die now than all of us later."

"I think he meant the passengers," the top man asked.

"Don't worry about the passengers, if it bothers you," Patrick said. "I'll take care of them personally. Especially that one named Trent."

Proctor tensed. Why did they want him dead especially?

"Who's the buyer for the ship when we reach Ireland?" Shelden asked.

"Dee," Patrick said. "His name is Dee."

Proctor was stunned.

"What is this Dee, some kind of privateer?" Shelden asked.

"Why do you got so many questions?" Patrick asked.

"You know me, I won't breathe a word, not even if Barry puts hot iron to my skin. I just want to know who we're dealing with, in case anything goes wrong."

"Nothing's going to go wrong, not to me," Patrick said. "And Dee's doing this because he believes in England and the empire. He says we're all Englishmen, we're all part of one empire, and that's the way it ought to be. He's spending his own fortune on it. You saw the gold he gave us."

Proctor was still shaking his head. How far was Dee's reach? If he truly spoke with angels and demons, could they see the future and tell him what to do and when to act? The Americans desperately needed the supplies aboard the *Lafayette*. Was this aimed at stopping that ship or was it aimed at stopping Proctor as well? How could you defeat a witch that powerful, with a reach that far?

"Spent all my gold drinking," the top man said.

"That's how Crooks and Mallady ended up in the brig," Shelden said.

"Well, they're out now," Patrick said. "We wait until tomorrow night, when we've left the bay, and then we strike on my signal. Got it?"

The other two understood. The top man climbed back up in the rigging. Shelden scurried off through the shadows also. Patrick rose to leave, but Hacker, the first officer, called out, "Who's fore? Name yourself."

Patrick crouched down on the opposite side of the chicken crates. The birds flapped their wings, raising the smell of damp feathers. Proctor peered through the crates at the ringleader. No talent at all in him, unless it was a talent for murder. But then they already knew that Dee would use anyone for his purposes.

Proctor was keenly aware of every sound—the footsteps on the quarterdeck, the creak of the wood, the slap of the sails, the strain of the ropes. Mostly he listened to the waves: every few rolls one thumped the side of the ship, sending water rushing over the rail.

The ship rolled, and Patrick crouched.

The wood creaked, and he made ready to dart to safety.

The wave thumped the side of the ship and Proctor tackled the would-be mutineer, slamming him to the deck. He sat on top of him, and clamped his hand tight around the other man's throat. Hands clawed at Proctor's face, but he had the longer reach, and punched the other man in the temple a few times until he was groggy.

The chickens squawked and flapped their wings, covering any noise.

Proctor dragged the man to his feet, torn in his intentions. He wanted to take him back to the captain and turn him over, but he wanted to question him about Dee first too.

Making up his mind nearly proved his undoing. The mutineer only pretended to be groggy. As soon as he was on his feet, he grabbed a belaying pin and swung at Proctor. Proctor dodged the blow and lunged back with a powerful shove just as the ship rolled.

The mutineer hit the railing and toppled over the side into the waves.

Proctor watched him go, trying to decide whether to tell anyone or not.

There was a fury of activity in the mast above Proctor, and then a voice called out, "Man overboard! There's a man overboard!"

"Heave to," ordered Barry. Men ran up over the deck, pulling in ropes and sails with a speed and order that Proctor couldn't follow. He wandered across the deck like a curious passenger.

Hacker yelled, "Who is it?"

"Patrick Duggan," the top man yelled.

All heads turned toward the rear mast.

"A tail tackle gave way," the top man yelled.

But though the ship stopped and searched for an hour, no further sign of Patrick Duggan was found. They resumed sail in the dark as a drenching squall blew in.

Proctor stood on the deck, letting the rain soak him to the skin. He had just killed a man and he had no strong feelings one way or the other. The man had been planning a mutiny, had been planning to kill him personally, but he didn't have to be murdered to be stopped. Proctor could have turned him in to Captain Barry.

He didn't know whether he should be more worried about what had happened to Deborah, or about what was happening to him.

He stopped and checked the cages one more time, but there were still no eggs. The hens were probably disturbed by the transition to the sea. It might be days before they started laying again.

Unhappily, he went below.

Chapter 24

With the ringleader of the mutiny dead, the other conspirators lost their will to murder, and late the next day someone went to Captain Barry and confessed everything. Proctor discovered it late that night when the captain shook him awake in his cabin.

"There's a mutiny hatching but I mean to step on its throat," Barry whispered. He offered Proctor the grip-end of a pistol. "Apparently the ringleader fell overboard, but I'm asking the officers, the marines, and every other man I can trust to help rouse the crew so we can get to the bottom of this. I figure, since you're willing to say *sir* these days, you might be willing to point a gun. Can I trust you?"

"You can trust me," Proctor said. He took the pistol and checked to see that it was loaded.

He bumped shoulders with the marines crowded on the quarterdeck, while the night officer dumped the crew from their hammocks and called them up to midship. Sailors were used to being roused in the middle of the night, so this didn't alarm them. When they had assembled and saw the row of guns resting on the quarterdeck rail and aimed in their direction, however, their mood took a different turn. Three conspirators—McElhaney, Shelden, and Crawford, the quartermaster—were strung up by their thumbs to the mizzen stay, stripped to the waist, and lashed in turns from dawn until they implicated other mutineers, which was close enough to noon that Proctor's stomach rumbled. The men they named were strung up in turn and flogged through the afternoon until the whole plan was laid as bare and raw as their backs.

It should have sat wrong with Proctor: it was as bad as the Inquisition, torturing men until they confessed whatever crimes were expected of them. It was no different from the witch trials in Salem eight decades before.

But Proctor felt nothing.

The would-be mutineers had made bad choices and brought it on themselves. He didn't know if all the men were guilty, but he knew enough to understand that some of them, at least, were only getting what they deserved. Just like Patrick Duggan.

He saw the blood, the wet cuts in the men's backs, the drops on the deck, the flecks that flew back across the bosun wielding the lash. He sensed the pulse in it, sensed it throb and fade. He heard the grinding teeth, the reluctant grunts of pain, the wretched gasps. But ever since he had seen men and women burned alive in the streets of London while demons danced in the flames, the stream of his feelings had been dammed.

Or maybe it had been the months that followed in prison, when he was locked away from his talent as well as his freedom.

He shook his head. None of those was right. It had started before that. It had started on the day his soul was yanked halfway around the world, when he fought a demon in the smoke and clouds over Salem in order to protect his wife and child. Even now, all this time later, he had no idea if they'd been saved, or if the demon had shimmied down that last rope of spirit to possess Deborah.

By the time the day was finished, three men were in chains in the hold, eight more had been whipped and put on probation, and the rest of the crew was angry and worried.

Two days later, the ship was approached by a pair of English brigs. The privateer sails appeared on the horizon at dawn while Barry was reading from the Bible to the crew.

The *Lafayette* was about a mile distant, and fell off at the appearance of the brigs. Barry beat to quarters and had his best crew put a warning shot across the bow of the first ship. The brigs ignored the warning and swept in for the attack.

The brigs think they're facing a leaderless crew, Proctor thought. They had knowledge of the mutiny and expected it to succeed.

He went to the ship's rail and watched the lead brig approach. It had its cannons aimed low. "They're going to try to hull us below the waterline," Barry said. "Aim for their sails."

But the roll of the ship and the narrow approach of the brig gave the advantage to the attacker. The *Alliance*'s cannons tore some holes in their sails but failed to slow the ship considerably. The brig turned broadside on them as the *Alliance* rolled to the other side in the swell. One well-aimed volley would wreck them.

Proctor leaned over the rail, counted twenty guns on the brig, and then drew on all his power. He had seen Deborah perform a spell, once, in which she deflected a volley of musket balls. He reached out and, as the cannons jetted smoke and fire, slapped his hands down.

The cannonballs dropped into the water. The momentum sent one or two skipping over the surface to bounce loudly off the *Alliance*'s hull, but no damage was done. The ship rolled the other way and, with its cannons aimed at the brig's deck, Barry yelled, "Fire!"

The deck shook, shot whistled through the air, and

bitter smoke obscured Proctor's view. When it cleared, the deck of the brig was cut to pieces. Barry had used chain shot. Sails and rigging were in tatters, the railing and deck were peppered with holes, and dead and injured men lay bleeding all over the deck.

Even this far away, Proctor could feel the blood call to him. It beat in him like a pulse.

He looked up to see Lydia watching him. He fought the feeling down and turned away.

The smaller brig tried to run for it then, perhaps realizing that it wasn't facing a bunch of mutineers. Barry chased it and forced a surrender. Their two-ship convoy had now become a four-ship convoy, joined by *Mars* and *Minerva*. It wasn't necessarily an advantage. There were more than a hundred prisoners in irons on the lowest deck, and part of the *Alliance*'s crew had to be sent to man the brig.

"We were shorthanded before the mutiny," the captain told Proctor confidentially on the quarterdeck one day. "I'll give Lieutenant Fletcher command of the brig, with a small handful of men, but he'll need to keep all the others locked up."

"Why not just send it back to France?"

"The American navy needs the ships and guns," Barry said. "American ships have had a difficult time crossing the Atlantic. They've been captured, like the ship that carried Henry Laurens, or they've simply disappeared, like the *Saratoga*."

"Or come close to sinking, like the ship that carried John Adams," Proctor said, remembering their own difficulty. "What do you mean *disappeared*?"

"Gone without a trace," Barry said. "Anything can happen at sea, and weather is always a danger, but that ship was seaworthy and built to ride out even a fierce storm."

Proctor stared out over the water at the dark horizon. "Looks like a fierce storm coming on us."

Barry turned his ruddy face to the dark clouds and clapped Proctor on the shoulder. "Don't you worry. It will take more than a storm to keep me from the American shore."

The storm hit them hard the next day, pushing them back toward Europe. The four ships hung lights to keep sight of one another and struggled on together through the wind and the rain. The *Alliance* tossed so much that only the hardiest men could keep any food down. Proctor was not one of them. Lydia and Proctor huddled together belowdeck.

"How powerful is Dee?" Lydia asked.

Meaning, *Could he have sent this storm?*

"I've seen Deborah pray up a storm this big once," he whispered. "But she had to use herself for a focus, and the effort left her drained for weeks." Drained nearly to the point of death. That had been right after the battle of Brooklyn, when Deborah had called in a storm they had seen forming over the ocean, to dampen the fighting with rain and bring winds that kept the British navy from cutting off Washington's escape.

"So maybe this storm is just a coincidence," Lydia said, bracing herself against the side of the cabin to keep from pitching over. "Coming days after a failed mutiny, and immediately after a failed attack by privateers. Maybe it's too much for even Dee to do."

"Maybe it is," Proctor said, but he had already had all the same thoughts.

The fury of nature was daunting enough, but the prospect that this storm was guided somehow, fed, by a witch not even present—that was more daunting still. If Dee, tapping into the power of all the witches of the Covenant, could draw this much weather, then he was beyond any power that Proctor could imagine.

"Maybe it is," Proctor said. "But maybe I should try to blunt the force of it anyway."

"Whatever I can do to help, let me know," Lydia said.

His effort from the cabin was useless. He could feel the storm raging around them, but he felt separate from it. So he went up the deck and pulled himself along the safety lines. When the wind ripped his hat away, he caught it and stuffed it into his belt. Rain pelted his face and burrowed through his clothes. With an elbow hooked around the rope, slipping and sliding as the ship fell off the peak of one wave and plunged through the next crest, he slowly made his way to the spot where the men had been whipped and the blood had stained the wood.

He had grown in power during his time in the Tower, but it had been from using blood as a focus. Now he would use it again.

He pulled his knife and drew it across his right palm—it was exposed and the easiest place to reach. He meant to drip the blood onto the deck and grind it in with his shoe, connecting him to the ship and its fate. Instead the wind and the rain tore the drops sideways as they fell from his hand. His severed knuckle throbbed.

The blood scattered in the storm, nothing compared with the volume of its fury, but it was enough to let him know that it was no natural wind. Dee had sent this. The storm had a purpose, and it was to see them sink.

Proctor had never been good with weather—that was Deborah's talent—but he would learn now or they would all die. The storm came at them from the deepest part of the ocean, so he reached out to the Continent for winds to come clear the clouds away. He spent a whole day standing there, soaked to the bone, trying to pull clear skies toward them. Crew members came and tried to persuade him to go back inside, but he growled at them until they went away. He could not let his focus be broken.

He thought through the Psalms for a good verse. "They cry unto the Lord in their trouble, and he bringeth them out of their distresses," he mumbled. "He maketh the storm a calm, so the waves thereof are still."

Yes, that was the verse. Proctor prayed it over and over again without ceasing, holding on to the image of clear skies reaching them from the Continent. He pictured the bluest sky he ever saw over England from the window of his cell, and he pulled it out over the ocean. "He maketh the storm a calm . . . He maketh the storm a calm . . ."

Hours passed, and Proctor reached the point of despair, and then continued. The world was big, the oceans were vast, and he needed to give the spell time to have an effect. Finally, in the middle of the night, the fury of the storm abated. The winds died down, and all that was left was a soaking downpour. It felt as if they were swimming through the sea instead of sailing over it. All four ships were battered but safe, their lanterns shining over the dark sea. They called to one another through the rain as Proctor limped back to his cabin. The captain sent him a bowl of hot beans and salted meat.

"I've never seen anything like that," Lydia said, spooning the food to him because he was too weak to feed himself.

"Deborah can do it better than I can," Proctor replied. It took all his effort to chew and swallow.

"Does she use blood magic also?" Lydia asked, keeping her eyes cast down.

"No, she used earth—what does it matter what she used?" he snapped. She held out another spoon for him and he swatted at it. She pulled it easily out of his reach, and he rolled over. It was one thing to grab a sheet and drag it across the bed. It was a different thing entirely to grab the sky and drag it over the ocean. Before he could pull up the sheet, he had closed his eyes and fallen asleep.

The sound of the rain beating on the deck jerked him awake. He was covered with a sheet and a blanket, and Lydia sat in a chair at his side. The wind had whistled back to strength again. The waves dropped the ship like they meant to break it, and water ran everywhere.

"It's not through," he said.

Lydia, her eyes wide, simply shook her head.

Proctor struggled back up to the deck and once again prepared to fight the storm.

The tops of the masts were invisible through the sheets of rain above him. A lantern lit the quarterdeck, where two men, bundled in heavy hats and coats, stood at the wheel. A few other men hunkered at their posts on the deck or the masts, but Proctor couldn't be sure how many. The rain combined with a wind-whipped mist that obscured even the bow and stern of the ship from his view.

"I can do this for another day," he told himself, and he stood at the heart of the ship and tried to draw better weather toward them, tethering his spell to the mainmast the way one might tie a kite to a lightning rod.

But though the storm ebbed and surged, it did not break that day or the next.

For two more weeks, the storm pounded the ship, waiting for them to tire or make a mistake. Even the crew muttered how unnatural it was. Every time it lessened, they would see the lanterns of the *Lafayette* and the captured brigs bobbing nearby. During the calm, Captain Barry ordered the ships to stay within hailing distance. Every time the storm lessened, Proctor would go below to eat and rest. Every time he did, the storm came back at them from another direction.

Nor was he the only one exhausted by the trial. For all the work that Proctor did keeping the storm at bay, the crew worked just as hard to keep the ship afloat and aimed toward America. With the weather, it was impossible to take a sighting, and so they had no idea if they had traveled a thousand miles or simply bobbed in place like a buoy. Every time Proctor thought he was spent, that he had reached the limits of his power, he would have to dig deep inside to find more will to fight.

During his breaks from the deck, Lydia would feed him and help him rest. He could feel her pouring healing strength into him, just enough to keep him going.

"Do you want to survive, even if the blood magic changes you?" she asked.

"Yes, I do," he said. He found he wanted to live more than anything else. He needed to know what had happened to Deborah and Maggie. He needed to stop the witches who had tried to hurt them. Not just stop them, but kill them.

Lydia kept her face expressionless. Finally, she said, "It may not matter. I don't think the storm will abate until we've sunk."

Of course not. The storm was set on them by a spell. It wouldn't let up until they had sunk. That's why every time he brought them a respite, it renewed its power from a different direction.

Proctor scooped another bite of cold meal and biscuit into his mouth and handed Lydia the bowl. She had given him an idea. What if he could make the storm think that it had won? He rummaged below the deck, looking for the things he needed—a piece of wood from the ship, a strip of sailcloth, a length of rope.

Blood magic. He needed more blood.

He knocked at the surgeon's cabin. Throughout the storm, the surgeon had been treating men injured by falls or blows dealt by snapped rigging, broken tackles, and the twice-sprung foremast. At least a dozen men carried fresh stitches on their faces and hands. A pile of bloody rags or bloody thread would give Proctor what he needed.

"I'm cleaning up," Proctor said, looking around at

the empty corners. "Do you have anything . . . bloody rags . . . ?"

The surgeon, a passenger volunteer like Proctor, was too green to speak and looked weak from days of not keeping any food down. He huddled in the corner and shook his head. "I couldn't take the smell," he croaked. "My mate tossed it overboard."

"Thank you," Proctor said, closing the door. Without blood, his spell wouldn't work.

He saw the faces of the ordinary sailors, floating like pale ghosts in the dim light below the deck. They were watching him closely to see what he was doing. Proctor didn't care. He looked for a familiar bearded face among the men. "Jack! Jack, are you there?"

There must have been a dozen men on the ship named Jack, but only one stepped forward, the huge brute who had traveled on the *Sensible* with Proctor. "Name's not Jack on this ship, but yeah, what can I do for you?"

"I need your blood soaked on this piece of sailcloth," Proctor said.

Jack licked his lips and looked over his shoulder. A murmur ran through the rest of the crew, and Proctor knew they were talking about witchcraft, but he could deal with that if they survived. The accusations would drown with the accusers if he didn't save the ship.

"Like an offering to the sea?" Jack said, loud enough so the others could hear him.

Proctor could accept those terms. "Exactly."

Jack nodded and stepped forward, pulling up a sleeve to expose his forearm. When he was close enough to Proctor, he said, "I saw what you did on the *Sensible* to keep the pump running. It warn't natural."

"Do you believe this storm is natural?" Proctor asked.

"No, I don't."

Proctor drew the knife across his arm and pressed the

cloth against it. "Which other sailors can I ask?" Proctor said.

"You need more?" Jack asked, rolling down his sleeve.

"Yes, as many as I can get," Proctor said.

"All right." Jack turned, bracing his legs and looming in the small deck where others crouched and stood bent against the violent rocking of the storm. "Get in line, all of you, and be quick about it."

A few of them shuffled forward, but more held back. The waves beat on the ship like mallets on a drum, knocking it from side to side. When they had regained their balance, one of the men said, "What's this for?"

"It's just like the surgeon with his lancets," Jack said. "It's for your god-damned health. So if you don't step over here and volunteer, I'll bloody your nose and we'll take it that way."

Outside, the storm raged harder. The men fell into line, pressing forward one after another while Jack jerked up their sleeves and held their wrists. Proctor slid the knife across each forearm, soaked up the blood, and took the next man in line. Men averted their eyes while Proctor worked. Some made the sign of the cross on their foreheads while others said the Lord's Prayer. Water sloshed around their feet before he was done.

"That should do it," Proctor said. "Thank you, Jack."

"Rupert," the big man whispered. "My real name's Rupert."

"Thank you, Rupert."

Proctor tied the bundle together, wrapping the blood-sopped rag around the wood, and tying it all together with the rope. He went back up to the storm, but Captain Barry stood at the hatch and tried to stop him from going onto the deck.

"It's the worst blow yet," the captain said. "You'll be swept overboard—if we don't all sink."

"Is that a Bible in your hand?" Proctor asked.

"Yes, of course," Barry said.

"Well, I'm going up there to pray, out in the rain where God can hear me," Proctor said. He pulled away from Barry and climbed up the ladder onto the deck.

The wind slammed into him at once, knocking him down. The ship rolled, and he slid across the deck as a wave crashed over the side. The water hit him harder than the wind, dragging him toward the railing and the ocean.

He reached out and caught a rope.

With the bundle still tucked tight under the other arm, he pulled himself upright with one hand and slowly made his way across the ship's deck. The bitter-cold fresh water of the rain stung him like hornets, while the salt water of the ocean grabbed him by the ankles and tried to drag him under. The wind buffeted him from every direction.

He reached the mainmast and the bloodstained deck.

With his elbow hooked tight around a rope, he lifted his bundle to the wind. "Sail and rope, wood and blood, let this sacrifice satisfy you."

The ship dropped into another trough and a wave crashed over the deck like a fist meant to break it in two. It carried the bundle out of Proctor's hand and over the side, while he held on with both hands just so he wouldn't be washed away.

The wind howled in triumph. Instead of easing, the storm increased its fury, like a dog with a rabbit in its teeth, trying to snap its neck by shaking it. Lightning sliced the air around them over and over again, and thunder shattered the sky. A huge ripping sound came from the front of the ship. Proctor looked up to see that the foresail had split, and as the wind twisted and tore at the fabric it carried away the foretop mast. Another ripping sound followed as the staysail split down the middle.

Proctor screamed back with equal fury, pushing back as he created a shield of safety between the ship and the storm. He was so immersed in magic after weeks of working the same spell that he merely had to think the thought to make it happen. The rain stopped falling on the deck, and the wind whistled around them though he was left standing in an eerie stillness. It was like looking at a storm through a window, safe behind the glass. Proctor felt the power course through him, more than he had ever felt before, as he held the storm at bay. He could not say how much time passed before it broke and he collapsed to his knees. He was kneeling, as if in prayer, when the clouds split overhead and the sun shone on them for the first time in weeks.

All around them, the sea was empty.

The captured brigs were gone.

The *Lafayette,* carrying everything the Americans needed to win the war, was gone.

Proctor was carried to his cabin, exhausted, where he passed in and out of a fever for days that stretched into weeks. He heard the surgeon's voice at one point saying, "It's something in his blood," and he felt the sharp end of a lancet pierce his arm and the blood drain from him.

A bright light and the smell of burning wood and flesh snapped him awake at one point. "What happened?" he croaked when he saw Lydia. His mouth tasted like it was filled with cotton, and his throat was as raw as sunburn splashed with salt.

"Lightning hit the mainmast," she said. "Shattered the mainyard beyond repair and burned a dozen men on deck."

He fell back. Was this just bad luck or was it another attack by Dee? Had Proctor's spell failed, after all?

Before he had an answer to his question, he slipped back into his blood fever. He was trapped in a dream of storm and battle, where the orange flash of the heavy guns looked like lightning, the boom of the cannons sounded like thunder, and the screams of wounded men sounded like the cries of the drowning.

He came awake alone. Hearing the sound of cannons and the cries of men, he staggered up to the deck.

The sea was as still as a cup of water. The air had no more breath in it than a dead man. Black smoke hung over the sea like a fog, but through a gap in it, Proctor saw two ships flying British flags. They sat astern of the *Alliance,* in a position where the Americans' guns could not be brought to bear, but where they could pound it with cannons and grapeshot. One ship had sixteen guns and the other fourteen, and Proctor ducked as shot whistled overhead.

He spun around as the shot hit the damaged masts, sending out a spray of splinters. The deck was a hopeless tangle of fallen rigging, spars, and sails. A musket ball whistled by and Proctor threw himself to the deck. The Englishmen were in their masts with muskets, picking off the American crew one by one.

"Where's Captain Barry?" he yelled.

Brewer, the marine sergeant, stuck up his head to answer. "He was hit by a canister of grape. He's below—"

His sentence went unfinished as a musket ball cracked his skull. Proctor crawled over to him, dragged the bloody body over to the hatch, and carried him below to the surgeon. "Help!" he called. "We need help over here!"

The surgeon stood over another injured man, tied to a table while he cut metal out of the shoulder. He nodded to his mate, who took one look at Brewer and then pried him free of Proctor and carried him over to a corner where other men lay dead with their eyes and mouths still open. More bloody men lay propped against the walls, waiting their turn with the surgeon. Lydia moved among them, easing their pain. Her eyes met Proctor's, and he saw exhaustion in them. The battle had been going on for some time. He still didn't see Captain Barry.

Lieutenant Hacker, an earnest young officer whom Proctor might have felt a kinship with before the war, came down from the deck.

"Captain Barry, sir," he said hesitantly. "The ship is in frightful condition. The rigging is damaged beyond easy repair, and so many men have been killed or wounded, I don't know if we could repair it. Even if we did, without any wind, we're at a distinct disadvantage. Do I have your permission to strike the colors?"

The man on the surgeon's table undid the stay that held him there, threw off the surgeon's drape, and sat up. It was Barry.

"Strike the colors?" he said furiously. "If the ship cannot be fought without me, then I'll come back up to deck. Go do your duty, sir."

Hacker saluted and ran back to the deck while Barry struggled to pull on his uniform. Proctor took one last look at Barry and followed Hacker. If all they needed was wind, he could provide that.

He crouched from one piece of shattered cover to another as the snipers in the British ships continued to pick off the Americans one by one. Proctor closed his eyes and reached out with his talent. There was hardly any wind to gather, but he felt a tickle of it coming from the south, and then another tickle, and he grabbed them as a man grabs a rope and reeled them toward him. He did not even have to think to draw on the power of the life's blood already spilled on the deck. It just flowed into him.

Sails snapped above him. Those not rent to shreds by the British attack filled. The men on the deck cheered, and Hacker shouted orders at them. He could hear feet pounding to the cannons as the ship turned. Proctor lifted his head and saw both British ships still sitting dead in the water as the Alliance's starboard broadside unloaded on them. The cannons were run in and out and blasted again, and the smaller ship's flag came down. A third broadside and the second ship surrendered too.

The American crew ran across the deck, leaping and cheering and shouting.

Proctor went belowdeck and found that Barry had already heard the good news. Proctor looked him straight in the eye, and said, "Captain, when will we sail for Boston?"

"The instant we're able to raise sail," Barry said. "We've done all we can on this voyage. The Lafayette is lost to us—we won't find it now. We'll have to find some way to beat the British with what we have."

On the morning of June 6, the Alliance, battered but not broken, raised sight of Boston Harbor. Proctor's own heart leapt with hope, and as soon as they were ashore he used the last of his coin to rent ponies for himself and Lydia. They rode through the night, with only the briefest of breaks, passing through Salem and coming to The Farm a day later.

As they crossed the hilltop, Proctor felt the tingle of Deborah's protective spell. He had a vision that everything was going to be all right. He would touch the charmed gatepost, the veil that hid The Farm would be lifted, and he would find Deborah with Maggie in her arms—no, Maggie would be holding Deborah's hand, running beside her.

The oak tree stood beside the road the same as it ever

had, marking their gate. He dismounted and put his hand on the gatepost.

The veil lifted.

Beyond the barrier, The Farm lay in ruins. The barn was shattered, the house reduced to its foundations, the gardens choked with weeds.

Proctor collapsed to the ground, sobbing.

Chapter 25

He crouched on his knees at the threshold for a long time, his body racked by sobs. He had gone so far to protect his family, he faced horrors he had never imagined for their sake, and he had come home to this. The early-summer sun beat down on him with the harsh, relentless light of truth. He had failed.

After a long while, he felt Lydia's hand fall on his shoulder.

"Come on," she said softly. "We best go see what we can learn."

He rose to his feet, but there was nothing to be learned. The damage had been done a year or more ago, at exactly the time the demon had been sent to possess Deborah. The land still showed signs of being scorched, the earth was churned and abandoned, the buildings were reduced to piles of stick and rubble. Not even the chicken coop had been spared. The remnants of the roof rested on the stone foundation.

Everything that he had built, everything that he had worked for, was destroyed.

He stumbled forward, barely able to take in the destruction. The only things still standing were the chimney from the new addition, the one that Proctor had built, the one that he and Deborah had protected with the spell. A single strip of fertile land ran from the chimney to a solitary tree in the orchard. Maggie's tree. It had grown so much, he scarcely recognized it.

There were chickens under the roof of the coop. They poked their heads out as Proctor approached, pecking at the grasses along the narrow strip of ground. With Deborah's protections still in place, no wild dogs or other predators had been able to get in to attack them. A rooster poked its head up and, seeing Proctor and Lydia, began to leap and flap its wings aggressively.

Proctor brushed his hand through the air, using magic to knock the rooster fifty feet away, leaving a trail of feathers behind it. The chickens ran, squawking, and hid.

"Was that necessary?" Lydia asked. The rooster stood up, dazed, and picked at its feathers.

"She's dead. Don't you understand? They're both dead."

"All dead, you mean," she said. "If Deborah and Maggie are, then Abigail is too. But we don't know that any of them are dead yet."

"Look around—how could she be alive?"

"I see the hearth and Maggie's tree still standing. Those were the most sacred places on this farm. If they survived, I think Deborah did too."

"That's wishful thinking."

"If you have a choice on how to think, then always choose hope over fear."

He walked away from her, shaking his head. It was hopeless. He had failed. He had not beaten the Covenant. He had not stopped the demon. Still, he had to know, and the only way he knew how to know was through scrying.

He began picking through the rubble of the house, tossing broken lumber and shingles aside until he found a bowl. It had a chip in the edge but it would do. Carrying it in one hand, he went over to the shattered wall around the well and found the bucket still attached to a rope. The wood was split, and would spill as fast as he could pour, but he dropped it down into the well. It smacked the water and grew much heavier as he hauled it hand over hand back to the surface. He dumped the water into the bowl before it drained out completely.

"What are you doing?" Lydia asked.

"The only thing I know how to do," he said. The thing he should have done a long time ago. Scrying was his only natural talent, the only thing he could do that he had not learned from Deborah or because of her.

He carried the bowl full of water over to the fallen coop, and reached under the roof looking for a nest. The chickens pecked at his hand, and it stung, but he reached around until he felt eggs in a nest. He scooped one up, felt it warm in his palm, and pulled out his hand.

A flap of skin fell loose and blood streamed over his thumb and wrist.

Once, to gain the foresight, he would have had to perform an elaborate ritual in preparation.

Not so today. He would have answers if he had to grab the future by the throat and wring them free.

With that thought in his head, he lifted the egg over the bowl and crushed it in his fist. The yolk squirted out of the shell, splashing water over the sides. Pieces of shell and egg ran down his arm.

Blood dripped off his hand, three droplets, framing the egg.

The vision hit him like a waking dream.

A huge brick mansion, like the homes of London, but set in a broad plantation at twilight. He recognized slaves in the yard, and a field planted with tobacco. Somewhere in the South, maybe Virginia.

The doors opened to the mansion. John Dee, with his gray hair and pointed beard, with his long, gray robes and ruffled collar, walked out of the house and down the broad staircase to the lawn. He was followed by the prince-bishop and Cecily, and by other witches that Proctor had seen in London.

But he didn't even notice them, so full of anger was he at Dee.

He launched himself toward the wizard, intending to kill him. A field of spears surrounded him. He lifted the spears into the air and hurled them at Dee, chasing along behind them to see the job done.

That's when Deborah appeared, wrapped in shimmering light, like a creature made as much of spirit as of flesh. She stepped in front of Dee and put up a protective shield, knocking the spears to the ground.

Proctor skidded to a stop.

Deborah? She had been taken by Balfri after all. It was almost a relief to know.

"What did you see?" Lydia asked.

The heat of the sun, the clucking of the chickens, the sharp pain in his hand, all rushed over him, bringing him back to the present.

His fist was still raised in the air. He flung the bits of the egg aside. His knees wanted to buckle but he would not fall another time.

"What did you see?" Lydia repeated.

"My last chance to stop this evil," he said. "I won't fail again."

He turned and walked back toward the gate, wiping his hands clean on his thighs.

Chapter 26

It was the third week of October, and bright red and orange trees stood out among the green during daylight. At night, everything blurred to gray, with the crisp, decaying smells of autumn mixed with the fecund scent of the swamp. Proctor, expecting weather like he knew in Massachusetts, was dressed for warmth, with a broad-brimmed black hat borrowed from a Quaker, and a long black coat. Over the past few months, his beard had also grown thick. But the Virginia temperatures never came close to frost, even at night, and the extra clothes only served to set him apart from the group of partisans that he and Lydia had joined.

Two dozen men and women followed a narrow trail through a swamp. They were only one day away from the new moon, so the road was dark. The stars stood out vividly against the night, and the Milky Way drew its band of pale light across the sky, but it wasn't enough to reach the ground below, where everyone was a shadow.

Proctor and Lydia had been traveling with this group for a few days now. They were mostly black, mostly runaway slaves, but they had fallen in with the poor whites and Indians who scavenged a living off the land.

Now and then, the wind played tricks and carried the sound of cannon fire to them from across the broad river.

The sound was music to Proctor's ears. George Washington had led the American army and their French allies in a forced march with few supplies down from the North. They had penned Cornwallis up against the water at Yorktown and battered him mercilessly. It was a desperate gamble: without the supplies from the *Lafayette,* the Americans might have only one chance to beat the British. But Washington had taken that chance without blinking.

Proctor tried to keep himself ready when his own chance came.

One of the black men turned and said, "Things are going bad at Yorktown."

"I was lucky to escape," said one of the other men, a runaway slave. "Swam across the river at night. Thirty of us went there from the plantation, and twenty were dead from the pox before I escaped. It was so bad, the dogs waited outside the surgeon's tent to eat men's arms and legs as fast as the doctor cut them off—"

"That's enough of that story, Jacob," one of the women said. "We've heard it enough times now."

"Cornwallis still has a chance if the British fleet arrives," another said.

"Banastre Tarleton holds Gloucester Point, this side of the river," said another slave. "That man fights like the devil himself had a lash at his back."

"What battles has he won lately?" said the woman. "None, that's how many."

"He hasn't had a chance to fight. You wait and see."

Proctor listened to them talk and tried to adjust to the difference. For these men and women, a British victory held out some small promise of freedom. Few of them expected the British to keep their promises to runaway slaves, but they had made the promises. No matter what happened in the war, they were sure to lose. Proctor knew the feeling. "Where's this plantation you were telling me about, Jacob?" he asked.

"Hard to tell, not being on the road and all, but it's not much farther, I'm sure," he said. "Just past the cross-roads."

Proctor had seen at least a hundred plantations, most in the twilight at dawn or dusk, or by the light of the moon at night, from the safety of ditches and trees, from the cover of the slave quarters at night. Since June, he'd been searching for the plantation he'd seen in the scrying. He'd been down the coast of Maryland and Virginia, all the way to North Carolina, inland along the rivers and back again.

"The big house is just ahead," said one of the Indians, a fisherman in a soft hat and oft-mended clothes. His skin was darker and his eyes folded at the corners, or Proctor would have taken him for just another poor white. In the moonless night, it was impossible to tell his race at all.

They came to a road and walked along the verge. Lanterns glowed in the distance, and Proctor's hope grew. He knew he would find the plantation, if only because he had scryed it. But he felt like he was close.

A hundred yards farther on, as the trees opened up and he saw the plantation in full, he shook his head and stopped. "That's not it."

Greek columns lined a broad porch, even with the ground, nothing like the place he'd seen in his vision.

The leaders of their little group withdrew into the woods off the road and whispered among themselves. Proctor sat apart from the rest, his arms resting on his knees. He could see them looking at him from time to time, a half turn of the head or a quick glance over a shoulder. A mockingbird leapt from shrub to tree to fallen log, imitating several other birds in quick succession.

"You aren't what you seem to be, are you?" Proctor said as the large bird emitted the call of a tiny wren.

At the sound of his voice, Lydia rose and came over to

his side. "They aren't trying to exclude you from the discussion," she said.

Proctor waved off the apology with a small motion of his hand. "I know they don't trust me because I'm white," he said.

"They don't trust you because you look and act like a crazy man," Lydia said.

He let that sink in. "Maybe I am."

"Some of them think you're a hoodoo man or a pow-wow man."

They weren't wrong, but he had not used his talent among them. "Is that what they say?"

"No, it's what they don't say, and the questions they ask me," she said.

"I understand. I can go on by myself. I've dragged you far enough."

"I haven't come for you," she said. "I've come for Deborah's sake, and Maggie's, and Abigail's."

"You may not like what we find," he said.

"Somebody's got to be there to remember them," she said.

The group of runaways and freemen rose and walked over to Proctor. The fisherman spoke for them. "The men here are divided. Some want to join the British garrison at Gloucester Point. They think that Tarleton will keep on fighting, and that the British ships will come, and they will have their freedom. Others want to turn around and go west to join the Cherokee in the mountains, though that is a long, hard journey, over land that I will not travel."

That urge for freedom. Proctor could see Lydia tense, ready to go either direction.

"I would not put any trust in the British," Proctor said. "Go west to the Cherokee, but don't stop there. Go farther west if you can."

Some of the men and women nodded among themselves. They had been thinking the very same thing.

Jacob stepped forward. "There's one more plantation, it might be the one you described. If we go back to the crossroads and follow it around to the river's edge, we'll come to it."

Proctor would visit every plantation in America if he had to, but there was no reason to drag these other people along. "How do you know of it?" he asked.

"It's called Rosewell. My master Thomas Jefferson stayed there in 'seventy-six, when he was writing the Declaration of Independence."

Proctor's skin goose-pimpled with anticipation. The residence where Jefferson drafted the Declaration of Independence would be exactly the kind of place where the Covenant would seek to destroy that independence. Crush freedom at its source.

"Can you take me there?" Proctor asked.

Jacob nodded. They all set out together, but as they passed the crossroads, Proctor noticed the others turn away. "They don't want to go this way," Jacob said.

Proctor didn't ask them why. He didn't have the right. "If you don't want to go on, just point the way," he said. "I'll find it myself."

Jacob tipped his felt hat. "Thank you for that. I'm going to follow the Dragon to freedom myself, I think."

"Follow the dragon?"

"Dragon Swamp," Jacob said. "We want to get a head start on that way west."

He turned and ran after the others without further good-bye. Proctor looked at Lydia. "Do you want to go as well?"

"I can't explain it," she said. "I feel a strong urge to go the other way. But I won't. I came to see this through."

Odd, but he didn't feel that at all. Instead, he felt drawn onward, as if he was headed to the place he was appointed to reach.

The road was dark and silent, curving through the

woods. The green smell of fresh water tinged the air. The trees grew thicker as they went, at least until Proctor stepped on a stick in the road. The branches were filled with hundreds of black crows that he had mistaken for leaves—at the loud snap, they flapped their wings and swirled into the sky before settling down again where they had started.

"Is that normal?" Proctor asked.

"I've never seen it before," Lydia whispered in reply. "But they're carrion birds, and there is a battle just across the river."

As if in response to her mention, the sound of cannons echoed over the water from miles away. The wind that carried the sound rummaged through the trees, ruffling feathers and sending autumn leaves tumbling to the ground.

This was the place. Proctor was certain.

They pushed on, down a long lane lined with trees. The woods were full of saplings, thick as a thumb, as if the clearing and mowing had been neglected. When the road opened out on acres of broad lawn, Proctor recognized the place at once.

A brick mansion on a foundation six feet tall, rising three stories, with each story twelve feet high, was framed by four massive chimneys, one at each of the corners. There were five windows across each floor, including the windows framing the entry door, and a light shone in every window. They spilled out over the structure, illuminating the fine brickwork and the elegant proportions. It was as if a building had been lifted from the London street where Lord Gordon lived, or even the neighborhood of Lord Shelburne, and dropped in the middle of the Virginia woods. The door was cracked open, and the sounds of stringed instruments came from within, and people whirled in the light as if dancing. Laughter echoed out across the grass.

A single figure stood on the doorstep.

He had long gray robes and a ruffled collar. He reached back and pushed the door open, saying something to those inside. Then he walked down the wide stairs to the lawn. A large man blocked the light streaming through the doorway. He was followed by a petite woman in an elaborate dress. They were both followed by a priest. The priest was followed by a beautiful young woman in a black dress of foreign, almost Oriental, cut.

One by one they walked down the steps and faced Proctor across the lawn.

John Dee. The prince-bishop, Philipp Adolph von Ehrenberg. Cecily Sumpter Pinckney. William Weston, the English Jesuit. Proctor thought the fifth one might be Erzebet Nádasdy. That was the only other name Gordon had given him that he remembered.

A blond boy in a tattered red coat skipped out of the woods laughing hilariously, slapping his chest and spinning around. The sleeves of his jacket hung down over his hands, but his pants were too short, and his ankles stuck out of the bottom. His hair was wild and unbrushed. As he stepped into the light cast by the house, Proctor recognized him.

"William."

William Reed. The orphan boy whom Proctor had lost to the prince-bishop at Trenton. The boy lifted his head at the sound of his name, even whispered from a hundred yards away. His eyes glowed like fire. He ran over to the prince-bishop, who wrapped an arm around him and stroked his head like a man with a favorite pet.

"Behold, the herald of Balfri, come in advance of his master," John Dee said with a sweeping motion of his hand. Though he spoke in a normal tone, his voice carried, just as Gordon's had, clear to Proctor's ear.

Four hooves thundered on the dark road behind Proctor. A man in a worn green jacket, faded and torn like the leaves in autumn, with a black cap upon his head, galloped past. A woman in a gray dress—gray like the color of Dee's robes—sat behind him. She glowed with a numinous light. *Deborah*.

Proctor had waited, frozen, too long.

He spread out his arm toward the hundreds of saplings growing in the woods. With one slash of his hand, all the branches and leaves were stripped bare. A second gesture—a spin of his fingers—whirled around the tops, sharpening them to pointed stakes. A third motion, his hands raised up, snapped all of them off at the ground and brought them up in the air like spears.

With a roar, he pulled both arms back and flung them forward. The spears flew toward the tiny group of witches and the little demon boy.

The woman in the gray dress—Proctor tried not to look at her; he didn't want to fight her—slipped off the back of the horse and passed her hand through the air.

The spears hit in an invisible shield just short of the witches and fell to the ground.

"No, Deborah, not like this," Proctor whispered.

But he ran forward, already launching his next attack. He saw two large boulders on either side of the lawn, amid other small ones.

He lifted the boulders, dripping dirt and grass, and sent them hurling toward each other like two mortar stones, big enough to grind the Covenant to bone and meal between them.

Deborah reached into the air and cast the boulders aside. They flew high up into the night sky across the river and out toward the bay. They boomed, cracking the air as thunder did, and then caught fire as they burned up like shooting stars. He had never seen that kind of power from her before.

"Don't stop me, Deborah," Proctor whispered.

He whirled his hand in the air, calling forth every piece of metal and silver from the house. There were knives and sabers, awls and saws, every kind of sharp tool or blade you would find on a large plantation. They flew out of the door like a nest of hornets. He spun the mass in a circle and sent it whipping toward the Covenant, too fast to deflect and toss away.

Deborah dropped her hands to her sides and walked into the path of the blades, blocking the way to the Covenant.

It wasn't Deborah, Proctor told himself.

She had been possessed by the demon Balfri.

Balfri must be destroyed. He was the only one who could do it. He had been prepared for it by his journey, brought by steps to a greater power than he had ever dreamed possible. Balfri had to be stopped, and he was the instrument of its destruction.

But he couldn't do it, not even if Deborah was only the shell of herself.

When the whirling blades were inches from cutting her to shreds, he flung them to the ground. He dropped to his knees a second later, exhausted. He had drained himself and accomplished nothing. He covered his face, and said he was sorry over and over again, not sure whether he was apologizing to Deborah for failing or for nearly chopping her to pieces.

The orphan boy—what did Dee call him? Balfri's herald—capered and laughed, clapping his hands with glee.

"Make way for Balfri," he shouted. "Lord of the red coat, the purifying flame, the scorching wind. Balfri, the bond and the fetter. Balfri, the covenant fulfilled and the master of mighty legions. Make way!"

Deborah walked across the lawn toward Proctor. She always seemed to glide, so sure and steady was her step. He could not lift his head to look at her face as she approached. When she stopped in front of him, he saw only the hem of her dress.

"I'm sorry," she said, sounding the same as she ever had. "I cannot let you harm them while they possess my daughter—"

He had turned his face toward her when she mentioned their daughter. She was the same Deborah he had always known. Her cap had fallen off, and her hair tumbled down around her shoulders. But she had the same determined set to her mouth, the same large eyes, the same numinous inner light.

". . . Proctor?" She reached out to him.

Words would not come to him, but he reached back. Their hands touched and, after a moment's hesitation, clasped. A pure light flowed through their grip. He jumped to his feet and wrapped his arms around her. She fit in his embrace, the way she had before. He pressed his face against her head—she smelled wonderful, familiar. There were bits of dried flowers falling from her hair.

"I'm so sorry," he whispered. "I thought you were—"

She threw her arms around his neck. "I didn't recognize you," she said. "I thought you were . . . I thought you were dead, that you were never coming back, that you had run off to Russia with that countess."

"What—? No!"

She held his head in her hands and started kissing his face, his eyes, his lips. He kissed her in return, feeling the tears roll down his cheeks.

"I would never leave you," he said. "I thought you had been possessed . . . I . . . I thought . . . I was wrong, I was so wrong . . ."

She didn't stop kissing him so he stopped speaking instead. He could feel the tears on her cheeks, mixing with his where their faces pressed against each other.

A shadow fell over them.

"Now that we are all reunited," Dee said, "it's time for us to begin. Balfri has already waited too long."

Chapter 27

Ropes slithered across the ground like snakes, tying them up. They were both too weak to resist. The ropes wound around them, binding them to each other, and then a single strand climbed straight into the air, as rigid as a pole, and looped itself over an invisible branch. The two of them dangled there.

"Why didn't you recognize me?" Proctor asked as he struggled against the ropes.

"You've changed—so powerful, the black clothes—I thought you were a rival witch."

"They have Maggie?"

"I sent her into hiding with Abigail, but they found them."

"What . . . where were you?"

"I had stopped their herald, and held him a prisoner—I was healing him, or so I thought—until tonight he escaped."

Dee moved like a mathematician writing out an equation. He stood in the center of the great lawn and spun slowly with his hand outstretched. Fire leapt from his fingertip, scorching a large circle in the grass. When the circle was complete, he slashed his hand in a series of five sharp motions, completing the pentagram.

The same symbol he had drawn in fire in London during the riots.

"The two of you might have been good students," Dee said. "If only you hadn't been born in this wilderness. The star is a powerful symbol to astronomer and astrologer, to the mathematician and the necromancer alike. It is from the Greek word *pentagrammon*, meaning 'five-lined,' but it is associated with the Roman word *lucifer*, meaning 'bringer of light and knowledge.' I consider myself a bringer of light and knowledge to this dark world."

"I know you wanted to speak to the angels," Proctor called to Dee. "But listen to yourself—only demons answered your call."

"Call them what you will, but one man's demons are another man's angels," Dee replied.

The Jesuit carried the rosary in his hand. He looked up, startled, mouth half open, as if interrupted in his prayers. His eyes were milky white, and he turned his ears toward them rather than his face. "God is in all things," he said. "Whether you call the beings of spirit angels or demons matters not at all, because God is present."

Deborah could not accept that answer. "But—"

"Would you find it easier to stay silent if I stuffed rags in your mouth?" Cecily said. She cupped her hands and wiggled her fingers.

Proctor felt the hem of his shirt unravel, with threads crawling under the rope like an army of worms intent on filling his throat. He kicked and strained, hoping to give them less room to move over his skin. Deborah choked off a cry and began to kick and struggle just as hard.

Dee waved his hand impatiently and the worms stopped. "It is not yet the darkest part of the night. We have a moment or two."

The prince-bishop stepped onto the point of a star, followed by the three other witches at three other points. "You are too much the professor," he said to Dee impatiently.

"And yet how much have you learned from me because of that, my friend?" Dee said. He never took his eyes off Proctor and Deborah when he spoke, as though they were either curiosities or dangers—*Please, God, let us be a danger,* Proctor prayed. "Did Thomas Digges tell you his proof, that the universe is infinite and all the stars are suns?" Dee asked.

Deborah looked puzzled, but Proctor knew that the longer they kept Dee talking, the better the chance they had to reconnect with their source of power and find a way to escape. "Yes," he said. "It must make you feel very small and insignificant."

"Not at all," Dee said, smiling. "Consider it mathematically. If the universe extends infinitely in every direction, then it forms a sphere, and I am the center of that sphere. The universe and everything in it revolves around me. If I am the center of the universe, then why should I not do exactly as I please?"

"We are all at the center of the universe," grumbled the prince-bishop.

"The universe is the sacred heart of God, and He holds all of us at the center of it," said the blind priest.

Dee nodded acceptance of these remarks. Cecily held her tongue, perhaps as the newest member of this group. Proctor wondered if she replaced the widow Nance. The fifth member—Erzebet Nádasdy—he was beginning to think of as the silent woman. Perhaps she had her doubts, just as the Countess Cagliostro had. Somewhere there had to be a crack.

The little boy possessed by the demon began to run around the circle with his arms extended like a bird's. "It's time it's time it's time it's time. Summon Balfri of the legions, summon Balfri of the blood-red coat!"

Dee turned his head away from Proctor and Deborah, and stepped onto the fifth point of the pentagram.

"My friends," Dee said. "By this act, we shall all live long enough to see the second coming. By this act, we shall all stay young forever, until the end of days. By this act, we shall, like Enoch, live to ascend to heaven without dying."

The five witches at the five points of the star held out their hands. Though they did not touch, a cold blue flame leapt out from Dee's left hand and ran around the circle until it returned to him. The light ran down his legs and traced the circle and star on the ground, making them all glow with a flickering blue light.

"Living without dying sounds great," Proctor mumbled to Deborah, "until you realize that they do it only by making others die in their stead."

"I can't touch my talent at all," Deborah said.

He shook his head. He couldn't either. "I can't even free my hands."

Dee tilted his head back and began speaking in a language that neither Proctor nor Deborah could understand.

"Ils diaspert soba vpaah chis nanbazixlai dodsih . . ."

The air shimmered as he spoke and an oval lozenge of blue light, as large as the entrance to a cathedral, blossomed into being. It floated above the earth, at the center of the star. As Dee continued to speak, it began to spin, and as it spun, it changed colors, from blue to white to yellow to orange to red, bright and twitchy, each one like a flame. The light of the star and circle scratched in the earth changed color with it. When it reached bright red, like a glowing coal, it stopped spinning abruptly. A loud clang sounded, like the chime from a broken bell.

The orphan boy cheered and leapt into the air. "Behold, Balfri!"

Proctor had faced demons before. So they were summoning a demon. He could face one more demon. A human shape, drawn in flame, twisted with horns and talons, tusks and tail, stepped through the oval door. It carried a cudgel formed from some giant bone. It was much larger than the other demons Proctor had seen, but it could be beaten.

"Is that all?" he said.

The demon marched out of the way, and it was followed by another demon, and another. They carried rough instruments of war—broken swords, spears with shattered shafts, shields with great chunks torn out of them. Demon after demon, they flowed across the lawn and into rows like an army marching. Hundreds. And then thousands.

The orphan boy looked at Proctor. "Balfri's other name is Legion," he said.

Dee lifted his hands to the heavens. "Let the words of the angels and of men be the same. O thou, the third flame, beyond the flame of flesh, the flame of spirit, whose wings are thorns to stir up vexation, and who hast twenty thousand living lamps marching before thee, whose God is wrath and anger. Gird up thy loins and hearken to my word."

Proctor twisted helplessly, looking from side to side. He had hoped that Lydia was still nearby, that she would come and cut them free. But he did not expect it of her and did not blame her for running. He hoped that she was far, far away before this horde was unleashed.

He and Deborah were bound side by side. In his struggle to get free, he had wiggled his hands through the ropes, so that his fingers could touch hers. He pushed through them now and closed his hand around hers. He felt a small, hopeful spark as they touched.

"Accept our humble offering, O Lord," Dee said. "Let all the rivers of talent flow into a single ocean, which is Your will. Take these soldiers and let the destiny of this country manifest from one ocean to the other. Make the world a single empire, under Your order, on which the sun never sets."

A final demon stepped through the portal, larger than the others. Its limbs were like the trunks of mighty oaks sheathed in flame, and it wore a red coat. Its eyes were as black as coals, and its mouth was a white-hot furnace ringed by the charred stumps of broken teeth. It carried a two-headed ax in its right hand. Wings unfolded from its back like vast clouds of smoke.

This was it then. This was the worst they could face. Proctor swallowed hard and found the determination to face it. "We have to stop that," he whispered.

Deborah nodded mutely.

The demon's left leg seemed to be stuck in the portal. Turning its head, it roared and the ground shook so hard that even the windows in the mansion rattled. With one final jerk, it pulled its leg through. There was a cuff around the ankle and a chain. At the other end of the chain was a second demon.

The second demon came through the gate. She was slender and whip-like, like a summer grass fire. Long black hair tumbled off her head like billowing smoke, and her wings spread translucent as flames torn free in the wind. She wore a long red coat like her mate. In her left hand, she carried a knife with a hilt as black as charred bone and a blade as red as blood.

The two demons connected by the single chain looked at Proctor and Deborah hungrily. Tongues of fire licked the edges of their charred mouths.

Dee held out his hands to Proctor and Deborah. "Let these vessels be a gift unto You. Let them be possessed by Your holy spirits, and by this possession see Your spirits made flesh, to lead this army of spirits and make this army flesh, to do Your will."

The legion of demons, thousands of them, in line upon line spread across the lawn, roared and stomped their feet.

Proctor could feel Deborah's fingers trying to push through the rope to take his hand.

Dee turned toward the house. "Bring the child," he commanded. "When they sacrifice the life of their own daughter, it will make the binding spell complete."

"Maggie," Deborah gasped.

The light of the house seemed cold and small and distant compared with the blinding flame of the army arrayed before it. On the top step, just outside the door, stood Abigail in her simple farm dress. She walked like a puppet with a small child firmly in her grip. The child cried and tried to pull away from Abigail, but she wouldn't let go.

"Maggie?" Proctor whispered.

"Don't let them have her!" Deborah screamed desperately.

The pair of demons shook as if they were chuckling, as if resistance made possession sweeter, as though any fight against them was futile. The little boy in the red coat—Proctor would not think of him as William; William wasn't present anymore—danced around their legs.

But Abigail was as stubborn as a mule, as tough to move as an old stump. The sound of Deborah's voice shook something loose in her, gave her a strength that she did not have alone. With a visible effort she shook off the control that Dee had over her body. She grabbed Maggie and shielded her with her body, turning to leap off the steps.

"Nein," said the German.

With a simple flick of his hand, he stripped Abigail's flesh from her bones. Skin, muscle, and organs were splattered in a streak across the lawn while her bones clattered in a pile on the steps. The silent witch licked her fingertips and then sucked on them. Proctor winced and caught his breath.

It happened so suddenly that Abigail's spirit did not know she was dead. Her dress was now pure white, but otherwise nothing had changed. She stood on the steps where her living body had been, half turned toward the house. Maggie dropped out of her arms, but she looked up at the familiar face as if that were all she saw.

Run, Abigail said, and she pushed Maggie toward the ring of trees nearest the house. Maggie toddled toward darkness. Nearby, demons chuckled.

Proctor jammed his hand through the ropes and clasped Deborah's hand in his. He felt a sharp shock as they touched. Deborah gasped. Alone, they were cut off from their talent, but together—

"Rain is the enemy of fire," he said. "Let it storm like it has never stormed before."

"Yes," she said.

More power surged through Proctor than he had ever felt before. Hours' worth of clouds rolled in overhead in a second, and the first fat drops of rain were followed a second later by a torrent.

The demons crackled and sizzled like doused fire in the sudden storm. The legions stomped their feet and writhed in agony, like creatures splashed with lye. Balfri, the paired demon, tried to go two ways at once, out of the rain, but was checked by the chain that bound it at the ankles. Angry and frustrated, they lashed out with ax and blade, scattering the witches of the Covenant.

Deborah lifted her head to the sky and cried out. Lightning struck the ground all around them, with thunder louder than the stomping of the demons. Rain fell in waves, as if the river had been channeled into the sky and emptied on them. It fell in sheets so thick that for a moment, Proctor could not see even as far as the house.

Proctor could feel the power flowing through him. He ripped through the ropes. As they fell off, limp and dead, he and Deborah dropped hard to the rain-soaked earth.

It was enough to shatter Deborah's focus. The rain lessened and Dee stepped forward out of the fog and mist.

"Enough," he shouted. "Bring forth the herald. Let him proclaim the reign of Balfri and be done with this."

The demons held their heads up against the lessening rain. Balfri stopped fighting itself and stood its ground with four vast wings outspread. The rain crackled and sizzled as it hit Balfri, like water on a hot skillet. The other four witches of the Covenant formed a line on either side of Dee, the prince-bishop and Cecily to his right, and the priest and the silent woman to his left. The wind whipped the trees into a confusion of green and black.

Proctor struggled to his feet, pulling Deborah with him.

The boy-herald stepped forward. "All hail, Balfri. Welcome, Balfri—"

The last words bubbled out of his mouth, drowned in blood. The point of a cavalry saber protruded from his chest. The boy grabbed at it, trying to pull it all the way through, but his hands kept sliding off the blade. He toppled forward, off the saber, and fell to the ground.

The demon, liberated from the boy's flesh, hopped from side to side, like an animal looking for cover. Before it could act, it faded and disappeared.

A British officer stood over the dead boy's body. He was of small build, with a boyish cast to his face. His dark green jacket and black cap blended in with the wet night so that only his face showed clearly in the dark.

"Tarleton," Deborah said, her voice cracked with sorrow.

He stared at the bloody saber in his hand. "I will not abide evil any longer," he said. "I will not have an army of men turned into the monster that I saw myself become, not even if that is the only way to win this war."

The prince-bishop staggered over to William and knelt, cradling the dead body in his lap. "Not you, too, my pretty boy, not you." The oval portal had faded to a mere line. With the herald dead, and the rain falling steady, the legion began to fade.

"Do something," Cecily demanded of Dee.

"The blood of an innocent, shed in violence, is a powerful focus," he said, walking over to the dead boy. Dipping his fingers in blood, he began writing letters in the air, where they hung like shimmering glyphs of fire.

"No," said Deborah. "I will not allow it."

She erased them with a sweep of her hand.

Dee's calm was finally shaken. He turned to Balfri and screamed, "Take them, just take them now."

Balfri growled and stepped forward. The male half smashed Dee to the ground and stepped over the mage's still body. The she-demon followed him through the rain, reaching for Deborah.

Proctor did not know if Balfri meant to attack Deborah or possess her. He didn't care. They weren't going to touch her. He blocked them with a shield of light. The she-demon struck at him with her knife, and he knocked it aside. The ax fell, and he lifted the shield over his head. The blow shook him to his knees. They attacked him furiously, but they had to come at him together, and he deflected each blow. Finally the knife and ax fell toward him at the same time, and he slammed them aside with a sideways blow of his shield.

The edge of the shield, formed of light and spirit, struck the chain that bound them together and shattered it.

The demons howled in delight and jumped apart. They prepared to attack Proctor from either side, but they shrank in size and power as they moved away from each other.

"What a stupid waste," the silent woman said. She looked over Dee's shattered body. "Balfri without the bond is not Balfri. The Covenant is no covenant once the promise is broken." She raised her head to the demons. "You are free. Go on your way. Seek your own purpose."

She took the blind priest by the hand, turned to the side, and they both disappeared. One moment they were there; the next they were gone. The legion of demons broke and scattered into the woods and across the river like an army under rout. Balfri started for Proctor and Deborah, and then both halves turned and fled in opposite directions. All that remained was the sliver of light above the faint scar of the pentagram and circle still glowing in the earth. Proctor and Deborah stood on one side of it. On the other, the prince-bishop cradled the dead boy in his arms. Tarleton stood over them both.

"I'll kill you," the prince-bishop said, pushing the dead boy aside. But as he rose to attack Tarleton, the cavalry commander stepped in and sliced off his head with a sweep of his saber.

"I think not," he murmured as the head rolled one way and the ancient body collapsed to the ground. It imploded on itself, leaving nothing but smoldering clothes behind.

The ring of knives and blades of all kinds, scattered on the ground where Proctor had dropped them to preserve Deborah, rose suddenly into the air. Cecily stood, soaked to her skin, her face contorted with rage. She pulled her arms back to hurl the weapons at Proctor and Deborah.

Proctor tried to summon the power to stop them and felt depleted again. He threw his body in front of Deborah to protect her from the worst of the weapons.

Before they came hurtling through the air, Cecily crumpled to the ground, the blades dropping with her. Lydia stood over her with a heavy piece of wood. Rage contorted her face just as it had Cecily's. She raised the log above her head again to smash it down on the other witch's head.

Deborah shoved Proctor aside. "Please, Lydia."

Lydia hesitated. "Did you see what she did? What she did to me? What they did to Abigail?"

"I won't make you drop it," Deborah said. "But I'm asking you to. There's been enough violence. Enough killing. We can only begin to heal these wounds with love."

"No." Lydia shook her head. "No, absolutely not." She pulled the log back over her head. "I will never love that woman. I will never forgive her."

When she brought her arms forward, she hurled the log into the darkness instead of bringing it down on the still form at her feet.

"Thank you," Deborah whispered. She walked over and embraced Lydia.

"I did it for you," Lydia said.

"You did it for yourself," Deborah answered.

Proctor grabbed them both by the shoulders. "We must hurry," he said. "Before the demons spread too far. We must call them back and return them to their own realm." He took Dee's position at the point of the star.

"What about Maggie?" Deborah asked, startled into the moment. Her head turned frantically in the dark. "We need to find her."

"We must do this first," Lydia said. "I don't want those creatures free in this world, not even one of them." She took Cecily's point in the star.

Tarleton stepped up to the prince-bishop's point. The bloody saber trailed from his hand, scratching a line through the rain-slicked grass. "I want to help."

"Throw away the sword," Deborah said.

Tarleton lifted the saber and looked at it. "I've trusted you for months. You protected me from that demon, even when you couldn't free him or me. I'll trust you in this."

He cast the weapon aside.

They only had four points of the star covered, but it would have to do. Proctor closed his eyes and stretched out his hands, trying to remember the words that Deborah had spoken in the orchard at home before he left for France.

When he opened his eyes, Abigail's spirit stood at the fifth point *What do we do now?* she asked.

She still didn't seem to know that she was dead. Perhaps that was appropriate. He lifted his face toward the sky and felt the rain falling on him. "Let us confront evil with justice and mercy," he answered. "Let us always answer fear with love. Let us turn every mark of destruction into a garden of hope."

A cool light, pure and white, flowed out of Proctor's right hand. It soothed the ache in his scarred finger, and for the first time in years he felt no pain in it. The light flowed from his hand around the circle and returned to him again, magnified to the fifth power.

"Yes," Deborah whispered.

The star and circle glowed like ice in the moonlight, healing the marks made in the earth by Dee and returning it to its natural condition.

"Let this world be for the creatures born to this world," Proctor said. "Let the world of spirit belong to the creatures born there. Let those who passed through the gateway here tonight be returned through the gateway to the world where they belong."

The thin line of light that hung above the center of the circle began to vibrate and glow. As it widened into an oval, it started to spin. When it stopped spinning, it was a door of pure light that felt both close and far away, as if it waited at the end of a long, dark tunnel.

Abigail's spirit gasped. *That is so beautiful.*

"Call them back," Proctor said. "Call back all those who passed this way once already."

From the open door of the house, a clock began to chime. From the portal, a second bell also chimed, deeper and more resonant. The hour was midnight. By the third stroke of the bell, the demons began to flow back through the gate. By the sixth stroke, whole files of the legion flowed through it, wailing and gnashing their

teeth. On the ninth stroke, Balfri appeared from two opposite directions, dragged against its will. The two halves
beat wings against the air, trying to slow down. They
grew in size and strength as they came closer together,
and the more they grew, the stronger they resisted.

"If they're not through by the twelfth stroke . . . ?"
Tarleton asked. He eyed his saber.

"Take them all," Proctor said. "Take them all back."

On the eleventh stroke, Balfri was sucked into the portal. Each half stuck out a hand and gripped the edge, re-
fusing to go through. Both of them started clawing their
way back out of the gate.

Abigail stepped into the circle and, spirit-to-spirit,
pried their fingers loose as the twelfth stroke fell.

Balfri flew into the portal and the light snapped shut.

The five of them were all standing in the sudden darkness, in the rain, while the wind swirled and twisted
around them. Tarleton squinted into the rain and said,
"Well, this is the end of the war. Cornwallis meant to escape across the river tonight, but in this weather he
won't be able to. He'll have to surrender to Washington
tomorrow."

Abigail dusted her hands and had opened her mouth
to say something when she suddenly noticed that she,
alone among all of them, glowed.

She blinked out of existence on the lawn and reap-
peared the next second on the steps of the mansion,
where she'd been standing when the prince-bishop killed
her. She turned and looked for Maggie.

Maggie, hiding in some bushes near the house, ran out
with her arms open, yelling, "Abby!"

Abigail, grinning, reached down to pick her up. The
toddler slipped right through her spectral arms. With a
confused face, she looked at her hands and blinked out
of existence. A second later she appeared again, looking
for Maggie.

Deborah sprinted toward the stairs, followed by Proctor. She grabbed up Maggie and held her tight to her chest, rocking her back and forth.

"She's beautiful," Proctor said. She looked just like Deborah.

The mansion stood with lights in every window and the door wide open. Inside, the residents, all finely attired, stepped to the door and looked at the sky as if surprised by the rain. They looked dazed, like people waking from a sleep. The finely parqueted floors gleamed. Oriental rugs with elaborate designs filled the halls between rooms. Finely carved furniture lined the walls; fine paintings hung over them while elegant draperies framed the windows. Candelabra filled every room with light. One of the musicians coughed and nervously plucked at the strings of his cello.

"May we help you?" asked the mistress of the house.

"If you have any scotch, that would be a welcome blessing," Tarleton said, stomping up the stairs. "You have a lovely place, but I would like to forget that I was ever here."

Deborah and Proctor stood on the bottom step, with the ghost of Abigail shimmering in and out of existence above them and Lydia in the flickering shadows below. Deborah hugged Maggie close, rubbing her face against the little girl's cheek until she was annoyed. "Here, say hi," she said and tried to pass Maggie to Proctor.

Proctor held out his hands, but Maggie squirmed back into her mother's arms and hid from him.

"Go on," Deborah said and tried again.

Maggie shook her head and clung to Deborah. She peeked over her shoulder at Proctor, and said, "Who man?"

"That's your father." Deborah's eyes met Proctor's. She started to apologize, but he stopped her.

"How would she know who I am?" he asked. "She's

never spent any time with me. I'll have to make that right."

Inside, the band struck up a lively song and people began to whirl and dance across the high-ceilinged room. Proctor stepped in close and wrapped his arms around Deborah and Maggie, hugging them both while the rain poured over them.

Chapter 28

It was midafternoon and Proctor and Deborah had been waiting since noon for the British army to arrive. Proctor had shaved and cut his hair. Deborah had found a cap and tied her hair back under it again. Both of them wanted to look their best for Cornwallis's surrender.

The American and French armies lined the road out of Yorktown. The Americans were as mixed as the colonies: some were in uniform and others were not, some carried their issued weapons and others carried their own, some were clean and neat while others looked like they had just crawled out of a swamp. But in their countenance they were unified. Every man stood at attention and every face beamed with open joy. The French stood on the left of the road, an unbroken line of men in full and matching uniforms, their weapons as regular and even as fence-posts. Their expressions filled a range from impatient to happy to smug satisfaction.

In one item, the two lines were identical. The French soldiers had pinned the black cockade of the American uniform onto their own cockade, and the Continental army reciprocated by pinning the white French cockade onto theirs. All hats on both sides were adorned with the black-and-white ribbons as a sign of union.

The hats—and both lines of soldiers beneath them—stretched a mile down the road, toward the English fort. Thousands upon thousands of soldiers. They were surrounded by thousands of civilians—old farmers in straw hats, poor women ringed by broods of children, young ladies in their finest hats and dresses, men and women slaves with bare heads and free blacks in homespun clothing, red men in the coats and trousers of local laborers, Chesapeake fishermen still wearing their weather gear, veterans on crutches or with their sleeves pinned up, wives in widows' clothing.

Proctor leaned over to Deborah and whispered, "I think there are more civilians than soldiers."

She glared at him and placed a finger to her lips. He looked over at Lydia, but she glared also.

They had a point. For two hours, not one of the thousands of soldiers had spoken, shifted out of line, or made another noise. Their joyful solemnity was contagious, and the crowd had fallen into the same mood of anticipation.

Only the horses seemed bored. Comte de Rochambeau sat astride his courser at the head of the French line, surrounded by his suite of officers. Their sky-blue-and-white uniforms matched the color of the autumn sky. His horse twitched its bobbed tail and seemed ready to run off to the next fight.

Proctor and Deborah had taken a position on a hill behind the French line so they could watch their friends and countrymen across the road. Washington sat astride his white horse, Blue Skin, the one he preferred for parades. He was surrounded by his closest officers and aides. Alexander Hamilton was there, still followed by his ghost. The Marquis de Lafayette stood with the American forces instead of the French. Proctor tried to catch the eye of his former commander, Tench Tilghman, who had been at Washington's side the entire time that Proctor had served, but Tilghman stared straight ahead, a model of military pride.

Maggie was quietly snuggling against Deborah's shoulder. At two years old, she was nearly too big for Deborah to carry for long periods of time. Proctor was going to offer to hold her when Maggie's head popped up and she twisted around. Pointing down the road, she said, "Dum!"

Proctor had his fingers to his lips to shush her when he heard it too. The melancholy *dum-da-dum* of drums at slow march. The soldiers in line continued to stand at attention, but the civilians all around them strained to see the British.

As the troops came closer, and the beat grew clearer, an old Irishman behind Proctor began to hum a tune. As it came to the end of a verse he mumbled the words of a song.

". . . Yet let's be content, and no more lament, you see the world turn'd upside down."

Proctor almost laughed. "I didn't recognize the music with only the drums. Is that the song they're playing?"

The old man shrugged. "I dunno," he said, then tapped his ear. "But that's the song I'm hearing."

That did make Proctor laugh. Although in his head, the world had stayed right-side up. Only if it fell to the Covenant would it be upside down.

As the British soldiers came closer, Proctor saw that they had their flags furled in surrender. They marched with their heads turned to face left, so that they were only acknowledging the French army. It was a petty slight against the Americans, or a sign of respect for their ancient enemy. Proctor accepted that there was nothing to be done about it, but suddenly pipes and timbrels sounded along the French line. Within a few bars, the French had started playing "Yankee Doodle," the closest thing to a true national anthem the young country possessed.

The British heads snapped face-forward. They would not acknowledge the French if it meant honoring the Americans. At that moment, Proctor loved France more than he had at any moment since he'd left the country.

Maggie started to bounce along with the song. "Yank we doodle came to down," she sang. Deborah's face lit up, and she started bouncing along with Maggie.

"I think that's the closest thing to dancing I've ever seen you do," Proctor said.

"Maybe you need to bring a French band home more often," Deborah whispered.

As the British troops approached within a couple hundred feet, their red coats stood out against the autumnal landscape. Every man was dressed in a bright new uniform that was clean and neat enough to outshine the French. The contrast with the American soldiers in their various gear could not have been more marked. The single general riding at the head of their troops seemed beaten and dejected.

As the rider came closer, the crowd pressed in behind Proctor and Deborah. They all wanted to see the expression on General Cornwallis's face. He was known for his noble features, and for his calm and steady disposition. It was impossible to guess what effect the loss would have on him.

And impossible to see. The British troops were led not by Cornwallis, but by his second in command, General O'Hara, a choleric man doing his best to appear stoic. Proctor was disappointed.

General O'Hara finally came to the end of the line. The British drums stopped. The army of Redcoats stretched out along the road for a mile behind him, all of them standing at a sort of restless attention as if they were eager to be done. The French and American musicians stopped their music also.

For a brief moment, there was perfect silence.

Into the silence rose Maggie's voice. "All gone song. More song!"

Deborah whispered something in her ear and gently bounced her. General O'Hara cleared his throat and dismounted, holding a sword and scabbard in his right hand. He turned neatly toward the Comte de Rochambeau.

"I offer my sincere apologies for the non-appearance of Lord Cornwallis on account of indisposition," General O'Hara said. "He sends his regrets, and asks me to present his sword."

He held out the sword in both hands.

Proctor was stunned. Not only did Cornwallis not show, but they were going to surrender to the French instead. They were trying to steal the victory away from the Americans.

Comte de Rochambeau bowed his head and removed his hat in one smooth and simultaneous gesture. Then he lifted his head and placed the hat back upon it.

"I'm terribly sorry, but you have the wrong general."

He held out his hand toward Washington across the road.

Proctor was close enough to see O'Hara's shoulders slump and notice the deep breath he took before turning around and walking with as much dignity as possible across the muddy ruts.

O'Hara repeated his practiced speech.

"I don't understand the point of all these ceremonies," Deborah whispered.

"It's a focus for the magic we call civilization," Proctor replied. "Now shhh."

He wanted to hear Washington's response. The general sat with his hands crossed on the front of his saddle while O'Hara spoke. When O'Hara was done, Washington did not bow or remove his hat or raise his hands. After a moment's pause, he said, simply, in his clear, steady voice, "General Lincoln would be honored to accept the sword from you."

Proctor almost laughed. If the British sent out their second in command, then Washington would defer to his. How sweet for Lincoln, after surrendering to Cornwallis at Charleston.

Lincoln dismounted at once and extended his hands. After a moment's hesitation, O'Hara presented him the sword.

The British had surrendered.

The crowd erupted in a cheer, throwing their hats in the air and spinning friends and strangers alike. Deborah and Lydia hugged, and then Proctor wrapped his arms around Deborah and Maggie and picked them both up off the ground. Maggie laughed and clapped her hands. Proctor kissed her forehead then put them down, and pulled Deborah close for a longer kiss. After almost two years apart, she tasted sweeter and more delightful than he remembered.

She pulled away, finally, grinning at him. "It's going to turn out all right, isn't it?"

"It is," he said.

He looked back at the soldiers. The British were stepping off the road into a field to ground their arms. John Adams or Ben Franklin might still have to negotiate a peace treaty, but for all intents and purposes the war was over here and now. America had won her freedom.

That thought sobered Proctor in a hurry. The war was over. That meant that the hard work lay ahead. If the country prospered or failed, they would now have nobody to blame or credit but themselves.

They moved with the crowd that was walking over to the field to watch the British finish their surrender. The British soldiers were not graceful in defeat. As more men stepped up to surrender their guns, they began to smash them into the pile. A flintlock snapped off one, and the stock cracked loudly on the next.

"Hey," Proctor said. "They're trying to break their guns."

"Let them," Deborah replied. "Let them break all the

guns forever. I'm tired of guns." To make her point, she deliberately walked away from the crowd. "How soon will you be ready to leave for Salem, Lydia?"

Lydia lifted her chin and stared over the tops of the armies to the treetops that marked the woods and swamps. "I won't be going back with you. I'd say I was sorry, but it wouldn't be true."

"Did something happen . . . ?" Proctor asked. He could sense Deborah watching him closely, as if she was wondering the same question.

"Not like that, no," Lydia said. She stepped over the furrowed field, waiting to be planted with winter rye. "But I've been thinking about the Quaker Highway."

The secret series of trails and farms that helped witches escape persecution in New England to start over again in other parts of the country. "What about it?" Proctor asked.

"I don't belong anywhere," she said. "And I never will. But I want there to be a world someday where I could belong, where I could live a free life without fear. The Quaker Highway doesn't have to lead one way, or be just for one kind of people. I've been thinking about using it to lead my people north to freedom."

Her people . . . ? Oh. Not witches. Slaves. The northern states had started banning slavery during the Revolution.

Deborah clasped Lydia's hand. "That's a wonderful idea. Most of the Quaker families we know are abolitionists. Proctor and I will do whatever we can to help."

Proctor thought about it for a moment, then nodded.

Deborah turned back to Proctor. "I'm ready to go. If we leave within a day, we could make it back to The Farm in time for Maggie's second birthday."

Proctor hesitated. He wasn't sure how much she'd seen or knew. "The Farm is destroyed," he said softly.

"Smashed to splinters," Deborah said. "There's not a

thing left standing except Maggie's tree and our hearth. That's all that survived. The parts that we made together."

"If we go back, we'll have to replant and rebuild everything else from scratch," Proctor said.

"That's true," Deborah agreed. "It's going to be very hard, especially the first year or two, and harder if Maggie has a little brother or sister." Without warning, she handed Maggie to him—this time, Maggie did not try to get away. "Do you have any other plans?"

Proctor bounced Maggie tentatively—she laughed and grabbed his cheek with wet fingers.

"No," he said. "Nothing this important. I've got no other plans at all."

Acknowledgments

My thanks must begin with the good people at Random House and Del Rey, especially my editor Chris Schluep. This book took longer and was more difficult for me to write than we expected, but he gave me the time and the guidance I needed and told me to write the best book I could, not the fastest. I am deeply grateful.

This book, more than the other two, deserves notes on the history. New England's "Day Without a Sun," described in chapter 14, actually took place in May 1780. People didn't know the cause and thought it was the end of the world. The voyages of the *Sensible* and the *Alliance* are far more interesting and colorful than I had room to explore. Captain John Barry isn't as well known as John Paul Jones, but he fought more successful engagements against pairs of enemy ships than any other captain of the time, winning repeatedly against superior odds. When he didn't have ships to captain, he served with the army, just to help the war effort.

Banastre Tarleton has been portrayed as one of the great villains of American history, and there is no doubt that he burned a church and was present for the massacre of prisoners at Waxhaws. It is also true that these events are at odds with the rest of his biography and his years of service to the British people. After the Gordon Riots, the mystically inclined Lord Gordon was freed from the Tower of London by the intercession of William Petty, the earl of Shelburne and one of the great patrons of the Enlightenment. Gordon later had himself circumcised, converted to Judaism, and moved to the Continent to study occult magic with Count Cagliostro. Shelburne became prime minister of Great Britain on July 4, 1782, and negotiated peace with the United States of America.

Nathan Hale is often seen as the first figure of American spying, but that honor ought to belong to Thomas Atwood Digges. Digges, the direct descendant of John Dee's most famous student, was born in Maryland and lived on the Warburton plantation across the river from George Washington's home. He left America under a vague cloud of scandal and traveled in South America and Europe before landing in London, where he anonymously published *The Adventures of Alonso,* arguably the first novel written by an American. Digges, using a variety of pseudonyms and disguises, worked tirelessly for America throughout the Revolution. He provided intelligence to both Franklin and Adams, helped hundreds of Americans escape from prisons in England, and stole advanced munitions and other desperately needed technologies from the British, which he shipped to the states through Dutch merchants and other third parties. Digges not only risked his life and safety repeatedly for the American cause, but also produced tangible results that helped the young nation stand on its own. Though cast under suspicion during the war because he could not account for how he spent all of the American funds, he eventually returned to the United States where he maintained close friendships with both Washington and Jefferson.

Only the ruins of Rosewell Plantation stand in Gloucester County, Virginia, today. At the time of the Revolution, Rosewell was considered one of the most elegant and refined homes in America, the equal of the good life in London. Today it is considered one of the most haunted of the surviving colonial plantation sites.

My own French is worse than Proctor's. I thank

Melissa Siah, her husband, Eric Blanchi, and Aliette de Bodard for helping me with translations. My employer was kind to give me some time away from work to finish the first draft. The good folks at Luck Bros' Coffee allowed me to make their front booth my office away from home, and kept me supplied with coffee and sandwiches during the many hours and days I spent there.

Once more, my sons proved understanding of long and frequent absences while I was working on this book. Coleman, in particular, is also an astute listener and asker of questions. He was helpful on numerous occasions when I needed to talk my way through scenes. I am especially grateful to Rae, who took on extra chores to keep the house running while simultaneously making time to slash into the manuscript with her red pen. It is a better book for all their contributions, though any flaws and mistakes remain my own.